D1395681

You-Jeong Jeong is the award-winning author of four novels, including the number one international bestsellers *The Good Son* and *Seven Years of Darkness*, which was named one of the top ten crime novels of 2015 by the German newspaper *Die Zeit*. Her novels have been published in nineteen countries.

Chi-Young Kim is a translator of Korean literature into English. She was awarded the 2011 Man Asian Literary Prize for her work on *Please Look After Mother* by Kyung-Sook Shin.

Also by You-Jeong Jeong

The Good Son

SEVEN
YEARS OF
DARKNESS

YOU-JEONG JEONG
Translated by CHI-YOUNG KIM

Little, Brown

LITTLE, BROWN

Originally published in Korean as *Chilnyeonui bam* by EunHaeng NaMu Publishing Co.
First published in the United States in 2020 by Penguin Books
First published in Great Britain in 2020 by Little, Brown

1 3 5 7 9 10 8 6 4 2

Published with the support of the Literature Translation Institute of Korea (LTI Korea).

A CIP catalogue record for this book
is available from the British Library.

ISBN 978-1-4087-1206-1

Designed by Meighan Cavanaugh
Printed and bound in Great Britain by Clays Ltd, Elcograf S.p.A.

Papers used by Little, Brown are from well-managed forests
and other responsible sources.

MIX
Paper from
responsible sources
FSC® C104740
FSC
www.fsc.org

Little, Brown
An imprint of
Little, Brown Book Group
Carmelite House
50 Victoria Embankment
London EC4Y 0DZ

An Hachette UK Company
www.hachette.co.uk

www.littlebrown.co.uk

CONTENTS

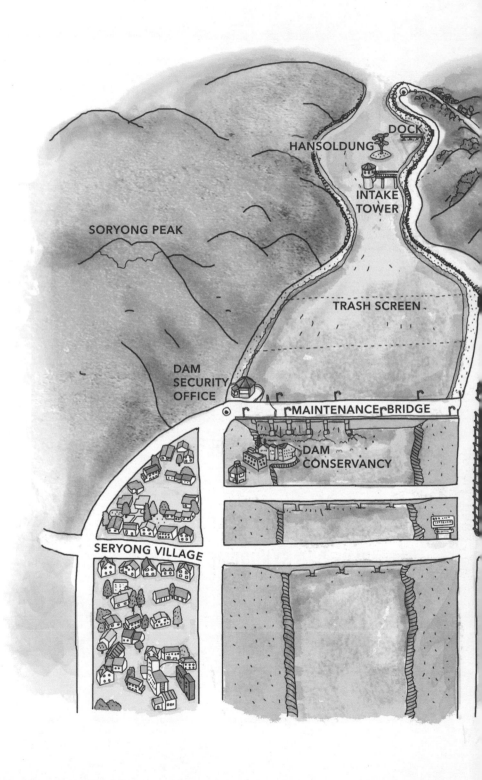

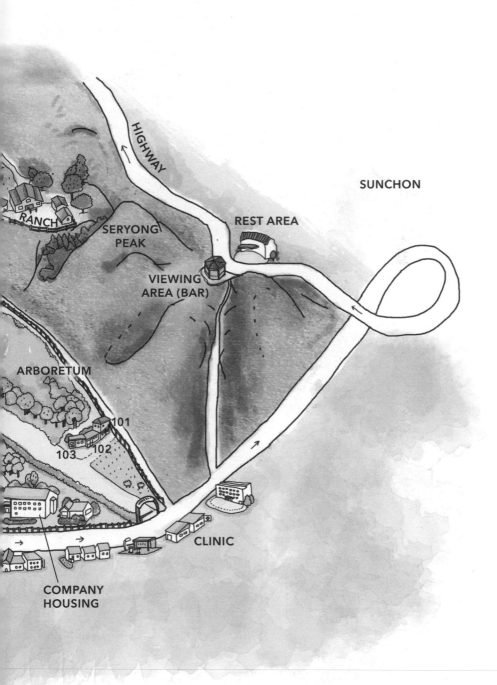

SUNCHON

HIGHWAY

RANCH

SERYONG
PEAK

REST AREA

VIEWING
AREA (BAR)

ARBORETUM

101

103   102

CLINIC

COMPANY
HOUSING

SEVEN YEARS OF DARKNESS

PROLOGUE

The early morning of September 12, 2004, was the last time I was firmly on my father's side. I didn't know anything at the time—not that he'd been arrested, nor that my mother was dead, nor what had happened overnight. Only as Mr. Ahn led me out of the barn at Seryong Ranch did I become certain that something was gravely wrong.

Two police cars blocked the road leading up to the ranch, the flashing red and blue lights bruising the alder trees. Insects skittered through the lights. The sky was still dark, the fog dense. "Keep it safe, okay?" Mr. Ahn whispered, referring to his cell phone, which he'd given to me earlier. An officer ushered us into a squad car.

I caught glimpses of the devastation as we drove through— the damaged bridge, the roads under water, the destroyed streets, the tangle of fire engines and police cars and ambulances, the helicopter circling the black sky. Seryong Village, our home for the past two weeks, had been completely destroyed. I was afraid to ask what had happened. I didn't dare look at Mr. Ahn; I feared I might learn something terrible.

The squad car pulled up to the police station in Sunchon, on the other side of the mountain. The cops separated us. Two detectives were waiting for me in a small room.

"Just tell us what happened to you," one of them instructed. "Not what you heard or what you imagine. Got it?"

I knew I couldn't cry. I had to calmly tell them what happened last night so that they would let Mr. Ahn and me go. Then we could go find Dad and check that Mom was safe.

They listened as I explained.

"So let me make sure I understand," the same detective said. "You played hide-and-seek tonight with a girl who died two weeks ago?"

"Not hide-and-seek. Red Light, Green Light."

The two detectives stared at me in disbelief. A little later, one of them took me to the entrance of the station; Uncle Jongu was there to take me home with him. But reporters were swarming out front. The detective held my elbow as he pushed through the crowd. Flashes popped all around. *Look up! Look here! Hey, kid, did you see your dad last night? Where were you during the incident?*

I felt dizzy. I thought I was going to throw up. The detective hustled me along. I thought I heard Mr. Ahn calling me. I shook off the detective's hand and looked back, searching for Mr. Ahn in the sea of faces. In that moment, all the cameras went off; I was an island in a sea of light.

Uncle Jongu opened the back door of his car and I hunched

low in the seat. I put my head between my knees and tried to hold back my tears.

People would refer to that night's events as the Seryong Lake Disaster. They would call Dad a crazed murderer. The story was so big that I, too, became famous, as his son. I was eleven years old.

LIGHTHOUSE VILLAGE

On Christmas Eve, a black SUV screeched to a stop in front of the pharmacy, and the driver walked inside. I was just about to dig into my ramen. It was three in the afternoon, but it was my lunch break. I forced myself to get up.

"Hey. I have a question," the man said, taking off his Ray-Ban sunglasses.

I reluctantly put my chopsticks down. Hurry up, man, I thought.

"How do you get to Lighthouse Village? I don't see any signs for it." He gestured toward the intersection.

I glanced at his big, powerful SUV. What was it, a Chevy?

"Hey! Did you hear me? Where's Lighthouse Village?"

"Don't you have GPS?"

"I'm asking since the GPS can't find it," the man snapped, clearly irritated.

"How would I know if the GPS doesn't?" I said, equally irritated.

The man left in a huff and gunned his SUV across the intersection.

I turned back to my lunch. Lighthouse Village was what the locals called Sinsong-ri. He should have turned left at the intersection, not gone straight through. I knew, because that was where I lived.

The village wasn't on any map; it was as though it was so insignificant that it wasn't worth calling out. According to Mr. Ahn, it was the tiniest village on Hwawon Peninsula. My boss, the owner of the pharmacy, said it was a dismal, out-of-the-way place that was impossible to get to. The village's so-called youth club president referred to it as the edge of the world. It was true that the place was remote—you had to drive down an unpopulated stretch along the coast for about ten miles before you spotted it. The lighthouse from which it had gotten its name stood at the end of the jagged, beak-shaped cliff that jutted over the sea. Rocky mounds rose from the water and a long, tall ridge enclosed the village from behind.

When we first moved here, I'd gone up to the top of the ridge with Mr. Ahn. From there, you could see the other side of the mountain, a treeless wasteland as vast as the sea. The government had purchased the land for a tourism complex, but so far nothing had come of it. I'd heard that it had been covered with sorghum once, with a small village at the far edge. It was the kids of that long-gone village who had come up with the local name for ours.

With only twelve residents remaining, our town was also facing extinction. That number included Mr. Ahn and me; everyone called us "the little ones" because the average age of the residents was nearly seventy. Most were sweet potato farmers; although we lived in a coastal town, everyone was far too old to fish. Sometimes they were able to cajole us "little ones" into catching something. The last baby born in the village was now sixty-one years old—the youth club president. He owned the sole motorboat in the village and rented us one of the rooms in his lodging house; he also rented out to scuba divers who came to explore the underwater cliff off the coast. That was why Mr. Ahn and I had first come here, before deciding to stay on. Perhaps the man in the Chevy had been lured by the underwater cliff, too, though I hoped that wasn't the case.

Even though Mr. Ahn was only thirty-nine, his hair was already thinning, and he had long white hairs sprouting from his eyebrows. His performance was pathetic at our version of Ironman, which we held every day. We would take the youth club president's boat to the rock island not far off the coast and anchor it. First, we swam around the island. Then we swept the ridge of the underwater cliff to fill our bags with sea squirts, clams, and sea cucumbers. After that, we played basketball; we had nailed a hoop to the trunk of a pine tree. The first to sink five baskets won. Mr. Ahn had lost nine out of the past ten games. Last week, he pulled a muscle in his neck when he tried to dunk. Since then, he was always muttering about how some bastard had shoved his head down when he was trying to score.

My boss came in around seven in the evening and opened the safe, which signaled the end of my shift.

"I'm heading out," I called out. I hopped on my bike, coasted through the intersection, and barreled down the meandering coastal road. It wasn't too dark; stars dotted the night sky. The sea shimmered, the waves crashed against the cliff, and a silvery seabird banked silently through the air.

I pulled up to the house to find the black Chevy parked next to Mr. Ahn's purple van. I could hear Mr. Ahn arguing with someone in the yard. "The current is strong and unpredictable, with undertows. It's like a maze around the island. It's too dark, and you've all been drinking . . ."

"Who are you to tell us what to do?" the other man interrupted.

I pushed the gate open. Four guys were facing off against Mr. Ahn and the youth club president. I recognized one of them; he was the one who had come into the pharmacy, asking for directions.

"Have you ever done a nighttime dive?" Mr. Ahn asked, crossing his arms. "If you're reckless you can get in serious trouble."

The guys laughed at him.

"Boys, he's trying to prevent an accident," the youth club president interjected. "He's our diving expert. Listen to him. I'll rent you the boat tomorrow morning, so let's call it a night."

I kicked the gate closed behind me, and everyone turned to look.

"Oh, hey," the guy from the pharmacy said. "It's the very helpful clerk from earlier. How did you manage to find your way here, when you couldn't tell me where Lighthouse Village was?"

"I don't think you should take them out tonight," Mr. Ahn said to the youth club president. With that, we went inside. Soon, we heard their van revving and driving off.

I shook my head in disgust and went to wash up.

~

They say a cat can sense thunder right before it rumbles. Perhaps the human brain has a similar sensory ability—the clock of anxiety that begins ticking when catastrophe looms. Later that night, in the room I shared with Mr. Ahn, I lay in bed but couldn't fall asleep. I drifted into my memories, back to that day seven years ago when the police had separated me from Mr. Ahn.

After they released me, my mom was cremated without a proper funeral, and I was entrusted to my dad's younger brother, Uncle Jongu, in Seoul. On my first day at my new school, before I could introduce myself, I realized that the kids already knew who I was. To them, I was the son of a crazed murderer who had killed an eleven-year-old girl and her father, thrown his own wife into the river, and then opened the floodgates of the dam above Seryong Village, drowning four police officers and wiping out nearly half the town.

My cousins, who attended the same school, came home in tears; their classmates had taunted them for being related to me. Uncle Jongu had to quit his job as a physical therapist. Soon, our landlord asked us to vacate the apartment. We fled to an apartment in Sanbon and I was given a room at the back, albeit with its own enclosed balcony. My aunt was terrified that people would find out I was living with them. My cousins avoided me at all costs.

I emerged from my room only when the apartment was empty or everyone was asleep. I ate if there was food and went hungry if there wasn't. I rushed to the bathroom, having held it in all day long, and washed. This became a ritual of sorts, my way of confirming that I wasn't a monster. I still had two legs, two arms, a pair of irises, a soul.

Back in my room, I curled up next to the window, alternating between napping and daydreaming. I missed Mr. Ahn. I wondered if he ever tried to contact me. I wouldn't know if he had; Uncle Jongu had smashed the cell phone Mr. Ahn had given me against the wall when he found it, telling me that I was forbidden to remain in contact with anyone my father had known if I wanted to continue staying with them.

Three months later, he sent me to live with his older sister. After three months there, I was sent to their other sister. Things were the same wherever I went. As time passed, the events of Seryong Lake faded from the collective memory, and fewer people recognized me. But eventually, someone would always figure it out, and they would drive me out of school.

The only person in my family who was kind to me was Aunt Yongju, my mother's younger sister. She took me in for a month longer than any other relative before or since. After I'd been there for four months, she sent me to her brother, Giju. "I'm so sorry, Sowon," she said, her eyes filling with tears. Maybe she would have let me stay longer if it weren't for her husband. He despised me. He would come home drunk, drag me out of my room, and pummel me. He would push his wife away as she tried to intervene.

I'll never forget what I overheard him say the night before I was sent away.

"Have you ever looked into the kid's eyes? He never cries. He just stares at you, blankly, even if you curse at him or beat him. It makes me crazy. It's not a child's gaze. It's the gaze of someone who would do something terrible. I can't have him here anymore."

Three months later on a snowy January morning, I came out of my room at Uncle Giju's, and he handed me two one-thousand-won bills. "You know how to get to your uncle Jongu's place, right?"

I figured I could find my way somehow. I nodded. He apologized for not being able to drop me off. They were moving that day, and they neglected to tell me where they were going. I threw my stuff in my suitcase, shouldered my backpack, put on my hat, and walked out of the apartment. The wind sliced through me. The streets were icy. My hands were cold and the tip of my nose was numb. But I didn't look back. I would not beg them to take me along. I didn't much care where I lived, anyway. I thought of Mr. Ahn again.

I found out later that my aunts and uncles had taken my inheritance and divided it among themselves for child-rearing expenses. They had taken everything, including my mom's savings account, life insurance, and our brand-new apartment. But that hadn't been enough to buy their generosity for more than a few months at a time.

I got lost on my way to Sanbon and it took me five hours to get there. When I rang the doorbell, I heard an unfamiliar woman's voice call out, "Who is it?"

I asked for Uncle Jongu, but she answered that nobody of that name lived there. I checked the unit number; maybe I had come to the wrong place. I went outside to check the building number. I wasn't in the wrong place. They, too, it seemed, had moved. I rushed to the phone booth at the entrance of the apartment complex, but Uncle Jongu had changed his cell phone number, too. I called Uncle Giju, but I couldn't get through to his cell phone or his landline. I stood there, stunned. Uncle Jongu had moved away from Sanbon before his turn came around again, but Uncle Giju had sent me there anyway. I called all of my aunts, but no one answered.

Snow swirled into the phone booth through the gaps around the door. My jacket was too thin and my jeans were too short—my ankles were bare. I had grown out of my sneakers, so I was wearing them with the heels folded down—like slippers. I hadn't eaten anything all day. I only had a hundred-won coin left.

There was only one number I hadn't tried—Mr. Ahn's cell phone number. There was probably no point, since he'd given me his phone and Uncle Jongu had broken it, but I dialed, cautiously hopeful. Maybe he'd bought a new cell phone after giving me his and was still using the same number . . .

It rang for a long time. Finally, a slow, clear voice said, "Hello?"

It was Mr. Ahn. I had never forgotten his voice. My throat closed up and I couldn't speak.

Mr. Ahn persisted. "Hello? Hello? Who is it?"

"It's me," I managed. "Your roommate."

~

I waited for what felt like an eternity for his purple van to pull up in front of the apartment complex, though in reality it was only an hour.

He was living in Ansan, not far from where I had been living. His place looked just like the room we'd shared in Se-ryong; it was as if we'd gone back in time. His desk, with his laptop, notebook, keys and wallet, the pack of menthol ciga-rettes, empty beer cans, sticky notes everywhere. He was the same, too—the same short salt-and-pepper hair, a hint of a smile on his face, his habit of taking off his socks and tossing them aside the instant he entered his room. The only thing that had changed was that now he worked as a ghostwriter.

Mr. Ahn didn't ask how I had been. My appearance must have told him everything. Instead, he said that he hadn't changed his phone number all this time, thinking I might call him at some point. I rushed into the bathroom when he said that; I didn't want him to see the emotion on my face. I didn't want him to know how relieved I was that he hadn't gotten married—if he had, surely his wife wouldn't have wanted me around—and that he was still living alone. I didn't want to let on how nervous I was; would he let me stay, or track down my relatives and send me away?

As winter turned into spring, Mr. Ahn completed the legal steps to become my guardian. I'm not sure how that was pos-sible, as I still had living relatives, but I never asked. The only thing that mattered to me was that Mr. Ahn wouldn't aban-don me.

In school, all I did was study. It was my silent vow to Mr. Ahn that I would be on my best behavior; I didn't want to give him any reason to cast me off.

I placed first in my class and fifth in my grade after my second-semester midterms. Mr. Ahn took me to a Korean barbecue restaurant to celebrate, clinking his beer with my soda. Just then, the television on the wall uttered my dad's name. His execution date had been set. My glass slipped out of my hand. Ever since that night, over the months and years when I'd been shuttled from one household to another, I had been hoping that he wasn't actually guilty of the crimes he'd been accused of. Perhaps it had all been some kind of misunderstanding, I thought naively; I dreamed I would be able to reunite with my father when the true criminal was apprehended. To keep that hope alive, I'd avoided the television, newspapers, and the internet. I didn't ask my relatives or Mr. Ahn about my father. For that reason, I still didn't know the full story. Sure, I'd heard rumors about the number of people killed, how they'd died, and my father's sentence. But that was about all I knew.

The following afternoon, I received a manila envelope that shattered my last vestiges of hope. The return address was a PO box. Inside was that week's issue of the popular *Sunday Magazine*. A single photograph was splashed across an entire page—a boy looking back at the camera, his mouth closed firmly. Me. Eleven-year-old me, standing in the sea of light at the Sunchon police station. It was part of a special ten-page feature: "The Seryong Lake Disaster." It included the judgment against my father, an in-depth look at the incident, and details of my father's life—his childhood, his twenty-year baseball career and his life afterward, and a detailed psychiatric analysis. Photographs of the crime scene were scattered throughout. At the end was a picture of my dad in the courtroom after receiving confirmation that he would be executed. He didn't cover his face in shame the way convicts usually did; he wasn't bowing his head, either. His inexpressive eyes staring at the camera reminded me of my own; it was that same blank gaze my aunt's husband had railed about.

Who would send me this? I looked up and noticed Mr. Ahn sitting near me. "This isn't true, is it?"

I watched his expression darken.

"It can't all be true, can it?" I asked.

After a long pause, Mr. Ahn spoke. "It isn't the whole story."

"So it's a mistake, right?"

Mr. Ahn didn't answer. None of this was a mistake, I realized. All of it was true. I felt my eyes well with tears. Mr. Ahn's eyes were moist, too.

The *Sunday Magazine* ruined everything. On Monday morning I entered the classroom and saw a copy of the magazine on every desk, opened to the article about my dad. The ruckus quieted at once. I walked to my desk and hung my bag on my chair. I picked up the magazine that had been left on my desk and went to chuck it in the trash. Then I sat down and opened a book. Thirty pairs of eyes bored into the back of my head.

Someone behind me started to read the article out loud. "'Execute me.'"

The words in my book swirled and blurred.

"The murderer Choi Hyonsu refused an attorney. He had a calm expression on his face, even at the very moment his execution was confirmed."

I looked over my shoulder. It was Junsok, the jerk who always made me go buy him snacks and who called me his bitch.

He stood up with the magazine in his hands. "In November

2004, during the investigation, Choi Hyonsu calmly showed how he had snapped the young girl's neck and thrown his wife into the water. The public was outraged by his composure."

I slammed my book shut. I grabbed my backpack and walked toward the door. My heart was pounding. Junsok kept reading. "Choi Hyonsu's son, who was eleven at the time, was hiding in an old barn in Seryong Ranch . . ."

I stopped beside him. He looked at me with disgust. I considered the situation. This kid was much bigger than me, and nobody would be on my side. All I had was my agility. I kept walking. He looked back down at the article. "Choi's son, who managed to avoid the disaster—"

I spun around, swinging my heavy bag. It hit him square in the face. He shrieked and fell out of his chair. The back of his head slammed on the desk behind him. I seized my chance and planted my heel on his chest. That was all I managed before someone tackled me. Everything grew faint and then turned black. When I came to, I was buried under a pile of kids.

Junsok was taken to the hospital and I was dragged to the police station. If the story of the Seryong Lake Disaster hadn't resurfaced in the news as a result of my father's sentencing, there's a possibility I could have been released with a warning—but there was no chance of that now. As the police saw it, the innocent child of an upstanding citizen had been savagely beaten by the spawn of a mass murderer, breaking his nose and ribs. Junsok's parents refused to drop the charges, and reporters rushed to the station. Mr. Ahn wasn't able to block my transfer to a juvenile court.

Four weeks later, I was given two years' probation. It was

a light sentence considering public sentiment at the time. Mr. Ahn had settled with the victim, allowing me to avoid juvenile detention, but it meant Mr. Ahn could no longer afford his lease. We moved into a sub-basement studio.

As we left the courthouse, Mr. Ahn held out some tofu, the traditional commemoration of leaving jail. "Don't worry," he said. "It's all over."

He was wrong. That was only the beginning. Our new landlord received a copy of the *Sunday Magazine* in the mail, this time along with an article about the fight, and we were kicked out. I was expelled from my new school. Mr. Ahn had to choose between transferring me to yet another school or letting me drop out.

In the end, I never managed to get a middle school diploma. After cycling through twelve different schools, I dropped out and took the middle school equivalency exam so that I could go on to high school. In my first four semesters of high school I transferred nine times. My identity was revealed the same way every time, with a copy of the *Sunday Magazine* and the article about my fight sent to everyone at school, the parent associations, and our neighbors.

We became drifters, usually staying in port cities. Mr. Ahn was an avid diver; he taught me how to dive, and the sea gave me a sense of freedom. In the underwater darkness, the world vanished, and nothing could reach me. I was safe from people's prying eyes and their malicious whispers.

The last school I attended was in Sokcho, by the ocean. I entered the class one day and found a copy of the *Sunday Magazine* on my desk. The kids stared at me silently. One never gets used to certain things, like ostracism. I walked out, enveloped in a cold blue blaze that burned as I crossed the yard and went out the school gates. I headed straight to the convenience store where I worked part-time.

My boss was there, and it was busy. I spotted a copy of the *Sunday Magazine* on the counter. I asked for my month's wages. My boss told me to wait as he finished ringing up a customer. I waited thirty minutes, which quickly turned into an hour. There were so many customers that day; my boss grumbled that I was in the way. I moved from the counter to the back door to the storage room to the front door, waiting all the while. I refused to give in to anger or humiliation.

By that time, I never got flustered or angry. I didn't expect anything from anyone, which meant I never panicked, no matter what happened. I knew it was normal to be flustered when you were surprised, to be angry when you were humiliated— Mr. Ahn kept telling me it was okay to live like that. I disagreed: I had to live, period. And to live, I couldn't panic or get angry or feel vulnerable. I had to withdraw further into the cold, remote core inside myself, and wait there, where I was safe. This tenacity was what kept me going—what kept me from killing myself.

When I finally got my pay two hours later, I was famished. I took a lap around the store, selecting a hamburger, rice rolls, a hot dog, a sandwich—as much food as I could afford with what I just got paid. I piled it all on the counter. It was enough to feed half the homeless people living at Seoul Station. I threw the cash at my now-former boss and headed to the pier.

No one was around. I stuffed the food down, watching the seagulls diving against the backdrop of the setting sun, the boats coming and going, the stray cats meandering with nothing to do, like me. Finally, night fell. It was time to go back to the Rose Inn at the end of a nearby alley, where Mr. Ahn and I rented a room by the month.

That was the day I was honest with Mr. Ahn for the first time. I told him I would drop out of school for good. The next time we moved, I wanted to be scrubbed from the world and forgotten.

Mr. Ahn shook his head.

"I give up," I said.

"You can't give up," was his retort. "It'll get better in college."

I almost laughed out loud. College? Was he serious? None of that mattered anymore. My life had ended the morning I left Seryong Village. I had been branded with my father's crimes and Mr. Ahn had been forced to become a drifter because of me. The *Sunday Magazine* would follow me everywhere I went; nothing would change. This was what my life was and would forever be. Why couldn't he understand?

"All I want to do is live quietly by the coast somewhere."

Mr. Ahn shook his head stubbornly. I stared at him.

He relented a little. "Okay, then take a year off. You can make a decision about school then."

"Okay," I said, taking a step back, too. I didn't feel like arguing.

We followed the sea, from east to south to west. Mr. Ahn drove and I navigated. We unpacked when we could find a room for rent and slept in the van when we couldn't. We ate when we felt like it and dived whenever we had the chance. We left whenever someone started to show an interest in us.

We came to Lighthouse Village in early January of this

year, and it seemed as though perhaps we had finally found a home. We should have done this from the beginning, I thought; I should have quit school sooner. Then we wouldn't have had to roam around all these years, rootless and searching.

I was beginning to hope again. Mr. Ahn would continue his ghostwriting gigs, I would work at the pharmacy, and we would live here for a long time, maybe even until we both grew old. But for that to happen, the outside world couldn't discover this tiny hamlet. That was why people like the guys in the Chevy made me so nervous.

Mr. Ahn was tossing and turning in his bed. I could hear the waves crashing in the darkness. The clock in the youth club president's room next door chimed. I closed my eyes. A vein throbbed in the center of my forehead, and the clock of anxiety inside my head ticked louder and louder.

THE PHONE RANG, jolting us awake. Mr. Ahn picked up. "There's been an accident by the island," he said. "One man's still missing." I got out of bed and turned on the light to get ready, though I'd started deep-sea diving only a year ago.

We sped to the lighthouse and ran down the path to the water. The youth club president was tying the boat on the mooring post. He had managed to find three of them, though one was unconscious. The last one was still underwater.

Mr. Ahn and I took the boat to the island. The wind was gentle and the waves were calm. We anchored the boat, put on our gear, and jumped in. The water was frigid. We paused at the ridge of the pitch-black cliff. Mr. Ahn pointed his thumb down, signaling descent. I gave him the *okay* sign.

Fifty feet, sixty, seventy . . . at a hundred feet, Mr. Ahn gave me the *stop* sign. We swam south along the cliff wall thick with black horn coral. A few minutes later, Mr. Ahn pointed at overlapping arches below, where a light was visible. We passed through an arch and saw the missing man, lying still in a cave-like space, his headlight still shining bright. Mr. Ahn signaled at me to kneel next to the body. Mr. Ahn crossed two fingers in front of his mask, telling me not to look at the dead guy's eyes, but he was a beat too late. I was already having trouble breathing, just like that time at Seryong Lake.

Mr. Ahn blasted his horn at me, wresting me from my memories. We went up slowly, holding the body between us. The beam from the lighthouse skimmed across the water, and sirens blared from far away.

TWO DEAD, two gravely injured. The survivors of the accident were taken to the hospital. Mr. Ahn, the youth club president, and I were taken to the police station for investigation. The police demanded details about the accident and the rescue, throwing around words like "willful negligence" and "manslaughter." Soon enough, they had figured out who I was. Even though it became clear that they couldn't charge us with a crime, the fact that I was the son of an infamous mass murderer made them keep digging.

We were finally allowed to leave at six in the morning. Somehow, reporters had discovered I was there, and they followed us to the van, shouting questions about what I had been doing these past several years and what I thought about my father's situation on death row.

The reporters flooding in meant that our idyllic life in Lighthouse Village was essentially over. Neither of us said a word on our way home.

~

I remember the first time I played executioner. It was the summer I was studying for the middle school equivalency exam. We were living in Gunsan, and I went to the library and spotted a book called *Theories and Practices of the Death Penalty*. I walked past it several times before finally taking it off the shelf. I opened it to the first page. I finished the whole book sitting there on the floor by the bookshelf. I put it back in its place and went straight home. Nothing mattered anymore. I wanted to forget the picture of the gallows I saw in the book. It was hot that day, almost ninety degrees, but I lay down and pulled a heavy blanket over me until all I could see was crimson darkness.

Then, I was in front of an old wooden building with a persimmon tree growing outside, the setting sun stretching beyond the roof, and the heavy wooden door blocking my way. I pushed it open and stepped inside. The room was bright, although it had no windows or lightbulbs. In the center was a table with a black cloth on it. A white curtain shrouded the back of the room. I heard a noise behind the curtain, so I crossed the room and brushed it aside. A man was sitting there on a mat, wearing a hood over his head. A thick rope hung around his sweaty neck. His hulking shoulders were trembling ever so slightly. I heard a weepy sigh from inside the hood. "Execute," I ordered. The floor opened up and the man vanished.

I threw off the blanket and sat up. I looked out. The burnt-orange evening sun hung in the darkening sky. The man I had executed was my father.

~

The next day, I finished tidying up and left the pharmacy at four. Mr. Ahn's purple van wasn't parked by the house. I looked through the window, but he wasn't in our room. Maybe he had gone to the fisheries co-op. But then why didn't he stop by the pharmacy, which was right next door? He hadn't gone to gather information for a ghostwriting project, since the bag he took to those meetings was hanging next to the door. I parked my bike in the backyard.

"When did you get here?" the youth club president asked, coming up behind me.

I straightened up with a jolt. "Oh, were you home? It was so quiet I thought you were out."

"I was in my room." Holding out a box, he told me that a courier had brought it not long ago. It was slightly bigger than a shoebox and didn't have the sender's name or address, only my name and the address of the lodging house.

"Where's Mr. Ahn?"

"Sunghwan? I don't know. We had lunch together, and then when I woke up from my nap he was gone."

I headed to our room but stopped to look back at the youth club president. Was it only a matter of time until he kicked us out, too?

I opened the box. Mr. Ahn's reporting notebook, the recorder watch he wore when he went out to talk to sources, a coin-shaped USB drive I bought him with my first paycheck from my job at the pharmacy, a bundle of letters, a scrapbook secured with a rubber band. What was all this? At the bottom of the box was a thick stack of paper. The first page was blank. I turned to the next. What was this?

SERYONG LAKE

PROLOGUE

August 27, 2004

The girl was waiting at the bus stop in front of the school, kicking at the curb with the tips of her sneakers. She was looking down. Only her pale, round forehead was visible as her long hair fluttered in the wind.

A dump truck rattled past her, obscuring her for a brief moment. Soon, a silver van drove up and stopped in front of her; it was the shuttle from the art school. A merry voice pierced the damp, heavy air. "I'm not going to art class today. It's my birthday and I'm having a party."

The van made a U-turn and drove away. The girl crossed the road forlornly, her shoulders drooping as she stared at the ground. Across the street, Sunghwan watched her from the beginning of the path to the rest area. The girl looked up. The August sun glinted off the hairpin holding her bangs to the side. She stared at Sunghwan nervously. Sunghwan almost greeted her: *Hello, young lady. Happy birthday.*

She walked toward the main entrance to Seryong Arbore-

tum. Sunghwan lit a cigarette. A few minutes before, at the
rest area, he had spotted some kids who lived in the company
housing heading into what seemed like a birthday party at
the McDonald's there. Everyone was holding a present. It
clearly wasn't her party.

He heard the traditional percussion quartet from Seryong
Lake, announcing the beginning of a rite to remember the
old Seryong Village, which was submerged a decade ago when
the dam was constructed. While the company kids were at
the birthday party, the kids from the low-lying village would
be there.

There were two classes of people now living at Seryong
Village: the natives and those who worked at the dam conservancy. The former had lived in the old Seryong Village; they
had resettled in the lowlands below the dam, along the east-
ern bank of the river. Employees of the dam conservancy and
their families lived in company housing across the river from
the village. Company housing was adjacent to the arboretum, and just north of the arboretum was the Annex, which
had three houses: 101, a two-story fortress, and 102 and 103,
smaller structures that were rented out to the conservancy
security guards. The birthday girl, named Seryong after the
lake, lived with her father in 101. Her father owned the ex-
pansive property containing the arboretum, the company
housing, and the Annex.

Sunghwan never saw the kids from the village playing with
the kids whose parents worked for the dam. The girl, Seryong,
didn't play with anyone. Though she was born in the now-
underwater Seryong Village, she lived in the Annex and was

therefore classified as neither a kid from the lowlands nor one from company housing. That was probably why she was alone on her eleventh birthday.

Sunghwan looked up at the sky, a cigarette between his teeth. Leaden clouds were brewing. The sun was hiding behind the clouds and the cicadas had stopped wailing. It was a hot, sticky, unpleasant Friday afternoon.

I dropped the manuscript. Mr. Ahn—whose first name was Sunghwan, though I never called him that—had written this. His style was as familiar to me as my own face. I could guess what loomed on the following pages. The *Sunday Magazine* had carved that story into my bones. I didn't need to read about it again. Why did he write this manuscript, which seemed to be a fictionalized account of what had happened at Seryong Lake? Why would he send it to me, when we lived in the same room? (I didn't recognize the handwriting on the box, but whose else could it be?) And where had he gone?

I biked to the lighthouse and sat at the edge of the cliff, looking out at the sea. Friday, August 27, 2004. The girl was still alive that afternoon. I couldn't stop my mind from going back to that summer seven years ago.

We moved to Seryong Lake on Sunday, August 29. My father had been transferred there as the head of security at Seryong Dam. There were only two bedrooms in 102 and Mr. Ahn was already living there. My parents took the master bedroom and I became Mr. Ahn's roommate.

Mr. Ahn showed me that path leading up to the rest area the first day we got there. We were on a mission to find my father, who had left the house to get some supplies. Two hours after he left, he still hadn't come home, and my mother asked us to go find him. Mr. Ahn and I climbed that narrow path and arrived at the highway rest area where my parents and I had stopped on our way in to Seryong Lake. I was confused. We had stopped at the rest area, then driven through the interchange that led to Seryong Village, and then traveled for another stretch before arriving at the lake. Mr. Ahn saw my puzzled expression and pointed to the path we had just taken. "It's a magic shortcut."

I almost believed him. You could walk up that path and get to the rest area in five minutes, while driving would take over ten minutes. That wasn't the only strange thing about this place. It was a basic highway rest area, but it was also the center of daily life for the people of Seryong. The rest stop eateries were their restaurants, the convenience store was their supermarket, and the tables topped with umbrellas on the observation deck functioned as the village bar.

It was there that we found my father, along with two empty soju bottles. We sat down next to him, looking down at the lake below.

"How does it work—the magic?" I asked Mr. Ahn.

"What magic?" my father asked.

"The magic of that path."

Dad looked at Mr. Ahn, who laughed. "Sowon, you know what a spiral is, right?"

I drew a whirl with my finger.

"That's right. Seryong Lake is at the foot of the mountain, with the new village beneath, in the lowlands. The highway travels along the mountain ridge. So if you can imagine the lake as the first floor and the rest area as the second floor, the highway is the spiral staircase linking the two floors. But the path is a ladder. If you take the path, you can climb straight up to the second floor."

Forgetting that we were supposed to bring Dad home, we stayed there awhile—I had a Coke, my father drank more soju, and Mr. Ahn had beer. The sun turned crimson and the shadows grew longer. A faint vapor rose from the lake. Mr. Ahn pointed to a spot far away where the plain met the sky. He said the ocean was out there, by Dungnyang Bay. On nights with a southerly breeze, if you opened our bedroom window, you could smell the sea. But when I did that, what drifted in instead was a voice—*her* voice. *Red light, green light.*

~

When I got home, Mr. Ahn still wasn't back.

"But something else came for you," the youth club president said.

It was another box. This time the sender was "Your friend." I didn't recognize the handwriting: it was neither Mr. Ahn's nor the same hand as on the package I'd received two hours before.

Back in my room, I opened it. Inside the box was a copy of that blasted *Sunday Magazine* and a yellowed Nike basketball shoe. Just one, size six and a half. A name was written faintly on the inside of the tongue.

Choi Sowon.

I'd owned a pair of Nikes exactly once in my life. I won an award in a math contest at school when I was eleven, and my father had given them to me as a present. He had written my name on them, and I'd lost them at Seryong Lake.

I closed the box. Who sent this? What did they want? If they wanted revenge, they should target the man on death row in Seoul Prison, not me.

I took out my mat and blankets and lay down, even though it was still early. More questions kicked around in my head. Where was Mr. Ahn? Why was he out so late? Why wasn't he calling? Who sent the *Sunday Magazine*? Was it a coincidence that Mr. Ahn's things and the Nike were sent on the same day? What was going on? Until this moment, I had assumed the person sending the *Sunday Magazine* to my neighbors and schoolmates was a relative of one of the victims. I figured nobody else would pursue me this doggedly. But the Nike proved me wrong. A stranger couldn't have known what it meant to me.

I called Mr. Ahn, but his phone was off. I turned on his laptop and plugged in the USB drive. A digital copy of the manuscript had to be on there somewhere. I needed to find the part I wanted, the part that would give me a clue as to who was doing this to me, without having to read the whole thing. Luckily, the drive contained two folders: "Reference" and "Seryong Lake." In the "Seryong Lake" folder there were ten Word files. I opened "Final Draft" and searched for "Nike."

Last spring, Sowon had won a prize in a math contest at school. Hyonsu bought him Nike basketball shoes to congratulate him.

I kept pressing "Find Next." A few more sentences went by, all with Hyonsu as the subject. Until I saw a different name.

Yongje took the Nike basketball shoes out of his bag. "Could these be your son's?"

Yongje. A man's face flashed in my mind. Our neighbor in unit 101.

My hair stood on end. That girl's father. He'd had the Nikes. Could he be the one sending copies of the *Sunday Magazine*? No, that couldn't be. He died seven years ago. The entire world knew that he died by my father's hand. A sickening confusion churned in my gut.

I glared at the name highlighted on the screen. I took a deep breath and scrolled back to the beginning.

SERYONG LAKE

PART I

Sunghwan opened the glass door that led from the living room to the veranda. The wind was coming from the south, and the salty ocean air flooded the dark room. The path in front of the Annex was blanketed in fog and it was starting to rain. It was quiet; nobody was out. He heard the tinkle of a music box: *Fly me to the moon and let me play among the stars . . .*

Sunghwan flipped open his cell and called Choi Hyonsu, but his call went straight to voice mail.

Choi Hyonsu was the new head of security at Seryong Dam. Starting Monday, he would be Sunghwan's boss. Hyonsu was planning to move in on Sunday, but he'd wanted to come by tonight, Friday, and take a look at the place his family would be sharing with Sunghwan. He was supposed to be here at eight, but it was nearly nine now. He couldn't have forgotten. They had just made these plans at lunchtime, and he hadn't called or texted to say he would be late.

Sunghwan closed the door and drew the curtains. He couldn't stop his new boss from coming so late, but he also didn't have to sit around and wait when he was being blown off. He didn't have the time or patience. He had things to do. He texted Hyonsu: The code to the front door is 214365.

Sunghwan went into his room, which faced the arboretum behind the Annex. He tossed his cell on the desk and began changing. Things would be easier if he got there already in basic gear—wet suit, BC, weight belt. He was strapping a diving knife around his calf when his cell rang, startling him. It was his father. He often called around this time of night after a drink. Sunghwan could already hear his voice in his head: *How long are you going to try to write a novel? At thirty-two years old, you're nothing but a security guard. We didn't all work ourselves to death to give you an education just to see you waste your life.*

Sunghwan put his sneakers on and climbed out the window, ignoring his cell. He slung his backpack, which held his underwater camera and other gear, on his shoulder. He put his headlamp on and started off in the direction of the secluded, unlocked gate behind unit 101 that led to a shortcut to the lake.

As he walked toward the gate, a half-open window of unit 101 caught his eye. It was Seryong's room, the girl he'd seen a few hours before, leaning against the bus stop and kicking at the curb. A mosquito coil was on the windowsill, smoke curling up. On the wall opposite was a portrait of the girl, her hair gathered on top of her head, her dark eyes staring straight ahead. She looked like a young ballerina in a Degas painting. Underneath the picture was a white desk on which glowed three votive candles: one green, two red. Next to them sat stuffed animals wearing party hats. A musical toy Ferris wheel with a lightbulb for a moon and a figure of a girl flying toward it rotated in front of the animal guests. That was the source of the tune that had been floating in the foggy evening air. Sunghwan hitched his backpack up and turned away, unsettled by the scene he had just seen. She must have thrown herself a birthday party before falling asleep. There was no way her dad would let her keep the candles burning through the night, and the window should have been closed. His white BMW was usually parked in front, but now Sunghwan couldn't remember if he'd seen it. In his mind, yellow flames, flickering in the breeze, leaped from one stuffed animal to another, devouring them instantly.

Sunghwan blinked away the imagery and kept walking. It would not be smart to hang around. He should slip out of the gate toward the lake.

~

S unghwan had taken the job on the security detail at Seryong Dam because of the perks: He was provided housing in the mountains near a lake. The pay wasn't bad; it was less than working for the railway but more than he'd earned as a stable hand at a racehorse ranch. It was a one-year contract position, so he wouldn't feel like a cog in a large organization.

The first time Sunghwan went up to the rest area observation deck, he felt he'd picked the perfect job. It was the first day of June, neither hot nor cold. It was hazy out, and only the rim of the sun was visible in the pearly sky. It was the perfect weather in which to view the lake below, which, he saw now, had been created by stopping up the river that snaked down from Paryong Mountain in the north to the South Sea. Two thin, straight peaks bookended each side of the lake: Seryong Peak, which was near the observation deck where he sat, and Soryong, which was across the way. At the foot of Seryong Peak was a thick alder forest and a shuttered barn.

Below the entrance to that ranch was a path that led to the dam. The lake was shaped like a woman's torso—the river looked like her long neck, and the dock was located near her chest, with an island, called Hansoldung, in the middle. The tributary below the floodgates split the fields in two as they flowed out to sea. Seryong Village hugged the banks of the tributary.

If he was lucky, he thought, he might discover a muse here, one who would facilitate his becoming a bestselling novelist and an answer to his father's questions. But in the two months since he'd arrived, Sunghwan had managed to write only two sentences: *Seryong was the most famous girl in the area. Wherever you went, you heard that name—Seryong Rest Area, Seryong Elementary School, Seryong Medical Clinic, Seryong Police Station, Seryong Arboretum.* That was as far as he'd gotten. That his book would be about the girl in 101 was a stroke of inspiration, though he didn't know yet what she would do or why she was in the story at all.

But Sunghwan soon grew bored. His job was monotonous and the weather was getting hot. The lake beckoned alluringly, but he wasn't allowed to enter it; he couldn't even dip a finger in. His diving gear stayed in his closet. Seryong Lake was a first-tier reservoir that sustained four cities and ten counties nearby. A barbed-wire fence surrounded it. Nobody was allowed to even climb Seryong Peak. Seryong Ranch, which used to raise goats, had been shuttered upon the dam's completion. The barn had become a haven for wild animals; it was illegal to build or tear down any buildings in the protected zone. The road that wound around the lake was partially closed to traffic. The lake was, in essence, a huge, sheltered well.

Guards patrolled the lake day and night. There were only six men working security, and four of them lived in unit 103. Sung-hwan shared 102 with the former head of security, an evangelical Christian who had pasted a sign that said *Believers of Jesus Christ* on their front door and devoted himself to proselytizing. Sunghwan was subjected to lectures day and night, and worse still, developed insomnia due to his writer's block. He panicked when he lay down to sleep, but was consumed by a dense fog when he got up and turned on his laptop. It made him fearful of the night. On sleepless nights he began wandering through the arboretum. He sometimes bumped into fellow nocturnal beings, like the old groundskeeper, who sometimes got drunk and wandered around at two in the morning, and Ernie, the stray cat who hung out by Seryong's bedroom window.

The first time Sunghwan encountered Ernie, the cat wasn't scared; he stared at Sunghwan with an expression of feline boredom before he turned and disappeared through the gate. Sunghwan followed the cat down the shortcut until they arrived at the lakeshore road. He watched Ernie saunter leisurely through the fog. He followed until they reached the old barn, a decent distance from the road. One part of the floor had buckled; a large wooden box lined with a pink blanket was laid inside. Judging by the bowls full of water and food, it was clear someone came here often.

After that night, Sunghwan had continued expanding his range of movement beyond the barn. He snuck out of his bedroom window so his boss wouldn't know and walked along the lakeshore road. But his wanderings didn't seem to be helping him coax his capricious muse back. His anxiety intensified.

Sunghwan was still stuck when his boss shared the news that he was leaving for a new job at Chungju Lake. In the office, as Sunghwan discussed how to split up the work with Park, another of the guards, Park told Sunghwan about the annual ceremony to commemorate the original Seryong Village, which was held each year on August 27, the date the old village had been submerged. The festival took place in the afternoon along the lakeshore road near the island, Hansoldung.

"Is it worth checking out?" Sunghwan asked. "I'm off that day."

Park stared at the CCTV monitor for a while, not responding. "This lake gives me the creeps."

Sunghwan looked at the monitor. As the fog began to dissipate, Hansoldung emerged like a gravestone in the center of the lake. A pine tree with a split trunk stood alone in the middle of the otherwise barren island. "What does Hansoldung mean, anyway? Single Pine Tree Hill?"

"Who knows?" Park replied. "I did hear the old village was right below it. They say it's still completely intact underwater. I heard the nameplates still hang on the gates."

Sunghwan blinked. The back of his neck prickled.

"At least, that's what they say. It makes sense, I guess. The dam was completed about a decade ago, but they didn't demolish the village first. They just flooded it. It used to be the second-largest village in the township, you know."

"Have you talked to anyone who's actually seen it?"

"No. The residents are very protective of it. They treat it like a holy site or something. They don't want anyone from the outside to come in and poke around. I figure it's superstition— they don't want to disturb anything since down in the new village they effectively live with a giant water tank above their heads."

"Do you think there's anything to it? That the lake might be sacred?"

"Sunghwan, you haven't seen her at sundown, have you?" Park asked, referring to the lake as though it were human. "Watch the screen for a minute or two after the sun sets. When the darkness settles over the water, fog wafts up around Hansoldung. Like it's smoke from the chimneys below." Park kept his eyes on the screen. "I sound crazy, don't I?"

"Well, no, but . . ."

"I can't wait for this assignment here to be over," Park muttered.

That night, Sunghwan drifted home. He lay down, but he couldn't fall asleep. The secrets of the old village would unleash his imagination, and he would be able to do what he came here to do. He would write his masterpiece. He could practically see the underwater village in front of him, the last embers burning in the houses' hearths. How could he get down there? Visions of Atlantis swam in his thoughts; maybe the lake had chosen him instead of the other way around. He needed to see the old village for himself. In fact, he would take pictures to help him lay out the scene in his novel. He couldn't climb over the fence with all of his diving gear. He had to get his hands on a key.

$\sim$

Sunghwan had left work that morning, after two consecutive nights on duty, with a copy of the key to the dock in his pocket. The keys were always transferred to the guards working the next shift to ensure that nobody could sneak them out, so Sunghwan had driven to a hardware store to make a copy during his shift, leaving the security office unmanned.

The village had to span from near the dock to beyond the intake tower, he reasoned, with Hansoldung marking the edge. This made the dock the ideal place to enter the water. That afternoon, he bought a fishing line, fluorescent paint, floats, and sinkers, spotting Seryong standing by the bus stop on his way home.

Who was at Seryong's birthday party? he wondered as he waited for darkness to fall, coating the sinkers with fluorescent paint. He waited for them to dry, then tied them to the fishing line, making sure to leave about a foot between each; it would be a makeshift depth gauge, so he could calculate how to safely ascend by accounting for pressure changes. The line would also be a guide; once he found the underwater village, he could leave it discreetly at the water's edge, allowing him to return, if he wanted to, the following night.

His new boss didn't show up even after Sunghwan completed making his depth gauge. He tried to calm his nerves with two cans of beer, but then realized that was foolish; it wasn't safe to dive while under the influence, and his anxiety had made him overlook that. He waited until nine, doing push-ups and pacing around the house, trying to clear the alcohol from his system. Tonight was the night; tomorrow he would begin writing again, before his workweek started. He had to enter the lake without anyone noticing him and take detailed pictures of the village.

He went out the window and past Seryong's bedroom, and through the gate to the shortcut. On the other side, Sunghwan turned on his headlamp. He made it as bright as possible but still couldn't see very well. The fog emanating from the lake was too thick; it smothered everything, like a snowstorm. It began to rain. He turned off the lamp at the end of the road, where he knew there was a CCTV camera. Darkness enveloped him.

He walked alongside the fence surrounding the lake and arrived at the dock ten minutes later. This was the sole point of entry to the lake: a pair of steel doors. It was the same height as the fence, and though there was a small gap between the sloping ground and the bottom of the doors, it was much too small for a person to crawl through. A thick chain was coiled around the handles and fastened by a padlock. Sunghwan turned his headlamp to the dimmest setting to unlock it. Once inside, he used the chain and padlock to lock himself in, ensuring he would not be interrupted.

The concrete ramp leading down to the dock was about twenty yards long, flanked by a tangle of shrubs and vines. The *Josong*, a barge used by the waste management company that serviced the dam, was tied to the dock. Sunghwan put his backpack down by the *Josong*'s cabin. He took out the fishing line, tied it to the pier, and prepared to enter the water. He tugged on his fins and slid the breathing apparatus into his mouth. He checked his watch; it was 9:30.

He entered vertically. Once submerged, he turned his lamp as bright as it would go and descended, carefully unraveling the fishing line. He passed the first thermocline and spotted the yellow center dividing line of a two-lane road at the bottom of the lake. The undercurrent was fairly strong, but visibility wasn't too bad. Sunghwan wrapped the fishing line loosely around a tree trunk and continued his descent.

Several minutes later, his feet were planted on the bottom of the lake. The water was cold enough to give him a headache. It was dark and quiet. Everything was colorless. Only the road, reflected by the light of his headlamp, glistened in silver. He could see glimmers of the old village in the far reaches of his light. Feeling both trepidation and excitement, he swam down the road into the darkness.

He was greeted by an engraved rock marking the entrance to the town. *Welcome to Seryong Village.* The frame of a bus shelter, its glass gone, was beside it. He looped the fishing line around a rusted sign pole and kept going. Underwater plants had grown thick on the ruins of a rice mill; fish swam through its walls. A telephone pole lay in the street and a rusted cultivator was stuck in the field. He wound his fishing line around each of these and continued on. He encountered a crumbled rock wall, dangling shingles, exposed steel beams, broken doorframes, scattered roof tiles, rotting, fallen trees, a stroller with a missing wheel, a well covered with a steel lid. Was this what the world would look like after humans went extinct? He was transfixed.

Like a fish, Sunghwan flitted around the roads and bridges and stone barriers, taking pictures with his underwater camera, documenting what he might otherwise have believed to be figments of his imagination. Where only the walls of a house were left standing, he could almost see an elderly couple enjoying a relaxed evening meal. He sat on the bench at another bus stop, listening to people make small talk as they waited, a young mother explaining how she had met her husband as she pushed a stroller down the street. His muse had finally arrived, he thought. He could piece these stories together and write something remarkable.

But time underwater flowed as capriciously as the current. In an instant, an hour had gone by. Sunghwan realized that he felt numb. Everything before him was shaking, and not because of the current. The village was suddenly painted in vivid colors. He felt ecstatic—he was starting to reel from the effects of nitrogen narcosis.

Last one, he told himself as he pointed his camera at the nameplate hanging on a house at the highest point of the village. He pressed the button, the flash popping over the dark letters on the nameplate. It vanished under the light and the letters floated up as though they were embossed.

It was 10:45 and he only had 120 bar of oxygen remaining. Sunghwan had to get up to the surface. He started to dump air out of the buoyancy compensator and began to ascend. He didn't have time to return via the same route he had taken in; he had to ascend directly above that last house. He looked down as he rose steadily at thirty feet per minute. Everything was starting to return to gray. His mind lingered on the final nameplate: *Oh Yongje*.

As he floated up to the surface, he thought back to his first Friday night at Seryong Lake, before his battle with insomnia and writer's block had begun. His boss had gone home to Seoul for the weekend and Sunghwan was alone in the house. As he was nodding off around midnight, he heard a piercing scream. His eyes flew open, but everything was quiet. He closed his eyes again, thinking he'd dreamed it. That was when he heard a quiet weeping from just outside his window.

He picked up his flashlight and peered out into the darkness. Cowering behind the entwined branches of a cypress tree was a young girl, her arms crossed in front of her chest. When he pointed his flashlight toward her, she curled in on herself and whimpered, "Don't look, don't look!"

Sunghwan nearly acquiesced. The girl looked as though she'd been attacked. Her nose looked swollen, and phlegm rattled in her throat each time she drew in a breath. Her body was covered in bloody gashes, and she was wearing nothing but her underwear. Suddenly, the girl collapsed. Regaining his faculties, Sunghwan climbed out of his window, wrapped a blanket around her, and carried her as fast as he could toward his car. He recalled having seen a twenty-four-hour clinic in the commercial district. Figuring out whose child she was and who had done this to her was a secondary concern. She needed medical attention.

The doctor, a young man with a buzz cut, examined her and took X-rays. He confirmed that the girl's nose was broken. "What happened?" he asked.

"I don't know," Sunghwan said. "She fainted just outside my window."

The police officer who arrived knew who she was: Seryong, the eleven-year-old daughter of the man who owned the arboretum. He took out his cell phone and made a call.

Not long after, a man in a navy suit and polished shoes appeared.

"Not coming from home?" the police officer observed.

"I was on my way home when I got your call," the man said, not bothering to so much as glance at his daughter. He stood blocking the door and looked at Sunghwan. His dark pupils were wide open. "And who are you?"

Sunghwan cleared his throat. "I live in unit 102."

"Since when? I've never seen you before."

Sunghwan felt his breathing grow shallow. He'd glimpsed something unsettling in the man's eyes—something like a challenge. "I moved in a few days ago," he said slowly, trying to calm down. "I didn't know she was your daughter."

"Why did *you* bring my daughter here?"

"Let me ask you this," Sunghwan retorted, his cheeks burning. "Why did your daughter faint outside my window?"

The girl's father turned to the doctor. "Is there evidence of assault?"

The doctor repeated what he'd told Sunghwan earlier. "Her nose is broken, and there are abrasions that look like she was beaten with something . . ."

"Is that it? What I see is that a strange man brought my daughter to the clinic half-naked in the middle of the night."

Sunghwan stared at the man in a daze. The optics of the situation hadn't even occurred to him.

The officer looked down at Seryong, who was stealing sidelong glances at her father.

"What did this man do to you?" her father asked. He turned to his daughter, pointing at Sunghwan. "Did he hurt you? Did he touch you?"

Sunghwan held his breath.

"No," whispered Seryong.

"How did you get hurt?" asked the officer.

Seryong's eyes searched the faces of the cop and the doctor.

She glanced at Sunghwan before returning to the officer. She seemed to be avoiding her father. Her large, cat-like eyes glistened, but not with tears. Sunghwan realized it was fear. She said nothing.

"Did you say your name was Ahn Sunghwan?" the police officer asked. "Please step outside for a moment."

Sunghwan couldn't do that; the girl had his life dangling between her small lips.

"You, too, Dr. Oh."

But Dr. Oh didn't move, his gaze fixed on his daughter.

"Both of you, now, please," the police officer pressed.

Dr. Oh and Sunghwan glanced at each other before turning toward the door.

"Don't go far, this will just be a minute," the officer said.

Dr. Oh sat in a chair just outside the door. He leaned on the armrest and looked down his nose at Sunghwan. His dilated black eyes and tense, coiled shoulders reminded Sunghwan of a wild animal about to pounce. Sunghwan sat across from him, trying to look calm and relaxed. Rational thought leaked out of his head, replaced by rage and humiliation and nerves. His breathing grew more ragged. He was desperate for a cigarette, but he couldn't step outside; who knew what these people would conclude if he wasn't there to defend himself. He couldn't hear anything from the exam room. Twenty minutes crawled by. By the time the police officer opened the door, Sunghwan was on the verge of passing out.

"She says she was playing Red Light, Green Light with a cat she came across in the arboretum and ran into a tree," the police officer reported, standing in the middle of the hallway. "When she tried to get home, she accidentally went to the wrong house in the dark. Her bloody nose made her feel dizzy and she fainted. She wanted me to tell you, Dr. Oh, that she's grateful to your next-door neighbor for bringing her here and that he never touched her."

Sunghwan stood up, rage burning his throat. "Are you saying this little girl was playing with a cat? In the middle of the night? In her underwear? Are you serious?"

"She said it's the cat's favorite game."

"And what about the gashes all over her? And her bloody shoulder?" Sunghwan demanded.

"The cat scratched her, she said. And she must have collided pretty hard with that tree. The X-ray shows that her nose is definitely broken. You'll need to take her to an ENT to figure out what to do about that."

Dr. Oh went into the exam room and carried his daughter out, wrapped in a blanket. He stared daggers at Sunghwan as he passed but said nothing.

The police officer took Sunghwan's elbow. "And you can come with me to the station."

Sunghwan shook him off. Bringing an injured child to a clinic didn't require a visit to the police station. Especially since the girl had cleared his name.

"Come on," the police officer said, taking his arm again and guiding him out of the clinic. "You reported this, so you need to at least file an official statement."

At the station, Sunghwan wrote down the events of the night, suppressing his urge to throw the pen across the room. His fingers cramped from the effort. His head whirred. Why was the girl lying about what happened to her? Why was her father trying to make *him* out to be the one who assaulted her? Why was the police officer so uninterested in finding the culprit? It was obvious that the three of them shared some silent understanding that he and the doctor weren't privy to.

Sunghwan reconstructed what must have happened. There was no doubt in his mind that Seryong had been beaten by her father. He had seen the violence in Dr. Oh's eyes and the fear in Seryong's. She fled but had nowhere to go. So she hid under a tree near his window next door. Her father must have gone looking for her. And that was the unfortunate moment when he, the nosy neighbor, had butted in. He imagined Dr. Oh watching as Sunghwan took off for the clinic. A little while later, he'd received a phone call from the police. The officer knew the girl was beaten on a regular basis and that the neighbor was in a sticky situation, but Dr. Oh was a powerful man, so he acted as if he knew nothing.

Sunghwan saw that Dr. Oh—and maybe the police, too—might try to implicate him in order to conceal the truth of what was going on in that house. But that didn't make any sense; parents were rarely sent to prison for hitting their children. Perhaps their reputation would suffer, but that was about it. The dad's reaction was disproportionate, like using a chain saw to remove some cobwebs. And it didn't come without risk; he could be held liable for making a false accusation against an innocent man.

Later, his coworker Park told him that Dr. Oh was in the middle of a contentious divorce. He was a dentist by trade and owned a medical building in Sunchon that housed eleven private practices, including his own. He was also the only son of an influential landowner in the region, and controlled the fields that were the livelihood of the village. Sunghwan understood that by making his veiled accusation in the doctor's office, Oh had been sending him a warning: Stay out of my personal life.

In the nearly two months since that night, no investigation had been initiated. Sunghwan had heard Seryong screaming a few times since, sometimes shrieking, "Daddy!"; but he knew there was nothing he could do.

His was the name Sunghwan had seen floating before him: *Oh Yongje.*

~

Hyonsu's cell phone rang. He glanced at it. Eunju again. This was her fifth call in the last hour, and she'd been texting him, too.

> Pick up.
>
> On your way, or are you there?
>
> You're not there, are you? Are you drinking with your friends again?

Hyonsu *was* drinking. With his friends. But he was at a soju bar in Gwangju, not in Seoul; he had just made a stop on his way out to Seryong Dam. That was why he didn't pick up. If he told her where he was and what he was doing, she would just get mad. He turned his attention back to the game. The Tigers and the Lions were playing at Daegu Baseball Stadium. The Tigers were getting beaten to a pulp. The camera showed the catcher, standing with his hands on his hips; his team had just given up a three-run homer.

Hyonsu had been there before. He had spent most seasons

as a backup catcher in the majors or in the minors for the now-defunct Hanshin Fighters.

His cell rang again, though this time it wasn't his wife. It was Kim Hyongtae, who'd joined the security company the same year he did. "Where the hell are you?" Hyongtae chided him irritably. "Your wife called. I told her we're not together, but she kept insisting that I hand over the phone. She said you're supposed to be at Seryong Dam tonight. Are you?"

"I'm on my way there."

"Then call her and tell her that, okay? You of all people should know about her temper."

Hyonsu wondered how famous Eunju's temper was. He stood with the phone to his ear; Hyongtae had already hung up, but he needed this excuse to leave. His two buddies glanced up at him. He pointed at the phone and began walking out.

"Excuse me, are you Choi Hyonsu? Did you play ball?" asked a man sitting at a table near the door.

Hyonsu looked back, amazed and a little embarrassed that someone had recognized him.

"I was in the forty-fifth graduating class at Daeil High," the man said, getting up.

Hyonsu slipped his cell into his shirt pocket and shook the man's hand. He autographed a piece of paper the man held out; he wanted it for his son. He turned down the fan's invitation to sit, instead downing the shot of soju he held out. He wanted to leave. He didn't want to answer a bunch of questions from a former schoolmate he didn't even remember.

His cell blipped with another text as he opened the car door. Where are you drinking? One of Eunju's favorite questions. The other was: Why? Hyonsu had never been able to answer that one to her satisfaction. Asking an alcoholic why he drank was like going to a grave and asking, Why did you die? There were as many reasons for a drink as there were bars to drink at. But he did have a good one this time. The pitcher he had played with since high school had opened a bar.

Kim Ganghyon had lasted three more years in the league than Hyonsu. He was a sidearm pitcher for the Fighters at one point, but after two years of cycling through operations and physical therapy, he was finished. Afterward he tried his hand at a number of businesses, but his failure was as quick as his fastball. This soju bar, near a college in Gwangju, was his fifth attempt at a comeback.

Hyonsu had been thinking of going by, but this particular visit wasn't planned. Eunju had given him the idea that morning, when she asked him to go check out their new housing situation before the official move on Sunday.

It was a long drive, but Eunju insisted. "We need to know the layout and how big it is, so we can figure out what to bring."

"There's nothing to figure out," Hyonsu protested. Her reasoning didn't make any sense to him. "It's the same size as this place."

But she would not relent. "Houses in the woods are usually smaller than they say they are. And the floor plan can be different."

As he put on his shoes, he asked, "So all you want me to do is go there and check it out?"

"Not just that. Didn't you say there's a young man who's already living there? You have to talk to him, okay? Figure out the bedroom situation and how we're going to share the bathroom and the kitchen, that kind of thing. We have to be clear from the beginning so it doesn't get awkward."

"So you want me to sit him down and go over whether we're going to share the washing machine and how we're going to split the water bill, that kind of thing?"

"Maybe you can convince him to move to the house next door. It's got to be uncomfortable for him to live with his boss's family, too."

Hyonsu stared at Eunju. How brazen she was. Was this inborn or consciously honed? He didn't have the skills to convince his new coworker to move next door. And he didn't really care much either way.

In any case, he called and told his new colleague, a man named Ahn Sunghwan, that he would stop by around eight o'clock. He figured he might as well pay Ganghyon's bar a visit along the way as a reward to himself for doing Eunju's bidding, especially since he was already heading toward Gwangju.

He arrived around six. He had planned to hand his old friend a small gift he'd brought, stay for one drink, and leave, but then he spotted three buddies from his high school team. None of them was still playing; they were all frittering away their time with meaningless jobs. They drank, ordered food, and then drank some more. They talked about the training camp where they had made a pact to be the best in the world and dreamed of stardom; they reminisced about how the handsome Ganghyon used to have legions of female high school fans. They recounted Hyonsu's famous three-run homer at the semi-finals of the nationwide high school competition. One bottle quickly became two and then eight, Hyonsu responsible for most of the consumption. Hours passed before the call came from Kim Hyongtae, catapulting him out of the bar.

Hyonsu's cell started ringing again as he reached the toll-gate to merge onto the highway. Eunju. She was going to call until he answered. Hyonsu turned off his phone. The high-way was choked with cars, maybe because it was Friday night. But when he passed through the tollgate, he spotted a pack of police cars. The back of his neck prickled. If this was a checkpoint, he was in trouble: his license had been revoked ninety-three days before for a drunk driving violation.

That day had not been so different from this one. He drank with friends at a soju bar and watched a game on TV, and Eunju had reached him by calling Hyongtae. He felt nice and buzzed when Hyongtae handed him his phone, smirking. Hyonsu felt his face flush. Eunju reacted almost pathologi-cally when he drank. Hyonsu was the only guy who got a call every hour badgering him to return home. After a certain point, he'd started ignoring her calls when he was out, but he couldn't wave Hyongtae's phone away. "Yeah?" he answered.

"Where are you? What are you doing? Are you drinking again?"

"I'm at dinner. I'm not drinking."

"Then why didn't you pick up?"

"I didn't hear it. You can't call Hyongtae, okay?"

"Then pick up your phone!"

Hyonsu could tell they were about to descend into a circu-lar argument. He quickly retreated. "What's up?"

"Sowon's sick. He's throwing up and he has a fever. A little while ago, he wanted me to help him get dressed. He said you promised to take him skiing."

Hyonsu's heart did a free fall. "Go to the hospital. I'll meet you there."

Hyonsu lurched out of the bar. He wasn't even aware that he was driving under the influence; he had forgotten he'd gone out drinking entirely until he was pulled over. He pleaded with the cop, explaining that his son was sick.

"I'm sure," came the reply.

He couldn't avoid blowing into the Breathalyzer; the machine screeched. Of course it did. Hyonsu suppressed the urge to speed away. His blood alcohol level was 0.09 percent, three times the legal limit. He was turned over to a local police station. Invoking his son's illness didn't work there, either. He was writing his statement when Eunju called again.

"Where are you?" Her voice was shrill.

"I'm on my way. I'm almost there. What did the doctor say?" Hyonsu whispered.

"He thinks it's encephalomeningitis. We need to go to a bigger hospital."

"So go!" Hyonsu shouted.

"What the hell? Of *course* I'm going! We're in a cab on our way to Donga Hospital right now. I called to tell you to meet us there!"

Having overheard their conversation, the cop became more sympathetic and sped through the process. As soon as it was over, Hyonsu hailed a cab and rushed to the hospital.

When he arrived, he found Sowon lying in a bed at the far end of the emergency room. Eunju was holding his hand. Sowon spotted Hyonsu first. "Dad."

"So you weren't drinking, huh?" Eunju sniped.

"What's going on?" Hyonsu asked, his eyes meeting Sowon's. He wanted to hold him, but he couldn't; the space between the beds was too narrow for a six-foot-three, 243-pound man. His hulking size was useless outside of a baseball diamond.

"Why are you so late?" Eunju asked.

"What's going on?" Hyonsu repeated.

"They say they have to do a spinal tap."

"A spinal tap?"

"They take . . ." Eunju glanced at Sowon and swallowed what she was about to say. "They tell me it's not dangerous, but they want me to sign a release saying they won't be liable if something happens to him. I was waiting for you. How can I make that decision all alone?"

Hyonsu wanted to shout, "Why *can't* you, when you always do whatever you want?" but stopped himself. "Where's the doctor?"

Eunju pointed at a man standing by the nurses' station in the middle of the ER. Hyonsu went up to the doctor, tempering his rage. The pediatric specialist said they had managed to control the symptoms with steroids for the moment but that he needed to perform the spinal tap. He would stick a long needle into Sowon's vertebrae to drain some fluid, thereby alleviating the pressure in his brain. They would use the sample for tests to figure out whether the infection was bacterial or viral.

"What's the difference?" Hyonsu asked.

"Viral meningitis is easy to treat, and he'll be fine," the doctor said.

"And bacterial?"

"He might experience some residual effects. It could be any-thing from hearing loss to developmental delays to epilepsy . . ."

Everything turned black before Hyonsu's eyes. His legs shook and he couldn't read the release. He dropped the pen several times before he could write his own name.

They wheeled Sowon away. Hyonsu went with them while Eunju remained outside. An assistant removed Sowon's shirt and had him curl into a fetal position while lying on one side. Sowon began to squirm. The assistant tried to hold him down, but it wasn't enough to keep the frightened child still. Sowon had glimpsed the long, thin needle. He looked up at Hyonsu with a silent request for help, and the doctor did, too. "Can you make sure he doesn't move?"

Hyonsu crouched next to the gurney, squeezing himself be-tween its side and the wall, sweating, his breathing ragged. "Sowon," he said gently. "Remember what I do whenever I get scared?"

Sowon stopped wriggling.

"Remember?"

Sowon pursed his lips as if to whistle.

"That's right. That's what we're going to do. I'll whistle out loud and you whistle along in your head. Once we finish the song, this scary thing is going to be over. Isn't that right, Doctor?"

"That's right," the doctor said, preparing a local anesthetic.

"What should we whistle?"

Sowon straightened his pointer and middle fingers, word-lessly forming legs. Hyonsu recalled the first scene of *The Bridge on the River Kwai*, a movie they often watched together. A unit of British POWs marched toward a Japanese prison camp, whistling the "Colonel Bogey March." Sowon didn't really understand the film, but he would rewind and watch that scene over and over again.

Hyonsu put his forefinger and middle finger on the edge of the gurney and whistled, their signal to begin the march. He began to whistle the tune, marching his fingers along the edge, tripping and twisting and wagging to the beat. A faint smile appeared on his son's face.

Sowon fell asleep as soon as the procedure was over. The doctor explained that he must be feeling more comfortable now that the pressure in his brain had eased, but Hyonsu remained crouched next to him, shaking. What if something happened to Sowon? What if he couldn't hear or walk or ride his bike or climb on the jungle gym or had seizures? It was a terrible night, the most terrifying of his thirty-six years. When he raised his head, Eunju's black gaze hit him like a wave of cold water, a mixture of disgust and resentment and fear and tears. He didn't know what to say to console her.

It turned out to be a viral infection, but Sowon was hospitalized for almost a month because the pressure in his brain proved difficult to regulate. They had to perform two additional spinal taps. All kinds of drugs were pumped into his small body.

Hyonsu commuted from the hospital to home to work. He brought food for his wife and son, ran errands, and took turns staying overnight. He didn't have the chance to tell Eunju about his suspended license. His anxiety about getting behind the wheel without a license gradually dulled, and by the time Sowon was ready to come home, he'd practically forgotten about it.

Everything went back to normal. Eunju went back to work at the high school cafeteria, and Hyonsu worked at the security company, went to the bar, watched baseball, and forgot or put off things he had to do, sliding behind the wheel at the end of each night. He continued to ignore Eunju's calls when he was out drinking and, like now, only gave any thought to whether he ought to be driving drunk when he was about to be stopped at a checkpoint.

~

Hyonsu peered out the driver's-side window. The line of cars in front of him began to move. It wasn't a checkpoint, thankfully—there had been an accident. The police had closed one lane and were dealing with the aftermath. An officer waved him through. He drove by carefully, but, as soon as he merged onto the highway, accelerated to seventy-five miles per hour. The engine whined and the body of the car shook, but Hyonsu didn't feel it; he just felt tired and depressed. He was thinking about the new apartment they'd just bought, or, rather, that Eunju had bought.

Ten days before, Eunju announced that she wanted to purchase a 1,200-square-foot apartment in Ilsan. Hyonsu studied his wife. She must be out of her mind. There was a cheap unit on the market, Eunju explained; the owner was going bankrupt and trying to sell quickly. It was in a nice neighborhood with good schools.

Hyonsu figured it was a good apartment if Eunju said so, but he couldn't square the cost in his head. It didn't make any financial sense. Even if they took the security deposit from their current apartment and drained their savings, they would still be short thirty million won. They couldn't possibly get a loan for that sum. And even if they could, what would they do about the taxes and how would they pay off the enormous interest? It would be better to eat three square meals a day in a rental, Hyonsu thought, than to suck hungrily on their fingers in a place they owned.

"That's why your life is the way it is," Eunju insisted. Her calculations were different. She set five account books down in front of Hyonsu.

"What's all this?"

"What do you think?"

It was money, a lot of money, that could cover the missing thirty million won and the taxes. Eunju began with what she said each time Hyonsu drank. "You think I scrimp and save for myself? No. I've been setting aside this money for us."

"What about the interest payments? How will we cover them?"

"We can put the new apartment up for rent."

"Then where are we going to live?"

"In housing provided by the company."

That meant volunteering to be stationed in the sticks somewhere. Hyonsu had his own reasons for not wanting to leave Seoul. He worked for a security company with contracts at important government facilities; he'd been with them since he retired from baseball. His first assignment was at a dam in the hills of Chungchong Province. The air was clean and tranquil, and the company provided free housing. The only problem was that all the amenities, from Sowon's kindergarten to the supermarket, were located in the larger town on the other side of the mountain. Eunju dipped into her savings and bought him a used Matiz. He was grateful for the car, but she had overlooked his physique when selecting it. It felt like he was stuffing himself into a suit of armor. He had to push the seat all the way back in order to be able to drive. Hyonsu wanted to insist on buying a slightly bigger car, but he knew he would only get shot down. He grumbled to himself about how everything in his life was so small and constricting.

The Matiz basically functioned as an ambulance all year. Sowon contracted illness after illness, from conjunctivitis to measles, and they would drive over that steep mountain in the middle of the night, Sowon burning with fever. On snowy days, their lives were at the tiny car's mercy. Hyonsu wasn't sure he was ready to go back to such a small town, especially after Sowon's bout with meningitis.

"For how long?" In Hyonsu's mind, two opposing feelings collided—the sweetness of the phrase "our apartment" and anxiety about dormant future crises.

"Three years. By that time we'll have paid off some of the loan, and then we can refinance."

"Why don't we buy something smaller? We can set our sights lower and still have our own place without stretching ourselves thin. It's only the three of us. We could do with less space."

"No. We need it."

"This is like building a house on thin ice. How do we know something won't happen to our incomes in the future?"

"I know what's going to happen in the future," Eunju said triumphantly. "We're going to sign the contract."

There was no room for compromise. Apparently this apartment was what Eunju perceived was a requirement to enter the middle class, something she fervently desired.

Hyonsu swallowed the sour tang of nervousness and submitted a form volunteering for an assignment in the countryside. He was immediately given a new assignment. Nobody
wanted to go to the countryside; everyone else was clamoring
to be transferred to posts in cities. His first day at Seryong
Dam would be August 30. Eunju bought the apartment and
found a renter that very day. Only one thing bothered her
about the arrangement: the young man living in the house
they were assigned to.

HYONSU GLANCED AT HIS WATCH. It was 9:03, an hour and
three minutes past the time he had told Ahn Sunghwan, his
new employee, that he'd be there. He took his cell from his
shirt pocket and turned it on. There were four missed calls—
two from Eunju, of course, and two from Sunghwan. Sunghwan had also texted him the code to the front door. Hyonsu
called him back, but he didn't pick up. He slid his cell back
into his pocket, cracked the car windows, and sat up straight.
A glow-in-the-dark skull grinned from below his rearview
mirror, dangling in the breeze. It had been a birthday present
from Sowon. He smiled. Other than the fact that he was also
a lefty, his kid didn't take after him at all. He didn't take after
Eunju, either. In fact, he was just like Hyonsu's late mother,
in both his appearance and his personality. Hyonsu liked
that. He imagined that Sowon was destined for something
different—something better. The skull wasn't just decoration;
it reflected his pride in his son, who was so different from him.
    Right after he passed a sign that said *Seryong Rest Area:
1 m*, a white BMW pulled up behind him and began to flash its
brights. They were on a winding uphill stretch of the highway

and three large trailers weighed down with steel plates were barreling along in the next lane. *Asshole*, Hyonsu thought, glaring at the BMW in his rearview mirror.

~

The Matiz slowly changed lanes and merged in front of a trailer, as leisurely as a dog that had just woken up from a nice long nap. Yongje leaned on the horn and blasted past. Why hadn't the stupid car move over when he flashed it? A car that slow shouldn't be in the fast lane to begin with. He looked back at it through his rearview mirror. A glow-in-the-dark skull grinned at him through the dark front window of the Matiz. Yongje took his hand off the horn and accelerated. The Matiz fell away from view and his thoughts returned to Hayong. Divorce, custody battle, restraining order, alimony. How *dare* she?

Only hours before, his lawyer had called him at his hotel room—he was in Seoul at an orthodontics conference—and told him something he'd almost never heard in his life: "We lost."

The opposing counsel was renowned for his high win rate. Throughout the proceedings, which Hayong hadn't even deigned to show up for, her lawyer had gone on at length about the ways a clearly "disturbed" individual named Oh Yongje had mentally and physically abused his wife and daughter over the past decade. Unfortunately, his story was supported by reams of documentation. Photographs of Hayong's naked body covered in lash marks, bundles of switches hanging throughout the house, Hayong's signed statement, doctor's notes for every single bruise leading up to her miscarriage. There were even recordings of their fights. More damning still was Seryong's taped deposition. The girl had a good memory, laying out in detail when, where, and how her dad had corrected her and her mother's mistakes. At the end, she expressed her frank, tearful wish that her mother be granted sole custody.

Yongje's lawyer's arguments about Hayong's practice of leaving the family whenever she wanted to, her lack of economic power, and her poor child-rearing ability had, apparently, not been persuasive. Hayong's lawyer entered trivial licenses into the record that pointed to her ability to support Seryong. A baking certificate? A cooking certificate for Korean cuisine? Yongje recalled how Hayong had gone to cooking classes in town about two years back; she had said she was doing it for fun. She left the house at the same time every week, taking the art class shuttle with Seryong and returning together with her. Yongje hadn't thought twice about it—it didn't inconvenience him and nothing about it raised his suspicions. He didn't mind her improved cooking skills. Never in his wildest dreams had he imagined that she was laying the groundwork for a divorce.

After a long explanation excusing his poor performance, his lawyer had added, "It seems you didn't know that woman very well."

Yongje stiffened. How dare this incompetent hack try to distract from his defeat by insulting him? He wasn't pleased with the way the attorney referred to Hayong as "that woman," either. Nobody was allowed to talk about his wife that way. Yongje advised his lawyer to call his own stupid wife "that woman" and hung up. He threw his phone down on the bed and stalked over to the window. Cars and people were moving about smoothly twenty stories below.

His own world had been orderly a mere three months before: people followed his orders and behaved according to his rules. But at the end of April, Hayong had vanished. It was the day they went to the coast to celebrate their wedding anniversary. They had dinner at a restaurant overlooking the sea, and everything had gone fine. The problem was when they called a car service to drive them back to the hotel. The driver requested more money than had been advertised, telling them the rate had recently gone up. Yongje gave him a piece of his mind. He wasn't about to be swindled. That was when Hayong did something truly shocking. Looking mortified, she took cash out of her own wallet and pressed it into the driver's hand. To top it off, she apologized. "I'm sorry. He's had a little too much to drink."

When they got up to the room, he slapped her around. Then he drove her up to Hangyeryong Peak. At the very top, he grabbed her wallet and cell phone and forced her out of the car. His plan had been for her to reflect on her behavior, not for her to leave him and file for divorce.

At first, he wasn't concerned when she didn't return; it had only been two days, she'd find her way home eventually. He was willing to take her back and administer the appropriate punishment if she begged for forgiveness. But after a week passed without a peep, he decided to find her and drag her back himself. He was ready to beat her until she was unable to walk for a month or two.

There were only a few places she could have gone. He contacted her father, her relatives, the few friends she had, and all the people she'd called from her cell phone recently, but he couldn't find her anywhere. Nobody had even seen her. Finally, he found a clue at a Sokcho hotel. They said she'd called the hotel from an emergency phone on Hangyeryong and asked for a taxi, saying she'd been in an accident. He tracked down the cabbie, who remembered her clearly. Hayong paid with a hundred-thousand-won bank check, he said. Yongje asked the driver if he'd written down the check number, but of course he hadn't.

Yongje turned to a company called the Supporters, which he had used in the past. These so-called professionals drained his funds for two weeks and still couldn't sniff out a single clue. A month later, at the end of May, he finally heard from Hayong in the form of court papers. Looking at them, Yongje laughed maniacally. First, because he was relieved that Hayong hadn't disappeared off the face of the earth, and then because it was so ridiculous. He was the one who had turned the daughter of an electronics repairman into a princess, showering her with luxuries. And here she was, repaying his kindness and generosity by filing for divorce.

He hired an attorney. First, he would win the proceeding, then he would concentrate on finding Hayong. The lawyer laid out a few guidelines. For the time being, he should stop correcting Seryong; he would be at a disadvantage if his reputation was sullied. Yongje abided by that for the most part and never left a mark on her. Except for that one time when the idiot in unit 102 interfered and almost made it an issue. He followed all of his lawyer's stupid rules, not looking for Hayong and not pressuring her father. After all that, he never imagined he might lose.

After hanging up on his useless lawyer, he took out a bottle of water from the hotel minifridge and sat down. He downed half of it in a single gulp. Where was Hayong? How had she gathered all of those materials and squirreled them away until she could deploy them in court? One thing was for certain: the recordings she submitted had been made over the past two years. The medical certificate about her miscarriage pointed to the exact time she started recording. That had been two springs ago, around the same time as that incident with the cat. Yongje put each moment of that day under a microscope.

Yongje didn't like spending time with people. He didn't go to alumni gatherings or play golf or go out drinking. His social life consisted of a monthly day of volunteer work with the other doctors in his building. In his free time he worked on his one true passion: constructing intricate universes in his basement workshop. Every spring, he would chop down a handsome cypress and embark on a new project. He would cut the tree into the desired lengths, shave off the bark, and dry them in the shade before slicing them into small, toothpick-like sticks. That was the only step in the entire process that was done by machine. Once he had the materials— perfectly sized sticks, tools, glue, and resin—he could realize a world of his own making: a forest, a wall, a hut, a church, a bridge, all coming together to form a fairy-tale village or a castle. He'd had this hobby for as long as he could remember. It was work that demanded artistry and patience, time and concentration. Every Christmas Eve he would unveil his new creation, and the awe that appeared on the faces of his wife and child more than compensated for the effort. He would feel content every time he saw his work displayed on the shelf in the living room under their family portrait. The following spring, when he started on a new masterpiece, the old work would be moved into storage.

Three years ago, he built an igloo-like dome. Inside, he created an entire city of houses and buildings, streets and parks. He seated a family on a bench—the husband holding a young son next to a wife and daughter. He carved the dolls down to their minuscule facial expressions, then painted them. He strung a small bulb on the streetlight to illuminate them. He created a constellation of stars on the ceiling of the dome with blinking lights. It was the best work he'd ever created; it housed the perfect family of his dreams.

The night before the unveiling, he was so excited he couldn't sleep. Over the last few years his family's enthusiasm for his work had begun to wane. To a layperson, their reactions would look the same as before, but he was an intuitive man who could tell the difference between imitation and true admiration. This time, he was sure Hayong and Seryong would praise him sincerely. His heart pounded as he imagined the moment. But when he revealed the model with a flourish, their reactions were tepid. Seryong's applause was limp and Hayong's smile was wooden, her eyes unsmiling. When he asked if she liked it, Hayong replied, "Of course I do." She might as well have said, "I hate it."

The next morning Yongje took the dome away. He threw a cloth over it and shoved it in the storage area. He brought back alder branches to use as switches and hung them around the house.

Winter departed and spring returned. The first morning of April, under the warm sun, Yongje opened the storage area, which had been closed all winter. It was time for a new project, time to forget about the painful Christmas experience and immerse himself in creating a new world. Whistling, he took out a folding ladder. He rolled his small cart away from the wall and grabbed a hatchet from his toolbox. That was when he heard something strange—whimpering or maybe meowing. Yongje froze in place. It was coming from inside the dome.

He crept over slowly and yanked off the cloth. Inside was a cat with the coloring of a lynx. It raised its tail and arched its back, hissing in warning. Behind it he saw three squirming kittens. The entrance to the dome was crushed, the walls had crumpled, and one side of the top had collapsed. The city was unrecognizable; the dolls that had formed the family on the bench were rolling under the kittens' paws.

He experienced a moment of pure rage. It was unforgivable. Anything that interfered with his creations had to be punished accordingly. He yanked a kitten out by its neck. Sharp claws pierced his shirtsleeves and dug into his arm, leaving behind hot trails of pain. He let go of the kitten. Blood beaded up from the long scratch marks. The mother cat was readying for a second attack, her legs hunched and teeth bared, hissing.

The sight of his own blood roused his fighting spirit. Yongje picked up the hatchet. He lifted the roof off of his beloved dome and flung it behind him. The cat leaped off its hind legs and flew toward his chest. His hatchet sliced through the air and the cat fell to the floor, its head almost entirely severed. He looked around for the kittens, but they had run away in the meantime. Holding the dead mother cat by the tail, Yongje turned to the door and saw Hayong and Seryong standing there, their faces pale. Their eyes were glued to the animal in his hand. He moved toward them and they slowly inched backward, as if he were holding a human body, not a stupid cat. He tossed the animal into the yard.

"Call Yim," he ordered his wife.

Hayong didn't answer. Nor did she budge. She just stood there with Seryong, staring at him. He thought he had taught her by now—that she shouldn't look at him with disgust, that she should always say yes when he asked her to do something, and that she should always follow directions within ten seconds. The clock ticked in his head. Four, three, two . . .

The two females were lucky, because right at that moment Yim, the groundskeeper, appeared as though summoned by telepathy. If it weren't for him, Yongje would have made the two dig the animal's grave with their pretty little hands.

After the others left, Yongje tore apart the storage area to find the kittens; he found two. He buried them alive with their mother in the hole the groundskeeper had dug. But he couldn't find the last one. It was as lucky as his wife and daughter.

For the rest of the day the house was silent. Yongje's emotions flared. These two females never did anything to contribute to the peace and happiness of the household, which was of the utmost importance for him. That night, it was as if they were conspiring to make his blood boil. Seryong gasped every time she met his eyes. If they brushed past each other, she trembled and inched backward. At night, Hayong provoked him. She was supposed to be waiting for him in bed, but he found her on the phone in the study. She sounded positively vivacious as she said, to whomever she was speaking, "I'll try." She hadn't used such a lively voice with him in years.

"Try what?" Yongje asked in a low voice, standing in the doorway. He saw her tense.

"Nothing." She hung up and turned to face him.

He felt the blood surging to his head. To him, that sounded like "You don't need to know." It was time to correct her manners. He was prepared to be severe, to instruct her about the kinds of things she shouldn't say to her husband. He would correct her in a way that even this stupid woman would be able to remember for a long time. "What did you just say to me?"

"Nothing—" Her eyes grew wide as she realized what was coming.

It was too late, of course. He was already in front of her, hitting her hard on the cheek with his fist. So hard that she fell against the corner of the desk, abdomen first, and collapsed on the floor.

"Say it again!"

"The women's group asked me . . . to teach them how to bake apple pie . . ."

He yanked her up by the hair and shoved her into the corner of the desk one more time. How dare she lie to him. He opened her cell phone and looked at her call history. A blocked number. "Who was it?"

Her mouth sealed shut and her eyes drained of emotion. Silence and vacant eyes were the tools Hayong used to evade his control. It drove him insane. There was only one way to deal with this. He would blow off steam by hitting her a little, then use the switch. Stripping her naked and whipping her didn't cause internal injuries that would necessitate medical attention, but would hurt and humiliate her enough to force her stubborn lips to open and spit out the words he wanted to hear, for her to beg, "Please forgive me." He never forgave her there, of course; the last step was sex. That was how he drove submission into her bones.

He followed his usual procedure. But that day, instead of begging for forgiveness, Hayong held her stomach and moaned in pain. When he saw the blood leaking from between her legs, he realized she wasn't faking it. He had no choice but to take her to the hospital.

She had been eleven weeks pregnant. The doctor asked if she had known. Hayong said no; she just thought her period was irregular. From her stunned expression, it seemed she was telling the truth. Yongje asked about the sex of the baby. The doctor replied that he didn't know. At eleven weeks, it was too early to say for sure.

A nurse wheeled Hayong into the operating room. Yongje sat on a chair outside and brooded. He was in as much shock as Hayong, if not more. Only one thing was missing from his life: a son. For nine years, he had tried to supply the missing piece, but Hayong couldn't get pregnant. Not even once. The doctor did some tests and found that neither of them was infertile. He said they should just relax and be patient. By now, Yongje had given up. He shuddered, imagining what was going on in the operating room. He felt as though his own body were being chopped to pieces. He became certain he had lost his son.

When he brought Hayong home, Yongje explained to her how her bad faith and carelessness had killed his son, about the shock and hurt and betrayal he'd suffered after the operation, while she slept peacefully. Apparently, that had been the turning point for Hayong: this conversation was the first she'd recorded and submitted to the court.

It was baffling. The woman he knew wasn't smart or detail oriented. She wasn't tough enough to use her daughter to win in court. She knew what would happen to Seryong if she left him. Hayong suddenly seemed incomprehensible to him. She had apparently ended her statement to the court with the following note: "I stayed in this awful marriage for twelve years because I was afraid my husband would kill my daughter and me if I asked for a divorce or ran away with Seryong. Now I realize that we will actually die if I don't end the marriage." What had pushed her from obedience to rebellion? Who had instigated this?

It had to be her father. Because of his attorney, he had done nothing to get the man to back off, despite his certainty that his father-in-law had been involved. He didn't have to sit back any longer. The trial was over and his lawyer was gone.

～

Yongje left his hotel and headed to Yongin. The electronics shopping district was deserted and his father-in-law's repair shop was even quieter. His father-in-law hung up the phone warily when Yongje stepped inside. "Where's Hayong?"

His father-in-law started to wipe down the screen of a TV with a rag. "She hasn't been in touch."

"I let you be for four months. I expected you would reason

with her and send her home. I only just found out you were the mastermind behind all of this."

A customer came in with a vacuum cleaner.

"Tell her she has one week. If she doesn't come back in a week, she'll never see Seryong again."

His father-in-law just stared at him.

"The trial has no particular meaning for me. Hayong should know what I mean by that."

Yongje drove home. He wasn't going to appeal. Instead of hiring a new lawyer, he would give the Supporters another chance. He would have them scour Korea to find her and bring her home, without harming a single hair on her head. Nobody else could touch her; Hayong was his. She had to return to her place, and that was where he would punish her. First, though, he would deal with the traitor under his roof before she was taken away from him.

By the time he got home, it was pouring rain. Yongje unfurled an umbrella and went slowly up the front steps. Inside, he caught sight of one of Seryong's shoes dangling on the ledge to the entrance of the living room. She must have kicked them off. Ill-tempered colt. He glanced at the dirt on the floor, at the smudge of her palm on the mirror above the shoe cabinet, and at her indoor shoe pouch and backpack flung haphazardly by the door. He could hear music coming from her room. He leaned his umbrella against the wall, turned on the living room light, and looked at the empty memo pad hanging on the wall. He had pasted eleven sticky notes on it before leaving that morning, and they hadn't fallen to the floor. The housekeeper wouldn't have touched them—she knew his preferences well. It was Seryong. She was always the problem.

He found them stuck to the family portrait above the sofa, pasted all over his face. The first was in the middle of his forehead. *Going to Seoul for a conference. Planning to be home tomorrow afternoon.* The second was on his left eye. *Everything must be in its place when I return.* The third was on his right eye. *Follow the rules.* The next eight hung from his mouth, like a tongue. *Make sure you don't track dirt into the house. Don't touch the mirror in the entryway. Pick up the phone before the third ring. Don't dress up in your mother's things.* He looked like an idiot with those sticky notes on his face. Seryong was mocking him. His pulse began to thrum behind his ears. A backstabbing wife and an ungrateful daughter—what a team.

Yongje tore off the notes and stalked into his bedroom. While he was away, she had done everything he'd told her not to—Hayong's face powder covered the vanity; lotion samples and open lipstick and mascara tubes were scattered about. He opened Hayong's closet, which looked like it had been ransacked. After placing his car keys and wallet on the dresser and hanging his jacket and tie in his closet, he rolled up his shirtsleeves and went to Seryong's room. He opened the door to a scene unlike any he'd seen in his house.

The floor was littered with a pair of crumpled-up shorts, an inside-out shirt, a rolled-up sock, remnants of firecrackers, pieces of construction paper, and a cluster of balloons. On her desk, three votive candles were burning, and her stuffed animals were perched next to them, wearing party hats. The model Ferris wheel Hayong had bought for her was slowly rotating in front of it all, churning out a repetitive melody. He thought he had thrown that toy away. Rain was coming in through the half-open window, extinguishing the mosquito coil that sat on the sill.

Seryong was asleep. Her hair was loose, her face painted in garish makeup, Hayong's white sleeveless blouse draped over her small frame like a dress. It barely covered her underwear. She looked like the child hooker from *Taxi Driver*.

Yongje sucked in a breath. Hot, wild anger churned in his gut, as though he had downed a shot on an empty stomach. He bent over Seryong's ear. "Seryong."

No answer. Her eyes moved slowly behind closed lids, on the boundary between a dream and reality. He reached out and stroked her throat with his thumb, her skin soft and supple to the touch. "Open your eyes."

Seryong's eyes froze under her lids.

"Daddy's home." Yongje watched as his daughter's eyelashes trembled. Her breathing became labored and the peach fuzz on her cheeks stood on end. But she didn't open her eyes. "Oh Seryong," he said, pressing his thumb into her throat, a warning that he would make her open her eyes one way or another.

She opened her eyes, which flickered nervously as they searched his face, trying to gauge whether she would be spared punishment.

"Happy birthday, sweetie." He tugged her by the neck to pull her into a sitting position. Seryong just stared as his fist flew into her face. When Yongje stopped punching, she lay limp on the bed. He grabbed her by the hair and yanked her back into a sitting position, then tugged her hair to force her to look at him. Blood was dribbling out of her nose and down her jaw. Her lips were stubbornly closed even as she groaned in pain.

"You had fun, I see." He shoved the eleven sticky notes in her face.

Seryong shook her head.

"You threw yourself such a nice party." Yongje slammed Seryong's face into the wall; on the rebound, she fell off the bed. Something resembling pomegranate seeds flew out of her mouth. Her front teeth, he thought, and turned on the light. He couldn't find them. Well, they would be of no use anyway. He snuffed the candles out with his thumb and forefinger and unplugged the toy; it felt nice and heavy in his hand. The perfect size.

Seryong scooted back toward her desk on her bottom, shaking her head, trying to smile, as if to beg, Please don't do that, Daddy, please don't. He hurled the Ferris wheel at her, which grazed her cheek and hit the edge of the desk before falling to the ground and smashing into pieces. Seryong, a forced smile still hanging on her face, stiffened as a tear rolled down her cheek. The bottom of the white blouse had turned yellow.

"Didn't I tell you not to touch your mother's things?"

An eyelid trembled. Yongje wondered if she knew that the steel toy had missed her because of his restraint, not luck.

"Get up. You need to be made to understand what you did wrong." He yanked his black leather belt out from his belt loops.

Seryong slid shakily up to stand, bracing herself against the wall.

"Take off your clothes." He heard a noise from the window and turned around.

A cat was perched on the sill, glaring at him, its hind legs bent, preparing to pounce. Its short fur bristled. It was as big as a lynx. It looked like that cat Yongje had killed a long time ago. Could it be that kitten that got away?

In that brief moment, Seryong reached over to the candles. Before he could anticipate what she was doing, a votive flew at him. He swung his arm to block it, but he was too late; it hit him square on the forehead and dumped hot wax in his eyes. The second candleholder struck his nose. The glass shattered underfoot. He grabbed his face and screamed, pawing frantically at the wax covering his eyes and nose.

When he regained his sight, Seryong was gone. So was the cat. Yongje grabbed a towel from the bathroom and wiped his hot, aching face.

Yongje wasn't a man who rushed; he always moved quietly and elegantly. But this was no time to be graceful. He ran to the kitchen, his footsteps heavy. He dug around in the freezer for ice and put some in a plastic bag, his hands shaking. He pressed the bag onto his face as he lumbered back into his bedroom for his car keys.

He sprinted outside and, with one hand still pressing the makeshift ice pack to his cheek, threw the car into reverse, skidding backward down the sloped driveway. When he hit the road, he spun the car around and zoomed toward the main entrance of the arboretum. That was the only place she could go; the rear entrance would be locked.

The arm of the main entrance gate went up as Yongje roared toward it. Rage coursed through his veins, incinerating whatever rational thought remained—the only thing that separated humans from beasts.

His eyes narrowed; he hunted Seryong as if she were an animal, his senses alert to her traces alone. How would he punish her for this? His pulse thundered. His eyes bored down side streets as he drove. The gate to the elementary school was locked, the medical clinic was dark, and the few stores along the road all had their shutters down. They must have closed early for the ceremony on the lake. Only the gas station and the police station remained lit. Through its glass facade, he could see that there was no one inside except an old cop dozing away, his legs propped on his desk. The fog thickened, but he was used to it. If he couldn't see something, it was because it wasn't there. His daughter was nowhere to be found.

He circled the low-lying village. Everything was eerily quiet. The bad weather must have forced the festivities to wrap up quickly.

He headed toward the maintenance bridge and called Yim, who was drinking at the rest area. He asked if Seryong was there.

"Haven't seen her," the old man replied.

Yongje headed toward the dam conservancy and ordered Yim to go lock the main entrance to the arboretum, search the premises with the security guard, and call immediately if they found her.

He drove to the security office of the conservancy. The guard on duty looked out the small window. Yongje had bumped into him a few times in front of the Annex. What was his name? Park?

"Has my daughter come by here, by any chance?" he called out the window.

"In the middle of the night?" Park asked.

"Did she come or not?"

"No."

Yongje looked up at the maintenance bridge. Streetlights lined the sides of the bridge, but he couldn't see anything else; the fog had thickened and was now interfering with his search. "Can I go up there?"

"I don't think a kid would go there in the middle of the night."

"Listen," Yongje said, exasperated. "I'm telling you to remove the chain from the entrance of the bridge so I can drive up and take a look."

Park shook his head. "I can't leave the security office unstaffed."

Yongje didn't like this man's attitude. Yongje almost reminded him that he owned the house Park lived in, but he suppressed his mounting rage and walked up to the bridge. Nothing.

He called Yim again, who hadn't found her yet, either. There was only one other place she could possibly be: the lakeshore road.

Even with his brights on, he couldn't see more than ten feet in front of him. It was even foggier along the road and it was still raining hard. He spotted something whitish near the entrance to Seryong Ranch. It wasn't a form; it was a movement. But when he arrived at the entrance, he saw nothing. He rubbed his makeshift ice pack on his forehead, which was starting to peel. Had he really seen that movement, or had he misjudged the flow of the fog? A person couldn't just vanish. Where would she have gone?

Yongje took out a flashlight and ran up to the old ranch house. It was too quiet. The roof of the old house had caved in; she wouldn't have gone in there. He went up to the old barn and opened the door. He was assaulted by the rotten stench of old waste and a swarm of mosquitoes. She wasn't there, either.

Yongje returned to his car and careened back toward the dock. He swung the car around at the steel doors and grabbed his flashlight. This was the last place she could be. He kicked the doors with his foot; the entrance was locked. He saw a gap about a foot high under the doors; Seryong could have crawled underneath. He shined his light through the fence and scanned the banks. Vines and scrub covered the ground. The bank stretched all the way to the dam; it was probably over half a mile long. He'd have to recruit the entire village to search that area. "Seryong, I know you're there."

No response.

"You can come out now. I won't punish you." He softened his voice with a herculean effort. "You see, Daddy just had a bad day today." A damp breeze wafted up from the lake, rustling the vines. He stood close to the fence and swept his flashlight methodically across the banks. "And then Daddy came home, and nothing was in its place. Daddy just wanted to relax after a long day, you know?" Yongje paused, seething. What the hell was he doing? He was standing there whining in the rain, getting drenched. What he'd really wanted to say slipped out: "And you made everything *worse*, you little bitch!" He clenched the flashlight between his teeth, grabbed the fence with both hands, and shoved the tip of his shoe into a gap to pull himself up. Then he thought better of it. He didn't want to climb over the barbed wire on top of the fence. It was unlikely he would find her here anyway. What eleven-year-old would hide near a dark lake in the middle of the night? He knew his daughter wasn't that bold. She was probably in the arboretum somewhere. He rubbed his palms on his pants. "Seryong! If you come out on the count of three, I'll forget this ever happened. One . . . two . . ."

Nothing.

"Fine. Let's see how long you last out here." He whirled around and left.

Yim and another security guard, Gwak, reported that they had searched all over but hadn't found her. Hayong must have taught her how to disappear, Yongje thought bitterly, as he drove back toward the Annex. He would retrace his steps to see what he'd forgotten or overlooked. But when he got there, he saw that the living room light was on in unit 102. So that was where she was. He couldn't believe he hadn't thought of it before. She would have sought help from someone who had performed an act of kindness once before. He crept up the front steps and pressed the bell. No response. He rang again and again and again. Still no answer. He went down to the ground floor and listened, his ear cocked toward the living room. He heard faint TV sounds. Were the two of them hiding inside, peeking out at him? Or was that idiot actually touching her? If that was the case, he would bury the pervert alive. If he was just hiding her from her own father, he would make sure that asshole served ten years in prison for kidnapping.

Yongje circled around to the backyard. The bedroom window was closed but not latched. It was dark inside. He yanked the window open and hopped onto the sill. The room was empty. The bedroom door was slightly ajar, letting the living room light filter in. Yongje took off his shoes and left them on the windowsill before stepping inside.

A laptop was on the desk next to an empty beer can, a glass bottle filled with cigarette butts, a notebook, a ball-point pen, and a cell phone. The TV chattered away in the living room. He searched the master bedroom, the balcony, the bathroom, the basement, even inside the closets. Nobody was there, though it looked like someone had just been home. That idiot must have taken Seryong back to the clinic. This time he would know better than to call the cops; he would probably bring her back here afterward.

He pulled out a fistful of tissues from the Kleenex box on the dining table, wiped up the water and footprints he'd left throughout the house, and climbed back outside through the window. Back at home, he locked Seryong's window and turned off all the lights, then pulled a chair up to the living room window. He would wait for them to return in the comfort of his own home.

~

Hyonsu rubbed his eyes. It was raining too hard to open the windows of the Matiz, and he was getting drowsy. Cranking the AC didn't help. His mind kept drifting. He was driving around seventy-five miles per hour, but it felt as if he were moving very slowly, as though floating in a balloon. The words on the signs he passed by looked like abstract symbols.

That was how he missed the turnoff to Seryong Lake. By the time he turned around and reached the Seryong interchange again, an hour had gone by. He called Sunghwan. His new employee didn't pick up his cell or his landline. There would be no point in going if Sunghwan wasn't there. Then again, maybe it was better this way. He wouldn't have to broach awkward topics with his soon-to-be employee and he would be able to report back to Eunju that he did what she asked. I did go but was running a little late, he would say. Sunghwan was out so he just texted me the entrance code.

He slipped his cell phone back in his shirt pocket and buttoned it as always. He must be in the commercial district now, he thought. But it was late, and the few shops he saw were all closed. Fog choked the empty streets, obstructing his vision. He had never seen anything like it—this fog was like a living organism. He thought he might have missed the entrance when he finally came across the sign he'd been looking for.

He took a right and followed the road as it ascended. The fog poured from the black sky like an avalanche. Visibility grew even worse. The streetlights were useless. He searched for the entrance, his eyes heavy from the alcohol. The road was suddenly darker and narrower; he encountered a sharp curve turning nearly 180 degrees, but he didn't slow down. The car hurtled around the bend, teetering, barely able to handle the centrifugal force. A second curve was suddenly upon him. He slammed on his brakes and jerked the steering wheel. By the time he saw a flash of white emerge from the fog, it was too late. He heard the screech of his tires as they skidded on the road. His visual acuity, honed by countless baseballs hurtling toward him at over eighty-five miles per hour, allowed him to witness every moment of this nightmare.

A long white object had struck his hood, then slid onto the road, where it landed with a thud.

Hyonsu thought he heard a sharp scream. Or did *he* make

that sound? His head snapped back and then lolled forward, the seat belt digging into his ribs. His breath caught in his throat. His vision swam. It took a while for the shock of the crash to leach from his body, and twice as long as that for him to be able to raise his head.

Hyonsu didn't move, his hands still gripping the wheel. His eyes were fixed straight ahead, but his mind was six years in the past, reliving the day he realized nothing in his life was going to go as he planned.

Jamsil Baseball Stadium, top of the ninth. Runner on first. The Fighters, down by three runs, tied it up. The coach sent in a pinch hitter for the catcher, who hit into a double play to end the rally. Before the bottom of the ninth, the coach pulled a double switch for the catcher and pitcher. The announcer boomed: "Now pitching for the Fighters, Lee Sangchol. Now catching for the Fighters, Choi Hyonsu." Anticipation and fear dogged Hyonsu as he went out onto the field. He looked up at the crowd behind the first-base line as he took his position. This was the first time Eunju had come to see him this season. Five-year-old Sowon was next to her.

At one point, Hyonsu had been a star player. Everyone said that he had the makings of a great catcher. At least, that was what they said while he was in college. Once he started playing baseball for a living, he started to falter. He committed errors at decisive moments.

The main issue was his left arm, which seized from time to time. It was something he had dealt with since his high school days, but it had worsened during his mandatory military service and become chronic in the minors. He would be charged with a passed ball. He couldn't do anything about it; all he could do was fumble around and wait for his control to return. Nobody understood what was going on. For him, it was a shameful secret, something that scared him. The orthopedist couldn't explain it and the psychiatrist concluded it was a symptom of psychological pressure. He was advised to avoid stress, which meant he would have to take off the catcher's mask. He didn't want to do that. He wanted to succeed—not just for himself, but for Sowon. He wanted his son to see his father be celebrated for a home run in the majors. He wanted Sowon to be proud to be his son. But pitchers didn't trust him; position players tensed when he strode onto the field. He wasn't called up to the big leagues, though he tried everything. He was relegated to the minors with its rows of empty stands, poor pay, and anxiety about being traded or released.

He had recently been called up to the majors, and today Sowon was here. This was his chance to make his dreams come true. He needed to focus. The leadoff man was at bat. Hyonsu signed for an inside slider. The ball grazed the batter's helmet and caromed behind home plate. Runner on first. The next batter squared up to bunt. From the dugout came the sign to bring the infield in. Hyonsu signed for an outside curveball. But Lee was clearly off his game and continued to miss his marks. Ball four; another free pass. The third batter stepped into the batter's box. He kicked the dirt in front of the plate. Hyonsu watched him from the corner of his eye. This guy was known for his line drives to the opposite side. From the dugout came the signal to pitch for a strikeout; next up was the cleanup hitter. The problem was that Lee couldn't seal the deal. He couldn't hit his spots. Ball one away, second pitch in the dirt. As he blocked the ball, Hyonsu's heart sank. Things were getting worse. He had to approach the mound, calm Lee down, and get him out of this rut.

Hyonsu signed for a changeup, Lee's signature pitch, which was supposed to fly in straight before dropping in front of the home plate. The ball came in low. With a crack the ball shot toward center field. It was just a single, but the guy on second rounded third and was headed for home. The center fielder threw the ball to Hyonsu as he blocked home plate. The runner slid in, one cleat in the air. Everything turned black. The spikes had impaled his shoulder. Hyonsu rolled on the ground and the ball rolled out of his glove. He couldn't stop it from happening. He couldn't move his arm. It was as if a heated metal hook had bored into his shoulder. A hush fell over the crowd.

In the years since, Hyonsu never forgot that moment. Not the split second that felt like an eternity nor the oppressive silence in the stadium as his hopes and dreams were crushed. The only sound was Sowon's voice crying out: "Daddy!"

Hyonsu pried his hands off the wheel. Did he just hear Sowon scream? He wiped his sweaty palms on his shirt. He couldn't take his eyes off the limp white thing on the road. Maybe it was just a road sign he had hit, or a wild animal. But he already knew what that white thing was. A child wearing white. A girl, who flew at him, her long hair lashing his windshield, materializing out of nothing like a ghost.

He staggered out of the car. He heard his feet splashing in the rain. He smelled something as he walked through the fog.

The smell of salt, of the ocean. It triggered his memories: sorghum fields swaying bloodred under the moon, the ocean breeze wafting over the stalks, the glimmer of the lighthouse beyond the mountain at the far edge of the field. A boy walking through the fields, clutching his father's shoes and a flashlight.

Hyonsu stopped. The girl was lying a few steps away. Half of her long hair was covering her face, while the other half was swirling limply in a puddle. One leg stuck straight out from under her white dress, while the other was bent awkwardly at an unnatural angle. She didn't seem to be breathing.

Was she dead? He didn't dare touch her. He wasn't even thinking about calling a hospital or emergency services. His throat closed. His impulse was to turn around, get back in the car, and drive as quickly as he could out of this horrible nightmare. He looked around. There were no houses nearby. He didn't see any cars. Only the streetlights illuminated the road. He looked at his car. He thought he could see Eunju and Sowon sitting side by side through the cracked windshield, their faces shocked and sad, just like the day he'd gotten his shoulder injury. He thought of their new apartment, their new life, now on thin ice.

Hyonsu backed toward his car, thoughts leaping incoherently into his mind but coalescing in a specific direction. He looked behind him at the girl's body lying in the road. If someone else drove through here, they would spot her instantly. What would become of him—and of Sowon—then?

Hyonsu returned to the girl and knelt beside her. Through the long hair that covered her face, he noticed that she was wearing a lot of makeup. The heavy eye shadow made her eyelids look like dark holes. He could see toothless gum between her bruised lips. What had happened to her?

This wasn't right. It wasn't fair. He'd never even killed a mouse. He'd never committed a crime, never taken anything that wasn't his. After his baseball career ended, he'd never even wished for something grand. All he'd wanted was to be able to support his family, make his son proud, and have a shot of soju from time to time. Was that so much to ask? The rage that had been simmering beneath his terror swelled as he looked at this girl. Who the hell was she? Why didn't she just throw herself into the lake if she wanted to die? Why leap in front of him, a father who had struggled for years just to be able to barely graze the middle class?

Minutes later, he stood on the bridge to the intake tower. He was shaking, his teeth chattering, his arms limp by his sides. What had happened? What did he do? He retraced his steps in his mind: he remembered the limp weight of her in his arms as he walked through the fog, and he remembered watching her fall into the lake from the bridge. He still heard the whisper ringing from the lake below. *Daddy?*

Sunghwan paused his ascent once he felt the water turn warmer. He wasn't entirely sure of his location in the lake since he hadn't retraced his route along the fishing line. He decided to decompress there and checked his watch: 10:50 p.m. The gauge on his air tank indicated that he had enough air for about seven minutes. He relaxed and closed his eyes. He would stay there until he was nearly out of air.

Sound travels four times faster through water than air, which is why it is difficult to tell where sound is coming from when underwater. Five minutes into his decompression, Sunghwan heard something: a small, gentle sound. It had to be either someone diving in or something being thrown in the lake. He tensed and listened for movement.

Sunghwan looked up and caught sight of something flapping like a broken sail near the water. As it neared him, he took in the flowing dark hair, pale face, white dress billowing around the body, legs stretched up as if kicking. A person. A girl. Descending straight down, headfirst.

His eyes met the child's, which were wide open. He felt his breath catch in his throat. A small, bare foot brushed against his shoulder before she sank.

It was her. Seryong. Sunghwan felt as if he were being sucked into a whirlpool. He had to be sure. He turned and kicked, forgetting that he was decompressing. He didn't pay attention to how much air he had left. He reached out his hands, feeling around, as he dove into cloudier water. He spotted something dark and snaking: her hair. He turned her right-side up, her small face coming to meet his.

It *was* her. Cradling the back of her head, he saw that her eyes were bruised, her top teeth were knocked out, and her lip was busted, but it was Seryong. Sunghwan felt paralyzed. In that moment she slid out of his grip and sank deeper into the water. He let her go. He was left with something small and hard in his hand, but he soon forgot about it. He couldn't breathe. But it wasn't because of his shock; his tank was empty. He finally came to his senses. He ditched his weight belt, tilted his head up, and kicked his fins, beginning an emergency ascent. He had gone farther back down than he'd thought.

At the surface, cold rain greeted him.

He floated on his back. The back of his neck hurt, and his teeth chattered. His body felt frozen; only the hand that had grabbed Seryong's hair burned hot. What had happened? What had he seen? He looked around, but he was blinded by the fog. Thinking the dock must be behind him, Sunghwan began to swim toward shore.

Back on land, he checked his watch; it was 11:15. He had left the house just a couple of hours before, but it seemed like a day had passed. He took off his headlamp, mask, and fins and shoved them into his backpack. He had the feeling he'd forgotten something, but he wanted to get out of there right away. He unlocked the padlock, unlooped the chain from the steel doors, and secured them again from the outside. He trudged along the rainy road, thinking about what he'd seen. He couldn't report this, not with the bad blood between him and Yongje. He would be the prime suspect. The police would question what he was doing trespassing in the lake in the middle of the night. The earlier insinuation of rape was a joke compared to this. Everyone would think he had killed her. If only he'd finished his dive when he planned to and followed the fishing line back to the dock. If only he hadn't come to the lake tonight, if he hadn't succumbed to his curiosity, if he had never heard of Seryong Village . . . he regretted it all.

The arboretum and the Annex were quiet. Yongje's white BMW was parked in front of unit 101. Seryong's window was closed and her curtains were drawn. He couldn't see a single light on in the house.

It was clear what must have happened: Yongje had beaten his daughter to death and thrown her in the lake.

Sunghwan climbed back into his own unit through the window and collapsed onto the living room sofa. What good would it do to report this? She was dead; calling the police wouldn't bring her back. The body would float up in about five days, and then it would be the cops' job to catch her killer. He would leave such complicated matters to the experts and avoid implicating himself. He would take a bath and go to bed.

But something kept nagging at him. He went back to his room and picked up his cell. He'd missed two calls; the first was at 9:03 and the second was at 10:30. His new boss. He wondered if he'd come by the house after all, if maybe he'd heard or seen anything. But it was too late to call back now.

His body ached and he felt chilled to the bone. He filled the tub with lukewarm water. He took the compass out of his pocket, and with it came a hairpin decorated with a crystal star. What was this? Then he remembered cradling Seryong's head, the hard object that slipped into his hand as she drifted away. He must have pocketed it without thinking.

As he sat in the bath, his muscles began to gradually relax, and his brain started to work again. If Seryong was swept along by the current toward the dam, she would be caught in the trash filter screen. But if she sank toward the wall under the intake tower—

Seryong Dam had a water pipe under the intake tower with a diameter of about five feet. When the floodgates opened at dawn, she might be swept through it, and with her the evidence of what had happened . . . Sunghwan slid into the bathwater until his head was fully submerged. *I didn't see any-thing*, he told himself.

~

H yonsu's cell phone was turned off. He must have turned it off after Eunju called Kim Hyongtae to get in touch with him. This was his way of telling her that she was embar-rassing him. Her thirty-six-year-old husband was acting like an insolent teenager. She tried Hyongtae again. He swore they weren't together.

"He said he was on his way to Seryong Lake."

The only time her husband didn't answer was when he drank. This habit of his was incredibly irritating, and even her intense nagging hadn't been able to fix it. She closed her eyes for a moment to calm her anger. Did he really go to Se-ryong Lake, or was he at a bar somewhere? There was no way to know, no one else to call. Kim Hyongtae was the only per-son Hyonsu had befriended at work; his baseball buddies were scattered throughout the country.

She called home, just in case he'd shown up.

"Dad isn't home yet," Sowon reported. "He hasn't called."

She flipped her cell phone closed and walked into the new apartment building. She got off on the nineteenth floor and paused in front of the blue-gray steel door of unit 1901, for-getting about her husband for a moment.

When she first came to see it, she had realized instantly that this apartment was her home. This was the first time she had visited as its owner. The previous owner had moved out that very afternoon. Tomorrow morning, their renter would be moving in. But for a few thrilling hours tonight, the unit was entirely hers.

Eunju took a folded piece of paper out of the pocket of her jeans with the code to the door: 2656940. She pressed the numbers, followed by the star key, and the door unlocked with a beep. She stepped inside. The motion-sensing lights turned on. She stood there beaming and looking around, like an actor at a curtain call. This entryway was the perfect place for Sowon's bicycle; it would look even better with a ficus tree in a planter. She flicked on the lights and saw shoe prints on the floor. She decided to keep her shoes on, too.

Eunju took her time in every room. She went through the house slowly, looking with satisfaction at the bathroom, which had lavender tiles and a tub; the room by the front door, where she planned to create a study space for Sowon; the glassed-in veranda with its nice view; the large, clean living room; the master bedroom, which had its own bathroom; and the kitchen, which had a dishwasher. This was more than worth the two hours by subway and bus it had taken her to get here. Then she placed her purse on the kitchen counter and headed to the window. Down below, she could see a playground with a jungle gym and seesaw, swings and monkey bars, and a sandbox. She thought of the playground in her childhood neighborhood in Bongchon-dong.

Charged with caring for her younger siblings, seven-year-old Eunju would sit on the playground swing in the dark with her year-old baby brother, Giju, on her back, trying to rock him to sleep as he pulled her hair with his tiny hands. Her four-year-old sister, Yongju, would play by herself under the streetlight. Eunju spent those endless evenings praying for time to leap ahead, to be able to grow up quickly so that she could leave home.

They lived in a converted bus where her mother, Jini, sold rice wine over a couple of tables. Jini was a masterful singer who performed "The Tears of Mokpo" coquettishly, accompanied by a beat she made with chopsticks. Her large breasts strained against her *hanbok* blouse, and she never said no to a man, whether it was a hand or a tip that slipped into her blouse. She laughed uproariously, her mouth wide open, and waddled like a duck. She got into scuffles with the other neighborhood women.

Eunju could go home only after Giju fell asleep. Jini would hit her if her baby brother cried. The three children slept at the back of the bus, blocked off by a piece of plywood. Eunju's responsibilities for the day came to an end when she laid the sleeping baby on the electric blanket. She would try to ignore the singing on the other side of the flimsy wall and dream of her friend Hyon's house, which she had visited exactly once. Hyon lived in the nicest house in the neighborhood—clean, nice smelling, and big enough for each person to have their own room. Eunju knew this level of comfort didn't come easily. She decided then and there that she wouldn't live like her mother.

Years later, in her ninth-grade ethics class, her teacher explained the concept of free will. "People who believe in their own futures can create their own lives," she said. Eunju evaluated herself objectively that day—what she was good at, what she was just okay at, what she needed to do in order to get what she wanted, and how she would do it. She looked at her reflection in a small mirror. She wasn't cut out to be an actress. She was cute, sure, but not so beautiful that she could make a man faint in his tracks. Her report cards confirmed that she wasn't a genius and she didn't excel in art or sports; she couldn't carry a tune, she was clumsy, and she couldn't write any better than her classmates. But at least she knew what she was living for. She had drive. She was hardworking and self-reliant. Those were plenty of reasons to believe in her future.

She made plans for herself: she would live at home until the age of seventeen, when she graduated from high school with a diploma; she would leave home the instant she landed a job, ideally one that offered affordable housing; she would save for three years to be able to afford first and last months' rent on a room of her own; she would never look back.

And that was what she did. After graduation, she got a job as a bookkeeper at a textile factory in Gwangju, the farthest possible place from Seoul, in her mind, and packed her things that night. She felt bad about leaving Yongju and Giju, both still so young, but she had to get out. She lived in a dormitory for factory girls and diligently saved her money. In three years, she got herself a basement room on a yearly lease, just like she had planned. But the joy of achieving her first goal made her forget her vow to never look back. She thought about her siblings every night; she missed them. Did Yongju manage to enroll in high school? Were they even eating regularly?

She found herself on a bus to Seoul bearing gifts, a dress for Yongju and a wristwatch for Giju. She was going to see just the two of them and leave quickly, but she couldn't avoid her mother. Jini packed a bag for Yongju and gave it to her. A year after Yongju started living with her, her mother burst in with Giju and all their belongings. All three of them stayed with her in Gwangju until Eunju was twenty-seven. That year, Jini succumbed to cancer; Yongju got a job as a middle school English teacher; and Giju departed for his mandatory military service. That was also the year she got married.

Her husband was three years her junior, but it may as well have been thirteen. He didn't know anything other than baseball. After his retirement, he came home drunk nearly every day. She forced him to get a job, and she took care of him while working all kinds of jobs, as a waitress, a supermarket cashier, a home health care aide, a school cafeteria worker. For Eunju, this apartment, which they managed to buy after twelve years of marriage, was much more than a home: it was proof that she wasn't her mother. It proved that she had made something of her miserable lot, and it was her promise to her son's future. She wouldn't send him out into the world with nothing, as she'd been.

Eunju went back into the living room. She didn't want to leave, but it was time to go. She paused at the front door and looked back at the apartment one last time. She would be back soon enough. Three years. Until then, she would do anything it took to make this her reality. She took an eyebrow pencil from her purse and squatted by the front door. She felt under the doorjamb and picked up the edge of the linoleum. In large letters she wrote *Kang Eunju* and *Choi Sowon* on the cement floor. She hesitated before adding the final name. She'd include him, too, why not. *Choi Hyonsu.*

Down on the ground floor, she flipped open her cell and

called Hyonsu again. This time the phone rang, but he still didn't pick up. The warm feeling of contentment she'd had in the apartment evaporated. This had to be a talent, the ability to drive his wife crazy without so much as lifting a finger or opening his mouth. Maybe he'd turned on the phone to talk to someone else, Kim Hyongtae or another friend. It didn't matter what the reason was; the important thing was that he was only ignoring *her*. A puff of pungent hot air wafted up from the sewer grate in the street. Eunju looked at her phone: 10:50. *Fine, Hyonsu,* she thought. *Let's see who wins this one*. She pressed the call button again.

SERYONG LAKE

PART II

An alarm startled Hyonsu awake. He swept his hands around until he realized that it was coming from his cell phone in his shirt pocket. He fumbled with his pocket, took out his cell, turned off the alarm, and threw it down next to him as if it was a piece of burning coal. His body was covered in sweat. He was panting. It was a long time before he was able to focus.

He was in the driver's seat of his car. Outside, it was raining lightly. Cars came and went through the mist and people walked by under umbrellas. He could see an apartment complex through the car window. He realized he was in Ilsan, near the neighborhood park across the street from their new apartment. He found a tollgate receipt in the glove compartment; it told him that he'd gone through the Seryong interchange at 11:08 p.m. The clock on the dash read 5:10 a.m. Six hours had passed. What had he done during that time? And why was he here, of all places?

Getting out of the car, he saw that his shirt was covered in blood. Dark stains were on his hands, up his arms, and by his waist. The hood of his car was crushed, the windshield cracked like a spiderweb. Did he drive this wrecked car on the highway all the way here? Why? There were gaps in his memory. Each piece he could remember was more nightmarish than the last. The fog, the rain, the girl who flew at him like a specter, the screech of the brakes, him walking through the rain with her body in his arms.

Thankfully, nobody was in the park. Hyonsu popped the trunk and took out his work uniform. He was thinking clearly for the first time since the accident. He needed to solve the immediate problem of his appearance. He spotted a bathroom between the gingko trees. He changed in a stall, then shoved his bloodied shirt deep into the trash can and washed the blood off his skin. After double-checking that he was clean, he went into a small convenience store and bought a pack of cigarettes. He lit one under a tree in the park. He'd quit about six months before because of Eunju's haranguing, but right now he was desperate for a hit. He ducked his head and took a long drag. The ground appeared to be shaking; he was shaking. He leaned against the tree and questions rushed at him like rapids. What if he hadn't gone down to Seryong Lake? What if he'd been sober? What if his license hadn't been suspended? He wouldn't have thrown her in the lake and fled, right? The cigarette slipped out of his fingers.

Hyonsu fled to his car. He picked up the phone and checked his missed calls. Eunju had called twelve times last night. The seventh time was at 10:48 and the next one was at 10:50. He remembered now how the phone rang without pause as he crouched beside the girl, adding to the clamor in his head that was telling him to get away, to save himself, to make this go away. He couldn't understand how he could have done such a thing. If he was afraid someone would hear, he should have turned off the ringer; instead, he had picked the girl up and walked to the lake.

He put his phone down. He couldn't undo the events of last night. Thinking about it wouldn't change anything. He had to find a way to scrub last night from his life. But how would he do that? They were scheduled to move tomorrow. The only way for him to avoid going back to Seryong Lake would be to quit his job. And the only way to convince Eunju that it was the right thing to do would be to tell her everything. How would he do that? What would he say? That he went to see the house but ended up mowing down a little girl? That he was driving too fast, that he was drunk? That he panicked, threw her in the lake, and fled, and now they couldn't start their new life, the one she was so firmly set on, had been dreaming of for years? No. Eunju wouldn't understand. But maybe she would find a solution. She was the kind of woman who kept five bank accounts secret from him. Maybe she would present him with five solutions and tell him to pick one. Maybe she would worry with him, feel for him a little. They weren't madly in love with each other, but they had been through a lot in twelve years together, and he was the father of her son. That had to count for something.

Hyonsu took his car to a nearby car repair shop and was told that it would be ready by three. He spent those hours in a sauna. A few bottles of soju on an empty stomach put him to sleep, and he woke at five in the afternoon.

When he went to pick it up, the car looked brand-new, as if the accident had never happened. He was feeling much better. Everything would be fine, he told himself. There was no proof he was involved. He'd put it on his credit card, the one she didn't know about, and never tell her.

"So, you're alive," Eunju said the moment he walked through the door.

Hyonsu looked around at the boxes piled up in preparation for their move.

"You don't answer the phone, you ignore my texts, you don't come home." Eunju stood in front of him, her posture rigid, her arms crossed, barring his way into the rest of the apartment. "You just do whatever you want these days, don't you."

He stood awkwardly in place. "Well, it sort of happened that way." *Let me in*, he wanted to say. *I have to tell you something serious.*

"And you didn't even go there. You told Ahn Sunghwan you were heading there and didn't bother to show up."

Hyonsu flinched. "You talked to him?"

"Why not?"

"How did you get his number?"

"You don't think I can find a phone number? Not that you care, but I arranged everything. He said he'd prefer not to move and that he would rather share a room with Sowon, so I told him that was fine. I agreed to cook for him, too—he said he'd pay. Why can't you handle anything? I told you it was important."

Hyonsu stiffened with rage. If she could have just handled it over the phone, then why did she ask him to go in the first place? Did she understand what had happened because of her? Before he could control himself, his hand flew at her cheek.

"Did you seriously just do that?" Eunju's cheek was already

starting to swell. "You *hit* me?" Her eyes were darkening, and her voice was thin and high. It was then that Hyonsu noticed Sowon standing behind her, a shocked expression on his face.

He turned and left. He walked and walked and ended up at a soju bar. As he drank, he thought of his father, Sergeant Choi, a huge man who would smash furniture and beat his wife and children every time he had a drink. Anytime Hyonsu failed to know his own strength, he was reminded of him—when the bottle neck broke off instead of the cap; when the stove knob fell off; when the door came off the hinges as he opened it.

But he wasn't like his father—or so he used to tell himself. Unless he went completely insane, he thought, he would never lay a hand on his wife or child. But now that had turned out to be a delusion. Or maybe he had gone mad. Otherwise, how could he have killed an innocent child with no remorse, and then gone home and hit his wife? He had to acknowledge it: he was a murderer. But as he began to feel the alcohol, his self-reproach and disgust dissipated. Things happened, he reasoned. He should go home, take a shower, and then have a nap. When he woke up, things would be back to normal, and he would be able to go down to Seryong Lake and start his new job. He could forget what he had done and resolve again to lead a good life. Yes, that was what he would do, he thought as he left the bar, humming to himself as he crossed the street.

Yongje stood up. He'd spent the night waiting by the window. Seryong and that asshole from next door hadn't returned. He hadn't taken his eyes off the path in front of the Annex; he hadn't even dozed off. He'd left his chair exactly twice, once to go to the bathroom and then to get some water. The security guard and Yim would have been watching the CCTV from their posts, and they were supposed to call him if they saw anything. But neither had called.

Yongje went to Seryong's room. There were bloodstains on the blankets and on the wall, and green candle wax and pieces of metal and glass were scattered across the floor. Then he noticed something: a smear of blood on the curtain. Seryong must have hoisted herself out the window, smearing blood from her bloody nose onto the curtain. If he'd seen it earlier, he wouldn't have gone around the neighborhood looking for her. Her window faced directly onto the unit next door; he would have gone straight there.

Why hadn't he seen it? He hadn't thought to look around her room; filled with rage, he'd run out the front door without thinking, inadvertently giving the asshole next door time to hide her.

The woods were misty. All was quiet next door. He didn't see a light.

Keeping an eye on the house, Yongje called Yim. "Bring the EMF meter and come over right away."

Ten minutes later, they were outside 102, knocking on the door. The idiot opened the door, bleary-eyed.

"I apologize for intruding so early in the morning," Yongje said politely.

The asshole looked at him and then at Yim, confused.

"We detected a leakage. Can we take a look?" Yongje nodded at the device in the groundskeeper's hands.

"Right now?" he asked before begrudgingly stepping aside. "Okay. But can you make it quick? I'd like to go back to bed."

Yongje towed Yim through the unit, searching every nook and cranny, but Seryong wasn't there. He didn't come across a single clue. Everything was the same as it had been the night before. Inside the closet he spotted a backpack that he hadn't seen before, but just as he moved to look inside it, the asshole appeared alongside him.

Yongje didn't want to leave. He'd been certain she was there. She had to be. But Yim had finished his "work," and he had no choice but to go. He lingered just outside the front door. "You live here alone? I thought there were two of you."

"My former boss was just transferred to Chungju. The new boss moves in tomorrow." The idiot rubbed his nose and wiped it on his undershirt. Disgusting.

Yongje craned his neck toward the living room. "You must have been lonely since he left."

"I didn't have time to be lonely. I was pissed. The Tigers just lost big to the Lions."

"I thought you were out last night. Where did you go?"

The moron leaned against the doorframe. "Like I said, I was here watching the game."

"Huh. We got a leakage signal last night, but when I called, nobody answered."

"Oh, well, I did go up to the rest area," the asshole said, after a pause. "I ran out of beer."

Yongje recalled the empty beer can next to the laptop. Maybe this guy had entrusted Seryong to a fellow security guard. They went over to 103 under the same guise of checking for a leakage, but had no luck there, either.

Racking his brain for where else he might have stashed her,

Yongje drove to the clinic. The doctor came to the door, still half-asleep, and informed him that nobody had come in after six p.m. the night before. Yongje would have heard about it if the idiot had called emergency services, and he couldn't have taken her to another hospital, since he didn't have a car. Just to be sure, Yongje called the local taxi company and asked if any cars had come to Seryong Lake last night. None.

Finally, he went up to the store at the rest area. "Did a young man come by last night and buy beer? He's thin, average height, and starting to go gray."

"Dozens of people who look like that came in," the employee told him.

Yongje's head throbbed. He was certain that the asshole in 102 had been involved, but he couldn't find any proof. He started asking around about where Seryong had gone after school the previous day. The shuttle driver said she'd never gotten on, and not a single kid of the parents he called had seen her, though that wasn't all that surprising—she had always been a loner, and she was completely different outside their house. The girl he knew was a miniature version of her mother: stubborn, clever, rude. But everyone else knew her as reserved and meek. He'd been hearing that for years.

He looked at her phone records and discovered that she hadn't used her phone at all in the last three months. Poring over the bills from the two prior years, he saw that she'd never called anyone other than her mother and home. Yongje grew even more incensed. Not at his daughter, but at Hayong. *She* had raised his daughter to be a loner. She had been more focused on the divorce proceedings than on being a good mother.

Having exhausted all the leads as to where Seryong might be if she had remained in the area, he called the bus company. Only one local bus from Sunchon came through Seryong Lake; if a barefoot girl in a white dress, heavily made-up, her face beaten to a pulp, had taken a bus that morning it would be impossible for the driver not to remember her. But nobody had seen her. That meant she had to be here somewhere.

He knew what he had to do. First, he let his office manager know that he wouldn't be coming in for a few days. Next, he went to file a missing persons report. Then he printed flyers with her picture and his phone number and pasted them everywhere. He formed his own search party of twenty villagers and two dogs. He split them into two groups and sent them off in opposite directions.

Thanks to the director of operations at the dam conservancy, he was able to borrow a key to the dock so they could see if there had been any suspicious activity there. The director was the only person he was personally acquainted with among all the conservancy staff. Two years back, the man had brought his eldest daughter to Yongje's dental practice; he remembered the girl had sharp, chimp-like teeth. Yongje did several million won's worth of orthodontic work for a nominal sum, figuring it would be useful to befriend the man for when he had to negotiate with the conservancy about the fees for letting its staff use the housing on his land, or when he had to deal with their trivial complaints. He was right, though not for the reasons he'd anticipated. Yongje made a copy of the key, not wanting to have to ask for a favor again.

The search continued into the evening, though the rain that had been coming down for two days straight made it harder. In the end, the only possible trace of Seryong they had found was a pink blanket she'd apparently laid inside a wooden box in the old barn. Yongje knew this pink blanket very well; it was a comfort object that Seryong had been unusually attached to as a little girl, and that she still took into bed with her at night.

The blanket was covered in cat hair and had been found alongside an empty bowl. It was clear to Yongje that this was the hideout of the cat that had appeared out of nowhere the previous night—the one whose mother and siblings had destroyed his city. Seryong must have been caring for it all along. He stood up. Was there no end to their betrayals? He asked the man who brought it to him to put the blanket back where he'd found it. He wanted the cat to return. Once he found Seryong, he would take care of the animal; he would do it in front of her. But only after he dealt with the person who'd helped her hide from him.

After the search party dispersed, Yongje returned to the arboretum to look at the CCTV footage. Four days before, one of the guards had gotten into a car accident, so Yim was filling in at the security office.

"Did you find her?" Yim asked.

"The cat that's been hiding out in the barn—you knew about it, didn't you?"

Yim didn't answer.

He felt rage fanning up from below his ribs. Yim's family had managed the arboretum for two generations. The old man had been good friends with Yongje's father, but that wasn't the only reason he'd kept him on. There was nobody else like him, with his landscaping talents, knowledge of trees, and love for the arboretum. He excelled at fixing things, including electrical or mechanical work, so Yongje never had to hire anyone else for those tasks. But still, he couldn't forgive someone who was helping keep a secret from him. Yim was number three on his list.

Yongje checked the CCTV footage from the night before. Judging from the toll receipt he'd found in the cup holder of his car, which was stamped "9:20 p.m.," it must have been around 9:40 when Seryong ran away. The rear entrance was locked beginning at nine, and nobody had gone in or out through the main entrance. Where could she have gone? There was nowhere around here for her to hide for an entire day.

It came to him suddenly: the lake. That was the only place they hadn't looked. But this premise was predicated on her death. It would mean she was permanently beyond his reach. He couldn't think about that. He had to put them back in their places, Hayong and Seryong both.

Yongje left the office and got into his car. It was 9:20 again now. He decided to go home and try to put himself in Seryong's shoes to figure out where she had gone.

Reflecting on it now, he knew why the girl had been fully made-up, wearing her mother's clothes. She missed Hayong. She had done the same thing not long ago and he'd punished her for it. Yesterday was Seryong's birthday, and that would have made her miss her mother even more, especially since she didn't have anyone to celebrate with.

Back at home, he went into Seryong's room. Yongje opened the window a crack. He sat down and took off his socks. Seryong had been barefoot last night. At precisely 9:40 p.m., he climbed out the window, the damp dirt cold on the soles of his feet. The rain was still coming down and the fog was even denser than last night. The arboretum was dark. He would walk into a cypress without a light, but he didn't turn on his flashlight since Seryong hadn't had one. He looked around swiftly. The way toward the main road was dark; it was too far from the streetlights. Unit 102 was dark. He knew a light would have been on last night, but he disregarded it. The only other light, however faint, was by the gate at the edge of the arboretum. On the other side was a dark road. The street in front of the Annex was closer and brighter, but Seryong would have known he would be coming out to look for her. That was where she would have run.

Yongje went out onto the back road. He strode on, feeling the chain-link fence that bordered the lake with the tips of his fingers; that was surely how she had found her way in the dark and fog. As he approached the intake tower and the dock, he tried again to put himself in her shoes. She would have known it was him when she saw the car's headlights coming toward her through the fog; she would have looked for someplace to hide. Yongje turned on his flashlight and looked around. He was two steps from the doors to the dock. He headed to the doors. Could she have seen the gap under the doors? Had she already known about it?

Yongje unlocked the padlock with his copy of the key, pulled the chain out, and went inside. He imagined Seryong crawling under the steel doors and his car speeding past the very next second. What would she have done next? Would she have gone down the banks to the lake? The fog was thick. He sat among the vines that flanked the ramp down to the dock. Would she have done the same? She must have wondered if he'd seen her,

if he would come back this way and stop at the doors to the
dock. He turned off his flashlight. It was now pitch-dark. All
he could hear was water flowing through the floodgates. She
would have been hunched here, trembling at his voice outside
and the flashlight sweeping over the vines. She wouldn't have
had a moment to fear this gloomy lake. But what had happened after he left? Did she dart back into the street? Or head
to the barn? Did she look for a more hidden spot? Yongje
turned on his flashlight and looked around the lake. He saw
the *Josong* floating by the dock and headed there.

Crouched on the deck of the *Josong*, he looked back toward the entrance, the banks, the ramp. It was then that he
noticed something white on the surface of the water, caught
on the pillar of the dock. He jumped onto the dock, leaned
over, and pulled it up. It was a long piece of torn white silk,
just like the blouse Seryong had been wearing. But before he
could study it more closely, something flickered below the
surface of the water. He shined the light on it and saw a light
green fluorescent object, thin and long like a chopstick, floating at an angle. He bent down and stuck his hand in the
water, and his fingers snagged on a thin line. He pulled gently
and out came a fishing line with fluorescent floats and sinkers
tied to it. It seemed to have been caught on something. He
followed the line to where it was tied to the pillar. He cut it
with his teeth and undid the section attached to the pillar.
The length he had was around three yards long, with three
sinkers and three floats spaced about a foot apart. There was
no hook. This clearly wasn't used for fishing, and it wasn't
trash that had accidentally drifted here. Maybe the conser-

vancy or the waste management company had installed it. He would find out.

Back home, he studied the scrap of fabric. He had bought the blouse for Hayong for her birthday a year before, a sleeveless top with narrow pleats from the neck to the hem, and a zipper down the back. He remembered helping her zip it up because she couldn't reach it. Yongje tried to imagine how it had gotten into the lake. He pictured her running up the banks, trying to slip back under the doors. Her clothes could have caught on something and ripped, and the rain might have washed the torn piece down to the lake. But then where would Seryong have gone? He'd looked everywhere, followed every lead. Yongje rethought his hypothesis. Could someone else have been out there on the dock when she was there? He thought of the last time he'd seen her, her long, disheveled hair, pancake makeup, the blouse hanging off her shoulder, her feet bare. An image flashed through his mind. Last night, when he stopped the car by the dock, had there been a chain and a lock on the doors? He remembered thinking the doors were open and pushing against them, only to find them locked from the inside. But this morning, when he went with the search party, the chain had been secured on the *outside* of the doors. His pulse thrummed. Someone had been out on the dock last night. Someone else had a key. Now he understood: she had been sexually assaulted and then murdered, thrown in the lake. He had to find whoever had left that line in the water.

Yongje was in his basement workshop as day broke. He could hardly wait till the tackle shops opened to pursue this latest lead. He drove into town with the fishing line, but nobody he showed it to knew what it could be for. Finally, at the last place he tried, he learned something useful: that fluorescent paint on the floats and sinkers might mean it was used for night diving. Yongje drove straight to the local diving club and asked to speak to the owner. "It's a depth gauge," he explained. "It's useful when you dive in dams or reservoirs in the mountains. At high altitude, normal depth gauges don't work very well. The paint tells me it's used for night diving. The floats might have also functioned as signposts."

"What do you mean?" Yongje asked.

"If you tie the line along the way with brightly colored floats and sinkers like this, you can find your way back out the way you came in."

"So this isn't the work of a novice."

The owner shook his head.

Scuba diving was prohibited at Seryong Lake, Yongje thought as he drove home. That was probably why the diver had gone in at night. But he still didn't know if he'd been in the water when Seryong ran onto the banks, or on another night altogether. He had to find the diver.

He went upstairs to shower, shave, and change. Then he went to see the director of operations at home.

"Were you able to find anything?" asked the director, sitting across from him in the living room.

Yongje shook his head. "Does anyone at the conservancy scuba dive?"

The man looked surprised. "Why? Do you think she fell in the lake?"

"I'm not sure, but she could have."

The director of operations hesitated for a moment. "Have

you considered the possibility that it could be a kidnapping? That might be more likely, given your wealth . . ."

"Then we would have heard from them by now. It's been almost two days already. I'm looking into all possibilities, and that's why I'm here. I'm wondering if you know anyone who could help search underwater."

"I'm not sure. There are diving clubs at other dam conservancies, but not here."

"There must be someone on staff who does it for fun. We're so close to the ocean."

"If someone did, I think we'd know about it."

Yongje nodded. "Can I ask for another favor?"

The director of operations looked uncomfortable but nodded.

"I'd like to see the conservancy CCTVs. To check the lakeshore road from 9:45 p.m. on the twenty-seventh."

"I'm sorry, that won't be possible. The tapes are kept in the system control room, and only staff are allowed in."

"Don't you let school groups in?"

"That's different. A field trip requested through official channels makes it part of official duties. We can't let people in for any other reason."

"Even if a child goes missing?"

"Listen, I know how you feel. A hundred times over. That's why I gave you the key to the dock."

"And thank you for that. Since you've been so helpful, I was hoping for just one more . . ."

"I could get in trouble just for giving you that key."

Yongje had to back down. "Then could you look through them and tell me if you see something?"

The director of operations began to look irritated. "We won't be able to see anything. The cameras by the lake aren't infrared, so they're useless in the dark. And it was foggy."

"But you'd be able to see car headlights, right? Or a flashlight?"

"Why don't you call the police? If they request them, we will of course show them the tapes."

"I've already filed a missing persons report. I can't wait around for the police. How would you feel if *your* daughter went missing? Would you just sit tight and wait for the cops?"

The director of operations glanced toward the doorway, where his elder daughter was eavesdropping, and shooed her away.

"Please. Could you just look from 9:50 to 10:50 that night?"

Finally, he acquiesced. "Fine. We can take my car."

He left Yongje by the security office at the main entrance and drove into the conservancy to review the tapes. Yongje spotted the guard on duty through the small window; it was Park again. Yongje approached him and asked for a cup of water. When Park placed a paper cup on the ledge outside the window, Yongje thanked him and asked, as casually as he could muster, what he did on his days off.

Park said he slept or went home to see his family.

"No hobbies?" Yongje asked. "I heard some of the guys at the conservancy are into scuba diving."

Park squinted at him.

"That's an expensive hobby. It's hard enough to live off our wages as it is."

"What about that young man in 102? Is he a diver?"

"I don't know. He doesn't talk about himself much."

That was all he could get out of Park. He didn't even invite Yongje to come wait inside. After staring at the CCTV for a while, Park suddenly stood up. Yongje saw the director of operations heading back in his car.

He stopped to pick Yongje up. "Okay, so there were cars that drove by during that window of time."

"Did you see which? What kind?"

"It was too dark. But at 10:02 there were lights on the road that, judging from their speed and orientation, have to be the headlights of a car."

Yongje nodded. That would have been him.

"I have to say, it's strange," he continued. "Not many cars ever come down that road, but that night there were two."

Yongje held his breath as the director of operations pulled up in front of his house. "The second pair of lights appeared around 10:40. They were going really fast, then stopped suddenly, and then left about twenty minutes later."

"Was it near the same place as the first car?"

"Hard to say. I'm no expert. I hope that's helpful."

"Yes, thank you." Yongje got out and headed to the arboretum security office. Nobody was there. A second car. Stopped for twenty minutes. What could it mean? He found the resident file for the idiot in 102 and copied down his citizen ID number. His instincts were telling him to start there.

～

Night shifts were like being in exile. From six in the evening until eight in the morning, Sunghwan spent fourteen long hours all by himself. Nights were too quiet, too dark, and too long. He could only hear water flowing through the floodgates. There wasn't much to do other than patrol the building. Usually Sunghwan read a book or went online or tried to write. Tonight, though, something else caught his interest.

There were eight CCTV cameras along the lakeshore, four near the screen blocking the trash from entering the reservoir, one each on the intake tower, the dock, Hansoldung, and the point where the lakeshore road came to a dead end. Unlike the ones they used inside the conservancy or on the flood-gates, those eight cameras were old, maybe ten years old, and when darkness fell, the CCTV screens turned black. All one could see were headlights from cars driving along the lake-shore road. Usually it was because they had taken a wrong turn; there was nothing down that way, and they generally turned around at the dead end. He rarely saw any other kinds of lights. This was one of those rare times.

It was a little after ten. Sunghwan was sitting at the desk with a cup of coffee, staring at the screens absentmindedly when he noticed a white light at the dock. It was so faint that he could have easily missed it. He held his breath, watching. The light stopped then moved, roamed all over the place, then disappeared. It had to be a flashlight. Someone had gone onto the dock and come back out. Who could it be? He automatically retraced his own path the previous night. His light had probably drawn a similar arc. He had to hope Park had dozed off or been otherwise occupied that night; his co-worker hadn't mentioned having seen anything during his shift. He leaned heavily back in his chair. Could it be Yongje, out on the dock? There was no way Sunghwan was going to go out there to confirm. His thoughts turned to his neighbor, bursting into his house that morning with the groundskeeper. He had thought it was odd for them to look for an electrical leakage with such urgency. If Yongje hadn't killed his daughter, he must have been looking for her; if he had, it was the perfect opening act to cover up his crime. The daylong search would have been the first act of his pantomime as a grieving father.

The rain stopped around dawn. By the time he headed home after work, the fog had dissipated a bit. Sunghwan trudged along the lakeshore road, staring at his feet, and came face-to-face with Seryong's image by the rear entrance to the arboretum.

Missing Child

Name: Oh Seryong

Female, 11 yrs., fifth grader at Seryong Elementary School

Last seen around 9:40 p.m., Friday, August 27

Long hair, pale skin, coin-sized birthmark on left side of neck, wearing adult's white blouse as a dress

In the picture, she was dressed in a ballet costume, but his mind flashed to how she had looked when he'd encountered her underwater.

He took off down the street, running as fast as he could. There were loose ends he needed to tie up, things in the house that could cast suspicion on him—the wet suit in the dryer, the underwater camera and strobe light in his backpack, his diving gear. Yongje hadn't found any of it that morning, but his new boss and family were due to arrive in two hours. And who knew when the police might come knocking.

Sunghwan downloaded the pictures of Seryong Village from his camera and saved them in the cloud, then deleted them off his camera. He put the diving gear and wet suit in a box; he would send it to his brother in Suwon. Just as he was writing the address on the box, his cell phone rang. It was the police officer he had met in the clinic, asking him to come by the station for questioning regarding Seryong's disappearance. He shoved the box in the closet and headed into town.

As soon as Sunghwan sat down at the police station, the officer cut to the chase. "You know the girl Seryong." He nodded. "Did you see her at all on Friday evening?"

"No."

"You live right next door. You didn't see her?"

"Why don't you ask her dad how his kid disappeared in the middle of the night?"

The cop slammed his hand down on the table. "She's missing. Nobody's seen her since Friday evening. Think about how he must feel. As a human being, you must sympathize. You really didn't see her?"

As the cop continued his pointless line of questioning, Sunghwan was beginning to feel antsy. His boss was supposed to arrive soon.

The officer squinted at him. "Looks like you're anxious to

leave. Okay, that's it for today. But I wouldn't leave the area if I were you."

"What's that supposed to mean?" Sunghwan demanded.

"Just some friendly advice," the cop said magnanimously. "You're not from around here, and there was that incident with the girl before."

This seemed ominous. He wondered again if he should have reported what he'd seen in the lake. But it was too late now. He lived next door, he wasn't from around here, and he had gotten mixed up in their family matters before. He didn't have to guess what would happen if he suddenly came forward with a different story.

The village was plastered with flyers seeking information on Seryong's whereabouts. He walked home with his head down so that he wouldn't have to see them. Entering the arboretum, he stopped short. A boy he'd never seen before was standing in front of a Welcome sign by the main path, looking at a poster of Seryong, his thumbs hooked through the belt loops of his jeans. It was then that Sunghwan noticed Yongje watching the boy from across the road.

"Hey," Yongje said.

The boy looked up.

"What are you doing here? I don't know you."

The boy turned to face Yongje.

"This is private property. You need to leave now."

The two of them stared at each other.

"My dad's the head of security for Seryong Dam, and we just moved here," the boy said. It was Sunghwan's new boss's son. "Who are you?" the boy asked calmly.

The kid's mother had mentioned that he was in the fifth grade, so he couldn't have been older than eleven. But he didn't seem at all nervous standing up to a man his father's age. He must have been born with a certain boldness.

Even Yongje seemed impressed. "Cute," he said.

"Only things like ducks are cute," the boy said.

"And which wise person said that?"

As if to answer that question, a white Matiz pulled up from the opposite direction. Sunghwan walked toward the boy as the Matiz stopped in front of Yongje. A huge man extricated himself from the tiny car. With his crew cut, ruddy face, and wide shoulders, he looked like an athlete, Sunghwan thought.

"Dad," the boy called. "Did you find Mr. Ahn?"

His new boss crossed the road in three strides. "Not yet." He glanced at the poster. He was about to introduce himself, but Yongje cut in.

"I'm Oh Yongje, the owner of this arboretum."

Hyonsu stiffened. "Oh, yes. I'm the new director of security for the dam," he said vaguely, as though he were waking up from a deep sleep. "We're moving into 102 today."

"I thought I saw a moving van come in," Yongje said. "I'm in 101. Did you notify the management office?"

"I will, after we finish moving in," Hyonsu mumbled. Sunghwan found himself wondering if his new boss was ill, or maybe extremely introverted. The boy looked angry and disappointed; he must have hoped his giant of a father would grab this rude man by the collar and shake him.

"Do it now. You'll need to get all-hours access to the property and get assigned a parking spot." Yongje glanced at the Matiz and walked toward his house.

It was only then that his new boss's gaze settled on Sunghwan.

He strode toward them. "I'm Ahn Sunghwan," he said. "I'm sorry I wasn't home to greet you when you arrived."

"Oh, I'm Choi Hyonsu," the giant man said, offering his hand.

Sunghwan took it. Hyonsu's palm was cold and damp.

"And I'm Choi Sowon," the boy said, sticking his hand out.

"So you're my roommate," Sunghwan said, shaking the kid's hand.

"I am," Sowon said. He glanced at Yongje walking away and began talking in a loud, clear voice. "My dad's high school roommate was the pitcher Kim Ganghyon. You know him, right? The submariner for the Fighters?"

Yongje turned to look back at them. Sowon mimed a perfect sidearm windup. The invisible ball shot toward Yongje; anyone could tell it was aimed squarely at his chest.

"My dad was the Fighters' best catcher. If he didn't injure his shoulder he would have been the greatest slugger ever."

Yongje stood there, not angry at the boy's bragging but not exactly amused by it, either.

"Go up with Mr. Ahn," Hyonsu said, clapping a giant hand on Sowon's shoulder. "I'm going to the management office."

Sowon nodded. Sunghwan liked this kid.

"It's near the rear entrance to the property," he called. "The management office is behind company housing."

Hyonsu got in his car and drove off. Yongje was still standing in place as Sunghwan and Sowon walked up the path toward unit 102.

Choi Hyonsu . . . Sunghwan didn't recognize that name. If he had been a starting catcher, Sunghwan would have at least heard of him. Maybe he had been a backup catcher. He knew a little about Kim Ganghyon; he had played on the national team. Sunghwan made a mental note to look up his new boss later.

Just then, they passed Yongje, who was still standing in the middle of the path. As they walked by him, Sunghwan felt a chill. Yongje's wide, black pupils were locked on Sowon, looking like the tunnel below the intake tower that sucked in everything in its vicinity.

~

Hyonsu's eyes flew open. He stared up at the ceiling, breathing hard. The voice calling his name was gone, but the dream stayed with him. Sorghum fields the color of blood, rustling in the warm breeze; the salty tang of the fog and the sea; the light of the lighthouse glimmering beyond the horizon. He lay there, blinking, until the scenes dissipated. Eventually he realized that he was lying on the floor of his new living room. He didn't have a pillow or a blanket; he was drenched in sweat and his back ached. He sat up, his left arm hanging lifeless beside him. He had thought that his arm had been getting better since he quit playing. This was the first time in six years that it was completely paralyzed when he woke up.

Nobody was home. Hyonsu went into the bathroom and turned the shower to scalding. He took his shirt off and sat on the edge of the tub, leaning forward so the spray hit his left arm. His body kept tilting forward and his head pounded. He felt cold and his nose was stuffy. He'd drunk himself into a stupor the previous night and fallen asleep on the living room floor. Eunju hadn't even bothered throwing a blanket over him. He had brought this on himself. If he could, he would have told her that he couldn't bear to live through yesterday sober.

Hyonsu was exhausted by the time he arrived. The liquid courage he'd felt the night before reuniting with Eunju and Sowon evaporated. As they drove to Seryong Lake, he felt as though he were looping a rope around his neck and jumping off a bridge. When they arrived, Sunghwan wasn't home. Hyonsu unlocked the front door for the movers and went out to find Sunghwan; it was preferable to roam around than to argue with Eunju over where things should go.

The poster at the entrance to the arboretum stopped him cold. It was her. The face in the photograph and the one he remembered were vastly different, but he still recognized her immediately. He stood there in shock. When he bumped into the girl's father talking to Sowon on the other side of the property, and learned that not only did he own this entire place but that they were going to be next-door neighbors, his shock morphed into panic.

Hyonsu didn't go to the management office. He didn't want anyone to know he was there. He wanted to run away.

But where could he go? Eunju had given him a list of things to buy—water, trash bags, milk, lightbulbs, a clothesline— so he might as well get started on that. He went to the convenience store at the rest area, and ended up having a few drinks. The next thing he remembered was Sowon and Sung-hwan coming to retrieve him. He vaguely remembered the two of them helping him up.

Hyonsu looked down at his left arm. Sensation was gradu-ally returning; tingles spread upward from the tips of his fin-gers. Good, he thought. He could go to work.

Arriving at the security office, he realized he'd forgotten to shave. Sunghwan, who had gotten to work early, grinned sympathetically and lent him a razor.

The next few hours sped by. He met his team, went to in-troduce himself to the folks over at the conservancy, and got an orientation about the interior of the conservancy building and the dam systems. Around eleven, he finally had a mo-ment to himself; he took a bundle of keys from the drawer.

"Where are you off to?" Sunghwan asked.

"The director of operations at the conservancy told me I should take a look around the dam."

"Want me to come with you?"

Hyonsu waved him off. "No, no. I can do it on my own." He wanted to look at the scene of the accident by himself. He could also take a good look at the lake. He was afraid to con-front his memories, but he had to make sure he hadn't forgot-ten anything there. He wrestled with wanting to go and check and wanting to run away. Absorbed by his own thoughts, he didn't recognize the man standing by the chain-link gate that led to the trash screen until they were practically face-to-face. It was Oh Yongje.

"Checking out the dam?" Yongje asked.

Hyonsu cleared his throat, feeling claustrophobic. Yongje

was the last person he wanted to see. He made a show of checking the gate, which was secured with a chain and a padlock. Four CCTVs were installed on a metal pillar on the bank, all pointing in different directions. Neon balls floated across the surface of the water, marking the screen's location.

"Do you have the key?" Yongje asked, gesturing toward the padlock.

Hyonsu pretended he hadn't heard.

"What do you think that is?" Yongje said, pointing with his long, thin, pale finger at the screen. Something white was floating there. When Hyonsu still said nothing, Yongje continued: "You know what I think? I think it's the blouse my daughter was wearing."

Yongje stared at the object expressionlessly. Hyonsu felt a chill. Did this man have hawk eyes? How could he tell from the other side of the fence?

"Let's go check," Yongje suggested.

"You want me to take you in there?" Hyonsu's voice sounded strained even to himself.

"I'm just a civilian. The head of security should lead the way, shouldn't he?"

Reluctantly, Hyonsu unlocked the gate and they walked down the wooden stairs side by side. Yongje broke off a long branch and approached the pillar. The white thing was stuck on a neon ball about two yards from the pillar. Yongje held on to the pillar with one hand as he stretched the stick toward the object. It was close but not quite close enough; by the time he caught the object on the stick, he was leaning far out over the lake. Hyonsu felt a terrifying urge rise up from inside. He wanted to shove Yongje deep into the water and hold him down so he would never have to see him again. Sourness pooled under his tongue and his left hand trembled.

Then something white flopped by his feet. He stepped back, startled. Yongje was back on dry ground, a vein bulging in his forehead. His lips had curled up in an odd way and his voice was low. "I was right—it's hers. Now we can report it."

It took twenty minutes for the police to arrive. The conservancy immediately allowed a search, and within hours, four divers were scouring the lake, starting in the northern part of the lake, in the area nearest where the shirt fabric was found.

Bystanders began to gather along the fence. Soon, the crowd was giving advice to the four divers; one old man began yelling that they shouldn't go disturbing the lake at all, and he didn't stop until people pulled him away.

The divers surfaced every five minutes, exchanged hand signals, and went back in, moving southward in increments. Each time the divers resurfaced, Hyonsu's veins burst with adrenaline. When they went back under, he could smell his own sour sweat as he glared at the surface of the water. He forgot all about Yongje. He didn't even realize that Sunghwan was standing next to him until the younger man said, "Don't look." He didn't understand what Sunghwan meant, and he didn't care to.

Sunghwan continued to whisper, "Once you look into the eyes of a corpse, you're done. Look somewhere else, like the other side of the lake or the sky . . ."

The sky grew dark. The sun disappeared behind leaden clouds. A damp wind began to blow. Hyonsu wasn't standing by the lake anymore; he was with his mother in front of the old well in the sorghum fields. There was no sound in the well; the rope tied to the diver's back snaked down. The man holding the other end of the rope at the mouth of the well kept wiping sweat off his face. The air felt sticky and the sweet scent of sorghum made him feel queasy. Hyonsu heard the villagers murmuring behind him.

"I knew something would happen."

"That well should have been closed up a long time ago."

"It's not the well's fault! He was just a drunk fool who slipped."

"What are you talking about? What kind of person takes off all his clothes and folds them up neatly and then *accidentally* slips into a well?"

"He wouldn't kill himself. I bet he was possessed. I bet he thought it was a reservoir and went in for a swim."

"His poor wife. What will she do now? And the four little ones . . ."

The rope draped in the well swung to and fro, and people stopped talking. Fog rushed into the fields as the wind shook the blood-colored sorghum stalks. Mother gripped Hyonsu's arm. Hyonsu felt dizzy.

Everything overlapped and broke apart; through those gaps, reality seeped in. He heard someone shout, "They found her!"

Two divers bobbed up to the surface close to Hansoldung and swam toward where Hyonsu was standing. Between them was a clump of long, dark hair. As they moved closer to shore, Hyonsu could see thin, white arms. Then he saw the shoulders and back. Soon, the girl was heaved up onto the bank. She was clad only in white underwear. The divers placed her in a black body bag. Her head was turned to one side; she stared at him with her dark, empty eyes.

Hyonsu stopped breathing. The memory he had tried so hard to suppress was roaring toward him like a train. He backed up, blinking hard. His face was burning. Her eyes were branding him so that he couldn't willfully forget, so that his subconscious couldn't cover it up: *he'd killed her.*

"That's my daughter," Hyonsu heard Yongje say. That pulled him back into the present.

Yongje covered his daughter's body with a white cloth. His eyes looked exactly like hers.

～

W ould you like one?" the detective asked, holding a cigarette.

"I don't smoke," Yongje replied.

"Ah." The detective slid the cigarette between his lips and settled in front of Yongje.

Yongje leaned back, watching him search for a lighter. He was in his midforties, with a strong build, a protruding forehead, and large, square front teeth that looked like the floodgates of the dam. His younger partner handed over a lighter. The detective exhaled a long plume of smoke in Yongje's direction.

The detectives had appeared on the scene an hour after Seryong's body was recovered. They were from the Sunchon Police Department; apparently, the incident was serious enough that it had been referred to regional headquarters. They went about setting up a temporary base at the local patrol station.

Yongje was called in first. They said they needed a statement from him.

"It's all in the missing persons report," Yongje said.

"Please humor us. And please try to remember even the tiniest detail."

Yongje looked out the window at the setting sun. There were still a few hours before it would get too dark to see.

Earlier that afternoon, Yongje had spotted Ahn Sunghwan standing next to the new head of security by the lake. He nearly grabbed him by the shirt and shoved him into the water; he wanted to yell, *You* go in and find her, asshole.

Yongje had received a message from the Supporters that morning; they hadn't found Hayong, but in a single day they had unearthed everything there was to know about Ahn Sunghwan, down to his shoe size. Two pieces of information in particular had grabbed his attention: *Son of a professional diver. Began diving at age eleven. Discharged from the Ship Salvage Unit after completing military service.* So, his neighbor was a diver with a special forces background . . .

Yongje didn't know anything about diving, but he did know that, if left untouched, drowned bodies would float to the surface between three and five days after death. That was why he'd gone to the lake that morning; it had been almost three days since Seryong went missing. He figured she would float up around the trash screen, where, unless stones had been tied around her ankles, she would have been moved by the current. Hayong's blouse scrap had been caught on the screen, so he'd been half-right. When he saw that, he was certain she had been raped, murdered, and thrown in the

water. It took all of his willpower to leave Sunghwan alone—
for the moment. He couldn't prove anything simply by the
existence of a fishing line. Even if he could prove it was
Sunghwan's, it didn't conclusively prove that Sunghwan was
at the lake exactly when Seryong disappeared. Yongje would
have to wait. He needed proof. Then he would take him
down.

Yongje was so focused on sleuthing that he hadn't absorbed the fundamental truth that, whatever had happened,
all signs were pointing to the fact that his daughter was dead
in the lake. When he saw her body, the reality of her death
hit him; he felt as if he were falling through air. He staggered
back, shoulders shaking. He was outraged that his daughter
was lying naked in front of spectators. How dare his world
be destroyed this way? But he could do nothing about it. He
clenched his jaw and glared at the body bag as the zipper
went up. They would place her on a table and the coroner
would mutilate his daughter's body to determine the cause
of death. He wanted to pull her up and slap her across the
face. Wake up right this instant and get home, he wanted
to yell.

"Mr. Oh," the detective said now, studying Yongje.

"When will we get the autopsy results?" Yongje asked.

"A few days," the detective said, not taking his eyes off
Yongje. "Then we'll have a pretty good idea whether it was
an accident or not."

"What do you think?"

"I think it's possible she was murdered. What do you think?"
Yongje didn't answer.

"Did you know she was in the lake? The new head of security said he bumped into you right where the clothing was found."

"I just figured it was the only place left."

"Why? She could have been somewhere else. She could have been kidnapped, for one."

"Do you have a daughter, Detective?"

The younger detective glanced at him as he continued typing on his laptop.

"You're saying it's a father's intuition," the older detective said.

"Yes."

The detective nodded. "Okay. Let's start from the beginning. What time did she leave the house?"

"Probably around 9:40 at night."

"And what was she doing before then?"

"Sleeping."

"Are you telling me she sleepwalked out of the house?"

"No, I'm saying she woke up and then ran away."

"And why would she do that?" the detective asked.

"I don't know. But she didn't come home all night long. So the next day I reported her missing and put a search party together. We looked all over the arboretum and the village, the woods, the ranch, the dock, and even the banks of the lake. But we didn't find anything."

"You found nothing?"

"No."

"Can you explain to me how finding nothing made you think that she had fallen into the lake?" asked the detective.

"If she wasn't on the ground, where else could she be? As far as I know she couldn't fly."

They let him go two hours later. The story had gotten out; reporters were beginning to arrive in the village, and so was nightfall.

When he got home, the Matiz was parked in front of 102. What a pathetic car for a giant like Hyonsu to drive. It made more sense for the guy's wife. Yongje noticed the glow-in-the-dark skull hanging from the rearview mirror. It looked familiar, but he couldn't place it.

He thought of the day before, when Hyonsu had pulled up in the Matiz while his son was studying Seryong's poster. Yongje didn't like how the boy was looking at his daughter. He wanted to kick him in the seat of his pants and tell him to get away from her. The giant in the Matiz had pulled up right then, and though he was initially cowed by Hyonsu's size, he quickly saw that the man was timid, self-conscious, and flustered. But the kid had balls; he more than made up for his loser of a father.

Had Seryong ever defended her father with that much loyalty? Yongje combed through his memories for a while but gave up. What was he doing? He was standing in front of his dark, empty house, searching for proof that his dead daughter had loved him. Did Hayong even know her daughter was dead? Seryong's death was all over the news, and her so-called mother hadn't even called. Who was the better parent now? He was used to rage coursing through his veins, but now the exact opposite feeling overtook him. A cool wave of sorrow made him stagger and he sat down on the steps.

Yongje stared vaguely at the cars parked in front of him: his BMW, the Matiz. White Matiz . . . skull. A memory so trivial that it had almost trickled away finally floated to the surface. Three trailers had been transporting steel plates. A

Matiz had changed lanes to let him pass near the Seryong rest area. He had honked and sped by. That glow-in-the-dark skull had been grinning at him through the Matiz's windshield. That was Friday night, the night Seryong went missing. Could it have been Hyonsu's car? How many people had a white Matiz with a glow-in-the-dark skull like that? If it was, what did it mean?

There had been a second car on the lakeshore road that night when he went out looking for Seryong. The second car had sped along before suddenly stopping, then disappeared after about twenty minutes. What had happened in those twenty minutes? He imagined Seryong screaming in terror, crawling through the gap under the doors. Or maybe she had jumped out onto the road right when the car drove by . . .

Yongje stood up and walked to the lakeshore road. A red-orange full moon hung in the dark sky. He walked slowly into the night, listening to the water and his own footsteps.

⁓

Sunghwan entered the dock area. He was about to sling the chain and padlock on the inside of the doors but changed his mind. This shouldn't take more than a minute or two, he thought. At the end of the dock he stopped and listened for a moment. Cicadas. He kneeled at the edge and bent over, feeling below the pillar. Nothing. His heart sank. He felt the other pillars. He remembered precisely where he'd tied the line, but he felt around just in case he was mistaken. It wasn't there. He swished his hand around in the water in vain. He turned his flashlight on and shined it on the water. Still nothing.

Only today, when the divers started searching the lake, had

he realized that this was what had nagged at him when he left the lake that night, the thing he'd forgotten: the fishing line he'd tied along the sunken streets.

Sunghwan made an excuse to Park and rushed over to the lake. He didn't have a plan; it wasn't as though he could check on the line when the entire village had descended on the shores. He couldn't do anything even if the divers found it. But he also couldn't just sit still in the office, waiting.

When he arrived, he found Hyonsu standing on the banks, pale, sweaty, staring. The man was barely holding it together. If he looked into the eyes of the corpse, that would be the end of him. He'd seen it before; the man would become haunted.

When the onlookers called out that the divers had found her, Sunghwan wanted to cover Hyonsu's eyes with his hand, but it was too intimate a gesture; instead, he again whispered to him not to look. He watched helplessly as Hyonsu was pulled into the horror of death, his consciousness narrowed to a pinpoint.

What surprised Sunghwan was Yongje's reaction. During the search, Yongje had stood watch, his gaze calm and his expression cool. But when the body was recovered, his behavior changed dramatically. A grieving father in shock. Which was real, the coolness or the panic?

He'd dragged his stunned boss away, then waited for nightfall, when he could go back and look for the fishing line. He decided to wear his uniform, in case he encountered someone. At least then it would look as though he were there as part of his official duties.

But now, swirling his hand around in the water, he couldn't find it. Maybe he hadn't tied it as tightly as he thought and it had sunk. He thought it was highly unlikely that the divers wouldn't have recovered it, but he hadn't heard anyone mention it yet. Maybe they assumed it belonged to a maintenance diver. Or maybe the police weren't revealing all the details of the investigation to the public. But deep down he feared Yongje had found it. If he had, Yongje would certainly bring it up with the police, as well as reminding them of the night when Sunghwan had brought the girl into the clinic. Sunghwan's heart sank. He felt dizzy.

He stood up and nearly fell over again in shock. Yongje was right behind him.

"What are you doing here?" Yongje asked, cocking his head.

Sunghwan was mute. His heart was pounding. He was surprised he didn't scream.

"Fishing in the middle of the night?"

"I'm on a night patrol at the conservancy's request," Sunghwan managed, glad he'd thought to wear his uniform.

"Ah. You patrol inside the water, too?" Yongje stepped in front of Sunghwan, blocking his way. "What can you see by leaning over and splashing around?"

Once his shock dissipated, he knew: Yongje was trailing him. Why else would they both be here at this time of night? "A long time ago, before there were police divers, there were people who recovered bodies from the water as a profession," he began.

Yongje stuffed his hands in his pockets and listened patiently.

"We call ourselves crocodiles." His father had taught him to throw his wallet at a mugger and run away. He would do the same with Yongje; he would give him what he was look-ing for, but on Sunghwan's terms. "There are superstitions we abide by. First, you don't go in the water when it rains. Second, you don't go in after having a drink. Third, you don't touch a body that's upright."

"Interesting. A body that's upright . . ." Yongje's forehead glowed in the red moonlight.

"Those are taboos specifically for those who handle corpses. There's a saying that a crocodile blinded by the promise of money dies the same day he touches a standing corpse. Some-times they were discovered underwater, arm in arm with the body. A standing corpse is a water spirit, waiting to find some-one else to bring into the afterlife."

"What does this have to do with anything?"

"I'm the son of a crocodile. But that night, I was home drinking beer and watching baseball in my living room. And it was raining when the game ended." With that, Sunghwan walked toward the doors.

Yongje didn't stop him. He was busy trying to piece to-gether the implications of the fishing line and Seryong and crocodiles.

He called after Sunghwan, "Let me ask you something."

Sunghwan turned around.

Yongje strode over to him. "That night, didn't your new boss come here?"

This was unexpected. What was going through this man's head?

Yongje added, "To see the house before moving in, maybe?"

"No."

"Is he from around here?"

"Why do you ask?"

"Oh, I think we've crossed paths before, is all."

"Why don't you ask him yourself? Sniffing around is what dogs do." Sunghwan turned and went out the doors. He knew it was safer to duck and cover after throwing a punch. Yongje didn't follow him. Sunghwan locked the doors from the outside. That asshole could crawl under or climb over— he didn't care.

Sunghwan stopped in front of the intake tower and took his notepad and pen out. Standing in the bloodred moonlight, he scribbled a note. *Hyonsu and Yongje met before. When?* He flipped through the notes he'd taken. He needed to organize all of these fragments, from Friday afternoon when he saw Seryong by the bus stop to just now. Everything from what he saw to what he knew to even the most fleeting of feelings. He had to protect himself. And to do that, he needed to see the entire picture.

When he stepped through the front door, Eunju greeted him with an attack. "Why are you alone? Where's Hyonsu?"

Sunghwan froze.

Eunju's mouth was smiling, but her eyes weren't. Sowon stood behind her with a pointer finger on either side of his head like horns and winked.

"I don't know. I got held up at work," Sunghwan mumbled.

"I thought you were together. Hyonsu isn't picking up and I couldn't get in touch with you, either. You don't know where he went?" Eunju stood rooted to the ground, as though she would never move aside.

"Mom, Mr. Ahn must be hungry," Sowon said, tugging on his mother's arm.

She shook him off. "Your dad needs to be home before we start eating." She'd said that the previous night, too, as though it were Sunghwan's job to go find him and bring him back.

It was clear they'd gotten into a huge fight before they arrived in town; Hyonsu and Eunju didn't look at each other once all day. After Hyonsu disappeared, it was Sunghwan and Sowon who had to go to the rest area to find him. Sunghwan would have to do the same again if he wanted to eat tonight.

"Should I go look for him?" he offered.

Eunju spun around and went into the kitchen. "I'm sure he'll be home." She had a gift for getting people to do what she wanted without asking for it directly.

Sunghwan turned around to leave, and Sowon quickly dashed out with him. "Mom, I'll go with Mr. Ahn!"

"Don't even think about it," she shouted, but Sowon was already scampering down the path in front of the Annex.

The path up to the rest area was pitch-black. Only the spire up at the rest area threw off a bluish light above Seryong Peak.

"Your mom seems really angry today," Sunghwan said, turning on his flashlight.

Sowon stuck close to him. "Yeah, because Dad broke his promise."

"What promise?"

"He promised he would stop drinking. Mom says you could build a castle with all the money he's spent on bottles."

Sowon sounded glum, so Sunghwan changed the subject. "How's your new school? Do you like it so far?"

"It's really small. There's only one class per grade."

"How many kids?"

"Thirteen kids in my grade."

"That's nice, I guess. Everyone must be friends with each other."

"Not really. The kids from the village don't talk to the kids whose parents work for the conservancy. I don't know what side I should be on, since the conservancy kids don't talk to me, either."

"None of them?"

Sowon shook his head. "They call me the Annex kid."

Seryong had also been called "Annex kid."

As though he'd heard his thoughts, Sowon said, "There's a picture that girl drew, the one who . . . went missing, on the bulletin board. I think it's a very . . . artistic picture."

Sunghwan smiled despite himself. "Yeah? What's it a picture of?"

"A cat on a windowsill looking out at the woods. The full moon is making the trees glow, and behind one tree there's long hair fluttering, as though someone just ran to hide there. You can see a girl's legs running between other trees. And there are bare feet walking up to the sky. She wrote a title on it, 'Red Light, Green Light'—I think they're playing that in the woods behind the Annex, and the parts of the girl are supposed to be what the cat sees of her." Sowon paused and looked up at Sunghwan. "That girl—she died, right?" he whispered. "I saw her."

Sunghwan was puzzled; he didn't remember seeing him by the lake. "When?"

"The kids from the village went to watch the divers after school, so I went, too."

"Did you watch the whole time?"

The boy nodded, his expression dark. Sunghwan felt a chill.

"I was coming down toward you and Dad when they pulled her out. I didn't recognize her. Her face looked weird. I thought I was going to throw up. I wanted to leave, but I couldn't move. A grown-up covered my eyes and said, 'Don't look.' After they put her in the ambulance, he took his hand away and told me who it was."

Sunghwan looked up at the spire of the rest area, feeling worried.

"Her cat must not know she's dead. He was waiting under her window earlier tonight."

"You saw Ernie?"

"How do you know his name?"

"I heard her call him that before. How did you know that's Seryong's room?"

"I brought him a can of tuna. He didn't run away. I said, 'Hi, kitty,' and he thumped the ground with his tail. He ate all the tuna. While he was eating, I looked up through the window and saw her picture. That same picture from the poster. I wanted to stop looking, but I couldn't. I thought maybe she would say something to me."

"You were scared."

Sowon shook his head. "No, I thought maybe she wasn't really dead."

They had reached the rest area. Sunghwan led the way toward the observation deck. "What do you mean?"

"The girl in the picture," Sowon said, hesitating. "She's just so pretty."

The streetlight illuminated the boy's face; Sunghwan saw that he was blushing.

Hyonsu was standing barefoot on the tallest point of the observation deck, leaning precariously forward on the railing, looking down at the darkness below. Sunghwan stopped. You could see Seryong Lake during the day, but right now the fog had rolled all the way up to the top of the ridge. What was he doing? Where were his shoes?

"Dad," Sowon called.

Hyonsu flinched and slowly turned to look at them. He looked pale and stunned; his eyes were wide, looking at Sowon, but it was clear he wasn't seeing him. He looked the way he had when he'd seen Seryong's body, like he was seeing a ghost.

⁓

Eunju bought a bag of apples from a truck at the rest area. Each bag had ten apples, freshly picked from a nearby orchard, and was only three thousand won, an unimaginable price in Seoul. Her anger subsided a bit.

She went to the observation deck and put the apples on a table shaded by an umbrella. She sat down, picked the reddest, juiciest-looking one, and rubbed it on her blouse. Just as she took a big bite, her phone began ringing. It was her sister, Yongju. The apple in her mouth was too big to swallow, and it would be wasteful to spit it out. She pressed the call button and mumbled "Hi," but it just came out as a groan.

"What?" Yongju asked. "It's so loud! Where are you?"

Eunju chewed and swallowed. "The observation deck."

"Why are you there? I thought you said it's where all the drunks go."

Eunju had come to look for a job. By the end of the day on Monday, she'd finished unpacking, made some food, and cleaned the house. On Tuesday morning, she visited Sowon's new school to ask about vacancies in the school cafeteria. There were none. Her next idea was to apply to be a cashier at the restaurant at the rest area. The pay would be terrible, but it was at least close to home; well-paying jobs were generally all in Sunchon, over the mountain.

That morning she'd gone to the management office at the rest area to submit her résumé. "Leave it there," the young woman behind the desk said carelessly, too busy applying a coat of powder to her face to so much as look at Eunju. Did she mean leave it there and wait, or leave it there and go?

Eunju waited for a long time before asking, "Miss, shouldn't I get some sort of receipt, or . . ."

The woman closed her compact and looked up. "*Ajumma*, I said leave it there. You can go."

Ajumma? It was a debasing word for a woman of one's parents' age. She wasn't deluded enough to think she could be mistaken for a student, but there was no way she was as old as this brainless bitch's mother. Why should this girl look down on her, anyway? She was applying for a job, submitting her résumé—it wasn't like she was begging. She had her own home in Ilsan, and she had a youthful disposition. She picked up her résumé again, doing all she could to keep her composure. "I'm Kang Eunju, not *ajumma*."

Yongju laughed as Eunju relayed this conversation.

"Do I look like an *ajumma*?" Eunju asked.

Yongju ignored the question. "Are you still not talking to Hyonsu?"

"Not really."

"And he hasn't apologized?" Yongju asked.

"I think he's gone a little crazy."

"He's probably too intimidated to apologize. Why don't you say something first?"

"Look, the worst kind of person in the world is the kind of man who drinks all night and beats his wife. Even if he begs and tries to make it right I might not forgive him. Why should I?"

"Because it was the first time ever. And it was just a slap," Yongju countered.

Sure, it had been just a slap, but the blow had sent her flying from the entryway to the living room. Hyonsu didn't know his own strength. In her mind, forgiving him would be like admitting her life didn't matter.

She felt like it was all her fault, that she'd made him this way. Whenever he apologized, she forgave him, and even though she knew he wouldn't keep his promise, she always believed him when he said he would stop drinking. She had spoiled him. Now she was waiting for the right time; when he came to her demanding a truce, asking her to talk, that would be her chance to put an end to everything. All of it, from the daily drinking to the smoking he'd taken up again recently, from his irresponsible behavior to his refusal to answer his phone.

Eunju felt her anger bubble up. Her sister always took Hyonsu's side. Yongju got along better with her brother-in-law than with her own sister. They were the same age, and their minds worked the same way.

Eunju met Hyonsu the summer she was twenty-seven. Yongju had introduced them, though not intentionally. Yongju, as pretty as a flower, had just become a middle school English teacher, and she was going on dates almost daily. That summer, Yongju went on a short trip to Jeju Island with some guy, while Eunju began her vacation lying in front of the fan at home. As Eunju was weighing whether to put rice cakes or dumplings in her ramen for lunch, she got a call from her sister. Yongju told her she was at the Jeju airport, and that she'd forgotten that she was supposed to go on a blind date that evening. She asked for Eunju's help. The blind date was with a Choi Hyonsu, a twenty-four-year-old baseball player, a rookie who had just completed his mandatory military service. He was in the minors but was expecting to get called up to the majors soon. Eunju knew next to nothing about baseball.

"So you want me to go on a date with a child?" Eunju asked.

"Everyone's dating younger guys now. And he actually makes a living playing baseball! You've got to be at least a little bit curious."

She *was* curious. What were baseball players like? She was intrigued that he had gone to a prestigious university, even though he probably got in because he was an athlete.

So, around dinnertime, she sat in an upscale coffee shop at the foot of Mudung Mountain. If someone asked for Kang Yongju, she would raise a hand elegantly. But she forgot about that plan when he arrived. She'd never seen such a large man in her life. It was as if one of the coffee shop's marble pillars was striding toward her.

"Um . . . are you Kang Yongju?" he asked.

He was wearing a baseball cap and dusty sweatpants, as though he'd run out in the middle of practice.

She stood up. "Nice to meet you."

He took his hat off and bowed politely, as though he were greeting a teacher. His head was shaven and he looked very young. Eunju stared at him, and as he put his hat back on, he smiled awkwardly, like a boy. He seemed sensitive for such a big man, and his gentle eyes made an impression on her.

Was it possible for a tiger to bed a cat? If she slept with him, would she be flattened? "My name is Kang Eunju."

Hyonsu pushed up the brim of his cap, looking surprised.

Eunju coughed. Her words tumbled out over each other. "I'm Yongju's older sister. She . . . she's on a plane . . . I'm also very busy . . . but anyway I came instead."

"Oh," Hyonsu said. He didn't ask any questions and answered Eunju's in monosyllables. His reticence made her wonder if he wasn't into her because she was older. But it didn't seem like it. Whenever their eyes met, he blushed and smiled.

It wasn't until they got up to leave that she finally heard him utter a complete sentence. "So . . . I have a game at one tomorrow."

She took it as an invitation.

It was a hot day, and the stands were nearly empty. She sat alone in the outfield bleachers. She couldn't see Hyonsu's face; she was too far away and he was wearing a catcher's mask. She couldn't follow the game and ended up dozing under the hot sun. Until a ball landed by her feet and her eyes jerked open in surprise. She looked up and saw number 25 rounding second base, glancing up at her. She could tell it was Hyonsu. She watched as he sped past third, his thundering footsteps threatening to split the dry earth.

Hyonsu's home run won the game. Afterward, he came up to the bleachers. "Give me the ball," he said, without a hello or a thank you for coming. She handed it over, dumbfounded. He took a pen out of his pocket, scribbled something on the ball, then gave it back to her. "I have to get on the bus."

She didn't have a chance to say anything; when she looked up, he was already jogging out of the exit. On the ball was written in English: *I believe in the church of baseball. Choi Hyonsu, August 1992.*

As soon as her sister returned home from Jeju Island, Eunju showed her the ball. Eunju knew enough English to read it, of course; she just didn't get it.

"What do you think?" Yongju asked. "Is he Tim Robbins or Kevin Costner?"

That made even less sense than what he'd written.

"His vibe. Which one is he like?"

Eunju didn't know how to answer. He didn't seem like a Kevin Costner. She didn't really know who Tim Robbins was. And what did that have to do with anything, anyway?

Yongju studied her. "You're no Susan Sarandon. First of all, your boobs are the size of plums."

"What are you talking about?"

"He believes in 'the church of baseball.' That's a line from *Bull Durham*."

"*Bull Durham*?"

"It's a baseball movie. Susan Sarandon plays an English instructor and her hobby is maturing a rookie in bed."

"So that's what he's saying? That we should do it?" Eunju asked, shocked.

Yongju laughed. "No, not necessarily. He might just like the saying. In the movie, she's interested in two players, played by Kevin Costner and Tim Robbins, and tries to see who she likes better."

"So he's saying he wants me to sleep with him."

"No, I'm telling you it might not mean that. Why don't you set something up so we can all meet? I'll figure it out for you."

Eunju studied Yongju, an English teacher who had a new boyfriend every week. She was more of a Susan Sarandon than Eunju would ever be. But she couldn't deny that she needed her sister's help.

Hyonsu called two days later. He said he was headed to Busan in the afternoon and asked if he could see her before he left. Eunju said she was spending the day with her sister but would be glad to see him if she could bring her along.

"Tim Robbins," Yongju whispered to Eunju as soon as she saw him.

When Hyonsu went to the bathroom, Eunju turned to her sister. "What does Tim Robbins look like?"

Yongju summarized his character in the movie: six feet, five inches tall, boyish smile, a lovable doofus.

When Hyonsu came back, Eunju studied him carefully. He did seem to fit Yongju's description. Then again, the phrase he wrote on the ball made her think he was a vulgar jerk feigning innocence.

Yongju broke the silence, smiling. "'I believe in the soul, the cock, the pussy, the small of a woman's back, the hanging curve ball, high fiber, good scotch, that the novels of Susan Sontag are self-indulgent, overrated crap. I believe Lee Harvey Oswald acted alone. I believe there ought to be a constitutional amendment outlawing Astroturf and the designated hitter. I believe in the sweet spot, soft-core pornography . . .'"

Eunju felt her face grow hot. What the hell was wrong with her sister—why was she saying these things?

But Hyonsu smiled boyishly. "'. . . opening your presents Christmas morning rather than Christmas Eve. And I believe in long, slow, deep, soft, wet kisses that last three days.'"

Eunju finally realized that they were quoting from the movie. Yongju put a hand on her cheek and pretended to swoon. "Oh, my."

The conversation continued between just the two of them, from baseball in movies to various catching strategies. There was no way for her to turn the tide.

"I heard that a catcher's first training session involves learning not to blink when the ball hits him in the mask," Yongju said, flashing her dimples. Hyonsu looked more engaged than he'd ever been with Eunju.

Eunju felt inferior, annoyed, and excluded. Yongju had gotten all of their mother's desirable traits—big breasts and seduction skills. All she'd given Eunju were half-baked life lessons and, she supposed, survival skills, thanks to Jini's neglect. Her sister had been able to go further in her education, had a better job, and even had a more easygoing personality. As Yongju seduced the ballplayer with her dimples and easy conversation, Eunju couldn't help but feel anxious. She liked Hyonsu.

As they parted ways, Hyonsu shook Yongju's hand. He said it was the most fun he'd had in a long time. To Eunju, he said, "I'm away all of next week. We have a game in Daejon on Saturday. That's not too far, is it?"

Later, Eunju asked her sister how she knew so much about catchers.

Yongju laughed. It sounded like pity to Eunju. "Remember how I was supposed to go out with him?"

"Yeah," Eunju said begrudgingly.

"I read some articles online. So I could use it when I met him."

That night, Eunju rented *Bull Durham* from the video store. After Yongju went to bed, she sat in front of the TV. But she was distracted by her fears about whether her sister and Hyonsu had fallen for each other.

There were a million reasons why she decided to go to Daejon that weekend. Because she had nothing else to do, because it was pathetic how she was spending her vacation lying around the house, because she wanted an answer, because she didn't want Jini's younger, prettier daughter to mature Tim Robbins in bed.

The field at Daejon was almost as empty as the game in Gwangju. In the end, his team won seven to four against the Eagles. But this time, Hyonsu didn't get on the bus after the game.

That night, she learned a lot of things. That the autographed ball he gave her had been his first homer since he'd made the minors. That he lost his father when he was eleven. That his mother ran a restaurant on a construction site, where she lived with his three younger siblings. That he lived with most of his fellow players in housing sponsored by the team. That he only earned eight million won a year, most of which he sent home to his mother. That he'd gone on the blind date because his friend had pestered him to, but he wasn't in the market for marriage. She even found out that a cat didn't get flattened like a rug even if it spent all night under a tiger.

Sowon was conceived that very night. And on this hot summer day, thinking back over their history, her anger returned. Because the man she had thrown herself at, before she had ever been with anyone else, turned out not to be Tim Robbins at all. The only similarity was his "five-cent head."

Walking home through the arboretum, still on the phone with Yongju, she spotted a poster advertising a job opening for a security guard position at the arboretum. She'd seen it the day they moved in but had passed blithely by. She'd never worked as a security guard before, and she hadn't been interested. Now that she'd spoken with the rude girl at the rest area and imagined what it would be like to actually work there, her calculations were a bit different.

"Yongju, I'll call you back later," she said and hung up. She read the ad carefully. Nothing said it had to be a man. She didn't think twice: she believed in the church of bank accounts, and she had emptied hers to buy the apartment. Luckily, she had another copy of her résumé in hand. She walked into the arboretum maintenance office.

Oh Yongje was sitting there alone, on the phone. Eunju

hesitated by the doorway. She'd heard from Sowon that this man's daughter had met a terrible fate; she didn't want to bother him with something as trivial as a job application now.

But just as she was about to turn around, he noticed her, and he hung up. "Yes?" he said. He looked calm, not like someone who had lost his daughter mere days before. The shirt he was wearing looked clean and wrinkle free, the sleeves rolled up tidily.

She held out her résumé. "I'm here to apply for the security job."

He looked at her silently. She began to wonder if he would respond. "It's not an easy job," he said at last.

"I know."

Yongje glanced at her résumé and launched into an impromptu interview. He was well-mannered and seemed highly educated, though his eyes were cold. Eunju didn't pay much attention to that, though; the wages here were double that of the cashier job at the restaurant.

"When can you start?" he asked.

Eunju was so relieved to have found a job in this remote area, right by her new home, that she almost said "Tomorrow." But she had to maintain her dignity. She lowered her eyes primly. "I can start Sunday."

~

D ad, it's 8:20!" Sowon shouted from just outside the bathroom.

Hyonsu was sitting on the edge of the tub, wrestling with his bad arm. The numbness had come and gone ever since his injury, but never with this frequency; it had visited him four times in as many days. Even when the sensation returned, it took him hours to recover his grip. The previous day, it had happened at work. He'd gotten himself a cup of coffee and was about to sit at his desk when his left arm suddenly went limp, the coffee cup smashing to the floor. Park had looked at him, surprised, as Hyonsu flushed and began massaging his arm. "It's okay," he'd explained. "This happens from time to time. It'll get better soon."

But it was still limp an hour later. Hyonsu was at a loss. None of the tricks he usually used were working. At the end of the day, when the feeling still hadn't returned, Park asked him if he could try something. He picked up a box cutter, grabbed Hyonsu's left hand, and pressed the blade into his middle finger. Dark red blood spurted out. Before Hyonsu could react, feeling shot back into his elbow, and a few minutes later his grip returned.

He clenched and unclenched his fist, embarrassed and amazed. "How did you know to do that?" he asked.

Park shrugged. "It happens to my mother sometimes. Not her arm but her legs. She's had a hard life, and she has a lot of repressed emotions. Sometimes she can't move her legs at all. This is the only thing that works for her." He put the box cutter back in his desk drawer. "You must be dealing with stress, too."

In his bathroom, Hyonsu opened the medicine cabinet and dug through the first aid kit in search of something sharp. But there was nothing. Even the scissors and tweezers had rounded safety tips. His arm was completely limp, like a dead snake.

Sowon continued pounding on the bathroom door. If Hyonsu didn't go out soon he'd make him late for school. Finally, Hyonsu noticed the tumbler that was on the edge of the sink. He smashed it, sending shards of glass skittering across the floor. He picked one up and stuck it into the end of his middle finger. Drops of blood appeared and merged into a thin stream that dripped through his fingers. Hyonsu let out a groan; it felt freeing, as if something that had been congested inside of him was finally leaving his body. His finger ached.

There was another knock on the door. Hyonsu quickly washed off the blood and put a bandage from the first aid kit on his finger. He gathered the broken bits and threw them in the trash. He opened the door and stepped out, expecting to see his son. But it was Sunghwan who practically shoved Hyonsu out of the way as he ran into the bathroom.

Sowon was waiting by the front door with his backpack on. Eunju had her back toward him, washing the breakfast dishes. He was glad. His plan to confess had long vanished. Only useless regrets looped in his mind. He shouldn't have come here, even if it meant quitting his job. It was foolish of him to think that he would be able to handle it. The girl continually materialized before him, lying limply in the road, plunging into the dark lake. He couldn't escape what he'd done. He felt alone. If he told Eunju, she might want him to go to the authorities, and he couldn't do that. What scared him the most was the possibility that Sowon might become known as the son of a murderer. If she told him to kill himself, he'd more gladly do that. No, he couldn't tell her. It was better to grapple alone with the specter of the girl. He had done this before, when he was a boy, fighting the voice calling his name from inside the well. He had to keep going. Time would solve everything. He was sure of it.

"Let's go," Hyonsu said, putting his uniform hat on.

Sowon put on his baseball cap. "What about Mr. Ahn?"

"He's in the bathroom. I think we should just go ahead."

The morning was hazy with thick fog. Under the streetlight in front of the house, two strangers were studying his car. The middle-aged one peered in the windshield while the younger one examined the bumper. "Wait here." He left Sowon by the stairs and crossed the street. "What are you doing?" he asked.

"Just looking," the younger man said, flashing his police badge.

"For what?"

The middle-aged detective came around to stand next to his partner. "I like your choice of decor," he said, nodding toward the skull.

Hyonsu tried to look at them calmly, but his eyelid twitched. "My son gave it to me."

"Oh, is that him?" the middle-aged detective asked, looking in Sowon's direction.

Hyonsu didn't answer. He didn't like how the detective had looked at his boy.

"When did you move here?"

"I already told you. On Sunday."

"You told me?"

"I told two other detectives," Hyonsu said.

"Ah." The detective scratched his nose. "When did you officially start work?"

"Monday."

"August twenty-seventh, then."

"No, the thirtieth," Hyonsu corrected.

"And you didn't come here before?"

Hyonsu glanced at Sowon, still on the stairs. "No."

"Interesting. People usually take a look at the house they're going to live in before they move."

"Well, I didn't."

"When did you get your car fixed?"

Hyonsu was caught off guard, missing the moment to reply.

"Did you get into an accident?" continued the detective.

"A few months ago."

"Wow, those guys are pros! Looks like it just got fixed a few days ago. Where did you go? I should start using them myself."

"Look, I need to get to work," Hyonsu interrupted.

The detective nodded. "And the girl. Did you see her before she died?"

Hyonsu wanted to scream; when he answered, his voice was louder than he would have liked. "What kind of question is that?"

"What do you mean?"

"I told you I started work on the thirtieth."

"Oh, that's right." The detective tapped a finger on his temple. "Sorry. When you get older, you start to forget things like that."

"Are we done here?"

"Well, I can't guarantee that. But you can be on your way." The two detectives turned and headed to the street.

As they walked away, the detective grumbled, "What's wrong with that asshole? Do you think he's lying? Otherwise, why is he acting so hysterical?" The detective clearly wanted him to overhear. Hyonsu felt the blood draining from his face. He glanced surreptitiously down at the car window. He could see his face reflected in it. It didn't make sense. He hadn't been there when it happened, at least not officially. So why were they sniffing around? He could still see them walking away, the older one lighting a cigarette.

"Dad? Are you okay?" Sowon was standing right beside him.

It startled him so much that Hyonsu bellowed. "What?"

"Never mind. Sorry." Sowon pulled his hat down over his eyes and looked straight ahead, his cheeks reddening.

Hyonsu regretted it immediately. He almost never yelled at his son. He swallowed hard. "Want me to take you to school?"

"If you want." Sowon's head was still bowed.

Hyonsu took Sowon's backpack in one hand and placed the other on his son's shoulder. Sowon hesitated a moment before hooking two fingers through one of Hyonsu's belt loops.

Hyonsu matched his stride to the boy's as they walked down the path. The streetlight turned the fog yellow. Just then, a cat crossed the street in front of them. "Ernie!" Sowon called out eagerly.

The cat glanced back at them before disappearing into the woods.

"He's someone's pet?" Hyonsu asked.

"No, he lives alone, up in the barn at Seryong Ranch."

"How do you know that?"

"That's what the kids say," Sowon explained. "When the adults went looking for the girl from next door, they found the place where she'd been hiding him."

Hyonsu was mute for a second. The cat belonged to the dead girl?

"Ernie comes to my window at night. I put a can of tuna on the windowsill and he hops up and eats it. Can you get me some cat food? If I keep taking tuna, Mom's going to notice."

"Where would I get cat food?" Hyonsu asked.

"There's a pet store in town. Can you go at lunch and put it in my closet? Without Mom finding out?"

"What if she opens the closet?"

"It's Mr. Ahn's, too, so she won't."

Hyonsu nodded, and Sowon beamed, his face brimming with love and trust. This face was the light that kept Hyonsu going.

"I heard Ernie was her only friend," Sowon said. "You know, if she didn't die, she would have sat next to me at school."

"You sit next to her seat?" Hyonsu stopped short, suddenly angry. Why would the teacher put a new student next to a dead child's seat?

"She doesn't have a seat anymore. The teacher moved it to the back. The other kids felt bad for her," Sowon continued. "They said her mom ran away, and that she probably ran away that night because her father beat her up. They say he did it all the time. That's the guy who picked a fight with you the day we moved in. He doesn't sound like a nice guy. You shouldn't be friends with him."

Hyonsu was lost in his thoughts. She was running away from her dad the night she died?

"Anyway, I'm worried about Mom. She's going to work for him."

Hyonsu's eyes widened in horror. "What?"

"Yesterday, I was coming home from school and bumped into Mom, on her way back from the company houses. She said she got a new job as the security guard there. She said she has to work because we have so much debt because of the apartment. Dad, can't you make up with her? Can't you tell her she shouldn't work there because he's mean?"

"Yeah," Hyonsu said, dazed. They were outside the school now. Sowon looked up at him. "Yes, I'll take care of it."

Looking relieved, Sowon disappeared into the school.

AT WORK, Sunghwan was on the computer. He'd gotten there faster since he didn't walk with them to Sowon's school. Hyonsu spotted a news photo of Seryong being pulled from the lake on the screen. He looked away and went to the sink to shave.

"Sunghwan, I've been meaning to tell you that I received a request for us to increase our weekend hours for a while."

"The conservancy asked us to do that?"

Hyonsu took out a disposable razor and rubbed soap on his chin. "Is that okay with you? I'll take some shifts, too, don't worry."

Sunghwan frowned.

"Because of all the media scrutiny and law enforcement demands. We'll get paid overtime."

"Why didn't you come here last Friday, like you said you would?" Sunghwan asked suddenly.

Hyonsu glanced at Sunghwan through the mirror. "Something came up. Why?"

"Someone was asking a few days ago. Whether you'd come to check the place out before you moved."

"Who was asking, a detective?"

"The girl's father."

Hyonsu turned on the faucet and rinsed the razor. "And what did you tell him?"

"I said you hadn't, and then he asked me if you're from around here. He thought you might have crossed paths before."

Had they? Where? Hyonsu was confused. The man hadn't looked familiar, and given what he knew of him, he was confident they traveled in different circles.

At lunchtime, Hyonsu went to town to buy cat food. He was feeling more optimistic. Maybe Yongje had been making small talk. He was worried he would bump into Eunju at home, but thankfully the house was empty. He hid the cat food in the closet and crept out of the house. On his way down the stairs, he stopped short.

Yongje's BMW was parked in front of his car. He suddenly remembered Sunghwan's words. It wasn't that they had *met* before. He'd said "crossed paths." Was it possible Yongje could have seen him on the road that night? He shivered. But Yongje didn't know what he looked like then, who he was. And he wouldn't have paid any particular attention to Hyonsu's car; it wasn't some rare foreign model or anything. He looked back at the Matiz. The glow-in-the-dark skull grinned at him from the windshield. That was when he remembered what the detective had said earlier that morning. "I like your choice of decor." "Interesting. People usually take a look at the house they're going to live in before they move." "When did you get your car fixed?" "And the girl. Did you see her before she died?" Anxiety fogged his brain. Maybe Yongje had noticed the skull. Did they know he was there that night? Did they know he was lying? Did Yongje tell them to investigate him? The skull kept smiling.

~

L et's go back to before your daughter ran off," the detective said, turning the recorder on. "What time did you say it was?"

Yongje settled into his chair. He clasped his fingers and rested them on his thighs, listening to the clock ticking on the wall. He had been called into the substation at three in the afternoon and was greeted by a new detective. They were adding more and more detectives to the case. "It was probably around 9:40."

"And you say she just up and ran away?"

"Yes."

"Well, the autopsy results are in," the detective continued. "Would it surprise you to know that her pelvis was smashed and her teeth were knocked out? She suffered a subarachnoid hemorrhage. Any idea what could have inflicted this kind of damage?"

Yongje was momentarily dazed. "So you're saying something like a dump truck crushed my daughter?"

"A truck wouldn't have been necessary. A BMW would have sufficed," the detective said. "Look, we know your wife filed for divorce because you were beating her and your daughter. And that the day your daughter died, you'd lost the case."

"Are you seriously suggesting that I ran over my own daughter and threw her body in the lake?"

Yongje's breathing grew labored; he felt punched in the gut.

"I'm not saying anything yet. Let's get back to what we were talking about. Start with when she ran away."

Hit by a car. Bones crushed. He remembered what the director of operations had said about the CCTV footage by the lake. The second set of lights speeding, stopping, then disappearing.

"Well?" the detective prodded.

"Was there any evidence of rape?" Yongje asked.

"None. But I did want to ask you about what she looked like before she died. Why was she wearing a woman's silk blouse? And so much makeup?" The detective leaned forward expectantly.

Let him wait. He had to think. If she'd been hit by a car on the lakeshore road, it couldn't be someone from around there; nobody drove down that road that late at night. Maybe it was someone who wasn't familiar with the area, someone who'd gotten lost. He thought of the Matiz and the grinning skull. Was it possible?

"I've read about it in novels," the detective said. "About pervy dads who dress their young daughters in grown-up clothes and put makeup on them. Do you like novels?"

"What are you insinuating?" Yongje snapped.

"Oh, you know. I'm just curious about your literary tastes."

Yongje needed to get out of here so he could get to the bottom of this. He started answering quickly. "She was dressing up in her mom's things. She'd done it before and gotten in trouble, but she kept doing it."

"Was that what set you off?"

"I didn't like it when she wore my wife's things. I told her that very clearly. But that day it was a more serious problem. She fell asleep looking like that, with candles burning. And her long hair was loose. She could have caught on fire. And the house could have gone up in flames. I didn't control my anger, and I slapped her. She threw hot candle wax at me and ran. But just because we fought doesn't mean I killed her."

The detective said nothing, tapping his pen on the back of his hand.

"I demand some respect! I'm the father of a dead child. If you want to treat me like a suspect, you need evidence."

"How's this for evidence? We know your car was on the lakeshore road twice that night."

"No, it was just once. I stopped in front of the ranch and by the dock. I drove down that road at 10:02. When I came back home, it was 10:35."

"That's very precise. Do you check the time like that every time you go somewhere?"

"No, I confirmed the times after. We have top-of-the-line CCTVs at the arboretum, you see. The footage is kept in our management office. It was foggy, but you can make out the license plates. Take a look for yourself; it will confirm my movements that night."

The detective nodded, looking irritated. "And what did you do after that?"

"I'd looked everywhere I could think of to look, so I went

home and waited. I thought she'd come back on her own. I would have been caught on camera if I left again."

"I heard there's no camera on the back path by the woods," commented the detective.

"Didn't you say she was hit by a car? You can't drive that way."

"Well, I'll have to take a look at your car regardless," the detective said, pursing his lips.

"Go ahead," Yongje said. He took his keys out and put them on the table. "When can I see her?"

"I'm sure right away, now that the autopsy is over."

Yongje walked home from the station. The Matiz was in front of the Annex. From what Yongje had observed of his routine, Hyonsu wouldn't be home for another few hours. He called a mechanic and offered to pay extra if he came immediately.

A half hour later, the mechanic confirmed that the entire front of the car appeared to be brand-new.

"How new?"

"Hard to say exactly, but it looks pretty recent."

"Would you be able to pin down the exact date?"

"Nah, you'd have to check the books at the shop that did the repair. Was it somewhere around here?"

After the mechanic left, Yongje went down to his workshop. Run over by a car, then thrown into the lake . . . He painted glue on a stick and placed it on the fortress wall, his fingers trembling. *Did you have to run away to die like that?* he asked, silently addressing his daughter. He glued on another stick. Sunghwan didn't have a car. He'd never even seen him drive. But his background check had shown that he had a driver's license. He did dive from time to time, but the man had insisted he was home that particular night. Maybe Yongje's stubborn belief that it had to be him had been blinding him to the other possibility that was right in front of him.

He went over the night again, from the very beginning, through the prism of his new neighbor as the suspect. He had exited the highway at 9:20, which meant he must have encountered the Matiz around 9:15. The second car appeared on the CCTV at 10:40. It didn't make sense that the Matiz would take over an hour to get from where he saw it to the lakeshore road. Maybe Hyonsu had stopped somewhere first. Or maybe he'd gotten lost. The road to Seryong Lake was easy to miss at first glance, especially on a foggy night, and he didn't know the area. If the Matiz had taken the wrong turn and headed to Paryong Lake, that would explain the delay. Yongje needed to find out more about his new neighbor. He also wanted to check the CCTVs at the Seryong interchange. But how would he get his hands on that footage? He went up to the living room and called the Supporters. "I need you to find out two things . . ."

~

Eunju made rice, sautéed zucchini, and sliced cubes of tofu into the bean-paste soup. She wiped the table clean. Her shoulders ached. She'd gone to the market at lunch and lugged back instant ramen, eggs, canned tuna, snacks for Sowon, ingredients for side dishes . . . She would have to make food in advance now that she had a job. She was going to announce her new position at dinner. She felt a little bad about Sunghwan, who was paying for his meals, but she decided not to dwell on it. There was no point. It would just make her feel worse. The three of them could manage just fine with the prepared food.

Just as she was about to taste the soup, the front door opened and Hyonsu walked in. Her good mood vanished. His face was red; he must have already had a drink. She looked away and dipped her spoon in the soup.

"Hey, I have something to tell you," he said. Now he was going to ask for forgiveness? Five days later? She wouldn't accept his apology. She placed the spoon on the counter, retied her ponytail, and took out the envelope from a kitchen drawer, divorce papers she'd filled out in preparation for a day like today, when she would need to issue an ultimatum. Her ace in the hole, as people said.

She crossed her arms, hiding the envelope by her side, and waited.

"Don't take that job."

She blinked. "What?"

"Just stay home."

"Since when do I have the luxury of just staying home? Have you ever brought in enough for me to do that?"

"There are more important things than money," he insisted.

Eunju's temper flared. "Do you even know how much interest we have to pay for the apartment? We'll never be able to move in if we don't save now. And what about Sowon's education? Don't you want to send him to college? Can we manage that on just your salary?"

"Get out." His voice was low.

"What?"

"Get out."

"Who do you think you are? How dare you tell *me* to get out? When we got married you were only making eight million a year. I had your child, I kept your house, I worked and saved and managed to buy property. And now you're telling me to leave?"

"I don't care. You can keep it all. Take whatever you want and just get out."

Eunju was stunned into silence. Her body burned and she couldn't open her mouth. She was the one who should tell *him* to get out. How dare he say that to her, when he stumbled home drunk every night? Was he insane? But he wasn't yelling or getting worked up. He didn't seem drunk. His voice remained low and calm. "You're nuts," she heard herself say.

He said it again. Clearly and calmly, as though speaking to someone who was hard of hearing. "Get. Out."

Eunju stared at him as he walked out. The front door opened then closed. Shock engulfed her. It was impossible to accept what was going on. Was that really Hyonsu? She went into the bedroom and sat down on the edge of the bed, her legs shaking.

"He doesn't talk much," her mother-in-law had told her when they first met. She had been right. Eunju had never been able to see all of him; there were certain parts he never revealed. It felt like the more she tried to learn about him, the more he withdrew. He was single-minded and rigid, and though he looked gentle, he was stubborn. He seemed conscientious and yet she soon discovered he was irresponsible. If she had known all of this about him from the outset, maybe he wouldn't have driven her so crazy during the first years of their marriage. Unfortunately, they hadn't had much time to get to know each other; they'd met in August and married in December, as Sowon was already growing in her belly.

As a condition for marriage, she demanded that he stop sending money home to his family. If he kept it up, there was no way they could support themselves and a new baby. Hyonsu wasn't thrilled about it but accepted her demand. Their wedding was a far cry from what she had dreamed. They got married under a tent on a baseball field, and the reception was at a pub. Her half-basement rental studio became their home. Still, she was hopeful. There was a possibility that Hyonsu, who had been drafted in midseason and hit twelve home runs, would be called up to the majors the next season.

Perhaps he might have, were it not for their terrible car accident on their honeymoon. They were driving along the East Sea, down a road hugging the coast, when all of a sudden the car jolted and they were flying through the air. When Eunju opened her eyes, the car was upside down. Hyonsu got out first and then pulled her out, his face frozen with concern. She thought that expression was love. She hugged him, telling him she was fine. And she was, other than being shaken up. She took in her surroundings. They were in a ditch between the road and the sandy beach. Dusk had obscured the ditch, and Hyonsu had assumed that the road adjoined the beach. Now they had to pull the car right-side up. People from the beach gathered and gave them all kinds of advice: that it would take over an hour for a tow truck to come, that it would be expensive. Amid the commotion, a bus honked from the road and offered them chains. They hitched the car to the bus and the driver started the engine. The car was righted with a lurch. But because it was yanked out so powerfully, it skidded toward Eunju. For a moment, she lost her sense of reality, standing there frozen in place as her husband threw himself between her and the car. The car stopped and Hyonsu rolled on the ground.

He had ruptured his thigh muscle. The injury wasn't too grave, considering he'd thrown his body in front of a car, but it was a fatal injury for an athlete who was trying to make it to the majors. He didn't recuperate in time to join spring training a few months later. His consolation was that he had managed to protect his wife and, most important, his son.

Eunju still remembered, vividly, the first time Hyonsu saw his son. He reached for the baby's finger, his huge hand shaking, as he murmured, "My son . . ." Joy, fear, and nervousness mingled on his face.

Not "our son," but "*my* son." He didn't let her make any decisions about Sowon. He had her bathe the baby when he thought she should. When he came home after a game, he would stare into the baby's eyes and laugh and talk with him, barely sleeping. When it was time to nurse and he had to give the baby to her, he looked so sad; it was as if he wished he could feed Sowon himself. When he was on the road, he would call repeatedly to ask, "What's Sowon doing?" What did he think an infant would do, other than sleep, eat, cry, or dirty his diaper? Of course, he never asked about her.

Still, at first, she was grateful to see how much he loved his son. After a few months, however, his obsession with Sowon began to grate. Once, she joked, "You married me so that you'd have a son, right?"

His eyes grew wide.

"Come on, admit it, you're obsessed with him."

"I'm not obsessed."

"You are. I've never heard of a dad as attentive as you."

"I promised myself when I was young that I wouldn't be like my dad."

"Why, what was your dad like?" she asked, but he didn't answer. He always clammed up when his father came up in conversation. That was one of the things he never shared with her.

Another was his struggles with his arm. When Sowon was three, she discovered prescriptions from a neurologist in Hyonsu's pocket. He'd been going for a few years and had never told her. The doctor said that his problems were a physical manifestation of his stress; that the mental pressure of wanting to get into the majors had brought on an illusory illness. And now it was a self-fulfilling prophecy: his arm would go dead, and he would ruin the game, and that was why he couldn't make it to the majors.

To Eunju, stress was a coward's excuse. Everyone experienced pressure; if your survival was threatened, you had to fight until you drew blood. That was how she led her life. By contrast, her husband allowed his fear to control him. In fact, as soon as he quit playing baseball, his problems with his arm disappeared.

After he retired, she realized she had married a child. He didn't know anyone; he couldn't even get a job as an elementary school coach. All he managed to get with his prestigious university diploma after half a year of unemployment was a gig at a security company. And as soon as he started there, he took up smoking and drinking. She did feel a touch of sympathy. How depressed must he have felt when he was booted from the sport that had been his entire world? But he had brought this failure on himself. He had to lead a respectable life even if he came to it late; a man in charge of a family's livelihood couldn't drive drunk all the time or return home comatose or pound on the front door. She couldn't keep getting calls from the police, asking her to come take her husband home.

The biggest mistake of Eunju's life was marrying Hyonsu. Once she admitted this fact to herself, she could live with the various ways her husband disappointed her. She was a warrior with an iron will. She was in charge of her own life. She never forgot her childhood dreams, and she would make them happen with or without his help.

But now, when Eunju was *this* close to realizing her dreams, this drunk nutjob was pissing all over everything. He had hit her and continued to drink, and now he had the gall to tell *her* to get out. Eunju looked down at the divorce papers still in her hand. They weren't her ace in the hole; they were useless. If he didn't care whether she stuck around, what could she do to get him to shape up?

The doorbell rang, wrenching her from her thoughts. She realized the rice was burning and the soup was about to boil over. At the same time, her cell started ringing on the dining table. She turned off the stove and answered the phone. She heard Yongju say, "It's me."

"Hi," she said, heading to the front door. "Hold on a second." She opened the door.

Two detectives were standing there.

"Hello," the younger man said, flashing his badge.

She took the cell phone off her ear.

"We need to ask you a few questions."

~

Sunghwan and his boss were headed to work that Saturday morning when they stopped short on the stairs in front of the house. A line of cars was coming up the wet street, led by Yongje's white BMW with black mourning insignia. Next was a Cadillac hearse, then a large van, television trucks, and passenger cars.

"You have a lighter?" Hyonsu asked, cigarette in his mouth.

Sunghwan took his out and flicked it on. The flame danced with the breeze. Hyonsu blocked it with his bandage-wrapped hand and took a hard drag. He looked dejected; the shadows under his eyes were dark.

"Did it rain last night?" Hyonsu asked.

"It was pouring," Sunghwan said, an eyebrow cocked. "You didn't hear it?"

"I drank too much, so . . ." Hyonsu headed down the steps. "Let's go."

Sunghwan followed him. The streetlights were on and a damp wind rustled along the cypress tree hedge. Hyonsu walked with his eyes on the ground. Sunghwan sped up to match his gait. What was up with him today? How did he hurt his hand again? Two days ago, it had just been his middle finger that was taped up. Yesterday it was three fingers; today, it was his entire hand. Was he smashing soju bottles at the observation deck every night?

Hyonsu had come home drunk the night before. Again. Eunju left him to sleep on the living room floor, repeating the routine they'd had since they'd moved in. Around three in the morning, as it began to rain, Sunghwan heard sounds from the living room, then the front door open and close. He opened his bedroom door and looked out. Hyonsu was gone; only the blanket was on the ground by the sofa, like the shell of a large animal. Where did he go, in the middle of the night, in the pouring rain? He wondered for a moment if he should go after him but was drawn back to his laptop. He was finally beginning the project that had been on his mind since he came to this place. A document titled "Seryong Lake" was open on the screen.

> The girl was waiting at the bus stop in front of the school, kicking at the curb with the tips of her sneakers. She was looking down. Only her pale, round forehead was visible as her long hair fluttered in the wind.

He looked up when he heard the front door open. Four in the morning. He heard a thud and peeked out. Hyonsu was lying below the sofa again. Sunghwan decided to go check on him. Hyonsu was drenched, his feet bare and his ankles muddy. His heels were bloody. "Boss," Sunghwan whispered. Hyonsu didn't answer. Sunghwan shook him by the shoulders, but Hyonsu didn't open his eyes. He looked peaceful, as if he were enjoying a nice dream. What was going on?

Sunghwan had wanted to walk with Hyonsu this morning so he could ask where he'd gone last night. But now he was perplexed; it seemed that Hyonsu didn't even know it had rained.

"That girl . . . is she being buried?" Hyonsu asked suddenly as they neared the gate leading to the lakeshore road.

"I heard she's being cremated today," Sunghwan reported. "And they're going to do one of those rituals to bring her soul out of the lake." He was referring to the traditional ceremony to release the drowned soul from the Dragon King's grasp and send it off to the afterlife.

Hyonsu took out a second cigarette and put it in his mouth. "Have you seen a ceremony like that before?"

Sunghwan took his lighter out again. "When I was a kid."

"When you were a kid? They don't usually let kids watch stuff like that, do they? Aren't they afraid they'll get possessed by a ghost?"

"My father was a diver who pulled bodies out of the Han River. Whenever he got a job, I would go with my older brothers to help. All three of us started diving when we were eleven. So I've seen a few of these rituals. Have you?"

"Once, when I was young. Not the full thing."

"It'll be quite a show today," Sunghwan said. "If Oh Yongje planned it, it's guaranteed to be."

Hyonsu threw the cigarette butt in a trash can about twenty meters away from the security office entrance. "See you later."

Sunghwan touched Seryong's hairpin in his pocket as he watched Hyonsu head down toward the conservancy. He had planned to throw it back in the lake, but he hadn't had a chance to do it. Today was the same. He took his hand out of his pocket and unlocked the door to the security office.

By ten a.m., the villagers had gathered on the banks of the lake; Sunghwan could see them on the screen of the CCTV. The ritual was starting. A shaman with a white cloth around his head walked onto the dock, shaking a bamboo stick. A piece of long cloth wound on the end of the bamboo stick fluttered in the wind. Yongje followed, holding a straw doll with something long dangling from its head. Musicians playing traditional instruments brought up the rear. The procession was large, more like a cultural festival than a shamanistic ritual.

Sunghwan searched for the latest coverage of her death.

> Seryong Lake—11-year-old girl found dead in the lake, suspected hit-and-run . . .

> Seryong Lake—The investigation of the death of a local 11-year-old girl is proving difficult. Five days after the incident, no suspects have been identified . . .

On the screen, the shaman walked to the end of the dock and began stabbing the water with his bamboo stick.

Sunghwan downloaded his video file titled "Atlantis" from the cloud. He planned to edit it down a bit. Now that there were more eyes on the lake, he couldn't make another dive. The images he'd captured the night of the incident were all he had to work with.

Hyonsu showed up right as he opened it. Sunghwan quickly hid the file below the news items.

"Hey, what's that song you were listening to with Sowon?" Hyonsu asked. "The one you made me listen to? Night something or other . . . the one that sounds like howling wolves?"

Sunghwan swallowed a smile and took his MP3 player out of his pocket. His boss was talking about a goth metal song. "You sure you want to listen to it?"

"It's got to be better than the noise from down there. Why can't they do it somewhere else? Doing it right in front of the camera . . ."

"At least it's not at Hansoldung, like they'd wanted initially. If the conservancy had made an exception for this ritual, the lake would be filled with boats."

Hyonsu looked at the island in the middle of the lake on the screen. "Why there?"

"It's like a shrine for people here. They bow toward it, wishing for good water levels."

"What does Hansoldung have to do with the water level?"

Sunghwan explained. The water level had to be maintained at all times for the proper operation of the dam, and Hansoldung was a water level indicator that the villagers could always see. During a drought it became a hill; at the maximum water level, it looked like a small burial mound; and during a planned flood it sank completely underwater.

"But why would they do a ritual in the middle of the lake?"

"The old village was submerged a long time ago, and Hansoldung was the highest point in the old village. I guess the girl was born there and her body was found there. I'm sure Oh Yongje gave the director of operations a hard time when he didn't agree . . ."

Hyonsu blanched and charged out of the office. Sunghwan got up and ran to the door after him, but he was already too far away. When he returned to the office and checked the screens, he realized why Hyonsu had reacted that way. Sowon was facing the shaman, holding a black plastic bag. Other people had encircled them, giving them space, as though they were about to fight. That must have been what had so alarmed Hyonsu.

What was Sowon doing down there to begin with? Sunghwan wondered. Then he remembered something.

Last Thursday, Sunghwan had returned home after eight. He had been reading everything he could about Seryong online at work and lost track of time. The house was strangely quiet; the table was only half-set and the master bedroom door was closed. Sowon had locked their bedroom door, too. Sunghwan knocked.

"Mom?"

"No, it's your roommate."

Sowon opened the door, and Sunghwan realized why the boy had locked it. Ernie was eating on the windowsill. Sowon opened the closet and showed him a gigantic bag of cat food. "Is it okay if I leave it there? I have to hide it from my mom— she doesn't like cats."

Sunghwan nodded. Ernie was chomping happily. Sunghwan started salivating, suddenly hungry. Right then, Eunju walked in without knocking. Sunghwan and Sowon instantly stood side by side, shielding the window from view.

"You should knock, Mom," Sowon said.

"Who knocks on their son's door?" Eunju craned her neck to look behind them.

"But it's Mr. Ahn's room, too."

Eunju ignored that comment and pushed Sowon aside. "What's this?"

Sunghwan glanced at the windowsill. Only the dish was there; Ernie was already gone.

"Cat food?" Sowon said sheepishly.

Eunju crossed her arms and stood next to Sowon. "Mr. Ahn, you have a cat?" she asked belligerently.

"It's the next-door-neighbor girl's cat," Sowon offered.

"The *dead* girl's cat?" Her eyes were still glued to Sunghwan.

"It's a stray, but they were friends. And now he's friends with me, too," Sowon explained.

"So, you're letting a dirty animal inside the house? If you give them food and play with them, you might get sick. Do you know how filthy they are?"

"Dad said it was okay."

"Oh, did he? Did he also buy the food?"

"Yes," Sowon said, his voice small.

Sunghwan could see Eunju stiffen with anger. "How about we feed him outside the window?" Sunghwan attempted.

"No, if you begin feeding them they'll come back with their friends. They'll rip up all the trash bags outside. And I'll have to clean it up. I'll have even less time to deal with things like that from now on. I was going to tell you later, but I'll be working as a security guard for the property starting Sunday." With that, she told them dinner was ready, turned, and left.

"Ernie's going to be hungry. He didn't get to finish," Sowon said, near tears. "He might not come back here again."

Sunghwan patted the boy on the shoulder. "Well, you can take some food to him."

"Will you tell me how to get there?" Sowon's moist eyes sparkled with excitement.

Sunghwan agreed under two conditions: that Sowon could only go during the day, and that he couldn't stay too long.

Back in the security office, Sunghwan realized: it was Saturday—no school. Sowon must have been on his way to Ernie with the cat food—that would explain the black bag— and been drawn to the dock out of curiosity about the ritual.

Sunghwan quickly locked up. Something was wrong; he needed to get down there.

But it was too late. By the time he got to the dock, the shaman was struggling to rip Hyonsu's hand off his neck, Hyonsu was looking murderous, and people were trying to separate the two. Sowon was calling for his dad to stop, Ernie's food rolling beneath their feet. Sunghwan pulled Sowon from the crowd. The boy shook him off and looked back at his dad.

"Choi Sowon," Sunghwan said firmly, shaking his shoulders to force him to look at him. "If you promise to stay here, I'll go get your dad."

Sowon nodded, and Sunghwan ran back, closer to where the two men were still struggling. He yanked out his phone and called Park at the dam security office. A moment later, the emergency siren began wailing from the speaker on the intake tower, and Hyonsu let go and looked up. The shaman sprawled on the ground, coughing, and everyone stepped back. Hyonsu was staring, dazed, at his bandaged left hand.

Sunghwan dragged Hyonsu off the dock. Thankfully, he regained focus when his son came into sight. He shook Sunghwan off. "Are you okay?" he asked Sowon.

The boy nodded.

Hyonsu looked up at Seryong Peak, still flustered. "Let's go." Father and son held hands as they left the dock.

Something made Sunghwan look over his shoulder. He saw Yongje watching Hyonsu with an odd smile on his face. Could Yongje have created this raucous performance for a sinister purpose? What that could be, he couldn't begin to guess, but the oddly knowing smile suggested he was up to something.

At the maintenance bridge, Hyonsu stopped. "Can you take him home for me? I don't think it'll be good for his mom to see me right now. I'll take your post at the floodgates until you're back."

Sunghwan handed his boss the office key. Hyonsu's legs swayed as he turned around. Surprised, Sunghwan reached out to steady him, but Hyonsu forged across the bridge. They heard the faraway sound of a gong announcing the continuation of the ritual. "Let's go," Sunghwan said, taking Sowon's hand.

Sowon stopped suddenly near the rear entrance. Before Sunghwan could ask him what was wrong, the boy threw up, vomit splashing his own jeans, sneakers, and part of Sunghwan's shoes. Sowon looked up limply, on the verge of tears.

"It's okay. We can wash up at home." Sunghwan took out his handkerchief and wiped Sowon's chin. His little face was so pale that it looked almost blue. His skin felt damp and cold to the touch. "Want me to carry you?"

"I can walk," Sowon said, but in the end Sunghwan had to carry him on his back.

A large tent was set up in front of the storage shed by the Annex. A table laden with food was ready for the rites. A few women from the village scurried between 101 and the tent, holding trays of food.

Sunghwan propped Sowon by the front door of their unit. "Do you know where your mom is?"

Sowon shook his head.

"Want to go to the clinic?"

Sowon shook his head again.

"Okay."

He took Sowon to the bathroom and washed him, helped him change, then got him into bed to rest.

"Mr. Ahn," Sowon said, then paused. "She probably got a nice farewell, right?"

"You mean Seryong?"

"Yes."

"Is that why you went to the ritual? Because you were curious?"

"No, I was going to bring her a card on my way to feed Ernie . . ." Sowon hesitated. "She died on her birthday. I felt bad for her. The kids at school didn't like her and they said she was always alone. Nobody made her a birthday card. Nobody even knew it was her birthday."

"So you wrote her a card?"

Sowon nodded.

"What did it say?"

"I didn't know what to say, so I just wrote 'Happy birthday, I hope you'll be happy in heaven and thanks for sending Ernie to me.' I also wrote that she shouldn't come see me anymore."

Sunghwan's heart froze. "She came to see you?"

"In my dreams. When I fall asleep I hear her voice. I lift up the curtains and I see her hiding in the shadow of a tall tree, and her hair's down her back . . ." Sowon lowered his eyes and his voice grew small. "She doesn't have clothes or shoes on, she's just in her underwear. She tells me to come play Red Light, Green Light."

"Do you?"

"No, I just watch from behind the curtain. I want to tell her to stop coming, that she has to go to heaven now. But I can't."

"Because you're scared?"

"I'm not sure. When she comes I just can't talk."

"Who were you going to give the card to?"

"Her dad. But then the shaman took it from me and read it and started yelling at me. He was holding me by my neck."

"What did he say?"

"That she can't go by herself, that she has to go with me. He shook his bells and glared, putting his face real close to me. I glared right back at him—I wasn't scared. But then Dad . . ." Sowon trailed off.

A while later, he spoke again. "Maybe it would have been better if we never moved here. This is a really weird place."

"Did you think that before you moved here?"

"I never saw it before. Mom was curious about it. Dad was supposed to come check it out, but he didn't."

"Why didn't he?"

"I don't know. They fought because of it. Mom wanted to know whether you would give up your room and how big the place was. Dad didn't do what she asked; instead, he got drunk and didn't come back until the next night."

Sunghwan looked at his watch. It was almost two. He had to get back to work. But how could he leave this sick kid alone?

As though reading his mind, Sowon said, "Mom's actually next door. That girl's dad asked her to help with the funeral, but Dad told her not to work there."

Relieved, Sunghwan stayed until the boy closed his eyes and drifted off to sleep. Then he slipped out of the room and out the front door.

The path in front of the Annex was busy; by now, the ritual had moved to Yongje's house. Dry straw was burning on the ground, and the housekeeper was combing the straw doll's hair. Sunghwan watched as the shaman lit the doll on fire with a handful of burning straw. The doll's legs began to burn, a plume of gray smoke rising into the air.

The villagers surrounded the shaman, watching and murmuring. They considered Seryong's death an ominous sign; the body was found in the underwater village, and the emergency divers who had found her were outsiders. They had all come to the ritual to pray that no bad luck would befall the village.

Sunghwan walked through the throng of people. Next to the flower garden, an old man in a black suit with neat, slicked-back hair was standing like a shadow, leaning on a walking stick. He resembled Seryong; he must be her grandfather on her mother's side. Sunghwan had heard that Yongje's father passed away long ago.

Eventually, he found Eunju near the back of the storage area, sitting in front of a brazier with a cauldron hanging on it. She was holding a poker and tending to the fire.

"Hi," he said.

She turned to look at him.

"You might want to check in at home."

"Why?"

Sunghwan searched for something to say. "Sowon's sleeping there by himself."

"It's fine, don't worry," she said dismissively and turned back to the brazier.

THE SECURITY OFFICE was empty when he got there. The key was on the desk, the news sites were still open on the computer, and the chair was pushed a few feet back from the desk. Sunghwan went to close his browser windows when he heard a knock.

Two men poked their heads in. "Mr. Ahn Sunghwan?" a middle-aged man asked.

"Yes?"

The younger man showed his badge. They were detectives. The older man glanced at the news articles open on the computer.

"Doing some research?"

"What's this about?" asked Sunghwan.

The older detective sat down. "Where were you on the night the girl was killed?"

"I was home watching baseball, like I told some detectives a few days ago."

"Not diving in Seryong Lake?"

This was the interrogation he had been dreading.

"You know what I think?" the older detective asked. "I think you were at the lake when the incident occurred. You entered the water from the dock, surfaced near the intake tower, then swam back to your entry point. I'm not guessing—we have it on CCTV."

It was a precise description of his dive that night. Sunghwan began to feel nervous, even though he knew better than anyone else that nothing could be seen on the CCTV footage at night. The younger detective perched on the corner of his desk, studying him.

"Can you show me the footage from the camera that supposedly caught me?"

The older detective smiled. "You're the only employee here who knows how to dive."

"Employees aren't the only people who live around here."

"I hear that the gear alone weighs more than eighty pounds. You couldn't throw an air tank over the fence, and I can't imagine you climbed over the fence with it on your back. The gap under the steel doors is too narrow. So there's only one way in. Through the doors. And to open them you would need a key. Who would have access besides an employee of the dam?"

Sunghwan didn't answer.

"Why don't you take some time to think? You might remember something."

"I don't need time. I haven't been diving since I got here."

The older detective stared at him. Sunghwan felt goose bumps forming on his neck. He tried to keep his mind blank so that the detectives couldn't analyze his facial expressions.

"Well, there's nothing I can do if you won't cooperate. I'm just asking you to tell me what you saw." The detectives finally stood up. "But the fact that you're lying to us makes you a suspect."

Sunghwan managed to swallow the breath that caught in his throat and tried his best to maintain an opaque expression. This was all just a bluff, he told himself. All the detectives could have seen on the CCTV was a blip of light. They probably brought in a diving expert and asked for help in mapping out a possible arc of movement. The only real evidence that he had been there was the fishing line—the bait shop in town would have a record of his purchase of the line, floats, and sinkers just before the incident. But they never mentioned that, which meant that no one had found the sunken portion of the line in the lake and—more troubling— that Yongje was keeping that information to himself for some unknown reason.

Sunghwan closed his browser windows and stopped cold. The "Atlantis" file had appeared on the screen. It had been open on his desktop this entire time, just behind the news sites. "My god," he blurted out. He had insisted to the detectives that he had never gone into the lake while he had the evidence open on the computer, barely concealed. Had Hyonsu seen this video?

~

The rest area was quiet. Not many cars were coming or going, and the local drunks who usually sat on the observation deck weren't there. Hyonsu was alone. Every time he came up here, he vowed it would be the last time. But the next day he would find himself sitting there again, booze in hand. He had become a full-blown alcoholic, he thought. He couldn't do anything about it. Getting drunk was the only way he could find relief.

He wasn't in his right mind when he went to the security office by the floodgates to take over for Sunghwan. He'd lost control of himself again—anyone who saw him would know he was deeply disturbed. Horrified and ashamed, he asked Sunghwan to take care of Sowon; he couldn't look his son in the eye. He was still in shock from his realization: the night of the incident, there had been a witness.

He couldn't remember how he'd come across the video, what he had been looking for. He watched, transfixed, as the camera tracked through the underwater village. The last scene was a close-up of the name Oh Yongje, then the screen went dark. He recalled what Sunghwan had told him: *I guess the girl was born there and her body was found there.* He went to the last frame and spotted the time it was filmed, imprinted at the very bottom: 10:45 p.m., August 27, 2004.

He watched it again from the beginning. The camera coasted down a long road before arriving in front of the entrance to the village. His hand, holding the mouse, began to tremble. He remembered what Sunghwan had told him: *My father was a diver who pulled bodies out of the Han River. Whenever he got a job, I would go with my older brothers to help. All three of us started diving when we were eleven.* Sunghwan had filmed this. It struck him immediately what the time and location signified—Sunghwan was underwater at the time Seryong's body entered the lake.

Hyonsu rushed to his post at the conservancy before Sunghwan returned. He stayed there all afternoon, thinking. His brain was working for the first time since he got to Seryong Lake. One thing was clear: if the younger man had seen something, he hadn't reported it to the police. Otherwise, Hyonsu would be in jail right now.

What kind of person was this Ahn Sunghwan? Hyonsu went over their interactions, but he couldn't recall anything out of the ordinary. Then again, his week had been chaotic. He hadn't had the energy to notice anything about him. There was no reason for Sunghwan to keep quiet if he'd seen everything. But if Sunghwan hadn't seen *who'd* done it, he would have wanted to conceal the fact that he was diving illegally at the time of the murder. He would have wanted to avoid being named a suspect.

Hyonsu had opened and closed his cell phone countless times since Saturday. He felt anxious each time he bumped into Sunghwan. He knew he should try to find out what the younger man knew, but each time he hesitated. It was so hard to casually say, "Hey, want to grab a beer?"

Returning home from the rest area after midnight, Hyonsu thought, Just let it be. Even if he did see me, what proof could he have?

He collapsed on the bed. It was Eunju's first night at work, and he felt at ease without her there. Good for you, Eunju, he thought bitterly. Go make your money and leave me in peace.

$\sim$

S uddenly he was walking barefoot through fields of sorghum, holding his father's shoes in one hand and a flashlight in the other. There was a full moon; the fields had turned red and dogs barked in the distance. He stopped at the well, drew in a deep breath, and threw a shoe in the well. The shoe slapped the water, waking the sleeping well. A hoarse male voice called out, *Hyonsu. Hyonsuuuu*. He threw in the other shoe. Take that. The well swallowed it; this time, he heard a girl's voice. *Daddy.*

Hyonsu opened his eyes. He'd fallen asleep in the bedroom, but now he was lying on the floor by the sofa in the living room. He sat up. His left arm was limp. Again. He turned on the light. He wasn't completely soaked, the way he'd been the previous night, but the hems of his pants and his feet were dirty. A flashlight was on the floor and his muddy footprints were smeared everywhere. Hyonsu went outside. It was already morning, and the rising sun revealed more tracks on the stairs. Below, the footprints emerged from the flowerbed out front, one pair of prints going out and one coming back. He followed the prints that led away from the house. He clambered over the low wooden fence separating 102 from 101, passed through the backyard of 101, and went toward the lakeshore road. This was the same route he'd taken after fighting with Eunju last Thursday night. The footprints stopped on the maintenance bridge leading to the intake tower, just where he'd thrown Seryong's body into the lake.

Hyonsu crumpled to the ground under the railing. A terrifying conviction was dawning on him: the recurring dream he'd had every night for the last three nights was not a dream; it was reality within a dream and a dream within reality. The memory of the well that had haunted him as a boy, the dreams he thought he'd left behind when he left home, had returned to destroy him. He wanted to resist it, but he knew it was true. All he could do on this Monday morning was to stand up and go home, before the guard on night duty appeared and asked him what he was doing.

When Hyonsu stepped back into the house, Sunghwan was on his way to the bathroom, a towel slung over his shoulder. The younger man gaped at his boss. Hyonsu didn't have the energy to try to explain himself, not that he could have if he'd tried. He was just glad Sowon wasn't the one who had caught him coming back into the house. "You mind if I wash up first?"

Sunghwan moved aside, still looking shocked. "Go ahead."

Once in the bathroom, Hyonsu began working on his arm. He took out the box cutter he'd hidden in a corner of the bathroom, grabbed his left arm with his right hand and placed it on the washing machine, and pricked his left hand with the blade. But the sensation didn't return even after he made three incisions at the base of his thumb. He couldn't go to work with his arm like this. He brought the blade to his wrist, to where the thick blue vein ran through. He had to be careful not to nick the artery or his tendon. It had to be shallow, narrow, quick. But when the blade sliced his wrist, his vein gushed blood like a geyser. A hot, sharp sensation shot down his left arm, and Hyonsu felt suddenly elated.

"Boss!" Sunghwan's voice rang out, as though from far away. Hyonsu's ecstasy evaporated as Sunghwan barged in. "My god. What are you doing?" Sunghwan sounded panicked as he wrapped a towel around Hyonsu's wrist, then shoved him against the wall and raised his hand above his chest.

Hyonsu let him do it, though he was annoyed. Why was he

making such a fuss? Had he never seen blood before? "I'm fine," he said. He could barely hear his own voice.

"It's really deep." Sunghwan applied a fresh towel to the wound and told Hyonsu to hold it in place. He applied a pressure bandage around Hyonsu's wrist. "We need to go to the clinic."

"It's just a little nick."

Sunghwan looked at Hyonsu with exasperation. "Is this why you've had a bandage around your hand all week?"

Hyonsu was frustrated; he didn't know how to explain his bad arm. He didn't want to appear hysterical or suicidal, but it would be a major problem if any of this was linked to the case.

"Listen, sometimes I can't move my left arm. It's a problem I've had since I played ball. The orthopedist says there's nothing wrong with my nerves, but sometimes I lose all sensation. If I let out some blood, it gets better. I was just making a small cut. I wasn't trying to kill myself." Hyonsu stopped, embarrassed.

"Well, we have to go to the clinic."

Sunghwan pushed him out of the bathroom. At the front door, he opened the shoe cabinet and looked around. "That's strange."

Hyonsu put his shoes on. "What is?"

"My sneakers aren't here. I thought I left them here last night."

Hyonsu winced. Eunju had said the same thing yesterday: "That's weird. Where are my shoes?" She'd given Hyonsu a look, as if he'd hidden them so that she couldn't go to work.

"Stay here," Hyonsu said quickly to Sunghwan. "Sowon's going to wake up soon. I can go by myself." He opened the front door, then paused. "Don't tell Eunju. She'll try to have me committed if she finds out."

Sunghwan stood there staring at him, an unreadable expression on his face. Hyonsu knew the younger man was frustrated. He understood; he was frustrated himself.

At the clinic, the doctor examined the wound. "How did this happen?"

Hyonsu was embarrassed; he knew the explanation was more psychological than medical. He looked down. "My left arm gets numb sometimes. It gets better when I let some blood out."

The doctor squinted at him suspiciously and lectured him while he stitched the wound and put Hyonsu's arm in a sling. "Keep this on for a while," he advised. "The more the hand is elevated, the faster the swelling will go down."

Hyonsu left the clinic with some painkillers. He paused out front to smoke. He was facing the road, but in his mind's eye he was watching a man walk toward the lakeshore road with other people's shoes tucked under his arm, tossing them in the lake from the bridge. It had been indoor slippers the first night, then Eunju's shoes, and last night it was Sunghwan's sneakers. Whose shoes would it be tonight? All he knew was that there was one pair of shoes that had to be protected from the man who emerged while he was asleep.

Last spring, Sowon had won a prize in a math contest at school. Hyonsu bought him Nike basketball shoes to congratulate him. But before the elated boy could try them on, Eunju snatched them away. "These are too small. I'll exchange them tomorrow."

"They're not," Hyonsu protested. "I bought a size bigger."

Eunju put the shoes back in the box. "Do you know how quickly his feet grow? For the price of one of these you could get five pairs."

Sowon looked disappointed.

"Just let him have them!" Hyonsu yelled.

"You really want to get him hundred-thousand-won shoes?" Eunju hissed. "Once hc gets used to expensive things he'll just ask for more."

Hyonsu yanked the shoes out of her hands, took a pen from his pocket, and wrote *Choi Sowon* on the insides of the tongues of the shoes.

He wouldn't be able to save them by writing his son's name in them this time. He would have to hide them, but where? Should he tell Sowon to hide them, so he couldn't even locate them with his subconscious mind? How would he explain that to his son? He rubbed his cigarette out with his foot, dizzy with despair.

RAPTURES OF THE DEEP

I put Mr. Ahn's "novel" down, flooded with memories. The day before the girl's funeral, I was in an agitated state. I remember counting down every minute of sixth period, bored to tears. I hovered by the bulletin board during breaks, stealing glances at her picture. I wished I could tell her, *Don't worry about your friend, I'll take good care of him.*

When I got home after school, my mom wasn't there. Instead I found a note stuck to the fridge: *I'm out. Don't forget to wash your hands and do your homework. Your snack is on the counter.* I wrote my own note in reply and stuck it on the fridge. *Finished my homework, going to visit Mr. Ahn.* I was certain Mr. Ahn would cover for me if she called to check up on me. I took my books out of my backpack and put in some cat food, mosquito repellent, a water bottle, and my snack. I slung it onto my back and climbed out the window.

I followed Mr. Ahn's directions to Ernie's hiding spot, the old barn. As I passed by the girl's window, I peeked in at her portrait. Her large black eyes greeted me coolly; maybe she was resentful that I ignored her when she called me from outside my curtains every night. I turned and left in a hurry, a creepy feeling spreading up my spine. It felt like someone was about to grab me by the back of my neck.

When I reached the barn, I threw the doors open and sunlight filtered in. Mr. Ahn had told me about the corner where the floor had sunken in. That was where Ernie's hideout was.

"Ernie," I whispered. "Ernie!" I didn't want to scare him away. I opened the bag of food and gently pushed it toward the sunken spot on the floor. I didn't have to wait long for Ernie to come out of the shadows. Like Mr. Ahn had said, he was more like a dog than a cat. He looked like a mountain lion, but he was as friendly as a mutt. After Ernie finished eating, he rubbed his face against my leg. I took that as an invitation to join him in his hideaway.

The box looked just how Mr. Ahn had described it, big and sturdy. Both of us could sit in there together. Mr. Ahn hadn't mentioned the pink blanket spread out on the bottom. A name was embroidered in black in the corner. My heart pounded as I read it. *Oh Seryong*. I leaned against the wall. It was hot and stuffy in there, but that didn't bother me. I felt safe. As Ernie snuggled up against me, I dozed off.

When I woke, I nearly yelped. A man was sitting on the floor above Ernie's hideaway, staring down at me. It was Oh Yongje, her father. What was he doing there? I didn't see Ernie anywhere; he'd been asleep on my lap. He must have instinctively gone into hiding as soon as the man appeared.

"What are you doing here?" he asked.

I clambered up to where he was. "What's the problem? This isn't on your property."

"My daughter's cat lives here." He looked at my bag and smiled. "Did he invite you?"

He was being strangely nice. But I was still wary. "What are *you* doing here?"

"I've been invited a few times myself." He stood up. "I'd rather you didn't use my daughter's blanket." He no longer had a smile on his face.

I shoved my hands in my pockets and looked up at him, saying nothing.

"Did you know that tomorrow is Seryong's funeral?" he asked suddenly.

I did, but I didn't say so.

"We'll be at the dock at ten, taking her soul out of the lake."

I stayed quiet.

"I hope you'll come. I want to thank you for taking care of my daughter's cat. And you won't be able to look into her room anymore after the funeral, since I'll be closing it up."

I flushed. I remembered the chill I'd felt every time I stood outside her window. He must have been watching me from somewhere. I took my backpack and walked out of the barn, trying my best not to run.

He stopped me by the door. "Will you come?"

I looked back at him and gave a quick nod.

"Let's keep this between us."

With everything that happened afterward, I had completely forgotten about this encounter. Only now, after reading Mr. Ahn's novel, did I realize that Oh Yongje had planned everything. He had arranged for the shaman to purposely provoke my dad. But why?

I had other questions. I sensed that the answers lay in Mr. Ahn's manuscript, but I didn't want to read any more. Why did Mr. Ahn write this? I wondered. Did he want to publish it? Or was it for me, so I would know the truth? I had no way of knowing what was factual and what he'd guessed or imagined. I supposed he could have pieced together my parents' sections through interviews. But Oh Yongje . . . who could have spoken to *his* inner thoughts? Both he and his daughter were dead and, according to the manuscript, his wife hadn't been at Seryong Lake at the time. At the end of the day, if Dad had really done what he was accused of, none of these details really mattered.

I opened the scrapbook, which had newspaper articles organized chronologically. I'd never seen them before, but they didn't tell me anything beyond what I had read in the *Sunday Magazine*. The only new information was about my mother.

My mother was discovered at the Seryong River estuary bank about forty miles away from the lake, four days after the village was flooded. The cause of death was head trauma. The article said that my dad killed her and threw her into the water, just as he'd done with Seryong. The prosecutors suspected that Oh Yongje had been killed with the same weapon as my mother—a wooden club with the blood of Oh Yongje, Mr. Ahn, and my dad was found at the scene. My dad was found unconscious and taken to the hospital. He had compound fractures on his right wrist, damage to the ligaments, a nose fracture, a depressed fracture to the lower jawbone, missing teeth, and septicemia from a foot injury that was a few days old. At the time the article was written, the police were still searching for Oh Yongje's body to confirm their suspicions.

Next were articles that detailed events I already knew: my dad's condition as he lay in the ICU for the tenth day, how he'd nearly died twice before managing to regain consciousness, how he was released from the hospital and transported to jail, and the trial. I shuffled through the pages again. There was nothing about Oh Yongje's body being recovered. If Mr. Ahn had clipped all of the articles about the incident, that meant it had never been found.

I closed the scrapbook and rummaged through the bundle of letters. They were all delivered to a post office box in Haenam, and had all been sent from Amiens, France. The sender was Mun Hayong—a name I'd seen in the manuscript. Oh Yongje's wife? She hadn't crossed paths with Mr. Ahn at all. Why would she have sent him letters—nine of them in total? I opened the first one.

I've been unable to sleep for the last few days. At night I go into the yard quietly so that my friend Ina doesn't wake up. I stand under the apple tree. Ina seems to be worried about me. She has figured out what I'm thinking about. Yesterday, she said to me, "Hayong, do what you need to do. Whatever it is, you should do it for yourself, not for anyone else."

I told her I would.

I've never spoken about my daughter since it happened. I was afraid I would sink into permanent despair. But I will tell you everything I know, even though I wasn't with her when it happened. I didn't learn that she died until much later. I was in Casablanca to extend my visa, and only found out when I returned to France. I was wrapped up in my own pain and worries. When I heard, it was after the funeral. I couldn't eat. I couldn't sleep. She must have been so lonely. So terrified. In so much pain. Outliving her felt like a betrayal, a crime. My guilt turned into rage at the person who killed her, even though I knew it wasn't healthy for me to hold on to that.

Your first letter enraged me again. How could you, I thought—a writer, doing research for your supposed novel—do justice to the story of my daughter and my husband? My father, who told me he'd given you my address, said you'd kept something of my daughter's and given it to him a long time ago. I was still angry. No matter how kind you'd been to her, you didn't have the right to demand something like this from me.

But when you sent the package, I was at a loss. The manuscript was thick and contained cruel truths I hadn't known. Why were you writing this, why were you tormenting me? For money? Or to make a name for yourself? I burned the manuscript, but what you'd written stayed with me. Still, I hated you, and vowed to burn any other letter you sent without reading it.

You're clever, though. You pasted that small picture on the envelope of your third letter. You knew I couldn't rip that picture to shreds or burn it. I knew that place in the picture. That place is what I see whenever I think about my daughter. The foggy path, the streetlamp, the trees, and a boy and a man walking toward the main road. They looked like father and son, and it made me open the letter.

You said: This child is his son. He's innocent, and
he's living at the margins of society. I want to tell him
the truth and finally set him free.

I didn't care. That kid should have to live in agony.
Just like me. But last night, as I stood under this apple
tree, I stared at the darkness until dawn broke. I saw a
boy in front of me, a boy the same age as my daughter,
a child I'd never met or even knew existed. Innocent,
just like my daughter. I recognized my husband's
cruelty in the enclosed magazine article and the boy's
abysmal school records. I understood the criticism and
the rage and the curses he would have had to face—
including mine.

So I will tell you what you want to know. I was with
my husband for twelve years. I know him as well as
anyone.

A final request: after you're done with the book,
please send me a copy. I want to know the truth, too.

Sincerely,
Mun Hayong

I slid the letter back into the envelope. It was dated January 20 of this year. I didn't look at any of the other letters; I was afraid. I was afraid of this woman's sorrow, of her generosity and compassion. I couldn't understand it. I didn't want or expect anything from her. I stared out the window, which was blurred with salt and dust. I was suddenly famished.

I put a pot of water on the stove. I opened the cupboard

and stared at the contents for a long time. My mind swam with questions. Was Oh Yongje *alive*? Mun Hayong had referred to him in the present tense. Did she have any proof? Did Mr. Ahn think Oh Yongje was the one distributing the *Sunday Magazine* article to my neighbors and classmates, too? That did seem to be the case, judging from Mun Hayong's letter. How long had he known? And if it were true, why hadn't he harmed me by now? He would have had countless opportunities.

I turned off the stove and sat back down at my desk, forgetting my hunger. I selected the USB window on the laptop. There were two folders on the drive: "Seryong Lake" and "Reference."

I clicked on the "Reference" folder. The first item was a video file titled "Atlantis," and the rest were MP3 audio files. I opened the MP3 file marked "1." Momentary static gave way to a deep male voice.

"I'm happiest when I imagine how Sowon would have grown up. I put the pictures from his birthdays, the ones you sent me, on the wall. It's amazing. How he was a boy at age fourteen and how he magically became a young man at fifteen. I'm sure I wouldn't notice that if I saw him all the time. I remember so clearly what he looked like on the first day of elementary school. Of the hundreds of kids in the auditorium, no other kid looked as poised as he did. When he became a man, I was going to tell him how proud I was that day . . ."

I quickly closed the file, my hands shaking. This was the voice I had tried so hard to forget. My father. The way he said my name was exactly how I remembered. I turned off the laptop. I never wanted to hear his voice again. I didn't want to read any more of the novel. He wasn't the confident giant I remembered; he was weak, a coward. I didn't want to know that person. It all made me so sad that I couldn't breathe. But I couldn't shut out his voice saying my name. "Sowon."

A gust rattled the window, and I heard him in the wind. "Sowon."

I had thought nothing in the world could knock me off balance again, that nothing could shock or move me. But that wasn't true. For the first time in seven years, I felt my father beside me.

~

I didn't want to read any more, or relive this terrible time in my life, but I was desperate to get my father's voice out of my head. I took out Hayong's letters. Seven of them had been sent over the course of two months; Mr. Ahn asked all sorts of questions, and Mun Hayong always responded in detail. She wrote about dating, marriage, his desires, his past, how he looked at his wife and daughter, his daily life, and even his sexual proclivities. Hayong had run away twice with her daughter before filing for divorce, and each time she was caught before two days had gone by. Oh Yongje had sat at his desk, put himself in her mind-set, and hunted her down. His pursuit of her was so relentless and precise that it made me feel queasy.

By the time I put the letters down, my hunger had returned with a vengeance. I was so famished that I felt I could eat a herd of cattle, but all there was in the fridge were two eggs, half a can of tuna, and a bottle of water. I should go to the store, I thought.

Wheeling my bike out, I bumped into the mail carrier. "Does a Choi Sowon live here?"

My heart sank. What now? "That's me."

He held out a letter from Seoul Prison. I stood there dumbly as snow began to fall. The sky was ashen, but my skin was burning. I brought my bike back into the backyard. I didn't want to read the letter. I went into my room and sat at my desk. It took me thirty minutes to open it.

Choi Hyonsu's sentence was carried out at 9:00 a.m. today, December 27.

The words blurred in my hands; there was more, but I couldn't read it. Spit pooled under my tongue. I stumbled to the kitchen and drank some water, but it felt as if I were drinking molten metal. I couldn't sit, but I couldn't stand, either. My legs shook. I leaned against the wall and tried to read the rest.

Family . . . pick up . . . after 9:00 a.m. on the 28th . . .

I dropped the letter, picked it up again, and dropped it again. Everything was fuzzy as I tried to wrap my head around what I'd just read. I could hear my father again.

I'm sure I wouldn't notice that if I saw him all the time . . . When he became a man, I was going to tell him how proud I was that day . . .

How did he die? Was he frightened? Did he finally understand the terror all those people must have felt as they died? Was he regretful? Sad? Calm? What were his last words? Did he beg to live? Did he call for me? *Sowon.*

I found my wet suit and put it on. I took my diving gear, ignoring Mr. Ahn's warning that I should never go in the water without a buddy. I had to extinguish the fire that was burning inside me.

The youth club president wasn't home. I opened his bedroom door and felt along the top of the TV for the keys to his boat. I caught the bundle and took it without hesitation.

Snow was falling over the ocean. The wind was calm, and the waves were gentle. I went down below the lighthouse and started the boat. Once I was far enough away from the rocks by the shore, I gunned the engine as fast as it would go. I couldn't see very well because of the snow, but I didn't care. I ignored the long band of current near the rock island. I anchored the boat near the island's western point and got into the water. The undertow tore at me, twenty times stronger than the flow I was used to. It smothered me and thrust me down. My breathing was ragged and I was light-headed. A column of water was pressing me down to the ocean floor, much like a waterfall. I didn't try anything—I didn't inflate the BC or look for a spot on the wall I could escape to or check the depth gauge. Death had me in its grip, and I didn't have the will to resist. I let myself go completely, engulfed in the white foam of water. I didn't even feel like sucking air through the mouthpiece. Soon, I didn't even feel the water or its pressure on my body; I was unburdened. I stopped descending. The white column of water roiled above my forehead and then dissipated.

A school of gray fish floated above. I saw enormous cedars. Long vines like electric wires. I was in the arboretum. I stepped onto the main road, swimming slowly along; I saw dark, rotten tree stumps and overgrowth where the concrete road had buckled. There was a flyer on the bulletin board.

MISSING CHILD

NAME: OH SERYONG

I was arrested by her picture just as I was the day I first saw it seven years ago, but I was now profoundly exhausted. My eyes drooped, and my body grew limp. I imagined lying down on the floor of her room and holding her hand. Moonlight poured in through the window. It was warm, her hand was soft, and I felt at peace.

"Sowon," a voice called. I opened my eyes; everything looked distant. It was my father's voice exploding ferociously: "Sowon!" I came to with a flinch, as though I had been slapped across the face. I looked around. She was gone. I couldn't breathe. I was suddenly freezing. I wanted to get up, but I was stuck. I had to think, I knew that much. Where was I?

"Stop. Think. Act." Mr. Ahn's rules for diving.

I stopped flailing and regulated my breathing. I was surrounded by black rock. I looked up, way up, and saw a long, uneven patch of sky, the edges of which were defined by shadows of coral. I checked the dive computer on my wrist. Total diving time: twenty-four minutes. Current depth: 160 feet. Nitrogen level rising very quickly. The water column had shoved me deep into a crevasse, and I was experiencing nitrogen narcosis, which could make me do something stupid and lead me to my death. I was feeling what divers called "raptures of the deep" or "the martini effect"—it was as though I were downing martinis on an empty stomach thirty feet below the surface of the water. At this point, I'd basically had five martinis. That explained my rapturous dream.

I checked how much air I had left—about three minutes. Shit. I hadn't refilled my tank with air after my last dive, and I hadn't brought any spares. This wasn't enough to get me to the surface. I ascended as quickly as I could, but I was using more air than usual, perhaps because I was tense. I depleted all of it fifty feet below the surface. I removed my weight belt in preparation for my first-ever attempt at an emergency buoyancy climb.

Those fifty feet felt like an eternity. My lungs felt as though they would burst as I shot up through the waves. I felt a searing pain in my bones and muscles; I hoped I wouldn't get the bends. Exhausted, I floated on the surface. I drummed the water with my fingers. They still moved. I could still feel my feet; I wasn't paralyzed. Snow was falling, and beyond the hazy sky, the fog light from the lighthouse flickered. I swam toward the red starboard light on the boat and managed to fling myself on board, weak and depleted.

Fifteen minutes later, as I approached the shore, I thought I saw a figure standing at the edge of the cliff, by the lighthouse. It didn't look like Mr. Ahn or the youth club president, but I couldn't be sure from this distance. Had someone been watching me?

When I got to the lighthouse, there was no one there, though I did notice tire marks on the ground that looked recent.

At home, I changed into dry clothes, wrapped myself in a blanket, and took out a portable air canister and mask. I drank in the oxygen and reread the letter.

Choi Hyonsu's sentence was carried out at 9:00 a.m. today, December 27.

Tomorrow I could go collect my father's body. The day after that was his birthday. I put down the letter and picked up the manuscript. I didn't want to read it, but it was time I learned the truth.

SERYONG LAKE

PART III

Yongje parked in the underground lot below the medical center. This was his first day back at work since the incident. He had a lot to do. The morning sped past as he saw patients, completed paperwork, made a list of those who had paid their respects, and had his secretary compose a form thank-you letter to be sent to them. Around noon, he finally had a moment to breathe. He took out Choi Hyonsu's file obtained through the Supporters to review the documents that had put him on high alert the last three days.

Choi's life didn't surprise him one bit. It seemed that he'd peaked in high school, as many jocks do, and after that everything had gone downhill. He was a failure in every respect: as a husband, as the breadwinner of a family, as a man. It infuriated him that someone so inconsequential had been the one to kill his daughter. Yongje was certain now: Choi had been driving drunk at the time of the incident. His license was suspended for driving under the influence, but he continued to drive without a license. He'd also recently purchased a home, and the interest payments were more than half of his monthly salary. Yongje marked that note with a star. Choi had also recently had his car fixed.

But there was one thing Yongje didn't understand. Why hadn't he just left her there and fled, simply turned around and driven away? Why throw her body in the lake?

That morning, on his way to work, Yongje had seen Choi smoking in front of the clinic, looking down the road. He had a bandage around his wrist and was wearing a sling. But he wasn't wearing a cast. Yongje called the clinic to find out more. "I'm Choi Hyonsu's younger brother," he lied, making use of another piece of information from Choi's file. "He visited your clinic this morning?"

The doctor let out a vague sound, neither affirming nor denying it.

"He hurt his hand," Yongje reminded him.

"Oh, yes."

"How is he? His wife is worried, but it doesn't sound like he told her much."

"I can't really get into it over the phone. Just tell her to come to the clinic, it's right down the street."

"It'll be hard for her to do that because she's working a double shift."

"Ah," said the doctor.

"I'm on a business trip myself," Yongje said, swallowing his growing irritation. "So, does he need to go to a big hospital?"

"Sorry, you said you're his brother?"

"Yes."

Satisfied, the doctor finally began going into detail. "He severed a vein in his left wrist. It's a deep cut, but thankfully the artery and tendons are fine."

"Do you think he was trying to hurt himself?" Yongje asked.

"I'm not sure. He said his left arm sometimes gets numb, as if it's paralyzed. Do you know anything about that? He said it's been going on for a long time. When he cuts himself, he says some sensation returns."

"Are you telling me that he cut his vein because he can't feel his arm?"

"He insisted it was a mistake. There are similar, smaller cuts on his left hand. They look recent."

"Do *you* think it was an accident?" Yongje asked.

"Cutting a vein is much different from pricking a finger. I don't know if we can consider that a mistake. This behavior might continue. And something serious could happen, even by accident."

"Do you think he needs a psychiatric consultation?"

"I think so."

"I'll try to convince him to go, but he might not listen to me. He might just go see you again. If he docs, please don't tell him we spoke. He's very proud," Yongje said.

After the call, he looked through the file again. There was no history of self-harm in his medical records, and he had never received any psychiatric treatment. He had been seen by a neurologist because of the intermittent numbness in his arm but had concealed it to continue his baseball career. He was left-handed; Yongje concluded the deep cut had to have been an accident. If he was really trying to kill himself, he would have held the blade with his dominant hand and cut his right wrist—at least that was what he told himself. Choi couldn't commit suicide. That would interfere with Yongje's plans.

He knew what he was going to do: he would get Choi to confess everything. He had wanted to know how hard he had to push Choi to get the man to lose control, and he discovered that all it took was a simple provocation—that was clear from the incident with the shaman. All Yongje needed now was definitive proof: he had to find the car shop that had fixed the Matiz. The Supporters were looking everywhere near Seoul. He had to be certain he had the right guy, and he also had to make sure Hyonsu wouldn't kill himself before he could exact revenge.

Yongje went over his schedule. This Friday was the day he volunteered at Hyehwa Orphanage with the other doctors from the medical center. That was also the day Kang Eunju was off work. He contacted the Supporters and told them to get ready for Saturday—that was when he would put things into motion. They would have to find the car shop no later than Saturday afternoon. At lunch, he met with the other doctors, who expressed their condolences. He suggested something special for the Friday volunteer session, and everyone agreed. The head of Hyehwa Orphanage was also grateful for Yongje's suggestion.

At four in the afternoon, Yongje drove to the elementary school. As he had requested, Seryong's teacher had gathered her things—her indoor shoes, recorder, art supplies, condolence letters from her classmates, and a framed picture she'd drawn. As she handed it to him, the teacher told him that the kids liked this picture—one child in particular, she said, had been sad when she'd taken it off the wall.

"That's nice. Who was it?" Yongje asked out of politeness.

"Choi Sowon," the teacher replied. "You might know him; he lives in the arboretum." Yongje bristled. Why was Choi's kid so obsessed with his daughter?

Yongje left the school and headed to the dam conservancy.

Choi Hyonsu was alone at the security office when he arrived.

Yongje pulled up to the window. "I'm here to see the director of operations."

Hyonsu picked up the phone. Yongje noticed that his left shoulder sagged, his left hand was red and swollen in the sling, and a flush was spreading under his stubble. He was clearly nervous. How could someone like this have been a professional catcher? No wonder he hadn't made it in the majors.

He hung up the phone and handed Yongje the visitor log. "Please sign in, and I'll need to hold on to your ID."

Yongje handed over his driver's license and wrote down his name and citizen ID number.

"Go ahead," Hyonsu said.

The conservancy staff looked ill at ease as Yongje walked through their offices. Not a single one of them had shown up at Seryong's funeral.

"I have to admit, I'm surprised to see you here," the director of operations said, standing up from his desk to greet him.

"I considered visiting you at home, but I thought you might still be at work," Yongje replied.

Someone brought them green tea. The director of operations hurriedly drank some, even though it hadn't steeped yet.

Yongje got straight to the point. "Some of us doctors at the medical center do volunteer work once a month. This month we were planning to go to Hyehwa Orphanage in Sunchon, but we decided to bring the kids to the arboretum on Friday instead," Yongje explained. "It would be nice if all of your kids could join us for a little party. It'll be casual. And I was hoping you could give the children a tour of the conservancy. We'll handle all the logistics, of course."

"That's certainly feasible," the director of operations said uneasily. "But it must be such a difficult time for you, especially with the ongoing investigation . . ."

"It is. But the kids were close to Seryong," Yongje said. "I took her with me all the time. Last spring, Seryong had promised she'd invite the kids over, and I want to keep her promise."

The director nodded sympathetically. "Well, they'd need to be here by three at the latest for a tour."

"That won't be a problem. Oh, and I have another request."

The director had stood up but awkwardly sat down again.

"Tomorrow is the third day after Seryong's burial."

"Has it already been that long? Time passes quickly."

"I was hoping to go out on the lake for a little bit tomorrow."

The director looked embarrassed. "I thought we came to an understanding about that. I'm sorry, but nobody can go to Hansoldung. You know we don't let anyone in, not even for ceremonies."

"I'm not planning to do anything like that. I'd like to circle Hansoldung on the *Josong*. Just once. I won't ask you for any other favors. All I need is ten minutes. I would like to say goodbye to her soul in private."

"I understand, believe me," the director said. "The problem is the boat. We can only move it when the service company comes, and they aren't scheduled to be here tomorrow."

Yongje felt the pressure of a migraine begin to percolate behind his eyes. This asshole never made anything easy; he always forced Yongje to grovel. "I'm sure they'll come if you call," he said, barely maintaining his composure. "I would be happy to cover the cost."

The director slurped his tea.

Yongje waited, saying nothing.

"What time were you thinking?" the director finally asked.

"Noon."

"Okay. But please don't bring the shaman like last time."

BACK HOME, Yongje parked the car in front of his house and looked up at 102. The living room windows and curtains were open, and he could see Eunju vacuuming. He took Seryong's drawing from the school and rang the bell to 102.

Eunju opened the door. "Dr. Oh," she said, surprised. "What can I do for you?"

"Is your son home?"

"No, he went to visit his dad."

Visit his dad? Yongje recalled what he'd stumbled across last Friday afternoon. If he told her that Sowon was probably at the old barn, playing with a stupid cat, what kind of expression would appear on this woman's face? He was tickled. "Oh, then could you give this to him for me?"

Eunju didn't take it. "What is it?"

"A picture."

"A picture?"

Yongje took Sowon's handmade birthday card out of his pocket. "Your son gave this to me during my daughter's funeral, when we were lifting her soul from the lake."

Eunju took it hesitantly. Her smile vanished as she read the card.

"This is a present for your son. Please have him open it himself, I think he'll like it."

Eunju took the picture reluctantly. She received this gift as haughtily and begrudgingly as Hayong would have. Yongje's hands itched. He wanted to yank it back out of her hands.

"Is that all?" Eunju pushed her bangs aside. Her forehead was flat, like it had been stepped on by a cow. Everything about this woman annoyed him, from her thin, shallow cheeks to her cold expression to her cunning eyes. Worst of all was her shapeless body, well past its prime. There would be a redeeming quality to her if she were at least sweet and deferential, but she was bold and brash. When she came to interview for the job, she had been eager to sing her own praises. She had also reviewed all of the benefits in detail, from the bonus to health insurance to how many vacation days she would get. He'd hired her anyway, because he figured it would come in handy to have access to and leverage over his two suspects, Ahn and Choi. He was impressed with his own foresight. She would be useful in a number of ways.

She was eyeing him suspiciously, fingering the edge of the card. Yongje felt his jaw set. If any other security guard acted so insolently, he would have fired him instantly. "On Friday, we're going to throw a party at the arboretum. The guests of honor are orphans I work with. An events company will handle the party, but we'll have to watch over the children. If the children damage the trees, that ill-tempered groundskeeper will go berserk."

"I'm not on duty on Friday," Eunju said instantly.

"We can't leave the security office empty. If Gwak wasn't on duty, it would fall to him."

"I have a life, too," Eunju said. "I can't work overtime whenever you want me to."

Yongje smiled gently. Fucking bitch. "That's why we pay overtime. Can I have the card back now?"

~

Sunghwan watched the CCTV screen for ten straight minutes. The *Josong*, which was usually launched only to clean the dam, was circling Hansoldung. He couldn't see the man's face, but he could tell it was Oh Yongje standing on deck. When the boat returned to shore, Sunghwan resumed what he'd been doing. He had taken a photo of Hyonsu and Sowon by the front door last Thursday; he'd made it the wallpaper of the computer. It was a good picture, down to the composition and atmosphere and the faded color. It looked like he'd taken it on an analog camera. He also changed the wallpaper of his cell phone screen to the photo. In the short time he had been living with his boss's family, he had grown genuinely fond of both father and son. He searched online for his boss's name, but he couldn't find an official profile. The Fighters had disbanded a long time ago, and Hyonsu wasn't playing professionally. He didn't know where to start. There were tens of thousands of Choi Hyonsus. He added "catcher" to the keywords. He clicked on links for nearly an hour before finally coming across something on a baseball blog.

Does anyone remember Choi Hyonsu, the catcher who had a streak of bad luck? That post had gone up only ten days before. He clicked on it. He saw a photograph of Hyonsu holding his catcher's mask and looking off in the distance, smiling. He looked so young.

Everyone knew the pitcher Kim Ganghyon when the Fighters were around, the post started. He was called the Submariner. He retired, then tried his hand at a couple of new businesses and went broke, or that was the rumor. I recently heard that he'd opened a soju bar near a university in Gwangju, so I organized a school reunion and made a reservation for eight p.m. last night. I figured I would bring him some business. I met someone unexpected there: Choi Hyonsu. People in their twenties might not recognize that name, but for those of us who went to Daeil High in Gwangju, the true legend of our school wasn't Kim Ganghyon. It was Choi Hyonsu, the catcher. He batted cleanup and Daeil went undefeated in the national high school playoffs. He was excellent in the clutch and once hit two walk-off home runs, twice in one series. But his true talents were as a catcher. He could read a game like he was possessed.

Movement on the bridge to the intake tower drew Sunghwan's attention back to the CCTV screen. He zoomed in and saw a man with graying hair, wearing a black suit, holding a walking stick. He remembered who it was. He screenshotted the post and saved it in the cloud, locked the office door, and hurried out toward the bridge.

"It's not too foggy today for once," Sunghwan said, coming up to stand next to the man.

"Do you work here?" the old man asked without looking at him.

"Not at the conservancy. I'm a security guard."

"Ah."

"You're Seryong's grandfather, right?"

The old man turned to look at Sunghwan.

"I recognize you from the funeral."

"Oh? I don't remember meeting you."

"We didn't meet officially. I thought you might be her grandfather because you resemble her."

"Did you know my granddaughter?" The old man seemed wary.

"Not well, but we did meet a few months ago under some unfortunate circumstances." Sunghwan looked down at a tree branch trapped in a small whirlpool below. "She was hiding in the trees behind the Annex in the middle of the night with a bloody nose."

As Sunghwan explained what had happened at the clinic, the old man looked pained. "It's all her father's fault. That's what I believe." The old man's voice trembled and his eyes reddened.

Sunghwan played with the hairpin in his pocket. Giving it to the old man would be the best way to get rid of it. But would he seem suspicious? "Here," he said finally. "It's Seryong's. I didn't get the chance to give it back. I think you should have it."

The old man took it and looked at it for a while. "What's your name, young man?" He didn't seem suspicious of Sunghwan at all.

"My name is Ahn Sunghwan."

"Thank you. I won't forget your kindness."

Sunghwan stayed there as the old man walked away, looking down at the lake. It was interesting to learn that Seryong's grandfather shared his suspicions about Yongje, but it barely registered—he couldn't stop wondering if Hyonsu had seen the video of the underwater village. There should have been some sort of reaction if he had; and besides, Park had told him that Hyonsu knew nothing about technology and had no interest in surfing the internet. But still, it wasn't enough to quiet his mind.

~

Phone call for you." Park was holding out the phone.

Hyonsu blinked. He must have fallen asleep for a moment at his desk. "Hello."

It was Kim Hyongtae. "How's it going?"

"Okay," he said drowsily. He had struggled not to fall asleep the previous night so that he wouldn't dream. He'd flipped through the TV channels but couldn't find something to focus on, and ended up drifting off. At least Sowon's shoes were still safe; he'd put them in the washing machine and placed a big basin of cold water on top of it. If the lid was opened, the basin would clatter to the floor. Even if he was in a deep sleep, the loud noise and the splash of cold water would hopefully wake him up. Thankfully, Eunju hadn't seemed to notice that anything was amiss, either.

"Is anything going on?" Hyongtae said. "I dropped my car off at the repair shop last night and the owner told me a detective came by on Friday."

Hyonsu sat up, his drowsiness instantly evaporating. The cops were looking into car shops now? "Two of them?"

"Just one. Apparently he asked if you'd come in to fix your car around the twenty-eighth of last month."

Hyonsu gulped, the wind knocked out of him. They might be close to finding the place he'd gone to. "And what did the owner say?"

"He told the guy everything was in the ledger and handed it over. What do you think this is about? Did you get into an accident?"

"No," Hyonsu said limply, trying to disguise his panic.

"That's a relief. But if something did happen, just handle it. Don't make it into something bigger."

I can't, thought Hyonsu. It's already bigger. He blotted his forehead with a tissue.

"Anyway, I'm calling about work," Hyongtae said. "The engineering team is going down there on Thursday."

"Yeah?"

"They're going to replace the CCTVs with the infrared kind and add searchlights."

"Why now?"

"The girl, you know. The conservancy is driving us insane, telling us they need more security personnel. So we're going to try this, and hopefully they'll back down."

Hyonsu didn't move for a long time after hanging up. He tried to gather his thoughts. He must be a suspect. A detective going all the way there must mean they were investigating him, and what they found was sure to implicate him. It was just a question of how long it would take. Meanwhile, what was he going to do about the witness living in his house?

At the end of the workday, he managed to gather the courage to call Sunghwan.

"Yes, boss?"

"Want to grab a drink with me?" Finally, the words he had hesitated over for days came tumbling out.

Later, Hyonsu bought two bottles of soju and a few cans of Budweiser from the rest area, put the beer on a table, and leaned on the railing of the observation deck. He drank two full cups of soju, waiting for the alcohol to kick in as he gazed down below. He would ask lightly, indifferently: What did you see that night?

But Sunghwan was over forty minutes late. Hyonsu began to feel anxious. Maybe it would be better if Sunghwan didn't come. Maybe he should leave before the younger man got there. What would he do even if he did come? He was so anxious that he might just tell him everything and that would be the end of it. He would lose everything. And he knew next to nothing about Sunghwan. How could he trust him?

Around seven, Sunghwan brought a can of beer over and stood next to him. "Sorry I'm late," he said. "I went to check on Sowon first."

Right. Sowon. He was home alone. "How's he doing?" he asked sheepishly. To Sowon, this near-stranger must seem more dependable than his own father.

"He had dinner and was watching TV. I told him I was coming to see you and he asked me to tell you he wants strawberry glazed doughnuts."

Hyonsu nodded.

Sunghwan raised his can. "How did you know I like Bud?"

"I saw it on your desk."

Sunghwan nodded. "Oh, that's right."

An awkward silence fell between them. Sunghwan looked down at the scenery, drinking his beer.

Hyonsu tried to find a way to begin. "So, why are you here?"

"You asked me to come meet you here, boss."

"No, I mean . . . here. At Seryong Lake." Hyonsu was already flailing. He didn't know how to get at what he was trying to ask.

Sunghwan smiled morosely. "I'm not sure, actually," he said.

Hyonsu looked at him, surprised.

"Things were hard for my family when I was young. We struggled. Diving was the only trade my father knew, and there's not much money in that. My mother worked as a housekeeper and managed to bring in some money. I still adored my father because he was the one who introduced me to a life in the water, but one of my older brothers didn't feel the same way. He was tired of being poor.

"He entered the military when I was in eleventh grade. He hated diving, but he applied to the Ship Salvage Unit. Like my father, it was all he knew. The night before he left, he told our father that I should go to college. That I would be the one who could lift our family out of our economic situation. He said that he would cover the entrance fees with his salary. I was shocked, to be honest. I never imagined that I would go to college. I thought I'd be lucky if I graduated from high school. My brother tended to overestimate my abilities. He treated every kids' literary prize I won like it was a big deal."

Hyonsu offered Sunghwan a cigarette.

"Do you know what it's like to be your family's sole hope?" Sunghwan asked. "To go to college when your family has sacrificed everything for you to be there?"

Of course Hyonsu did. Hyonsu lit his cigarette with Sunghwan's lighter. He had also shouldered his family's hope; he'd been offered a chance to go pro after high school, but his mother had wanted him to go to college first. Her choice was his and his failure was hers. She died the year after he quit baseball.

"It's like running a hundred yards in armor. I couldn't breathe. I wanted to quit. After my military service, I managed to get a job at the National Railroad Administration, but I didn't last two years there. I couldn't fathom just going to work, coming home, getting paid, focusing on promotions, having a family. I wanted more from life."

Hyonsu stared at the flickering light at the tips of his fingers.

"That's all bullshit, actually." Sunghwan smiled limply and scratched his head. "I just hated working nine to five. I realized that there was little difference between my elementary school–educated father's job and mine; both were tedious and unfulfilling. I should just do what I wanted to do with my life. Before I could change my mind, I quit my job. I basically betrayed my family and ran away." Sunghwan drained the rest of his beer.

Hyonsu finished his soju, too. "Sowon says you want to be a writer?"

"Yes, but my father doesn't approve. He says, where's the money in that? I guess that's how I ended up here." Sunghwan studied Hyonsu calmly, carefully. He seemed to be wondering why Hyonsu had really called him up here.

Hyonsu didn't know where to start. How could he ask his question naturally? He lost his courage as he picked up the remaining two cans of beer. Sunghwan was looking down the mountain, leaning against the railing. Hyonsu suddenly felt dizzy, as though a black hood was falling around his head. Sunghwan was just an arm's length away. He could easily push this witness over the railing. Hyonsu shook his head, stunned, and reality seeped back in.

Sunghwan turned to look at him.

He handed Sunghwan a beer. *Right now. Ask him. Ask him what he saw.* "So," he said at the exact same time as Sunghwan said, "Well."

Sunghwan took the beer and grinned. "Go ahead."

What should he say? *Did you make that video?* Or, *What's up with that video?* Should he say he saw it by accident?

Sunghwan's phone rang. When he answered, Hyonsu could hear a scolding woman's voice buzzing on the other end of the line. "Ah, yes," Sunghwan said, looking uncomfortable. He glanced at Hyonsu. "I know. Okay."

Hyonsu realized it had to be Eunju.

Sunghwan hung up. "So—she wanted to know why Sowon was home alone." Sunghwan didn't tell him the rest, but Hyonsu knew what she would have said. She would have ordered the younger man to stop drinking and go home. "Should we head down?"

Hyonsu nodded, frustrated that he had missed his chance.

Sowon was asleep on the sofa with the TV still on. Hyonsu put the doughnuts in the kitchen, picked him up, and carried him to bed. Then he went back into the living room. Like the night before, he hid Sowon's shoes in the washing machine and set his cell phone alarm to two in the morning. This would wake him up before his alter ego appeared. And, just in case, he dragged the dining chairs into his room and built a barricade in front of the door. If he tried to leave, he would stumble over it and fall.

He lay in bed and closed his eyes. He wanted to rest for a few hours, but now that he was lying down he couldn't fall asleep. He should have found a way to bring up the video. He could have reprimanded Sunghwan, saying, Were you in the lake that night? You know you're not allowed in there. But even if he knew what Sunghwan had seen, what would he do about it? What would he do if Sunghwan said, I saw *you* that night? Would he panic and throw him into the lake, too?

He turned over and looked out his window. The BMW and the Matiz were parked side by side. He recalled how he'd moved out of the way as the BMW sped by, honking its horn. Hyonsu groaned. He should have just gone back to Seoul when he got lost. The girl's eyes, two black holes, loomed in front of him. He turned over again and swallowed. His tongue was dry, and his throat burned. Maybe he could chase away the apparition with liquor. Maybe then he could get a few hours' rest. He moved the chairs away from the door and dug through the living room closet. He found the box that held his old baseball uniform. He'd hidden a bottle of Calvados inside his helmet in case he ever desperately needed a shot.

But when he reached for it, the bottle was gone. He pulled everything out of the closet. He found an iron, an ironing board, an electric blanket, various plastic containers, a folding table, a weed whacker he'd bought last Chusok, but no Calvados. He rummaged in the fridge, under the sink, in the drawers, and upended everything in the master bedroom. Nothing. Blood rushed to his head. Eunju. She was an old hand at finding what he'd secreted away; of course she'd found his emergency bottle. He slammed the drawer of the vanity shut and accidentally jammed his finger in it. He was in so much pain that the words he'd so often thought but never uttered, even in his dreams, leaped out of his mouth. "That bitch!" Fear and craving turned into rage so suddenly that he felt nauseated. He sucked on his aching finger and decided to go find Eunju at work and slap some sense into her. He was going to shake her until he felt better. Then he would go up to the observation deck and buy a bottle of soju.

He shoved his feet in his shoes and froze. In the mirror by the shoe cabinet was a man he hadn't seen in years—hair standing on end, thick veins bulging from his face, red eyes shining, pale lips trembling with rage. Sergeant Choi. He had become his father. He looked behind him. He saw the things he'd pulled out of the closet, the drawers open or thrown on the floor, things cluttering the table, their bedroom a wreck. He had seen this scene countless times as a boy, but this time his father wasn't the culprit; it was Hyonsu himself. His father's image jeered at him from the mirror. *What do you think, son, did you turn out any better than me?* Hyonsu fell to his knees, shaking.

~

As he was about to head home after work on Wednesday, Yongje received a call from the Supporters. "She left the country on May first and landed at de Gaulle Airport in Paris. There are no records of her returning."

Hayong was in France? He had suspected from time to time that she might have fled overseas, but France? How had she gotten there so quickly, two days after disappearing?

"Does she have any connections there? Any family?" the Supporter asked.

"Not as far as I know."

"Friends?"

Did she have any close friends? Yongje had never really met any of them. All the women at their wedding had looked the same and he'd only said hello to seem polite. "I'll have to think about it."

"Call us when you remember something."

At home, he went upstairs to the library and took out their wedding album. The first picture was at the Catholic church in Sunchon. Hayong was looking at the camera with dull eyes. He remembered a woman who had stood behind the camera, who crept over and slid a handkerchief into Hayong's hand right before they said their vows. She was the one who caught the bouquet. A college friend, maybe. He found her on the next page in a group picture. She was small and pale. He remembered asking about her, probably when they received the album from the wedding planner. Hayong had told him her friend was preparing to study abroad. That was all he remembered. What was her name? It wasn't a common surname: Eun? Min? Mo? No: it was Myong.

He called the Supporters. "I remember a friend of hers. Her last name is Myong, but I don't recall her first name. They might have gone to college together. I can send you a picture. Can you find her?"

"Of course," said the person on the other end.

Yongje's heart leaped. He couldn't sit still. He had finally gotten a clue to Hayong's whereabouts. Once the Supporters located her, he would go retrieve her personally. After he solved the situation there, of course.

Yongje heard the doorbell ringing. He went downstairs to find Yim standing outside, holding a log of cedar. Yongje had asked for it the day before.

"I couldn't find anything better because of the rain," Yim said.

"That's okay." He took the log and moved to shut the door, but the old man kept standing there. "What is it?"

Yim pointed at 102. "Late at night, I've seen Choi out by the back path toward the lakeshore road."

"What time?"

"Right when I start to do my rounds. Maybe 2:30? You should tell him he shouldn't take that back road in the middle of the night. It's so dark, he could hurt himself. What if he runs into a tree or something?"

Yongje sent the old man on his way and went down to his workshop. He began to shave the bark off the cedar, and a few hours later the wood revealed its smooth inside. If he carved it, sanded it, and painted it with resin, it would become a beautiful object. He went upstairs, planning to sleep a little. He set the alarm on his cell phone to 2:00 a.m.

At 2:30 a.m., he went into Seryong's room wearing black pants and a black waterproof jacket, a flashlight in his pocket. If Yim was right, Choi would come out soon. It was raining hard, and this weather was supposed to continue for some time. This was helpful; the universe was cooperating with his plan. He put a hand on the urn containing Seryong's ashes. Soon, he thought, everything would be back under his control.

Around three, when he had begun to think Yim had imagined everything, he spotted something white outside. Yongje stuck his head out the window. It was Choi. He didn't have an umbrella or a raincoat; he was wearing a white shirt, no shoes, a headlamp, and his arm sling. He held a pair of shoes and walked straight ahead. Yongje pulled the hood of his jacket over his head, shoved his feet into his boots, and climbed out the window.

Choi's pace was incredibly slow; it took him nearly ten minutes to reach the gate. He tripped and fell through the opening, landing face-first in a mud puddle with a big splash. That must be what it looked like when five-hundred-year-old cedars fell. Yongje watched as Choi raised his head. He hoisted himself up and began walking again, shoes still in his grip, moving stiffly and sluggishly, like a doll under a spell. He didn't seem to notice or care that he was drenched in muddy water. The fog was thicker by the time they made it to the lakeshore road. Choi stopped in front of the bridge to the intake tower, and Yongje stopped, too. Then Choi swung around suddenly, the light from his lantern catching Yongje's face, mere steps away. Yongje froze in shock. But the other man just turned around and kept going onto the bridge, seeming not to have seen him.

Choi stopped again in the middle of the bridge. Yongje walked toward him, feeling invisible. Choi stood there, glaring at the lake, then he threw the shoes in the water. Choi turned around as soon as he heard the splash. Yongje didn't have a chance to react; this time Choi collided with him directly, slamming into his shoulder. Yongje landed on his back and hit his head. By the time he gathered his wits, he was lying alone in the dark.

All the way home, Yongje couldn't shake the feeling that someone was following him. He kept whirling around to shine his light, but he didn't see anything other than fog, rain, and the occasional blue flash of lightning. He went around to the front of 102 and saw that the living room light was on behind drawn curtains. He stood under the crepe myrtle and listened, but he couldn't hear any movement. Was Choi sleeping? Was he sleepwalking? Whichever it was, this excursion had been useful for Yongje. He'd had a chance to experience Choi's strange behavior and physical strength firsthand. His shoulder ached. There were two things he had to do in the morning: get an X-ray, and come up with another way to handicap his adversary before the inevitable showdown.

$\sim$

After Yongje went inside his own house, Sunghwan emerged from the backyard. He crept toward the front and stopped between the two units. Unit 101 was dark; all the lights were off. Only the light in the basement window was on. He had seen that light on late at night before, and he had always been curious. What did Yongje do every night in the basement? He slunk into the flowerbed and stood with his body pasted next to the window. The blinds were down about two-thirds of the way. He could see Yongje's back through the window. Yongje was leaning over a table as if shooting pool. He saw shavings and bark and pieces of wood by Yongje's feet. Sunghwan crouched and brought his face to the window. A wood table with what looked like a model castle on it stood in the center of the room, and in the corner near the window was a piece of wood in a vise. The castle was large and intricately designed, seemingly constructed from tiny sticks of wood glued together. Judging from the pieces of wood and the carpentry tools, it seemed that Yongje had not only built the castle but was creating the materials with which to build it. Sunghwan was awed in spite of himself. But what Yongje was carving now didn't look like a part of the castle's architecture. Sunghwan considered its length, thickness, and rounded tip, and concluded, with a shiver, that it could be a club.

Yongje suddenly stopped and turned to look up at the window. Sunghwan jumped back and stood with his back to the wall, his heart pounding. Sunghwan was grateful for Seryong Lake's vicious fog; he didn't think Yongje had seen him. But he didn't dare bend over to look again.

He crept out of the flowerbed and climbed back into his room through his window. He was caught off guard by Sowon, who was sitting up in bed. Between the boy's legs was Ernie, tensely coiled.

Sunghwan took his muddy boots off. "Shh."

Sowon nodded.

"Sit tight," he whispered.

Sowon nodded again.

Sunghwan peeked into the living room. Hyonsu was asleep in front of the TV, his headlamp still on, drenched in mud. He looked peaceful, for once. Sunghwan placed his boots by the front door and was about to approach Hyonsu when he froze. Eunju was standing in front of the master bedroom, her arms crossed. "Were you two out drinking?"

He looked down at himself. He looked just like Hyonsu. "Oh. Well, no, but . . ."

Eunju spun around and slammed the door. Sowon was peeking out from behind their bedroom door, and he emerged when Sunghwan met his eyes. With the boy's help, Sunghwan took off Hyonsu's wet clothes, cleaned off what mud he could with a towel, and mopped up the water on the floor. Sowon brought out Sunghwan's thin mattress and Sunghwan rolled Hyonsu onto it like a log. Sowon covered him with a blanket. Sunghwan then went to take a shower.

"Mr. Ahn," Sowon said nervously when Sunghwan got back to their room. "My dad's sick, isn't he?"

"Sometimes he ends up sleepwalking. But it's just a nightmare he's having," Sunghwan said, trying to sound reassuring.

"Like the dream I have about the girl?"

Sunghwan glanced up at Ernie perched on top of Sowon's closet and nodded.

"I don't go out when she calls me, but Dad does. Right?" Sowon looked anxious and frightened.

"Right."

Sowon nodded and lay down.

SUNGHWAN WANTED TO BELIEVE his own words, that this was just a severe case of a sleep disorder. But he knew the truth. Earlier in the evening, Hyonsu and his wife had fought loudly. The door to their room was closed, so he couldn't make out all the words, but he could tell their emotions were running high. Sowon put his headphones on and trained his eyes on his book, trying to block them out. Sunghwan pretended to focus on his laptop. He heard Hyonsu leave.

Sunghwan waited until midnight, and still Hyonsu didn't return. He figured his boss was at the observation deck, but he soon grew worried; it was raining hard. Maybe he should go get him. He took his headlamp out of his bag but remembered something. He went back to that baseball site and checked the time of that post: 10:05 p.m., Saturday, August 28. His heart sank. Hyonsu had told him he didn't come down on the twenty-seventh because something had come up. But the man who wrote the post had bumped into Hyonsu in Gwangju at eight p.m. on the twenty-seventh. Seryong Lake was only an hour and a half away from there. Depending on how he drove, he could have gotten here in an hour. The first call he'd missed had been at 9:03 p.m. The second call had been at 10:30 p.m. His head began to race. Hyonsu's timid demeanor when he first met Yongje, the panicked state he'd been in when Seryong was lifted out of the water, Yongje telling him that he'd seen Hyonsu before, his dramatic reaction on the day of Seryong's funeral, his erratic behavior over the past week . . .

Sunghwan suddenly felt afraid. Things were beginning to fall into place. He put on a rain jacket and grabbed an umbrella.

Nobody was at the observation deck other than Hyonsu, dozing under the umbrella at a table. He was drenched, and his feet were bare. Three empty bottles were on the table, along with his shoes and socks.

"Boss?" Sunghwan called.

Hyonsu opened his eyes, but he didn't seem to recognize Sunghwan. He grabbed his shoes off the table and staggered through the rain. Sunghwan understood immediately— Hyonsu wasn't drunk, he was dreaming. He wouldn't look back even if Sunghwan called him by name; he was completely defenseless. All Sunghwan could do was make sure Hyonsu didn't stumble in the dark. He caught up to him and put his headlamp on Hyonsu's docile head.

Hyonsu went slowly down the path and bumped into the barrier at the arboretum entrance. He ducked under it and went up the path by the Annex. He walked through the gap between 102 and 101. Sunghwan stopped abruptly when he saw Yongje climb out of Seryong's window, wearing a black waterproof jacket and black boots. He had clearly been lying in wait.

Hyonsu led the way, Yongje followed, and Sunghwan trailed them both. When Hyonsu slammed into Yongje and the smaller man was briefly incapacitated, Sunghwan was forced to choose who to follow. He decided to wait for Yongje. Why had he been following Hyonsu?

After getting a glimpse of what Yongje was working on in his basement, surviving Eunju's wrath, and trying—probably fruitlessly—to comfort her son, Sunghwan turned off the light and lay down.

SUNGHWAN OVERSLEPT, probably because he had slept fitfully, tossing and turning all night. When he stumbled out of his room, Hyonsu and his family were already sitting around the breakfast table. Hyonsu looked haggard but was clean-shaven, his arm still in the sling. Nobody spoke. The silence felt like a ticking bomb. At work, neither Hyonsu nor Sunghwan was wearing his regular shoes, but neither mentioned it. In front of the dam security office, Hyonsu glanced at Sunghwan and opened his mouth as if he was about to say something. Sunghwan waited, but Hyonsu turned and set off toward the conservancy without a word.

~

D on't forget to clean the library this morning," Gwak said.

"I won't," Eunju said absentmindedly. What they called the library was really a kind of informal community center for the families living in company housing, where the wives could gather and the kids could play on rainy days.

"Make sure you do a good job. We don't want any complaints."

"Got it."

After Gwak finally left, Eunju texted her sister. Want to talk?

Her phone rang immediately. "What's up?"

Eunju took a deep breath; this wasn't the time to be proud. Yongju would be able to assess the situation objectively. Maybe she would even come up with a solution Eunju hadn't thought of. "So, last night."

The previous night, Hyonsu had handed her a stack of papers and said gravely, "We need to divorce."

She had smirked, thinking, He's finally gone mad. "Oh, really? Why?"

"I don't want to live with you anymore."

He didn't want to live with *her* anymore? Eunju started laughing and couldn't stop. She laughed so hard tears sprang to her eyes, her laughter verging on a wail.

"If you agree to it, it'll get processed quickly. Violence and my drinking are the grounds for divorce."

Her laughter rolled back into her throat.

"You can have it all. Sowon, the house, the car, everything. I may not be able to pay child support in the future, but I will for as long as I can. I'll send you my entire salary for as long as possible. You'll be able to keep him safe."

This wasn't an empty threat, she realized. He meant it this time.

Hyonsu took out an envelope and a bankbook. "This is all I have. There is cash in here and this is information for a credit line. You might be able to afford a studio near Gyonggi Province."

A studio? "Divorce?" she finally stammered. "Who says you get to decide? Do you think I stayed with you all this time because I wanted to? You think I couldn't live without you? I stayed because of Sowon. Don't you get that?"

"I know. That's why I'm telling you that you don't have to anymore."

Eunju tried to calm down. "You should be asking for forgiveness, not giving up. You should be saying that you'll get a grip on yourself and lead a better life. If you were in your right mind . . ."

"Are you listening to me? I can't be in my right mind as long as you're near me. I feel like I'm going to have a seizure just hearing your voice. I'm going crazy every hour of every day. Let me go. For my sanity. Please."

She felt a wave of sharp, hot pain that took her breath away. She felt as though she were breathing fire. She took the cash out of the envelope and rolled up the bundle—judging from the heft, it seemed to be about a million won. "*You're* going crazy because of *me*?" she said, slapping him with her free hand. "Am I that awful?"

Hyonsu grabbed her hand. The cash fell out of her grip and fluttered to the floor. His cold, cavernous eyes met hers. "Leave. Go tomorrow. Take Sowon. If you don't, I'll kick you out myself." He released her hand and left the room.

She slumped to the floor, feeling faint. Was he really demanding a divorce? How dare he?

She paced, waiting for him to return. Sowon's room was quiet, though she saw the light shining faintly under his door. At some point in the middle of the night, she heard the front door open, but it wasn't Hyonsu; it was Sunghwan going out. She waited in the living room, figuring he must have gone to look for Hyonsu. A long while later, Hyonsu came in by himself, barely glanced at her, and collapsed on the living room floor. He was barefoot and covered in mud, but he seemed to fall asleep instantly. She just stood in the doorway, staring at him. She was more confused than angry.

Then Sunghwan came out of his room, just as wet and muddy as her husband. Clearly he'd found Hyonsu and they'd drunk themselves silly. But Sunghwan would tell her nothing.

"Maybe he's having an affair," her sister said now.

"I'm not an idiot."

"I'm not saying you are."

"What kind of wife doesn't realize her husband's seeing someone else?" she scoffed.

"Then he got himself into trouble."

"What are you talking about?"

"Maybe gambling. Or embezzlement. Or maybe he beat someone up while he was drunk. He wouldn't act this strangely unless he got himself into some serious trouble, don't you think?"

"He doesn't even know any card games," Eunju protested. "He's not sophisticated enough to embezzle! He's never gotten into a fight. He's never even hit anyone."

"He hit you."

Eunju was angry. Why was her sister bringing that up now, when she had reassured Eunju earlier that a single slap meant nothing? She stopped herself from hanging up on Yongju; she needed help. "No. It's not that. If he was in trouble, he would have asked me for help."

"Think about it. You said he told you that you can have everything. That he may not be able to pay child support. That he would send you his entire salary for as long as he could. That he asked you to take care of Sowon. He wouldn't do that! He would *never* give up Sowon. He's gotten himself into something bad, something he can't fix. That's the only thing that makes sense. Maybe he's worried about his assets being seized. Divorce is the best way to protect you." She paused. "I mean, it's weird that he didn't tell you about it. But still. Try to find out. Call around and ask some questions. Just because he can't fix it, it doesn't mean you can't try."

Eunju remembered the detectives who had come by the previous Thursday. They'd told her they were there to ask about the dead neighbor girl, as a formality. Eunju had told them to go ahead. They asked her if she'd come there before moving.

They kept asking even when she said she hadn't. Isn't it common to look around a place before moving in, wouldn't your husband have come by, it looks like your car was fixed recently, was there an accident . . . Eunju didn't want to tell them that they'd fought because Hyonsu didn't come down and they were still not on speaking terms. Instead she told them that the car was in her name, and there was no way she wouldn't know if it had been in an accident. What kind of woman did they think she was? They dawdled for another thirty minutes before finally leaving. She hadn't thought it was anything serious, but she realized now how blind she'd been.

She hung up with her sister and started calling her husband's friends, starting with Kim Hyongtae. She asked if her husband had gotten into a car accident recently. His friend said not that he knew of, and that it seemed unlikely; after his license was suspended for driving under the influence, he seemed to be more careful. Eunju's heart sank. Driving under the influence? Suspended license? What other secrets had he been keeping?

She kept going down the list. Hyonsu's high school friend Kim Ganghyon told her that Hyonsu had stopped by his bar on the night he was supposed to come to Seryong Lake, and that they'd drunk together until around eight p.m. Then she called the car repair shop and asked if he'd been in. The owner asked what was going on, telling her that a detective had come by asking the same question. Eunju pretended she had bad service and hung up, afraid to find out more. Everywhere she looked, she learned something new that she had missed. What had Hyonsu been up to? She remembered him coming home singing drunkenly the night before they moved here. She'd never heard him sing before. All he liked was drinking and baseball. Nothing other than Sowon had ever made him happy. She had been so pissed about being slapped that she'd gone into their room and shut the door, ignoring him. But now she had questions that she wanted answered. She could ignore his strange behavior no longer.

Her rage and confusion began to subside as more unsettling questions presented themselves. Had he ever gone on a drinking binge as bad as that of the past two weeks? Had he ever hit her or said vile things to her before? Had he ever told her what job she could or couldn't take? No—he had never done any of those things. Until they moved to Seryong Lake.

She called Sunghwan. She asked if Hyonsu really hadn't come down to see the house the night of August 27. After all, he'd gone drinking in Gwangju, which was on the way here. Sunghwan said he hadn't. She let out a long sigh.

IT WAS PAST TEN A.M.; she'd lost track of time. Eunju ran to the library, where she vacuumed, dusted, and scrubbed, trying to keep her mind off what she'd learned. The other women came in just as she was wrapping up.

"Is your boy okay?" a freckled woman asked. "I heard the shaman grabbed him."

"I'm sorry?" Eunju asked.

The woman looked surprised. "Didn't you know? Everyone's talking about it."

"The shaman? The one who came for the girl's funeral?"

The woman's voice shot up. "Oh, my goodness! You really

don't know! I heard your husband tried to strangle the sha-man, but the young man who lives in your house separated them."

"I don't know what you're . . ."

The woman with the straight hair jumped in. "Oh, we didn't see it, either," she said, then told her everything she'd heard. "Gwak was patrolling and saw that young man run as fast as he could with your boy on his back. Weren't you home?"

Eunju felt hot. She remembered that day. Sunghwan had come to find her and had suggested that she look in on Sowon. She'd thought it was odd. The next day, Gwak had asked, "Your boy is okay, right?" She recalled the drawing Yongje had brought over; Sowon had explained that the dead girl had drawn it, and Eunju had taken that unlucky thing and shoved it in the trash. Sowon was not speaking to her over that. He just stared at her coolly and ignored her when she spoke to him. He was just like his dad sometimes; they both made her feel sheepish and alone. Eunju felt her rage rekindle. Was she the only one who didn't know what every-one else had known? Why had nobody told her? How could they make her out to be such a fool? She wanted answers from her so-called husband. She turned to leave.

The freckled woman called after her. "There's window cleaner on the bookcase. Since you're already here, can you do something about the windows? They're really dirty."

Eunju glared at her. She remembered how Gwak called this woman "ma'am." Who was she? The wife of the head of the conservancy? She pressed her lips together and found the cleaner. The women gossiped, mostly about the girl's family. They said that Seryong's father was the prime suspect.

"Remember when I said it's only a matter of time before she's killed by her own father? His wife did well to run away. She probably would have died with her daughter if she stayed," whispered the woman with straight hair.

The freckled one giggled. "Be careful with what you say. You never know who's listening." She glanced at Eunju. "Are you done?" she asked. "You can leave, then."

Eunju stormed out, so angry that her legs shook. She was being treated like the security guard she was. It was entirely her husband's fault. She didn't have the desire to go shopping like the other players' wives, but he could at least make enough money to ensure that she wouldn't be humiliated like this.

At home, Eunju made herself two packets of instant ramen and ate it all. As her anger diminished, anxiety took its place. She called Hyonsu.

"Yeah," he said, his voice low.

"I have just one question for you. That night I told you to come here and check the place out. Did you?"

After a long silence, he answered, "No."

Eunju was relieved. She decided to take him at his word. She hung up and went outside. She dumped the recycling bin and cleaned the trash area. She emptied the compost bin, swept the front path, and mopped the stairs. When there was nothing else left to clean, she cleaned everything again.

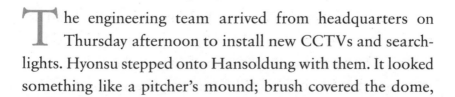

The engineering team arrived from headquarters on Thursday afternoon to install new CCTVs and search-lights. Hyonsu stepped onto Hansoldung with them. It looked something like a pitcher's mound; brush covered the dome,

and the pine tree in the middle was made up of two enormous trunks that were entwined. Together, they were three
times wider than his torso. Two new infrared cameras were
installed on a pole next to the tree, supposedly showing 180-
degree vistas. Hyonsu called the dam security office from
under the tree. "Can you see me?"

"I can count the hair in your nose," came the amused reply
from Park.

They also replaced the camera on the dock, and a large
searchlight was installed on top of the intake tower. Hyonsu
looked around at the new equipment, feeling unsettled. These
would reveal his sleepwalking habits to the whole world. How
would he get through the night? His only options were to stay
awake all night, or hope the invincible fog would render the
technology useless.

After the engineers left, Hyonsu swallowed two Tylenols.
His head pounded, his eyes were bloodshot, and his ears were
stuffed. He felt hot and his muscles ached. Had he caught the
flu? It wouldn't be surprising considering that he ran around
in the rain like a rabid dog every night.

Around dusk, as the fog began to roll over the lake, Hyonsu
got up from his post at the dam security office. He had dawdled as long as he could. He told Park, who was staying on
for the night shift, "I'll stop by the lakeshore on my way
home. Keep an eye on the screens and let's see which is more
powerful, the new system or the fog."

"How about I call you when I see you at the dock?" Park
asked.

At the first entrance, Hyonsu came face-to-face with a blinding white light. The searchlight must be revving up. It was like

the revolving, all-seeing beacon of a lighthouse. He turned the corner, went past the intake tower, and got a text when he reached the dock. It was Park. Gotcha. Cameras for the win.

Hyonsu took the road up to the ranch and perched on a bench under the persimmon tree. He needed to think. His head was still pounding. Leaning against the tree trunk, Hyonsu closed his eyes and drank in the cool night air. His mind drifted back to the events of the morning.

HE HAD OPENED his eyes with his alarm, realizing that a blanket was draped over his damp body and that he was sleeping on a mattress. It must have been Sunghwan's doing. That young man made him nervous. He must know where Hyonsu went every night, where his shoes had disappeared to, but he never said a thing. Hyonsu wanted to ask him why he wasn't asking any questions, but he couldn't. He hoped it meant that Sunghwan was on his side. He wanted to tell him things he'd never told anyone, not his mother or Eunju. He wanted to share the weight of the baggage he'd been carrying for the last twenty-five years with someone who would understand. He wanted to ask Sunghwan for help.

But Hyonsu was afraid that he was beyond rescuing—the only person who could do anything for him now was himself. All he could do was try to mitigate the fallout for Sowon, and the only way to do that was to send his family away. Once they were safe, it wouldn't be too late to decide whether to confess, wait to be arrested, or kill himself.

The previous day, he had opened a line of credit, emptied his secret fund, found a divorce lawyer, and filled out the papers. He knew it wouldn't be easy to get Eunju to agree. If he told her everything, she might agree to a divorce, but he still couldn't bring himself to tell her the truth. Instead he ended up confessing to something totally different. He'd dreamed of saying those words to her countless times.

Then Eunju called him at lunchtime. "I have just one question for you. That night I told you to come here and check the place out. Did you?"

He realized that she'd finally detected that something was amiss. This was his opportunity to come clean. But his staff was around, and the timing wasn't right. "No."

"Fine," she said and hung up without even a second of hesitation. That was it; he'd lost the chance to tell her forever. He knew she wouldn't ask him again. She sounded relieved. She didn't really want to know.

"Long time no see," a voice said, shaking him from his reverie.

Hyonsu opened his eyes and saw Yongje standing in front of him with a flashlight in his hand.

"Oh, no. What happened there?" Yongje pointed at his left hand.

"I tried to suck my own blood," Hyonsu said.

Yongje let out a laugh that was almost a bark; an odd glint of something sinister was hidden in it. "It must not be as bad as it looks, since you're joking about it."

"What are you doing here?" Hyonsu's voice was calm despite his inner turmoil.

"Just taking a walk. I heard the cameras on Hansoldung were replaced. Do they work well?"

"I'm not sure yet. We'll find out tonight when the fog rolls in." Hyonsu got up and turned toward the road. "See you later. I'm on my way home."

He walked on, looking straight ahead. He could feel Yongje's gaze on the back of his neck.

IT WAS DARK in the living room. Sowon's light was off. Two pairs of shoes were by the front door—Sowon's basketball shoes and Sunghwan's hiking boots. Hyonsu put his son's shoes in the washing machine again. He wondered if he should barricade the front door with chairs. Instead he would set his cell phone alarm for every thirty minutes. He put his headphones on so that nobody else would hear it and slid his phone in his shirt pocket. All he had to do now was watch TV and stay awake. After less than an hour, he felt his eyelids grow stiff. He kept losing focus. Hyonsu sat up straight at the third alarm. When the fourth alarm went off, he was dozing with his head on his chest. Just two days earlier, he had been drinking to try to get to sleep. The good old days, he thought. Without fail, sleep overpowered him. Hyonsu lifted his heavy head and tried his best to focus on the screen. Two more hours and the sun would rise. The sun would rise and . . .

Hyonsu felt the darkness surge inside him. He drifted out into the fog. All sorts of things rushed past—the lights in front of the Annex, a crepe myrtle with deep red flowers, the walls of 101 that looked dark in the rain, a window, and what he thought might be Yongje's face, but it was gone before he could fully grasp it. A full red moon hung in the sky. Sorghum fields were flaming in the moonlight. Hyonsu blundered forward.

Suddenly, he felt the searing agony of sharp, strong talons

sinking into his foot. He instantly snapped back into reality; his eyes flew open and he screamed. He was smothered by fog. His cell phone alarm was ringing loudly, a bright light shone overhead, and he saw that his bare foot had been ensnared in a large trap. Deep pain engulfed his leg and shot up to his waist. He fell hard, clutching his foot. He tried to pry open the trap, but it was impossible. As usual in times of distress, his arm wasn't cooperating. It hung uselessly at the end of his shoulder. He couldn't do anything with one hand. The more he writhed and tried to pry the trap open, the deeper it dug into his flesh. Blood soaked his foot and seeped into the ground. Hyonsu let go of the trap. He moaned through his teeth.

"Are you okay?" asked a voice behind him. It was Sunghwan. "Oh, my god," the younger man muttered over and over again when he saw the trap. He dropped his flashlight, heaved the jaws of the trap open, took off his shirt, and tied it around the wound. "Try to stand up, boss," he said, slinging Hyonsu's arm around his shoulders.

Hyonsu couldn't do anything. He felt dizzy. The trees flipped upside down. His consciousness retreated into the faint horizon.

"Please get up," came Sunghwan's whisper. "I can't carry you."

~

Hyonsu didn't even try to get up; he shook Sunghwan off and stretched his hand to feel along the ground. His left arm was still limp between his thighs. Sunghwan spotted Sowon's basketball shoes. One was by the gate and the other was under a tree a short distance away. As soon as he found the shoes Hyonsu closed his eyes. Had he fallen asleep? Or did he faint? Sunghwan couldn't carry his boss on his own. He'd have to wake him up and force him to walk.

Sunghwan sprinted back to 102 and climbed through his open window.

Sowon was sitting up in bed, looking tense and alert. "Where's my dad?"

"At the back gate." He didn't have time to explain. He ran into the living room and felt around Hyonsu's uniform shirt hanging on the sofa, looking for his car key. That man kept everything in his shirt pocket. He found his wallet and a notebook, but no car key. Sunghwan began to panic.

"What are you looking for?" Sowon was standing next to him.

"Do you know where your dad's car key is?"

"In the drawer under the sink. My mom took it away. She said he should walk to work to save money on gas."

"Can you go get them for me?"

The car key was in Sunghwan's hand in the blink of an eye. "Mr. Ahn, can I come with you?"

Sunghwan paused. He needed help, that was for sure. He'd seen Hyonsu in this state before; much as he didn't want to upset the boy, Sowon's father needed immediate medical attention, and having Sowon there would give him a sense of security. At least he hoped so. "If you can promise to stay calm, I'll take you with me."

When Sowon saw his dad on the ground, he didn't get upset or yell or cry. He knelt next to him and whispered, "Dad, wake up. Get up so we can go to the clinic."

Hyonsu opened his eyes, took Sunghwan's hand, and heaved himself up. It was a miracle. He leaned on Sunghwan and dragged his injured leg behind him, but he made it to the car.

It took more than two hours for the doctor to treat the wound, washing it with saline solution, stitching the top of the foot and the sole, taking X-rays, putting a cast on, running tests, hooking him up to an IV, and administering several shots. After it was over, Hyonsu fell asleep with Sowon beside him.

Sunghwan answered the doctor's questions in another room.

"This isn't the first time you've brought an injured person here in the middle of the night," the doctor said.

Sunghwan cast around for a simple explanation. "He's my boss. We live together."

"I informed his brother that he needs to be carefully monitored. How did this happen?"

Sunghwan stared at the doctor. "What do you mean, his brother?" Sunghwan asked.

"When he cut his wrist, his brother called."

Sunghwan cocked his head, confused. He had heard that Hyonsu's younger brother lived in Seoul. How had he known his brother had been injured?

"Anyway, he's a very lucky man," the doctor continued. "The wound is deep and there are hairline fractures on the bone, but it's not completely broken and the ligaments seem fine. When small animals are caught in those traps, their legs get cut off."

"Do you remember the caller's name?"

"Why, is there a problem?"

"I know for a fact that his brother didn't call."

"Then who was the man I talked to? He even gave me the patient's citizen ID number."

"Did you write the phone number down?"

"No, but it's probably still saved in the answering machine. It was only a couple of days ago."

"Could you find it?"

The doctor, looking uncomfortable, began searching. "I think this is it, judging by the time. It came right before lunch." It was a Sunchon area code at 11:50 a.m. on September 6. Sunghwan saved the number in his cell phone.

It was almost seven. He had to get Sowon home.

"He's getting painkillers so he'll feel better soon," Sunghwan explained as he entered the room. "It's a deep wound, though. He'll have to stay here for a while."

Sowon looked worried. "Here?"

"He'll have to go to a big hospital with an orthopedist on staff."

Sowon nodded.

"Go home and tell your mom exactly what I'm about to say, okay? Calmly, so she doesn't get scared."

"Okay."

"Tell her that he went on a walk in the arboretum this morning and got caught in an animal trap. We took him to the clinic, the doctor saw him, and now he's resting. Okay?"

Sowon nodded, and Sunghwan walked him to the front door. "Call me when you get home so I know you made it safe." Sowon nodded.

After the boy ran off, Sunghwan went into a telephone booth and called the number he'd saved in his cell. A woman's voice answered, "Thank you for calling Oh Yongje Dentistry."

Sunghwan hung up. Something was brewing, but he couldn't begin to guess what it could be. That frightened him. He knew what Yongje was capable of. He headed back into the clinic and went into Hyonsu's room. The man was moaning, weepy, as if he were having a nightmare. Sunghwan shook his shoulder. "Boss?"

Hyonsu opened his eyes and his body stiffened, his mouth open. He looked like he wasn't breathing.

"Boss."

Hyonsu's eyes drifted until they met Sunghwan's. A sigh leaked out of Hyonsu's dry lips. His breath was sour and hot.

"Are you okay? Do you want the doctor?"

"Can you get me some water?" Hyonsu asked after a long silence, sitting up in the bed.

Sunghwan poured water into a paper cup and set it on the bedside table. His boss gulped it down. He looked as if he wanted to say something. Sunghwan put a pillow behind Hyonsu's back.

"Have you ever been in a place where sorghum fields stretch all the way to the horizon?" Hyonsu suddenly blurted out.

"No, but I've seen small plots at the foot of mountains."

"In a field, sorghum grows tall and ripens into a blackish red in less than three months. On summer nights under a moon and in the breeze, it looks like a bloody, rolling ocean. I was born and raised in a place with fields like that, at the base of a rocky mountain. It was a dry, barren place, with fog coming up like smoke. Everything smelled salty because the ocean was just on the other side of the mountain. We would climb up the mountain and look out at a small village on the other side, and we could see a white lighthouse on a cliff." Hyonsu leaned back and looked out the window at the rain. "We called it Lighthouse Village. On dark nights when you couldn't see the moon, I would walk to the end of the field by myself to see the light flashing from the other side. I was eleven at the time, and I played baseball at school. I desperately wanted to go pro.

"The adults told us that we shouldn't go into the field when the moon wasn't out, since the sorghum was so tall and it was easy to get lost. Have you ever heard sorghum stalks talking?"

"No," Sunghwan said, pouring him a new cup of water.

"Sometimes, in the middle of summer, it can feel suffocating. The sun beats down and the air feels thick. Like you're trapped in a glass bottle. That's when you hear something strange, even though there is no wind. It sounds like waves or trees rustling.

"There was an old well in the middle of the field. It was really deep. If you leaned over the edge and looked down, all you saw was black. According to local superstition, if your shoes fell in the well, it would soon draw you in after them. Dozens of people were said to have become bewitched and jumped in; their bones were still inside. There was a kid who died in the well before my family moved there. After that, the villagers asked the owner to fill it up, but he refused; he just told people to stop trespassing. The owner lived in town, you see, not in the village." Hyonsu coughed.

"At night, I would sneak into the field alone. During the

day, my siblings were always with me. My father was injured fighting alongside the Americans in the Vietnam War, so my mother worked at the milling factory in town. My dad was a drunken lout and a good-for-nothing gambler. It always felt like we were walking on thin ice around him. What he liked and hated changed depending on the day. Like baseball. He loved baseball so much that he didn't even go gambling when a game was on TV. He would drink from a two-liter bottle of soju and stare at the screen.

"But as soon as I wanted to play, he started to despise the game. At the time, I was in charge of all the housework. I cooked, cleaned, and looked after my siblings. But when I started playing baseball, I would come home later in the afternoon, and didn't have as much time to devote to my other responsibilities. That's when he started beating me every day when I got home. I never understood why my mother was with a man like that. She never even gave us a cross look, no matter how hard things were. My father, on the other hand, was a mean drunk who beat whatever crossed his path when he was in a bad mood. Everyone knew when he came home drunk, because he'd sing at the top of his lungs. *Sergeant Choi, back from Vietnam . . .*" Hyonsu sang quietly as if reciting a poem.

"I wished someone would shut that mouth forever. And even when he wasn't around, things weren't easy; three kids were too much to handle for an eleven-year-old kid. Everything was my responsibility—when my sister broke our father's radio, when the baby got diarrhea, when Mother came home late. He beat me on behalf of everyone. When I complained, Mother would hug me, telling me that everyone depended on me. I was like my siblings' real father, she said, and she relied on me for everything. I didn't want to be a father or dependable. But I couldn't say that. I knew Mother had to work.

"That was why I went to the well in the middle of the night. I stood there and thought of the people I wanted gone, imagining I was throwing in their shoes: my father's, my brother's, my sister's, even the baby's colorful rubber shoes. Some nights I wanted to throw our entire house in. Afterward, I would feel terribly guilty, and I would take these bad thoughts out and throw them in, too. That gave me the patience to keep going another day or two.

"Then one Sunday around the end of summer, my gym teacher called the house. My mother answered, then told me to change into gym clothes and go to school. I went and there was a huge man, a baseball coach at some Gwangju elementary school. He'd heard from my gym teacher that I had potential as a catcher. That was the first time I tried on catcher's gear, and the first time I touched a real leather mitt. I was told to catch and throw and bat. The coach asked how old I was. I told him I was eleven, and he said it wasn't too late, and that I should practice so that I could be fully ambidextrous. He said I could bat left-handed, but I had to catch like a righty. He wanted to meet my parents—he said we should start now.

"I was anxious as I led him to my house. What if Father was home? At least my mother was home, too, I assured myself. My father turned out to be home that day. The coach

told my father that he wanted me to take up baseball officially, that I had the right physical build and a natural talent.
He said it would be harder for me to reach my full potential
if we waited until I was older. He said he'd heard a bit about
our family situation, and reassured my parents that he could
house and feed me. My father berated him until he left the
house. I followed the coach to his car, hoping he would take
me with him anyway. He seemed to feel bad for me. He took
a leather catcher's mitt out of his trunk, wrote his number on
the glove, and handed it to me, telling me to call him if my
parents changed their minds. I was so happy I couldn't sleep
that night. I cleaned and oiled it until it shined. I slept with it
under my pillow. I would beg my mother to give me permission, I vowed. But when I woke up the next morning, the
glove was gone. I found it cut into tiny pieces and scattered
all over the room. That asshole had come home drunk and
destroyed it. Tears gushed out of me." Hyonsu paused and
swallowed, his eyes red.

"He didn't come home that night. After midnight, I went
into the fields with a flashlight and my father's dress shoes.
He never wore those shoes and never had anywhere to wear
them to, but I was still expected to keep them shiny and polished. I walked through the dark, foggy field. It smelled
strongly of the ocean, and the sorghum stalks were chattering
loudly. I thought I could hear my father singing. I was so
scared, but I guess my hatred was stronger than my fear. I
thought I heard his voice when I got to the well. *Hyonsu*, it
called. *Hyonsu.* I threw one shoe in the well, shouting, *Shut
up! Don't ever come home again!* But then I heard him for
real: *Hyonsu . . . Hyonsuuu . . .* His voice was rattly, like he

had phlegm stuck in his throat. His voice grew smaller and bigger and kept calling me, over and over. I threw the other shoe in the well, shouting, *I hope you die! Just die. Don't come home.* His voice grew louder. *Hyonsu . . . Hyonsuuu.* I put my hands over my ears and ran away, but I couldn't get away from the voice and I couldn't find my way out of the sorghum. I thought I would be stuck in there all night. Maybe even forever. Then I realized I couldn't hear the voice anymore. I was in front of my house, sweaty, dirty, my pants torn.

"Only the following day did I learn that someone had discovered my father's clothes near the well. Everyone rushed into the field, and the head of the village shined a flashlight and thought he saw a body floating in the water below. A diver from Lighthouse Village came and was lowered down with a rope tied around his waist. From the bottom he tugged the rope twice and the men began to pull, until finally my father's body was hoisted out. I couldn't watch. He must have called me after falling in. So when I threw his shoes in, it wasn't the well calling me but my father.

"He wasn't the type of person who would kill himself, so everyone concluded that it was a drunken accident. We moved away soon after. But every night, in my sleep, I wandered the sorghum fields, taking shoes and throwing them in the well. The problem faded as I got older. But now it's back. The last six years were the most peaceful time of my whole life, and I didn't appreciate them. I realize that now. Even though I didn't achieve my dreams, I had Sowon. He's all I have left." Hyonsu hesitated.

Sunghwan patiently waited for him to continue.

"Can you give me a little time . . ."

The door flung open and Eunju flew into the room. Hyonsu stopped talking. Sunghwan stood up. She must have come straight from work; she was still in her uniform.

"What happened?" she asked.

"Aren't you late for work?" Hyonsu asked Sunghwan.

"Oh, right. Yes, I'm really late." Sunghwan made a show of looking at his watch. "I'll come back to get you after you're done getting your IV drip."

"Have you seen Sowon's shoes?" Hyonsu asked.

Sunghwan looked around. When they got to the clinic, Hyonsu had been empty-handed. In fact, Hyonsu hadn't had them when Sunghwan had taken Sowon to the gate. "I'm sure they're in the car. I'll find them."

They weren't there. They weren't on the path, either, or near the gate. He retraced his steps; Hyonsu had been holding on to the shoes when he left him to get the car key. But now they were nowhere to be found. It seemed they had disappeared while he was gone, when Hyonsu was out of it. Had someone taken them? The person who set the trap? There weren't normally animal traps in that area, so it was hard not to think it was intentional. Sunghwan wasn't sure what was going on, but he understood now that for Hyonsu, it would have been critical to protect Sowon's shoes. Throwing them in the lake would signify condemning his son to death. That was why he always hid Sowon's shoes in the washing machine.

SUNGHWAN PARKED HYONSU'S CAR by the dam security office. Inside, he sat at the desk and wrote all the information he had gathered about Yongje's recent actions down in his notebook. *Called the hospital and impersonated Hyonsu's brother. Followed him—knows about sleepwalking. Possibly laid a trap to get him seriously but not fatally injured. Possibly took Sowon's shoes. May have orchestrated incident with the shaman.*

The only explanation was that Yongje thought Hyonsu was the killer. But if he had evidence of that, why hadn't he handed it over to the police? Yongje had done the same thing when he found Sunghwan's fishing line. Was he planning to handle things himself?

Was he planning to use Sowon to manipulate Hyonsu?

He downloaded the "Atlantis" file from the cloud and began to review the video, looking for something he might have missed. He stopped, a chill running down his spine. He knew, deep down, that part of the reason he had been taking such diligent, attentive notes was purely selfish: this was the plot of a novel, better than anything he'd come up with in years. He felt weak. How could he even think of using such terrible events for his own gain?

～

On Friday afternoon, Yongje got a phone call from a Supporter as he was getting ready to go home from work.

"I found the car repair shop."

"Oh? Where?"

"Ilsan," said the Supporter.

"Near his apartment?"

"Yeah. It occurred to me that he might have gone somewhere near there when I was looking around Seoul. And I found it on my first try. It's the closest one to their building. He left it there the morning of August twenty-eighth and picked it up later that afternoon. Paid with a credit card. But it seems like the police are chasing that lead."

"What?"

"I heard two detectives came by earlier in a shop I stopped by before heading to Ilsan. One was in his midforties and the other was really young. I was a little faster this time, but I know they'll get there eventually."

The jock and his partner, Yongje thought. He hadn't seen them in the last few days. "Can we make sure the mechanics in Ilsan don't talk?"

"I don't know how. There are records."

Yongje sat down, dismayed. If the detectives got to Ilsan within the next day, all of his work would be for naught. They could call their colleagues here and arrest Choi immediately. But he couldn't set the plan in motion sooner. "Stake out that place until the twelfth. If they show up, call me right away."

The Supporter would have to distract them somehow, perhaps even ram his car into theirs. Yongje put a few 5cc syringes and one box of Peridol in his bag. He'd ordered them from the pharmaceutical company on Monday. He remembered to include the Valium.

A TOUR BUS and a dozen cars were parked in front of the conservancy. Kids were getting off the bus and lining up. Yongje nodded at his fellow doctors milling about and pulled up to the dam security office, where Park and another guard were on duty. He signed the visitor log. "Where's the head of security?" he asked casually.

"He's not here today," Park said.

"Oh, I didn't know that the head of security gets a day off on a weekday."

"He doesn't. He called in sick because he hurt his foot."

"Must be pretty serious for him to call in."

"He's just off for the day. He said he'll be back tomorrow night."

Yongje handed the visitor log back. "He's taking the night shift even though he's hurt?"

Park glanced at Yongje quizzically.

"I was going to invite him to the garden party," Yongje explained. "The kids want to meet the brave head of security who guards the dam."

"I don't know if that would be possible."

Choi had decided to do everything Yongje had hoped for. If he stayed home, an innocent guard would have to be sacrificed. Yongje assumed a disappointed expression. "All of you are working so hard, night and day."

"Yes, well." Park pointed to the main entrance of the conservancy. "Go on in. The deputy director is there."

The tour began with an exhibit about the dam. They listened to the deputy director give a long-winded explanation, showing them a digital restoration of the flooded village and the aerial view, and talking about how the dam was constructed and all the safety and security systems. Another thirty minutes were devoted to the hydroelectric power plant. "This is an automated power plant with remote-control systems. In the future, many power plants will adopt these systems. We're trying them out as a pilot project."

The kids walked around the second-story passageway that went around the turbine, looking curiously at the machinery below their feet.

"Any questions?" asked the deputy director.

A kid raised his hand. "If nobody's here, who controls the power plant?"

"Oh, it's done by headquarters. We have computers doing it."

"So they can see the dam all the way from headquarters?" the kid asked.

"Yes. A low-earth-orbit satellite conveys information to their screens."

"Can the satellite see inside the dam?"

"Yes, as well as the weather and rainfall. You sit at your desk and look at the information sent by the satellite."

"Maybe the head of the conservancy here can show us that," Yongje inserted.

The deputy director didn't correct Yongje's use of the wrong, inflated title, and he didn't look displeased by it, either. They trailed after the deputy director to the central control room. The deputy director told them what happened in the office outside the control room, explaining the water quality measuring device, the text display that showed rainfall amounts and water levels, the aerial view, and the warning systems for flooding. "Before we enter, please remember that we cannot touch any of the machines there. Listen with your ears, look with your eyes, and keep your hands by your sides!"

The staff in the control room left when the tour group filtered in. The windowless room wasn't that large. One wall was overtaken by large machines: the satellite video transmission equipment, along with the security system, the call system, the alarm system, and the floodgate monitoring box. On the opposite wall were CCTV monitors on wheeled cabinets. Five desks faced the door. Each desk had a computer monitor, printer, documents, and pen holder, and Yongje spotted several mini cactus plants. A CCTV for the interior and a flood forecast warning system were near the door. Two unidentifiable machines stood below them and two armchairs and a round table were in the middle of the room.

The children were most interested in the satellite video transmission system and the floodgate monitoring box. Between the two was a big pillar; the deputy director stood in front of it to address the group. "Who knew that Seryong Dam was made by blocking the river?"

"Me!"

"This dam is a lake with a lot of inflow, so the conservancy pays particular attention to the amount of water we send out through the floodgates. If the amount is more than usual or if the water level goes up, the evacuation alarm deploys automatically. The screen at the entrance to the maintenance bridge plays a role in maintaining the current water level. We try to maintain the level at one hundred thirty-five feet during flooding or normal pool level during drought, and this floodgate control monitor right behind me does the work of opening and closing the floodgates. We have five floodgates maintained by several security systems. The monitoring box is controlled both remotely, through satellites, and manually, at the gates themselves. You'll see that later."

The deputy director then turned to the CCTV, explaining

each part of the dam, zooming in closer on certain screens. Yongje and another doctor stood in front of the monitoring box, which was huge but simple to operate. Under the master button, there was a button for each of the five gates, with a ± symbol on them.

After the tour, the bus drove the kids up to the maintenance bridge by the floodgates. Sunghwan came out to greet the group. The head of the dermatology clinic stood next to the deputy director, asking all sorts of questions, and Yongje stood near them, listening. This was the first time he was seeing the floodgates up close. They loomed like buildings from their spot a hundred feet below the bridge. An emergency floodgate, called the stopper, was about three feet closer to the bridge. Between the two gates were several thick chains that were operated by pulleys. On the concrete wall was a ladder, and above the gates was a searchlight and a CCTV camera pointing down. That was where the manual switchgears were. The entrance to all of that was secured with a padlock.

"If there's a flood and you have to open all five gates, how much water would flow through?" asked the dermatologist.

"About two thousand five hundred tons per second," the deputy director said.

"Wow. That means in ten minutes it would be a million tons! Can the area below handle that?"

"Well, the evacuation alarm would go off and appropriate measures would be taken before anything like that ever happens."

"What if nobody's here? At night or on weekends."

"It's remotely controlled, which is more accurate than if a human did it."

"I see. But will there be enough time to evacuate once the alarm goes off? I live in Sunchon." The dermatologist looked nervous.

The deputy director reassured the dermatologist, saying that it would take an hour and a half for the water to travel seven miles. And though Sunchon was only eight and a half miles away, it was on much higher ground than Seryong Lake, giving the residents of that city plenty of time to evacuate.

"But that would mean it would be more of a problem for the arboretum and the village," Yongje interjected.

"As I mentioned, that's not something that would happen," the deputy director said confidently. "When we anticipate flooding, we discharge water in advance. Even if the water level goes a few feet above the normal pool level, the emergency manual assistance mode kicks in." He pointed to the stopper that was open. "And even if the floodgates opened by accident for some reason, it still wouldn't be a problem. Usually the stopper is open, like it is now, but in an emergency, it would block the gates and the water. Our security system is very advanced."

The dermatologist nodded, satisfied. The children clapped, though Yongje wasn't sure if they were happy because of the deputy director's answer or because the tour was finally over. Yongje looked down at the floodgates, pleased. He had gathered all the information he needed. The only thing that bothered him was Sunghwan. As he studied the stopper and the switchgears to the floodgates, he had the sense he was being watched; when he turned around, the idiot's dopey eyes were staring at him. Sunghwan didn't look away or appear embarrassed to be caught. Instead, he continued to observe Yongje carefully. Before Yongje got into his car, he looked back; Sunghwan was still standing there, watching.

The party was ready by the fountain in the arboretum. A cook was beginning to barbecue at one end of the long buffet table. Eunju ushered the kids in and seated them at the table, warning them that they couldn't talk or move until everyone got settled. She looked so grim, her face so pale, that the party quickly turned solemn. The dance music coming from the speakers sounded like a dirge. Everyone murmured, not daring to speak up. The kids were probably hungry, but nobody ventured to the buffet line.

Yongje went up to the front. "Welcome to Seryong Arboretum, everyone," he said into the microphone.

He was greeted by scattered applause.

"Let's have some fun now. We have karaoke, games, and a light show! Enjoy yourselves, and I hope you'll make some wonderful memories." He pulled some kids to the buffet line and the event company set off the fireworks. It was a little early, but it was effective in making the kids get out of their seats. Ten minutes later, the party was going strong. The kids who lived in company housing hadn't come, as Yongje had expected. Usually those houses sat empty on Friday nights, as the employees went home or on family outings on weekends. Today it seemed about two-thirds empty. Not many cars were parked in the lot.

Yongje snuck out and went home. It was time to meet the Supporters. He didn't love revealing his face, but he couldn't really avoid it this time; they had to synchronize their watches. At six on the dot, Yongje sat down with the two Supporters in his living room. They looked big and dependable. He hoped their brains were as reliable as their heft. He handed them two small parcels: one had three ampules of Peridol and three syringes, and the other contained a key to the dock and another to the *Josong*. He had borrowed the boat key from the garbage disposal company employee he met while he was circling Hansoldung and made a copy; the employee had understood the father's wish to bury his daughter's remains on Hansoldung, encouraged by the thick envelope of cash Yongje handed over.

"I'll keep the rear entrance to the arboretum open, and the CCTV won't be working, so you shouldn't have any problems. After it's done, wait at the rest area for me to call," Yongje explained.

They nodded.

"Did you go over the order of things?" Yongje asked.

They nodded again.

"Any parts you need clarification on?"

One Supporter played with the drugs. "Can't we do it our way and not use . . ."

"Do it my way," Yongje snapped. There was no room for mistakes. Four strong men lived in 103, and there were still some people in company housing. If it took too long or if people noticed, none of it would work. "You can forget about getting paid if you don't follow my orders."

IT WAS RAINING again the next day, a Saturday. By the time it stopped in the evening, what he'd worried about hadn't happened; the police detectives must still be running around Seoul. He called Yim and asked him to come by.

"You need to go to Andong," he said.

Yim looked at him in surprise.

"I heard about a five-hundred-year-old gingko tree at Sangsa Arboretum there. It looks like it'll go on the auction block. I'd like you to go down and take a look. If it looks good, we should get it for our arboretum."

"You want me to go now?" the old man asked incredulously.

"Yes. I just heard about it."

"I can go tomorrow. The tree won't go anywhere. Later tonight, I'm supposed to . . ."

"No, I want you to go now."

"But even if I do, I'll get there in the middle of the night. What good would it do to look at a tree in the dark?"

"Spend the night there. Then you can go in and look around discreetly first thing in the morning. I don't want it known that you're there to see it; that might alert the competition and drive up the price. Once you do, call me right away."

Yim left, looking unhappy.

It was seven. Yongje put the Valium in his pocket, took a flashlight, and left through the gate at the edge of the arboretum. He saw footprints on the muddy ground; it looked like they belonged to the kid from 102 based on the size of the prints. He imagined the boy rolling around with the cat in the barn. Yongje smiled. How happy would the two of them be if he let them spend the night together forever?

He headed to the barn. Nobody was there. One bowl was half-filled with food and the other bowl had clean water in it. He dumped out some water and mixed in the Valium. He left and walked slowly along the lakeshore road. Summer hung in the air; the breeze was hot, the air was sticky, and sweat beaded on his skin. Fog was blanketing the lake. The pine tree on Hansoldung looked like a solitary gravestone. He stopped by the intake tower and looked up at the CCTV. Was Choi at work by now? His cell rang, startling him. Was it his man in Ilsan?

It was the Supporter tasked with finding Hayong. "Is her friend's name Myong Ina?"

Yongje rolled that name on his tongue a few times. Myong Ina. Myong Ina. "Maybe."

"She lives in France. I haven't been able to confirm yet that your wife is with her."

Yongje's heart leaped. He managed to suppress his impatience. "Where does she live?"

"In Rouen, about eighty miles from Paris."

"And you have her information?"

"Yes. She works as an art therapist in a psychiatric hospital. Do you want me to head over there?"

"No, let's discuss that later. Send me the details first." Yongje hung up, his blood pounding in his veins. The bitch was swanning around France; meanwhile, her daughter had become a fistful of ash.

⁓

"Make sure to put the main entrance barrier down early," Yim said as he stood in front of the security office window. He was wearing a backpack and a hiking jacket, and holding a hat.

Eunju stood up. "Are you going somewhere?"

"To Andong, just for a day or so." Yim put his hat on. "Look, don't worry about doing the rounds. Nothing is going to happen if we don't do them for one night. Lock the door and don't open the window unless it's someone you know."

Eunju was surprised; Yim was generally gruff and quiet. "Why?"

"You're a woman here all by herself." Yim went off, grumbling, "That's why I said we can't hire a woman . . ."

Why the sudden burst of concern? Eunju wondered. Suddenly, she realized that she had never actually been on duty alone. The management office was adjacent to the security office, and Yim was always there; he could pop out if she pressed the call button. The refrigerator whirred, and she flinched and looked up. The streetlight was shining yellow in the fog, and trees rustled above the dark windows of the company housing units. Her heart began to pound. The arboretum suddenly made her wary. She'd never wondered why Yongje had hired her. It never even occurred to her that Yim would oppose her employment. She had just been relieved to have found a job. For the first time, she realized that an old man and a woman weren't nearly enough to effectively guard this place. A proper guard would have to patrol the vast, remote estate by himself in the middle of the night and be able to send away drunken strangers. He would have to watch the main entrance and operate the barrier for residents at all hours without falling asleep or becoming distracted. She really didn't meet the job requirements.

When she was on duty, Yim handled the night patrol. He

was also the one who let the cars in and out and monitored the CCTV. All she did was sit in the office and watch TV, talk to Yongju on the phone, or nap on the makeshift cot. She'd interpreted Yim's behavior as kindness. But she hadn't interviewed with the old man. He must have opposed her being hired after the fact, since it was obvious to him who would have to compensate for her. She had been foolish; she had focused only on her own situation and had been blinded by what she perceived to be her stroke of good luck. Why had Yongje hired her? Did all of her problems stem from her tendency toward willful blindness? She had ignored her husband's strange behavior, for one. But even now, she still wasn't ready to face the truth. When Yongju called back and asked if she'd found out anything else, she blurted out, "I did, but I don't know what it means."

"Tell me," Yongju said.

Eunju hesitated.

"I'll be able to look at it more objectively."

Eunju was afraid that her sister might reach the same terrifying conclusion that she had in her subconscious, but at the same time, she hoped that Yongju would tell her she was delusional. First, she laid out the information she'd discovered, then she told her what had happened on Friday.

At seven in the morning, Sowon had appeared at the security office to tell her about Hyonsu's injuries, clearly trying very hard not to forget a single word. She didn't have to ask who coached him; it had to have been Sunghwan. She was stunned, then worried, then angry. Why would Yim lay a trap in the woods, where people walked around? Why did Hyonsu go there in the dark? She wanted to run over to the clinic right away, but people were beginning to go about their day; she had to stay at her post. She called Yim to complain, but the old man said he hadn't laid a single trap in forty years.

As soon as Gwak came and took over, she ran to the clinic. She vowed to be nice to Hyonsu and figure out what was going on: how he got hurt, why he was acting so strangely these days, why he wanted a divorce. She wanted confirmation that it wasn't because of what she feared. She went over what she would say to him. *Hyonsu, tell me what's going on. I can help and I'm on your side. Don't hide anything from me; tell me everything. I'll fix it. All of it.*

She got to the clinic and went straight to the room where her husband was hooked up to an IV, deciding she would talk to the doctor later. Hyonsu was sitting up in bed and Sung-hwan was sitting beside him; they looked guilty when she entered, as if they'd just been complaining about her. Sunghwan left and her husband lay back down and closed his eyes. Eunju looked down at Hyonsu's foot. The cast went up to his calf, and his bloodied, blackened toes poked out at the bottom. This was a more serious injury than she'd expected.

"Hyonsu," she said as gently as she could.

He didn't respond.

She nudged him on the shoulder. "Hyonsu?"

"We have to send in the divorce papers today," he answered, his eyes still closed.

She stared at him as he breathed rhythmically, his expression peaceful, but she knew he wasn't asleep. She was standing in front of a door that never opened for her. He hid behind that placid expression every time they fought, and it made her crazy. The more she talked, the more he withdrew, his mouth closed and his ears plugged. "Hyonsu!" she ended up yelling.

A nurse opened the door and poked her head in. She pointed to a sign on the wall that said *Quiet*.

Thirty minutes later, she decided to retreat. It would be faster to poke around elsewhere than try to pry that mouth open. Outside, nobody was waiting in front of the exam room, so she knocked and walked inside. The doctor looked up from the desk. "Yes?"

"I'm the wife of the patient Choi Hyonsu." She sat down even though she wasn't invited to. "I heard you treated him this morning. What happened?"

The doctor put the chart down and stared at her over his glasses for a long while. "A few days ago, a man claiming to be his brother called about his arm and I explained the situation to him, then his staffer brings him in and tells me that the man who called earlier isn't his brother, and now you say you're his wife. Who's to say someone isn't going to come in after you and tell me the patient isn't married?"

Had Hyonsu been there before? She remembered the bandage on his left wrist. Hyonsu's brother? "This man who called a few days ago. Do you have his phone number? And anyway, shouldn't you confirm someone's identity before you release sensitive medical information to them?"

"Your housemate already asked about the impersonator's phone number," the doctor said grouchily.

Eunju suppressed her anger. "If I can prove that I'm his wife, can you tell me what's going on? I can give you my citizen ID number or . . ."

"The impersonator gave his own address and citizen ID number, and even gave me the patient's ID number."

Eunju's mouth hung open as she wondered for a moment if her brother-in-law had really called. It didn't make any sense; she talked to her sister every day and still didn't know her citizen ID number. Who would have their sibling's ID number memorized? "Why don't I call my brother-in-law?" She didn't wait for permission. She turned the doctor's phone toward her, punched in her brother-in-law's number, and hit the speaker button.

"Hello?"

"Hi, Jongu, it's your sister-in-law," she said.

"Oh, hi."

"What's the meaning of the Chinese characters for your and your brother's names?"

"Why do you ask?"

"It's for Sowon's homework," she said.

"Oh." Her brother-in-law laughed and told her what their names meant.

"By the way, did you call the clinic a few days ago asking about Hyonsu?"

"No, I didn't know you had a clinic there."

"Oh, okay. I'll give you a call later," Eunju said and hung up. "You see? Please, Doctor. Tell me why he came here before, what was wrong with him, what you told the man who called you, what his phone number was, and how my husband is doing."

The doctor acquiesced. "Do you know about your husband's left arm?"

"Yes, he calls it his bad arm. It freezes up sometimes."

"It freezes?"

"He was a baseball player, and his left arm used to go limp sometimes when he played. It got better after he quit. Did he come here for that?"

The doctor explained what had happened a few days before and showed her the phone number the impostor had called from. She entered it into her phone. That number was already stored in her phone as "Boss's office." She felt dizzy. She closed her cell phone and listened to the doctor in a daze. She got up, paid, and went home, still confused. Thoughts whirled in her head. Why was Oh Yongje so interested in her husband? He must have done a background check on Hyonsu if he had his citizen ID number. Was the trap a coincidence? How much did Sunghwan know about all of this?

Hyonsu didn't come home even after two. She called the clinic and was told that he was still getting his infusion. She called Sunghwan. "Something's going on with Hyonsu, isn't it? And you know what it's about, don't you?"

Sunghwan was silent. "I'm waiting, too," he said finally.

"For what?"

"I'm waiting to find out what this is all about."

She was more confused than ever. Since when had Hyonsu's bad arm come back? It's your fault, she told herself. You didn't care when he slept in the living room or why he was drunk every day. You didn't even care that he hurt his hand. Then again, she wasn't in the right frame of mind to ask him about it; once someone who drinks daily says he wants a divorce and insults her by saying how terrible it is to live with her, how could she focus on a bandage? She went to work her shift at the garden party, torn. Hours later, she cleaned up and went home to check on Hyonsu, and he seemed fine. Sung-hwan was teaching him a baseball game on the computer in the living room. She went into her bedroom to rest. But when she came out later to make dinner, nobody was there. She called the dam security office and her husband answered.

"Where is everyone?" she asked.

"Sunghwan and Sowon were here, but now they're on their way home."

"What are you doing there?"

"Night shift."

"But you're not well. And you're the director. Why not assign someone else?"

"It's none of your business. Just sign those papers." He hung up.

Eunju glared at the receiver. None of your business? All he did now was talk about the divorce papers. Why did he need a divorce that badly? She slammed the phone down and went back out.

Eunju finished her story. Yongju said, "Maybe . . ."

Eunju's heart sank. "Maybe what?"

"Well. Could he be linked to the incident somehow?" Yongju was voicing Eunju's deepest fears.

"What are you talking about?" Eunju snapped.

"I mean, why else would the detectives go all the way to the repair shop?"

"I don't know."

"Think about it," urged Yongju. "How weird is it that he asked you to take care of Sowon? He would never do that. You need to talk to him and get him to tell you everything.

The quiet ones are the ones who get into the most trouble."
Yongju sounded certain.

"There's no way," Eunju protested, but even she knew it
might be true. Everything was pointing to that. She remembered how odd he'd looked one morning, his clothes wet and
his feet muddy. He had a bandage on his hand and his face
was haggard and stubbly. He had been so deeply asleep that
she hadn't been able to shake him awake. She should have
known something was wrong when he first told her to get
out. He would never say that to her. Her rage and disappoint-
ments and disgust had gradually blinded her to his suffering.
She had been staring at the truth all along. If there was something Hyonsu would protect with his life, if he had to throw
everything away—including himself—to protect someone, it
would be Sowon. The shaman. The trap. Hyonsu's injury, his
insistence on taking the night shift, and now Yim's sudden
trip. Her hands began to shake. Her stomach churned. It no
longer mattered what Hyonsu had done. All she wanted to
know was what was going on. She wanted to know what Oh
Yongje was trying to do to her family.

"Are you listening?" Yongju asked.

Eunju heard a car pull up outside. It was a car from
C-Com, the security company servicing the arboretum. Two
men got out. "Hold on, the security company is here," Eunju
said, and she unlocked the window, holding the phone to her
ear. She looked down at the CCTV screen and noticed that
the camera at the rear entrance was out. The main entrance
barricade was down. That was strange. What happened to the
CCTV, and how did the car get in? Maybe she forgot to close

the rear entrance? She suddenly remembered Yim's warning. Don't open the window unless it's someone you know.

Everything snapped into place. Her eyes grew wide. Whatever Yongje was planning, it was supposed to go down tonight, right now. Before she could close the window again, one of the men reached in and dragged her across the sill. She tried to scream but couldn't make a sound; the world was falling away.

~

The game ended in two rounds. Hyonsu looked up from the monitor.

"No matter how quickly you go through, you probably won't get to the third level until tomorrow night," Sunghwan had said the night before as he taught him the game *Superhero*. He had been right; it wasn't easy. And Hyonsu only had his clumsy right hand to play with. But thanks to the game, he had managed to stay awake all night. He hadn't even dozed off. His head hurt, and his shoulder ached, but it was okay. The pain in his left foot was increasingly intense, though, and he felt feverish again.

He went back to the clinic in the morning, and the doctor took his temperature and cocked his head. He ran a blood test and told Hyonsu his white blood cell count was high, then cut a small rectangle in the cast to take a look at the wound. Signs of infection, he said, and told Hyonsu to go see an orthopedist. Hyonsu looked down at his foot, which was red and puffy. His toes looked like black skipping stones.

When he was playing professionally, Hyonsu used to frequent the orthopedist. He knew what the signs of infection meant; he would be admitted to the hospital. He couldn't go there right now, and there was no point, anyway; what he really needed was a single night without pain or fever. "Is there anything you can do?" he asked.

The doctor looked uncomfortable. "I'm an emergency medicine specialist, not an orthopedist. If we don't treat it, you could get septicemia."

"If you can make it so that I can get through today, I promise I'll go to the doctor tomorrow."

The doctor gave Hyonsu a look but acquiesced. He cut the cast off, washed the wound with saline, applied antibiotics, poured disinfectant on it, placed a thick bit of gauze, and secured a cast up to his calf with elastic bandages. He took the stitches out of his wrist. The wound had healed nicely. Then the doctor took a needle and poked the end of his pointer finger, but Hyonsu couldn't feel it.

"I'm not going to be here starting this afternoon. If this gets worse tonight, you have to go to the emergency room at a big hospital. And when you're there, you need to show them your left arm."

Hyonsu put his left arm back in the sling and nodded.

The doctor gave him antibiotics and a shot of painkiller and handed him some pills. "This should tide you over. Take two pills every four hours."

Hyonsu had taken the first pills around 9:00 at night, and now it was 11:25. He took his cell phone out and called Sunghwan.

"Yes?"

A shock of relief went down Hyonsu's neck. "Still not sleeping?"

"I was watching a movie."

"And Sowon?"

"He's sleeping."

Hyonsu felt a twinge in his heart. He wanted Sowon to sleep peacefully like this every night, to remember Choi Hyonsu not as a murderer but as his father. Would that be possible? "Okay." He hung up. He wanted to hear Sowon's voice, but it might be better this way. He wasn't going to call Eunju, either. If she said his name, he might not be able to control himself. She had been a source of pain for him for so long, but now he was grateful for her steeliness and her ability to fiercely protect their son. She was trustworthy, unlike him. He felt bad about putting her through this.

He went back to his game. He was trying to kill time, but he kept losing. His pain was slowing him down. He pushed his chair back and leaned against it, closing his eyes. Maybe he was nervous.

Eunju's voice, calling his name in the clinic that day, rang in his mind. There was a note of forgiveness in it. He was so touched by that. When she called his name again, he felt his will crumble. He really might have told her everything if she called him gently one more time, so he was relieved when she snapped, "Hyonsu!" That helped him recover. He'd thought he would have a chance to choose between confession and suicide, but when he stepped in the trap he realized it was all over. He hadn't completely lost consciousness, but, blinking in and out, he'd lost Sowon's shoes. Pain and insight dawned on him at the same time. Someone had put the trap there. It had to be Yongje. He was the only person who had a reason to want him to suffer so badly. As he told Sunghwan about his childhood, he had finally found the courage to do what he needed to do.

He tried to revive his focus and figure out what lay ahead based on what Sunghwan had told him about Yongje—pretending to be his brother, tailing him in the middle of the night, carving a club in his basement . . . He couldn't figure out the last piece of the puzzle: Yongje arranging the tour of the dam. Other than that, he came to the same conclusion he'd reached when he was lying by the gate. Yongje wanted Hyonsu to repay his debt in the way that he decided. That was why Hyonsu had volunteered for the night shift. If Yongje was the one who had taken Sowon's shoes, it had to be a warning, a preview of what might happen if Hyonsu refused to play along. If Yongje was coming for him, he wanted to be out of the house, so as not to endanger Sowon and Eunju. He hadn't decided how he was going to deal with him, but hoped he would know when the moment arrived.

Hyonsu fidgeted and let out a groan. His entire left leg felt like it was convulsing. It was 11:55. Time was flowing slowly. He took out the pills from his shirt pocket and slid them in his mouth. He got up and turned toward the water cooler but stopped. He had glimpsed something. He turned slowly to check. Yongje was standing in front of the small security window, a strange smile on his face. Hyonsu chewed the pills and swallowed them before opening the window.

"Are you okay?" Yongje asked. "You look pale." He was dressed all in black.

"How can I help you?"

"I was worried."

"About?"

"I heard you got caught in a trap in the woods." Yongje's eyes lingered on Hyonsu's left arm in the sling.

Hyonsu drew in a deep breath to stay calm. "So you came here in the middle of the night?"

"I found these nearby." Yongje took the Nike basketball shoes out of his bag. "Could these be your son's?"

This wasn't entirely out of left field, but it still knocked the wind out of him. "Yes, those are Sowon's," he managed.

Yongje placed the shoes on the windowsill.

Hyonsu leaned on the desk, watching.

"Can I use the phone?" Yongje asked. "I left my cell at home. I have to call the management office."

Hyonsu looked down at the phone. He needed to make his offer—I'll give you anything you want if you can guarantee what I need. Even though he was injured, it wouldn't be impossible to subdue Yongje; by the looks of him, he wasn't a fighter. Hyonsu picked up the phone. Balancing on his right foot, he twisted to set it down on the outer ledge of the window. Yongje reached out and yanked Hyonsu toward him. Hyonsu's head smashed against the stainless-steel window frame, hard. His eye, nose, and lips were smashed, and his teeth flew out of his mouth. A clot of blood rattled in his throat and everything grew fuzzy. Hyonsu plastered his cheek against the window and spat out blood.

Yongje took out his club. By the time Hyonsu saw it, it was too late. It came down forcefully on his wrist, bruising muscle and breaking bone. He felt a pillar of fire roar up his arm as his mind sank deeper into its swamp. Everything began to disappear. Through his shuttering eyelids, Hyonsu looked at his hand dangling from his broken wrist and saw a syringe stuck in his forearm. His visual field cleaved in two, turning red like a sunset, then spliced into four before disappearing completely. Right before he lost consciousness, a thought crossed his darkening mind, but then it vanished like a shooting star.

∼

O pen your eyes, Choi."

Hyonsu couldn't. Something sticky coated them. He could hear the hum of a machine. Where was he?

"Open your eyes." A hiking boot stomped on Hyonsu's left foot.

With a jolt of pain, his eyes opened.

"Awake now?"

Hyonsu gritted his teeth. He blinked away the blood crusted around his eyes. He was sitting on a chair, his arms tied behind its tall back. His torso, thighs, and ankles were tied, too. This was his office chair, but he clearly wasn't in the office.

"I know you killed my daughter," Yongje said calmly.

Hyonsu moved his right hand and felt a sharp pain shoot up his arm. He managed to stop himself from screaming. He ran his tongue along the tops of his teeth but felt only gums; his front teeth were gone.

"I don't want you to bleed out before we get to play."

Hyonsu wasn't afraid. He was prepared. It didn't matter whether he died by his own hand or by this man's. The only thing he cared about was striking a deal first.

"Look at me."

Hyonsu tried to recall the last thought that had flashed through his mind before he lost consciousness. It had been something important.

"Can you hear me? Do you need me to help you?"

Hyonsu looked up. Yongje stepped back to let him take a good look around. They were in the system control center. Yongje must have taken the keys from the security office. It suddenly dawned on Hyonsu that Yongje had used the tour of the dam as an excuse to assess the room beforehand.

The clock read 1:49 a.m. Nearly two hours had passed. Hyonsu was next to a desk, and one of the armchairs and the table that were usually in the center of the room had been pushed up against the wall. In their place was a CCTV screen. Yongje was sitting in the other armchair, his legs crossed. He held a remote control in one hand and the club in the other.

"You'll like this show," Yongje said. He chose one screen out of twelve and set it to full screen. It was just gray fog.

Hyonsu glanced at the machines around the room. He was surrounded by switches and buttons that controlled things like the floodgates, the alarms, the security systems. Of all the mechanisms, the remote-control monitoring box was the most important. It was still blinking green, which meant it was operating normally. Was Yongje planning to interfere with the floodgates?

If abnormal conditions were detected at the dam, the systems at headquarters would immediately take control. But he knew from his orientation when he started his job that the systems in this control center could override headquarters, and the manual switchgears at the top of the floodgates could override everything. The headquarters' system kicked in only when there was no resistance on the ground; either the changes to the water level had to be so minimal as not to be detected, or the situation would have to be such that any interference would be rendered useless. He squinted at the CCTV screen.

"Just wait," Yongje said. "The spotlights are going to go on soon. But before that happens, tell me about the night you ran over my daughter. She was still alive after you hit her. She would have died if you left her there. So why did you go the extra step?"

Why did he? Hyonsu had asked himself that very question hundreds of times.

Yongje stood up, shifting the club in his hand. "Answer." He struck Hyonsu on the chin.

This time Hyonsu couldn't even let out a sound; his eyes rolled toward the back of his head and the fragments of conjecture he had piled up to deduce Yongje's plan scattered. Something rattled, maybe a broken piece of jaw or a tooth. Hyonsu looked down, shaking, as blood poured out of his mouth. The floor turned red. Only his feet looked white; one bare and the other encased in a cast. Where was his shoe? Did Yongje take it off to bind his ankles together? What had he been wearing, his dress shoe? His boot? His sneaker?

A light began to flicker in his cloudy consciousness. As he tried to extract it, he forgot his pain for a second. A naked horror swept over him and his heart pumped violently. He had finally figured out what had flickered in his mind right before he lost consciousness: Sowon's basketball shoes. They hadn't just been a warning. They hinted at Yongje's revenge plan. That was why Hyonsu was in the control room—Yongje was going to force him to be a spectator, a helpless witness.

On the dark, foggy screen, a wave of light blinked and streamed in from the edges, cutting through the wall of fog. Hansoldung came into view, but the ground and the brush were not visible, only the old, twisted pine tree. The light moved like the second hand on a clock, passing along the branches and shining on the trunk, illuminating someone sitting, tied to it—terror-filled eyes, mouth covered in tape, water risen to his chest. Sowon.

Hyonsu's chest felt as if it would burst. The tendons in his neck bulged and his blood shot through his heart. Sowon's soundless scream cleaved his windpipe. His son's terror shredded his own body. He remembered what Sunghwan had told him. At normal levels, Hansoldung poked out a foot above water, while low levels revealed its long ridge. And when the water reached flood levels, the entire thing sank sixteen feet below the surface of the lake. Hyonsu's heart pounded and black clouds stanched the flow of his thoughts.

"Why did you throw her in the lake?" Yongje asked again, settling in the armchair.

Hyonsu searched for the text display indicating the water level. Shit. The screen in the control room that showed water levels was too far for him to see. His eyes bored into the CCTV. The searchlight vanished, and Sowon was hidden behind fog. Hyonsu couldn't move. His throat burned. "Let him go. Then I'll tell you everything." Hyonsu tried to speak calmly, but his voice came out strained and desperate. "You can kill me however you want. I'll do whatever you want."

Yongje smiled. "I know you will. But first you'll tell me why you killed my daughter, and then you'll watch your son die. After you tell me everything, I'll confirm that your son is dead and open the floodgates to gradually let the water out. The control systems won't react, because your son's too short for the alarms to go off. Don't worry, I'll bring his body back and leave it in your car. Your wife's, too. It would be too cruel for me to separate a family forever."

A huge wave lifted Hyonsu and crashed down; he'd completely forgotten about Eunju.

"With your family in the car, you'll drive at full speed into the lake. The murderer, unable to cope with his guilt, confesses to his crime and ends everything in a spectacular murder-suicide." Yongje took a voice recorder from his jacket pocket. "You like my plan?"

Hyonsu was shaking, enraged. He tried to breathe, struggling to regain his calm.

"Talk," ordered Yongje.

At the beginning of the semester, Sowon had been five foot two. How tall could his sitting height be? Two and a half feet? Hyonsu tried to remember. How high was the water now? If he could only see the display, he might be able to make some rough calculations.

"Didn't you hear me?" Yongje held up his club. "Do you need a little nudge?"

Hyonsu stared at the screen. The light was coming back. It looked foggier and Sowon appeared fainter, but he noticed something different. Sowon was scared, of course, but he was looking around the lake. He also saw glinting orange eyes behind Sowon's head, along with alert ears and a long tail. That cat.

"Choi Hyonsu," Yongje snapped.

As the light flashed across the screen, Hyonsu's rage cooled quickly. The objective reasoning he'd been desperately searching for returned as the screen grew dark. He was ready. Nothing would be gained from dragging this out. He had to talk and find an opportunity.

"It all happened so fast," Hyonsu said, leaning back and looking at Yongje. He couldn't look at the screen. Where was Sunghwan? Probably shut away somewhere or dead, Hyonsu thought, even though he hoped that wasn't true. He steeled himself. "The fog was so thick, I was lost, I'd had a drink, I was tired, and the road was slick."

Yongje sat back.

Hyonsu tried to flex his right pointer finger, but it was too painful. He realized that his left hand was supporting his broken right wrist. When had his bad arm decided to cooperate? "The turns were sharp, and I began to skid. Right then, out of nowhere, she ran out in front of me."

Yongje crossed his legs, leaning on the arm of the chair and resting his chin on his hand.

"I braked, but it was too late." Hyonsu held on to the desk behind him with his left hand. "Have you ever seen someone get hit by a car?"

Yongje didn't answer but kept glaring at him, his eyes narrowing.

"That was my first time. Her arms were open, like she

was hugging my hood. Her face was splattered across my windshield for a split second. Then she bounced off and fell onto the road. She lay there like a rag doll, not moving. Her body was crumpled and her head was smashed open. It was like a watermelon had dropped on the pavement." Hyonsu chose the most sensational descriptions he could think of and studied Yongje's expression. He inched his bottom to the back of the chair. The rope pinning him to the seat dug into his thighs and the pain from all his injuries was coursing through him.

"I thought she was dead. I was terrified. I thought about how I would lose everything. I'd had my license suspended but kept driving drunk, and now I'd hit and killed someone. I got out of my car and went toward her, thinking about my son and my wife and my job and our home . . ."

Hyonsu blinked hard, trying to get the congealed blood to flake off of his eyelashes. He needed to be able to see his target clearly; he had only one chance, one window of opportunity when Yongje, enraged, would lose control. "She opened her eyes all of a sudden. She looked at me, frightened. And she whispered—"

Hyonsu had managed to blink away the blood clot. He could see that Yongje was wondering what his daughter had said. "She wasn't addressing me. She thought I was you." Hyonsu placed his left palm firmly against the corner of the desk and scooted all the way to the back of the chair. "It was the most terrifying thing I ever heard."

Yongje uncrossed his legs and put both hands on the armrests.

"I've been hearing it over and over again for the last two

weeks. I hear it when I'm sleeping and when I'm awake. It's my most persistent hallucination."

"What did she say?" Yongje finally asked.

Hyonsu didn't answer.

"What did she say?" Yongje demanded.

"What do you think she said?"

Yongje's eyes flickered and opened wide.

"Come on, asshole," Hyonsu murmured.

"What?" Yongje leaned toward Hyonsu.

Now. Hyonsu pushed as hard as he could against the desk and shot toward Yongje, who raised his arms in self-defense, but a half beat too late. Hyonsu headbutted Yongje between the eyes. Thanks to Hyonsu's speed and weight, Yongje flipped over backward along with the chair. Hyonsu raised his bound ankles and kicked against the armchair to roll back to the desk. He tugged on the desk drawer behind him. Locked. He scooted over to the next desk. Locked. The desk drawer at the very end, next to the floodgate control mechanism, was open. He reached back and felt around. Ballpoint pen, ruler, calculator . . . box cutter. He cut the ropes.

Yongje was on his back on the floor, unconscious. Hyonsu limped toward the CCTV screen. The searchlight cut across slowly and reached the pine tree. By now only Sowon's neck and face were illuminated. Hyonsu ran to the floodgate monitoring box, but he didn't know how to operate it. He'd come in here a few times, but he'd never had to use this machine. He tried to calm down. There were buttons and knobs that operated each gate. Raise, Lower, Stop, EMG/Stop . . . Next to the buttons were plus and minus signs and numbers. He pressed

"Raise" for the first gate and then pressed the plus sign. The number went up from 1 to 2. He pressed the number button again, but nothing happened. He pressed the plus button again; it became 3. He worked quickly. He needed to open the flood-gates. It couldn't have taken more than a minute or two, but to Hyonsu it felt as if it were taking millions of light-years.

He went back to the CCTV. The lake should have been swirling, but the surface looked calm. His heart sank. He must not have done it correctly. He zoomed the camera on the floodgates. All five were going up. Something must be wrong. The stopper must be closed. He went back to the monitoring box in a panic. The knob for the stopper was gone. Yongje must have broken it off to prevent him from saving Sowon. That meant he had to get out to the floodgates and manually lower them.

He was rushing toward the door when the club decked him behind his ear. He ducked instinctively, groaning. Yongje swung the club at him again. Hyonsu punched him in the chest and sent the club clattering to the ground. Yongje fell. Hyonsu picked up the club, but the other man didn't move. Hyonsu poked him with the club. Nothing. He pushed him with his foot. Yongje rolled onto his back and the master key fell out of his pocket. Exactly what Hyonsu needed to enter the controlled area to the stopper. He pocketed the key and left the control room, taking the club with him.

It was over four hundred yards from there to the floodgates, and a steep uphill climb at that. Could he make it there in time? He broke into an awkward run, limping. His left toes felt as if they were going to fall off. With each step, his broken jaw clattered and his shattered wrist hit his thigh. He couldn't see very well; his consciousness was leaking away. But the thought of Sowon going under propelled him forward.

~

Sunghwan wriggled his fingers. He could feel them again. His body was gradually coming back to life, but he couldn't gather his thoughts. Random images blended together, then looped and disappeared. His heart pounded, but his limbs felt limp.

Where was Sowon?

When his boss called, Sunghwan had been sitting in front of his desk at home. He had told Hyonsu that he was watching a movie, but he had been writing. Hyonsu asked after Sowon. Sunghwan looked over at the boy, who was lying in bed, fingers laced together on his chest, asleep. He sounded sad, as though saying farewell, and hung up.

What could Hyonsu possibly do at this point? Confession seemed more likely than suicide—someone who was about to kill himself wouldn't ask a friend to wait for him. Hyonsu never mentioned it again. He seemed firm in his belief that Sunghwan would wait like he asked; Sunghwan didn't press him, either, not wanting to upset Hyonsu in his delicate state.

Hyonsu volunteered for the night shift, though they all suggested he rest up. Sunghwan figured he was afraid to fall asleep at home; he couldn't stay up forever playing games. If he were on duty, he could say he was on patrol even if he succumbed to sleepwalking. Sunghwan felt powerless to help Hyonsu and anxious about Yongje. Was he waiting to find

definitive proof before going to the police? Or was he planning some sort of direct payback?

Something clattered. Sunghwan looked at the window,
thinking it was Ernie. The curtain was flapping in the breeze;
the magnet stitched into the corner of the curtain must have
hit the sill. He turned his attention back to his laptop, but this
time the doorbell rang. Who would come there at this hour?
He went out to the living room and looked at the video monitor. He saw two C-Com security guards standing outside.
Their company car was parked behind them, lights flashing.

"What's going on?" Sunghwan asked through the intercom.

"The security guard lady said the emergency alarm kept
ringing in this unit. We're here to check it out."

Sunghwan glanced at the call button on the intercom. Why
hadn't she called home first, he wondered as he opened the
door, but by then it was too late. The two men rushed in and
pinned him against the shoe cabinet. He felt something sharp
prick him in the arm. With that, his legs gave way, his tongue
stiffened, and he lost consciousness.

Now awake, he realized his arms were tied behind his back
and his ankles were crossed and bound together. He was
lying under the basement stairs. He saw his old washing machine, the pot he used as an ashtray, a rubber hose, a plastic
bucket, and a set of cabinets. He had moved these things
down on Eunju's orders when his boss's family moved in.

Those men must be professionals. Yongje must have sent
them. Everything fell into place. They would have worn the
C-Com uniforms so that they could approach the security
office without raising suspicions. Sunghwan gulped. Yongje

must be after Hyonsu's whole family, including Sowon. Did
his boss know that? This possibility hadn't occurred to Sunghwan. Where was Eunju? Were they together?

Sunghwan tried to calm down. He was awake and alone.
Why hadn't they just killed him? He had to get up. His back
felt stiff. The door was locked from the outside. He looked
around. There was a lot of junk in here, but nothing that
would help him cut the rope. The window was up high; he
couldn't reach it. He needed to get up there. The cabinets
under the stairs were the best option. Eunju had brought
them from Seoul, but the living room was too small; he remembered struggling to carry them down to the basement.
They were far from the window, but he had no other choice.
Sunghwan scooted toward the two cabinets, which stood side
by side against the wall. As he remembered, they were incredibly heavy. And he was still weak from being drugged. He
pushed his foot behind the cabinets and pushed one away
from the wall. He squeezed behind it. That took at least
twenty minutes, and he was covered in sweat. He placed his
back against the wall and pushed the cabinet with both feet.
No matter how hard he strained, it only budged about a foot.
By the time he moved it to the window, he was aching.

He sat on the cabinet and pushed himself up with his back
against the wall. His shoulder now reached the windowsill
and the back of his head touched the middle of the glass.
One, two, three. He smashed his head backward and ducked
as the shards rained down on him. He crouched and felt
around for a piece of glass to use to saw through the rope. He
removed the window frame, brushed off the glass shards, and
climbed out. He stood in the flowerbed and looked into the

balcony. The living room lights were off, the door to their room was open, and he could see the bluish light of the desk lamp inside the room. It was eerily quiet. Nobody was home at the Annex that weekend; everyone in 103 had gone home to their families since Hyonsu had taken the night shift. If Yongje was home, he would have rushed out at the sound of breaking glass. Where was he?

Sunghwan went into the house. Nothing looked out of place. Not a single footprint in the living room. The bed was made, his mattress was on the floor, and his laptop was still open to the page he had been writing. His cell phone was next to the laptop. He flipped open his phone to call the police but paused; everything was abnormally, eerily quiet. He stood still, listening. He heard insects and branches rustling in the wind. He heard a dog barking from far away. It wasn't silent, actually. It was just that something was missing. With a start, he suddenly realized what it was: the sound of water flowing through the floodgates, which always overwhelmed everything else, was absent. That meant the floodgates were closed.

He'd heard that the last time the floodgates were closed was two Augusts ago, amid a severe drought. It didn't make any sense to close them now; it had been raining consistently over the last two weeks, and the dam had been collecting more water than usual. That meant someone had closed them, someone who had access to the control center. All at once, he understood. The tour of the conservancy. How had he not seen it before? Sunghwan's heart began to pound as his thoughts careened all over the place. Sowon's missing basketball shoes. Maybe Sowon was somewhere where his father couldn't reach him. Somewhere that would be the first to be submerged when the floodgates were closed. Hansoldung.

It was 1:30 a.m. Two hours had passed. How high had the water risen? It didn't need to reach flood levels, he realized; Yongje just needed the water to reach a few feet above normal pool levels to drown Sowon. Hansoldung was probably already underwater. Sunghwan snatched the headlamp from his desk, leaped out the window, and flew toward the back gate. He regretted all the time he had wasted standing stupidly in his room. If he was right, he had to get to the island before the lake swallowed the boy. He ran as fast as he could, but the path was muddy and his legs felt like lead. His heart thrashed in his chest. Sowon must be terrified. He was only eleven years old. He hoped Sowon was drugged and not aware of where he was.

It took exactly five minutes for Sunghwan to reach the dock. He opened his phone only once to check the time; he could call the police later. He climbed over the fence. The searchlight was slowly scanning the lake. He could see how high the water had risen; parts of the banks were already submerged. He could only make out the shape of the *Josong* in the fog. The lake was freakishly quiet.

The light swept past the steel doors to the dock and stretched toward the lakeshore road. Sunghwan left his cell phone under the doors and ran down the slope. He began to swim when the water reached his thighs and clambered onto the deck of the boat. He punched through the cabin window and unlocked the latch, switching on the light and looking around. There was a glass case on one wall with an inflatable raft in it. He smashed it with the attached ax and took it out. He threw the towrope into the water. The boat inflated upon contact, and he tossed a blanket and the ax onto it. Then he tied the towrope to his waist and jumped in, swimming toward Hansoldung.

Pitch-black darkness and fog blanketed the lake. Sunghwan's headlamp wasn't strong enough to illuminate anything farther than three feet in front of him. He stopped and looked around every time the searchlight swept over the lake, but he couldn't find Hansoldung. All he could see was an impenetrable wall of fog. Was it already underwater? Just as he was about to succumb to despair, a sound pierced the darkness.

A cat yowling loudly and fiercely.

He paddled toward the noise. The cat grew louder and more insistent until it was right in front of his face. His foot touched ground. The searchlight was coming back toward him. He saw a dark rounded shape behind the fog.

"Sowon!" he yelled, pulling the raft in front of him. The light revealed the pine tree. Sowon was in front of the tree, the water up to his neck, his mouth taped shut. But he looked strangely calm. His neck strained as he watched Sunghwan emerge from the water. He was all by himself in the dark, but staying so strong. Sunghwan felt a lump in his throat. *Good job, kid*, he thought.

Ernie was crouched behind Sowon's head, perched on a branch like an owl. How had he gotten there? "Don't move," Sunghwan said. "Stay still until I get you on the raft."

Sowon nodded. Sunghwan put the raft in front of the boy and put his headlamp on the raft, pointing it at Sowon. He leaned down and felt along the trunk. He found the rope with his fingertips and used the ax from the *Josong* to free the boy. He reached for Sowon, who was stiff. He lifted him into the raft and wrapped him in the blanket. He gently pulled the tape off his mouth. Sowon was shaking from the cold and staring intently at him, as though he thought Sunghwan would vanish if he looked away. Ernie hopped into the raft.

"Stay down until we get to the dock, okay?"

Sowon nodded. Sunghwan put the headlamp on the boy's head and began swimming. He moved toward the blinking light of the *Josong*. He was out of breath before he was even halfway there. By the time he got to the boat, he could barely move his shoulders. He pulled the raft up the slope. Ernie jumped onto dry land. Sunghwan carried Sowon up to the doors. He set him down and hugged him, patting him on the back. "You did good, Sowon. You're very brave."

Sowon nodded. He didn't cry or scream. Sunghwan was worried—Sowon had to release his emotions; otherwise the terror would curdle inside of him and poison him. Seryong Lake could become his well, an even deeper, darker, more powerful one than his dad's. "You can cry if you want to," he said, patting him on the back again.

"The red star by Seryong Peak is Jupiter, right?"

"Yeah," Sunghwan said. The boy was looking at him calmly. He felt a chill. What was wrong with him?

"When I opened my eyes, I saw Jupiter," Sowon said and hiccupped. What he said next was incomprehensible. "I thought I was in the woods at first. But then the searchlight found her. And I was always It."

Sunghwan looked up. He couldn't see a single star. There

was only a sticky, murky darkness. What was Sowon talking about? What had happened on Hansoldung? They would have a chance to talk about it later. Right now, he needed to send the police to the control center. He felt under the doors for his phone and called the police.

"What is your emergency?"

Sunghwan glanced at Sowon, who was looking down at his feet, listening carefully. He didn't know how to say what he needed to say so that only the police would understand. "Something's wrong with the dam. You need to send someone to the control center."

"What's wrong with the dam?"

Before Sunghwan could answer, a sudden roar emerged from below the maintenance bridge. The ground shook. The light of the *Josong* swung toward the bridge. The searchlight revealed a giant sinkhole of whirling water forming near the center of the reservoir—the dormant lake had suddenly come to life. His heart dropped and he let out a yell. Slipping his cell phone in Sowon's hand, Sunghwan rolled him under the doors and clambered over the fence himself. He would never remember how he had managed to run up the steep path to the ranch with Sowon on his back. For a long time after the incident, only the roar of the lake shaking the ground, the white searchlight bobbing over the trees, and the weight of the boy on his back stayed with him.

At the barn, he opened the door to an awful, musty stench. Ernie, who must have followed them, nestled in his box. Sunghwan pushed Sowon into the nook and wrapped the blanket tighter around the boy, who was still gripping Sunghwan's cell phone. "I'll be right back."

Sowon nodded.

"You stay here with Ernie. I want to stay with you, but . . ."

"You have to go save Dad," Sowon finished his sentence.

Sunghwan was at a loss for words. If Yongje had closed the gates, Hyonsu must have opened them. There was nothing left for Sunghwan to do if Hyonsu had triggered them from the control room; by the time he would be able to lower the stopper, the water would have already swept everything away. But if Hyonsu had opened the gates manually, maybe he still had time to reverse it.

"Just like you saved me and Ernie." Sowon's eyes anxiously pleaded with Sunghwan.

Sunghwan nodded. "You have to promise that you'll stay here until I come back for you."

"I promise."

Sunghwan reached the road and saw the searchlight above the lake and the roaring water. The banks were gone and water churned as if a tsunami had been unleashed. When he got to the maintenance bridge, he couldn't believe what he saw—nothing remained below the dam. Not the conservancy, not the village, not a single lamppost lining the commercial district. There was only a massive surge of water. Beyond that, white foam formed a mushroom cloud, its spray drenching the bridge. His legs buckled. What was the point of jumping into this, if the control center, the conservancy, the village, and its residents were all gone? He couldn't turn back time. But the searchlight roaming above the gates reminded him why he'd run over. He had to bring the stopper down and prevent further destruction. If he didn't, the water could engulf Sunchon.

He began to sprint. Near the middle of the bridge, he felt
something brush past him. He couldn't see anything through
the fog and the spray. But it felt like a person. He ran to the
controlled area by the floodgates. The gates were open. He
dashed to the emergency stopper and pressed the down button to lower it. He should have heard the whir of the pulley
engaging and the friction of the chains, but he couldn't hear
anything. He leaned over and looked down at the stopper.
He didn't notice someone approaching from behind. He felt
something whoosh above him and graze the top of his head,
and he ducked and rolled reflexively. When he righted himself, he saw Hyonsu, one shoulder drooping and dragging one
leg, approaching the switchgears. His face was distorted by
blood and swelling. His left hand gripped a bloody club.

"Sowon's alive!" Sunghwan screamed. The roar of water
surging through the woods drowned out his voice. "Sowon's
alive!"

He flung himself at Hyonsu. He had to tell him Sowon was
safe, and to do that, he would have to wrestle him to the
ground. But Hyonsu whacked him in the ribs with the club and
Sunghwan crumpled. Everything turned black. He couldn't
breathe. It occurred to him that Hyonsu was going to beat him
to death, or else he was going to fall into the water churning
below. He heard Hyonsu sob, and saw him bend down to pick
up the club. Sunghwan got to his feet again and rushed at
Hyonsu, aiming at his good leg, causing Hyonsu to fall. Sunghwan yanked his left arm behind his back and sat on him. He
put his mouth to Hyonsu's ear and screamed, "Sowon's alive!"

Hyonsu flinched and stopped struggling.

"Sowon's alive!"

Hyonsu turned to look back at him.

"He's alive. You can talk to him. You can call him. Trust me. Sowon has my phone."

Hyonsu didn't resist and eventually surrendered. Sunghwan let go. "I'll prove it to you. Let's go to the security office." He helped up Hyonsu, who swayed but didn't collapse.

The stopper was completely down; it had turned frighteningly quiet. Sunghwan could hear sirens blaring in the distance. In the office, he picked up the phone. Hyonsu blocked the doorway, determined to kill Sunghwan if this was a trick. Sunghwan began to panic. The phone was dead. He thought of Hyonsu's cell. "Give me your cell phone," he said, pointing at Hyonsu's shirt pocket, as his boss looked at him in a daze.

Hyonsu put a hand on his shirt, looking surprised.

"Hurry!"

Hyonsu fumbled with the button on his pocket and handed over his phone. Sunghwan flipped it open.

Sowon answered on the first ring. "Dad?"

Hyonsu snatched the phone out of Sunghwan's hand.

"Mr. Ahn?"

"Sowon," Hyonsu said hesitantly.

Sowon's voice grew animated. "Dad!"

Hyonsu keeled over as though he had been hit by a tranquilizer.

"Dad?"

RED LIGHT, GREEN LIGHT

As I spent that night tied to the pine tree on Hansol-dung, everything shifted—the scenery, even the flow of time.

Earlier that night, I'd heard something in my sleep. I opened my eyes and saw men in uniform in my room. I fell asleep again before waking to someone whispering, "Red light."

Thin white legs darted past. Tall cedars surrounded me, and straight ahead was a tower with a searchlight. I saw a red star in the sky. Mr. Ahn had told me it was Jupiter. The vast sky was a heavy, inky blue. Something grazed the back of my neck, as light as the wind.

"Green light."

I was tied to a large pine tree, my mouth taped shut. Something warm was in my lap, purring. Ernie.

Was I in the middle of the lake, on Hansoldung? Or in the woods?

"Red light."

I spotted the girl to my right, standing still under a low

branch. She looked the way she always did, her long dark hair covering her shoulders. This was just a dream.

The searchlight passed her and she faded away.

Wake up, I told myself. *Get up*. Suddenly I was lying under the blazing sun. I heard light, skipping footsteps. Ernie tensed and stood. He hopped onto my shoulder and then onto the tree, meowing.

It became dark again. I felt something odd on my neck. Her wet hand, tagging me. I was It.

"Green light."

She was now closer to me, but water was swirling under her bare feet. Her hand touched the back of my neck again. I was It again; I was losing without being able to play.

The cedars surrounding me suddenly loomed closer. I heard her skipping on the water, but I couldn't tell which direction the sound was coming from. I felt a chill. Somehow the water had reached above my waist.

I saw something black, whirling under the surface. I couldn't breathe. Large black eyes looked up at me from the water, then a pale forehead emerged. I realized that every time I lost sight of her, Hansoldung sank by another inch.

"Red light," she enunciated clearly, as if to chide me into paying attention.

The water hit my shoulders. The trees grew and grew, covering the sky. I grew sleepy.

"Sowon!"

I jolted awake. I panicked and looked around for her but saw nothing.

"Sowon!" That sounded like Mr. Ahn. I stared in the direction of the voice and finally spotted Mr. Ahn swimming toward me with an inflatable raft.

~

From that point until I got to the barn, my memories matched Mr. Ahn's novel. When Mr. Ahn called the police, I realized that Dad must have been nabbed by the same guys. And Mom—I clung to the hope that she was hiding somewhere safe. I opened and closed Mr. Ahn's cell phone countless times. I wanted to text Mom, but I wasn't sure if I should; if she was with the men in uniform, that would tell them where I was, and if she was hiding, the sound of her phone would expose her. I hugged Ernie, who purred and soon fell asleep. He was the reason I didn't get hypothermia, and how I was able to wait without succumbing to panic. I knew Mr. Ahn would save Dad. The girl didn't come back. I didn't think I could stand another round of that game.

I was dozing when Mr. Ahn's phone rang. I had to stop myself from running out of the barn when I heard my dad say my name. And when Mr. Ahn showed up on his own, I almost burst into tears. It could only mean that something was wrong.

"Are you okay?" Mr. Ahn said as he helped me up.

"What about Dad?"

"He'll be okay. He's on his way to the hospital."

"Can you take me to him?"

"Not now."

"Why not?" I was choking up.

"We have to go somewhere else right now."

"To see my mom?"

Mr. Ahn shook his head. "Later. You'll see your dad soon. I promise."

~

B ut Mr. Ahn never kept his promise. As I was pawned off from relative to relative, nobody brought me to see my dad. He refused visitors anyway, and once his execution was confirmed, I was the one who didn't want to see him.

"Let's go. He might agree to see you if we go," Mr. Ahn said, but I ignored him.

That night in the barn was the last time I heard my dad's voice. I didn't even get to say a proper goodbye to Ernie, who sat by the persimmon tree and watched us get into the squad car. I never returned to Seryong Lake. None of the village's residents survived, and the police who had been on their way to the scene also perished. And I became forever known as the son of the man who had caused the tragedy. I couldn't forget that fact no matter how much I wanted to. Now Mr. Ahn's novel forced me to face the truth: that all those innocent lives had been sacrificed for mine.

Why had Mr. Ahn written this account anyway? What did he have to gain by telling me this cruel truth? And it was unfinished; it ended with his own chapter. Where was my mother's story? I opened Mr. Ahn's laptop and clicked on a draft, but it ended at the same place. The only difference was that the draft had a blank page at the very end, titled "Kang Eunju." Why hadn't he written this last chapter? How did Yongje escape? Who killed my mother and threw her in the water? Mr. Ahn's notebook contained a list of sources, some underlined and others annotated. Nothing suggested my mother's or Yongje's whereabouts. Two letters from Mun Hayong and the voice recordings were all that remained. I hesitated to play the recordings, still afraid of facing my father.

I clicked on the second recording. I thought maybe it would be my father again, but it was a woman's voice I recognized. Aunt Yongju. "I don't think they had a happy marriage. Especially after they moved to Seryong Lake. Every night she texted me, asking me to call. That was so like my sister; even when she was desperate to talk, she didn't want to be the one to call and be charged for it." Over three recordings, Aunt Yongju recounted stories from my mother's life, many of which, I recognized, had made it into the novel.

The fifth recording was of Yim, the groundskeeper. "That day, as I left for Andong, I stopped by the security office. I was worried for some reason, even though she and I weren't that close. I told her: Put the barrier down, don't go out to patrol, don't open up for anyone you don't know. I heard about what happened on the news the next day. I rushed back and—there was nothing. Everything had been washed away.

"Now it's a dead place. They operate the dam from Paryong Lake. The residents who were away that weekend were awarded a small compensation, salvaged what they could, and left. They couldn't have rebuilt there even if they wanted to because new construction isn't permitted. The arboretum is just ruined. You'd have to whack your way through the vines for days."

The sixth file seemed to be an interview with a detective—the older one in Mr. Ahn's novel, it seemed. "We didn't find the car repair shop until the night of September eleventh. At the end of the night, we thought of checking Ilsan and found a shop near their new apartment. It was already one in the morning when we got there, so we went to get some food and soju. After we found out what happened, I felt terrible. If we found the shop a little earlier, I think we could have prevented this tragedy. My entire division was wiped out.

"I always thought it was strange that her blood wasn't on the club or on his clothes. And we never found Oh Yongje's body. The case went to the Seoul district prosecutor's office and the public outrage was pressuring them into a quick conviction. I objected, but I was shut down. Choi Hyonsu was fighting for his life in the hospital—he couldn't defend himself. And your statement and the kid's didn't make any sense; they were too fantastical. Anyway, it's all over now."

Recordings 7 to 25 were of all sorts of people, from the director of operations at the conservancy, who'd taken responsibility for the incident and stepped down, to doctors who knew Yongje. Also interviewed were the head of the orphanage and a teacher who had attended the garden party, a staff member of the events company, a dental hygienist who had worked at Yongje's practice, an employee from a pharmaceutical company, Yongje's relatives, and Mun Hayong's father. Some cooperated enthusiastically, some were filled with rage, and some warned Mr. Ahn to stop snooping around. The people interviewed were the same as the sources listed in the notebook. The only ones who weren't recorded were the Supporters and the office manager at Yongje's practice. Maybe Mr. Ahn never found them. There was no mention of my mother, nor any evidence that linked Yongje to her death.

In my mind, I tried to put the events of that night in chronological order. After my father left the control room, thinking Oh Yongje was dead or at least severely incapacitated, he went up to the floodgates. He would have been opening the floodgates while Mr. Ahn retrieved me from Hansoldung, and my mom . . . maybe she was tied up somewhere like Mr. Ahn and escaped.

It was my father again starting with recording number 26. He told the stories described in the novel in a low, hesitant, sometimes trembling voice, and spoke with a bit of a lisp I didn't remember. I tried to listen as objectively as possible.

"I realized what I'd done after I woke up in the hospital. I had nothing to say. What could I say? That I opened the floodgates to save my son? That I didn't even think about the villagers? I believed Oh Yongje was dead and I was the reason my wife was gone. So I just stayed quiet. I've been going over that night in my head for the last seven years, wondering what I could have done differently. But if I'm being honest, I would probably do the exact same thing again. I thought about killing myself every single day. And the well . . . I go there still. Sergeant Choi still calls for me and I still hear the girl.

"I think my execution date will be set soon. I kind of hope so. But Sowon . . . this is what I'd like to convey to him if I have a chance to say goodbye. If I don't, can you get this to him, anyway? Although I don't know if I'll be able to do this now, without my front teeth." My father began to whistle faintly. The "Colonel Bogey March."

I put my forehead on the desk, buried my ears between my arms, clenched my eyes shut, and pushed down all the memories the tune dredged up.

When I regained my composure, I finally opened Mun Hayong's last two letters. In the eighth letter, she explained how she'd prepared for divorce and how she'd fled. At the end, she wrote: "I don't think there's anything else left to tell you." But she had written another letter after that, six months later, on November 1 of this year.

I read your manuscript. I see the last chapter is missing; it's probably where the mother's story would go? You must not have figured out what happened to her. There's something I didn't share.

I found out he was alive two months after the tragedy. I was out of my mind with grief, and I had collapsed from exhaustion. My friend Ina was working as an art therapist in the psychiatric department at a hospital in Rouen. I had been admitted to the hospital, and on my second morning, I was asleep with an IV in my arm when I heard someone say my name. I felt someone's hands stroking my throat. I froze. There's only one person in the entire world who would do that. My husband always woke me up like that when he was angry. I hoped it was a dream; I refused to open my eyes.

I heard him say, "Mun Hayong, open your eyes." He was standing there, a gentle smile on his face. All I was thinking was how I would escape from him. Ironic, since only the day before I had refused food and water because I had lost my will to live. He grabbed me by the hair and pulled me up. "Don't you want to see Seryong?"

He put a picture in my hand; it was a picture of her in her coffin. I tugged on the emergency cord and began to scream. He grabbed me and punched me in the face, and I pulled the IV out and tried to run. I kept screaming and flailing. How dare he bring me a picture of my dead child?

A nurse and an orderly ran in, and I shouted in my stilted French that this man was trying to rape me. He was taken away and Ina came running into my room. We left Rouen immediately. After that, I wasn't able to lead a normal life. I couldn't go out alone, ever. Ina always accompanied me when I went to North Africa to extend my visa. I hid indoors, afraid that he would find me. But ever since I began writing to you, I've been thinking about the boy.

For my ex, family is the most precious thing in the world. I mistook that for love, but it was really a morbid obsession with ownership. We belonged to him, and he needed everything to happen on his terms. We were objects that he collected, raw material to shape like the wood in his workshop, and he forced us to obey his wishes. Any dissent would mean an assault on his entire worldview, a threat to the very core of his being. You don't have to imagine how he would react; you've already experienced some of it, and it's not over yet.

You said that Hyonsu's execution date was probably going to be scheduled for sometime in December. That means the boy is in danger, as are you. I can tell you he is planning to get the boy and the father at the same time. Why else would he live like a ghost for seven years, keeping the boy in his sights, pushing him slowly to the edge of the world? He's waiting for the execution. I don't know how he's going to find out when that is, but he will. He'll get rid of whoever stands in the way.

Please tell the young man to turn the tables on him, and to use me as leverage if he needs to. It'll work at least once. Here's my cell phone number: 0033.6.34.67.72.32.

It was a wonderful day yesterday; Ina got married, right here beneath the apple tree that I sit under every night. I made her a bouquet of roses. She exchanged rings with Philippe, who has lived with us since we got to Amiens. He's a producer who works on animations and has gotten me jobs that allow me to work without leaving the house.

I plan to leave France tomorrow. It's terrifying to leave by myself, but I have to try. I want to see what's left for me in this life. I haven't decided where I'll go yet. All I know is that I won't be returning to this place.

It's sunny today. I'm going to go down to the yard and say goodbye to the apple tree. Protect yourself. I wish you well.

So, Yongje was still plotting revenge against both me and my father. That much was clear. That was what he wanted seven years ago, after all. I stared at the letter from the prison on my desk. I couldn't breathe. Mr. Ahn vanished yesterday.

The letter came this morning. I was supposed to collect my father's body tomorrow morning. I read Mun Hayong's letter again. *He'll get rid of whoever stands in the way.*

Turn the tables. Use her. Her cell phone number. I couldn't grasp what I was supposed to do with all of that. What was clear was this fact: yesterday, Yongje got rid of the last person who stood in his way.

～

I reread Mun Hayong's letters over and over again. Mr. Ahn didn't come home. Every hour that passed confirmed my hunch, but I still held out hope. Maybe he would come home tomorrow morning unharmed. Maybe he had been running around, preparing for my father's funeral all by himself. He'd left me alone for two nights before. But my instincts knew this time was different. Questions flew around my head like a colony of bats. Had Mr. Ahn brought me here to Lighthouse Village knowing that it figured in my father's youth? Who had sent me his novel and materials? Where was Oh Yongje? Had he killed my mother? Could he really have gotten rid of Mr. Ahn? Why had he let me stay in this village for so long, in peace? Execution dates were not made known to the public; how could he have found out about the execution before it happened?

The wind rattled the window. I lifted the edge of the curtain to look out, but I couldn't see anything. Snow was piled in the four corners of the window, and the middle was covered in frost. I returned to my desk. Oh Yongje had bided his time for seven years, turning me into a vagabond so that nobody would care if I vanished forever. It couldn't have been easy for him to sit by and watch as the son of the man who'd killed his daughter lived on. I had never escaped his orbit. Mr. Ahn must have figured that out a long time ago, and Yongje would have known about Mr. Ahn's investigation. But did he know about the novel?

I made coffee and put aside my concern for Mr. Ahn. I mulled over Mun Hayong's advice. *Please tell the young man to turn the tables on him, and to use me as leverage if he needs to. It'll work at least once. Here's my cell phone number.* When day broke, he was going to come after me. I wasn't about to just wait around. And I refused to run away.

I took out a clean sheet of paper and picked up my pen. I had written this in my head countless times, so it only took ten minutes. People usually called this a suicide note, but I had a specific outcome in mind—luring Oh Yongje out into the open. I put the letters, the novel, Mr. Ahn's materials, and the USB drive in a box. I hid it above the ceiling fan in the bathroom. I left the basketball shoe and Mr. Ahn's laptop on the desk. I took out a blade from a disposable razor, ripped the back interior seam in the waist of my jeans, and stitched it loosely into the seam so that I could yank it out in a flash. I left the thread long and tucked it in. I put Mr. Ahn's watch on my wrist, the one with the voice-recording function on it. I put on my parka and hat, slipped the note into my pocket, and slid my headlamp over my hat.

I left home around midnight, slinging a buddy line over my shoulder as I walked toward the lighthouse. The beacon blinked above the ocean. The wind was strong. The horizon came into view between the flashes of light. I thought about the eleven-year-old boy, standing at the edge of the sorghum field, looking at the lighthouse beyond the mountain. What did he think about as he smelled the ocean in the fog? Was it him or his father who had imprisoned his soul in the well? Was he finally free?

The lighthouse was near a dense pine forest. I saw the tire marks from yesterday near the path. I recalled the man standing next to the lighthouse, looking down at me. I wondered if there was a car hidden in the woods now, but I didn't look; I had to behave like I was dazed so as not to alert them.

The door to the lighthouse wasn't locked. It glided open gently, as though someone had recently oiled the hinges. It was dark inside. I turned on the light and saw the spiral staircase curving upward along the walls. I went up to the second story. The door was locked. I went up to the third floor. I'd come here once before, wandering in while I was bored. I remembered a room with a balcony. It was where the lighthouse keeper lived a long time ago. I pushed the door open with my fingertips, stepped inside, and closed the door behind me. I flicked on the light switch and was surprised to find that it still worked. There were three doors—the door I'd walked through, the door to the tower, and the steel door to the balcony with a small window and shutters. The room still had the lighthouse keeper's belongings: a generator, a folding cot with a military blanket, a wooden chair and desk. On the wall opposite the entrance was a long, box-shaped steel furnace and a small amount of firewood. The lid was propped open. I saw singed wood inside. There were some newer things, too. An electric heater, soap on the sink, a towel on the wall, a trash can filled with empty convenience-store lunch containers.

I headed to the balcony with renewed courage. I opened

the door and the wind battered me. The rope on my shoulder slapped me in the face and I swayed backward. I closed the door behind me and squatted on the balcony. The steel beam felt sturdy. I looped one end of the rope around the beam and made a noose out of the other end. I put it around my neck. I stood up, looked down, and steeled myself to climb over onto the other side of the railing.

I felt eyes on the back of my neck. It was time. I lifted a leg, swung it over, and pitched forward. My breath caught in my throat and, in that moment before the wind flung me away, someone grabbed me from behind, his strong, firm grip practically strangling me. I began resisting, shouting all kinds of vulgar curses, writhing, kicking, thrashing, making sure all the while not to actually escape and fall over the edge. My captor let out all kinds of awful curses himself as he pulled me back onto the balcony. I didn't have to gauge the right moment to stop resisting, because I passed out.

～

When I came to, I assumed that I would be in a car, on my way back to Seryong Lake. But I wasn't; I was still at the lighthouse, my arms tied behind me and my ankles bound. Oh Yongje was sitting in the chair by the desk, his legs crossed. The man who had grabbed me was standing by the entrance to the room with his hands behind his back.

"You awake?" Yongje had short hair, black eyes with enormous pupils, a lean jaw, and a tall, slim build. He was exactly how I remembered him, as if he hadn't aged a day. I felt my veins throb. Here we were. Finally.

"It's been a long time. Seven years?" His voice was gentler

than I remembered. If he wasn't breathing so rapidly, I wouldn't have known that he was excited. On the desk next to him was my messenger bag. They had brought everything from my desk, but it didn't look like they had found the stuff I'd stashed in the bathroom ceiling.

"You were going to kill yourself."

I felt my right wrist. Mr. Ahn's watch was still there. I slipped a finger in my waistband and touched the edge of the thread. The blade appeared to be intact.

Yongje held out the letter from prison. "You can't be so impulsive. You have things to do tomorrow morning."

"I have nothing to do." I kept my eyes fixed on the edge of the desk to maintain my placid expression.

"How could that be? He was your father."

"I don't have a father."

Yongje smiled oddly. "Really? You loved your father."

"I don't care about him anymore."

"Now, now," Yongje clucked. "That's a dangerous mindset. That kind of thinking could end an innocent life, you know."

Was he talking about Mr. Ahn? I looked at him.

Yongje smiled. "He's an idiot, but he took you in and raised you when nobody wanted anything to do with you. He saved your life. It's time to repay the favor. You'll go to Uiwang tomorrow morning to claim your father's body, and then you'll go to Seryong Lake."

"I'm not going anywhere."

"You will. Because your Mr. Ahn will come with us." Yongje addressed the man guarding the door. "Bring him in."

The man hauled a figure over his shoulder and threw him

down by the furnace across from me. It was Mr. Ahn, slumped over, his arms cuffed behind him and his ankles bound by rope. He was unconscious, as I'd expected. But actually seeing him like that, completely vulnerable, terrified me.

"Don't worry, he's not dead. He's just taking a nice, long nap. Do what you're told and I'm sure he'll wake up."

Yongje was a dentist, I remembered. A dentist with access to anesthetics. I thought about the scene in Mr. Ahn's novel where Yongje goes to the barn and puts drugs in Ernie's water. Why had he drugged Ernie and tossed him onto Hansoldung with me? Why would he have gone to all the trouble? I thought back to the cat who ruined Yongje's sculpture all those years ago. Maybe his obsessive mind wouldn't allow him to leave any loose ends, no matter how small. However, Ernie had created a major unintended consequence for Yongje—that cat had saved my life.

The guard resumed his post by the door, awaiting orders. Was he one of the men in uniform who had kidnapped me seven years ago?

"Wait outside," Yongje ordered.

The man bowed and left. Yongje picked up my suicide note and read it, looking delighted. I glanced at Mr. Ahn, who was still lying there, immobile.

I needed to get Yongje to confess to my mother's death on tape. In the morning, I would go along with him to retrieve my father's body. In prison, even with him there next to me, I would have a chance to alert the authorities. It was possible that I would be putting Mr. Ahn in grave danger, but I couldn't think of a better option. But now that a near-lifeless

Mr. Ahn was right in front of me, I hesitated. Was this really the best plan?

"I want to ask you something," I said. I pressed the record button on Mr. Ahn's watch behind my back.

Yongje glanced at me.

"How were you planning to get rid of me that night? If you killed us, it would have been clear we were murdered. And you would have been the primary suspect. Mr. Ahn was still alive and knew what was going on."

"How kind of you to be concerned for me," Yongje said, smiling. "I didn't need to worry about your Mr. Ahn. If all went according to plan, he wouldn't have seen anything. Everything would have been your dad's fault."

"But why did you have to do that to my mother?"

"Your father killed her."

"I'm asking why you harassed her."

"Me? Harass that woman?" Yongje snickered.

"Whenever my mom was working in the middle of the night, you came up to her and hit on her."

"Who told you that? Your mom?"

"I heard her on the phone telling my aunt about it. That you went to the office every night and bothered her. She felt like she had to quit. Which is why Mr. Yim patrolled and did all kinds of other things for her. He even told her to keep the window locked and not to open it if you came by."

"That's what she said? That I, Oh Yongje, harassed someone like *her*?" Yongje looked insulted.

"She was really disgusted," I continued. "I remember her saying, 'Who does he think I am?'"

"Do you know what that bitch's problem was?" Yongje put down my note. "Her mouth. I wanted to wire that trap of hers shut."

I smiled. "I understand. My mother was more prudish than she looked. You were probably embarrassed when she rebuffed you."

Yongje's face tightened and his nostrils flared. "Listen, kid. I never wanted your mom. She was a nightmare; she couldn't follow the simplest instructions. She should have stayed in the library where she was tied up that night. Instead, she crawled out with a baseball bat and ran into me on the bridge as I was leaving the conservancy. Even then, she wouldn't stop berating me. I didn't have time to waste. She was in my way. When that bitch tried to hit me with the bat, I had no choice."

"So you killed her."

"I merely corrected her. For eternity."

I looked at Yongje silently.

"Let me ask you something, too," Yongje said, picking up the basketball shoe. "Where did you get this? I thought these were swept away along with everything else that night."

He hadn't sent them? Then who . . . I glanced at Mr. Ahn and I couldn't believe my eyes. He had a thumb up behind his back, making a whirling gesture. It was our diving signal: *Put up the SOS buoy.* I suddenly realized what I could do.

"Let Mr. Ahn go and I'll bring you my father's body." I knew he would never go for that.

"Kid, you're in no position to bargain."

"Then what about Mun Hayong?"

Yongje froze.

"Let's swap him for her."

Yongje began to laugh.

"Did you know she's having the best time of her life?" I said.

Yongje stopped laughing.

"She married a Frenchman last month. Philippe. Under the apple tree in their yard."

She was definitely a sore point for him. He stalked over menacingly and hit me on the temple with something. My ears rang and everything wobbled. I felt something warm trickle down my cheek. I managed to focus on what he was holding. A gun. With a silencer.

"What did you just say?" he snarled.

I recalled Mun Hayong's letter. "You went all the way to Rouen to find her, but you were arrested at the hospital. Philippe is the man who helped her run away. As you looked for an interpreter and a lawyer, she fell in love."

He swung the gun at me again. I felt woozy.

"Go on," he hissed.

Mr. Ahn was still flopped over, but now he was bending his leg back as if he were doing yoga, trying to untie his feet with his hands. I glanced at the gun. "How can I keep talking when you're holding a gun? I'm too scared to think straight."

This time he punched me in the throat with the hand holding the gun. My head buzzed. I felt a chill. Now I was genuinely afraid of this lunatic. He didn't seem to care that he might accidentally pull the trigger. How had Hayong lived with this nutcase for twelve years?

Mr. Ahn was working at the knots, but he wasn't making any progress.

"Talk if you don't want to end up with broken limbs. How did you hear about her?"

"I'm having a hard time talking, since you punched me in the throat," I murmured.

Yongje cocked his head. "What?"

"I said I wrote to her."

"You wrote to her?"

"I said I wanted to know about you. So she wrote back and told me all about you and your failures."

Yongje went back to his chair, aimed the gun at my face, and crossed his legs.

Mr. Ahn was back in his original position, seemingly unconscious.

Yongje gestured with the gun. "Go on."

"This is what she said: This wasn't the first time I ran away from my husband. I did it twice before, with my daughter. The first two times we were caught by the Supporters. They would locate us immediately but would leave me alone for a week so I would be fearful and anxious the whole time. When I ran out of money and started to panic, wondering how we would survive, he sent someone. He always welcomed us back warmly. He didn't touch me for a while and would be so kind that I would regret leaving him. And then, once my guard was down, he would become even more awful. That was how he tamed me. It wasn't hard to figure out where I went; we lived in a small town and while he bought me a lot of things, he never got me a car and never allowed me to get a license. I also had no money of my own. I wasn't allowed to work and I couldn't go anywhere without telling him. Living that way for twelve years, I no longer knew how to survive in the outside world."

His face twisted.

"Ina, who realized my predicament, told my father about my situation, and he began to look for a way to guarantee our safety and get sole custody. Beginning the night I miscarried, I began to lay the groundwork, following my attorney's advice."

Mr. Ahn had finally succeeded in bending backward and grabbing his ankles. I slid a finger into my waistband and lightly tugged on the thread; the seam burst and I held the razor blade in my hand.

"I gathered recordings, statements, and pictures," I continued as Hayong. "I got a passport and a driver's license, opened a bank account, and began saving for attorney's fees. I siphoned off our living expenses. Using a cooking class as an excuse, I accompanied my daughter on the art class shuttle and sold jewelry, gold, and even my watch in Sunchon. I bought similar fakes so he wouldn't notice. I did that for two years. I was afraid of him, but I was more afraid that I would go back to him."

I sawed gently at the rope so that my shoulders didn't move. Mr. Ahn was untying the rope around his ankles. Yongje's emotions were running high, and he seemed to have completely forgotten about the man tipped over in front of the furnace.

"Our wedding anniversary gave me the excuse to flee," I said, parroting Hayong's letters. "After I was beaten that night, I looked for an emergency phone along the road. I was prepared—after rape, my husband's second favorite way of correcting me was taking my cell phone and money and abandoning me somewhere remote. So I always kept emergency funds tucked under the inner sole of my shoe. That day, I had a few checks of a hundred thousand won each. I also had a credit card in my secret post office box. I made it to Incheon International Airport in Seoul and bought a one-way ticket to France. I got on the plane before I changed my mind."

Mr. Ahn's ankles were free.

"I should stop for today. Philippe is calling me from downstairs. Oh, I almost forgot. Next week I'm planning to move to Amiens. My new address is . . ." I stopped. The rope behind my back was almost severed.

Yongje pressed his lips together, holding his breath.

"I don't know French," I stalled, watching Yongje take a pen out of his pocket.

"Spell it out."

"Twenty-four, R-u-e d-e l-a L-i-b-é-r-a-t-i-o-n eight-zero-zero-zero-zero, A-m-i-e-n-s, F-r-a-n-c-e."

Mr. Ahn rose silently to his feet. His hands were still cuffed, but he looked sturdy on his legs.

Yongje eyed me suspiciously. "How do I know you aren't making this up?"

"I have her cell phone number. Why don't you give her a call and ask her yourself?"

He dropped his pen. "Give it to me. Now," he demanded. He took out his cell phone.

I drew in a short breath and double-checked the number in my head. "It's 0033.6.34.67.72.32."

Yongje dialed, his eyes dark. The gun was still aimed at my forehead, as though he would send me straight to my grave if she didn't pick up. I could hear the phone ringing. Then I heard a woman's voice. I couldn't make out what she said; I only saw Yongje nearly drool with rabid excitement. He stood up. "Mun Hayong."

I sprung my hands free. Mr. Ahn kicked the gun out of Yongje's hand and then hit him square on the chin. Yongje's head snapped back as he fell. The gun clattered and slid toward the door. I flung myself as far as I could—my ankles were still tied together—and grabbed the gun. I sat against the door and rapidly sawed the rope binding my ankles. The man outside began ramming his shoulder against the steel door. I braced against it. I was holding the gun, but I had no idea how to use it. I'd be lucky if I didn't accidentally shoot myself. And Mr. Ahn, who was probably a crack shot, was still in cuffs. At least two men were now outside. As I fought against the door, Mr. Ahn stomped on Yongje, who hit the back of his head on the furnace. Mr. Ahn continued to kick him until he grew limp. The men behind the door slammed against it and shouted, "Open up!" Mr. Ahn helped me push against it.

"Okay. On the count of three, move to the side and aim the gun at them," Mr. Ahn instructed.

I nodded.

"One, two," Mr. Ahn said. On three, we let go and jumped to the side. The door crashed open and two men rushed in. I pointed my gun at them. Neither was the man who had just been here. Their badges identified them as detectives.

"Oh," Mr. Ahn said. "You finally found us."

BLUE ORB SYNDROME

Mr. Ahn and I got into the ambulance with the detectives. They were the same ones who had investigated the Seryong Lake incident seven years prior. Fifteen minutes later, we arrived at a hospital in Haenam. I had a gash on my head but didn't need stitches. The doctors said Mr. Ahn needed to be admitted. I didn't understand how he'd managed to kick Oh Yongje into submission in his condition. Mr. Ahn was in intensive care. He lay in bed with two IVs running. The detectives sat by the bed. I perched on the radiator and told them everything that had happened, from when I opened Mr. Ahn's packages to right before they burst in. I took off the watch and gave it to them. I told them where I'd hidden Mr. Ahn's things. "I still don't understand who sent them to me," I concluded. "It didn't seem like Oh Yongje had sent them."

The older detective threw Mr. Ahn a glance.

"I did," Mr. Ahn said, looking at his feet.

"You?" I was the only one shocked by this revelation.

"I asked the youth club president to deliver them as if they'd come by messenger."

"Why?"

Mr. Ahn looked at me and then glanced at the detectives. I got it. He wanted to talk about it later. "I got a flat as soon as I left home," Mr. Ahn told the detectives. "Near the lighthouse. I got out to take a look. There was a hole in one of the rear tires. I was taking out the spare when a Jeep sped up and stopped really close to my car. I knew when I saw two guys get out. It was over as soon as they grabbed me. I felt a prick on the back of my neck, and then my legs grew weak and I lost consciousness. I don't remember what happened after that. I guess they had me sleep it off at the lighthouse. I thought it would be at the arboretum or the barn; I never thought it would be at the lighthouse."

"Yeah, we didn't, either," the older detective said. "After I got your call I began a stakeout near the pharmacy, but the tracker on you never went beyond the village. After midnight, it stopped moving. I watched it for an hour and then figured it out. We had them right in front of us all along. And our guys were waiting near Sunchon. I asked for reinforcement from the Haenam station and we rushed to the lighthouse. We caught someone under a pine tree and found your van and theirs in the woods. Do you know what was in their van?"

Mr. Ahn was quiet.

"A structure made of sticks. A coffin. It was on a piece of black marble. They were planning to drown you," the detective said, looking at me. "Both of you, probably. The innocent residents were going to be drinking corpse water." He stuffed his notebook in his pocket. "We should be getting back to the station. Do you have any requests?"

"My van—can you bring it here?" Mr. Ahn asked.

"Here? Are you planning to go to Uiwang?"

"We have to."

"You should probably pick up the body in a hearse, no? I'm sure you have a lot to prepare."

"I already have a portrait and a shroud. They should still be in my van. Could you get us suits?"

The older detective nodded and came up to me. He unzipped the collar of my parka, took out something the size of a lighter, and left with his partner. I stood there, puzzled, staring at Mr. Ahn.

Mr. Ahn looked nonchalantly at the wall.

"Do you think Mun Hayong is okay? She must have been shocked when he called," I said, just to get Mr. Ahn talking.

"You decide," he said, not answering my question. "Do you want to cremate him or bury him?"

I was stunned into silence.

"There's land here in the hills if you want to bury him. I spoke to the landowner already. He might be willing to sell us a plot under the right circumstances."

"If it were me, I wouldn't want to be trapped underground."

Mr. Ahn nodded and called Byokje Crematorium. He booked a five p.m. slot. He seemed determined not to say anything unless I asked him specific questions.

"Why did you keep working on the novel after the tragedy?"

"I was asked to." Mr. Ahn kept staring at the wall.

"Who would ask you to do that?"

"The boss."

I was unable to speak. My father?

"I wonder what would have happened if I'd managed to

get him to confess or if I'd reported him. None of what happened would have happened. But I waited. I kept telling myself that your dad was asking for time so that he could get his affairs in order before confessing. I realized that night at the police station what my motives had been all along. The detective said, 'You wanted to find out what happens at the end of your novel.' I had to admit it was true.

"You know the Blue Orb Syndrome? Agoraphobia you experience in the ocean, when you realize that you are alone on the vast ocean floor? You become so terrified that you forget to let your breath out. That was what the tragedy did to me. Every time I opened my laptop to write, I just saw the blue orb. The space became vaster and deeper the more I struggled to find my way out. That's why I took up ghostwriting. You don't have to find your own way, you can make sense of what someone else tells you. I was relieved I was still writing and making money off it, but it was hard to accept that as my lot. Was one book all I had in me? Every time I felt depressed about my career, I wrote about you. I could write about you without getting lost. I wrote down what you read, what your opinions were, what you ate, what you liked and didn't like, how you acted when you were sulking or angry or at a loss, how much your diving improved, how long you lasted at your latest school. At the end of every month, I sent that to your dad, even though he never wrote back.

"I wondered if Yongje was alive. I thought he must be the one chasing you down. I couldn't think of anyone else who would do that. And his body was never recovered. He isn't the kind of person who'd let you live in peace. But he didn't do anything for years. He just kept pushing you away from mainstream society. That felt stranger and more ominous. I searched for him, but nobody had seen him. Nobody, not his relatives or colleagues or the groundskeeper or neighbors. Last year, in July, when we were living in Taean, it suddenly occurred to me that I should look up his assets. In the middle of the night, I looked up the asset registrations online and saw that the medical center had been sold. Maybe it was him exercising his property rights, which meant he was alive. And that was around the time your dad wrote to me for the first time. It was just one sentence: We need to talk."

Mr. Ahn understood that to mean that my dad wanted to talk in person. When he went to prison for visiting hours, he saw an old, toothless man whose back was curved. His arms were secured to chains at his belt and he dragged one leg. A forty-two-year-old grandpa. Mr. Ahn said he was shocked.

"Oh Yongje is alive," my father told him. "He comes once a week to treat my teeth."

It did make sense—in prison nobody would know or care who Oh Yongje was; he was just another volunteer. The inside of my father's mouth was ruined, most of his teeth either missing or rotting. My father had never had strong teeth due to his habit of gritting his teeth when he put the catcher's mask on. And on the night of the tragedy, he'd lost a third of his teeth in his fight with Yongje. Prison life would have done away with the rest.

In June last year, my father heard of a volunteer dentist at the prison and went to see if he could get some painkillers. "He looked familiar to me even though he was wearing a cap and a mask," my father recounted to Mr. Ahn. "He beckoned for me to lie down, then pulled up a chair by my head. Our eyes met. I recognized him instantly."

Mr. Ahn told me he knew exactly what my father meant; that he himself remembered those pitch-black eyes vividly.

"Every time I read your letters I wondered," my father told Mr. Ahn. "Could he still be alive? Did he escape? Who else would go after Sowon like that? And now I knew for sure. I was scared. He was smiling behind his mask. He told me I shouldn't be anxious about the treatment. He said he would get me a set of dentures. I didn't want to ever see him again or think about him. If he had wanted to see me on death row, once was all he was going to get. I sat in my cell and looked at the pictures of Sowon I had on my wall. Any other time that would have calmed me down. That's what I did every time I felt guilt or regret, or dreamed about the sorghum field. But that day, I couldn't escape. A terrifying realization dawned on me. I knew what I had to do. I'd be the catcher one last time, reading the situation and analyzing and predicting behaviors to protect my team. I wasn't in my right mind at Seryong Lake. I didn't see what was coming. But in here, I've had plenty of time to think.

"For weeks after Oh Yongje first came here, I tried to figure out why he would take such a risk," my father told Mr. Ahn. "Turns out, you learn things when you're a volunteer at a prison. They call the volunteers, like the priests and the undertakers, and ask them to come early the following morning. Everyone knows what that means—an execution. I think that's why he's here."

"I'm not sure I understand," Mr. Ahn said.

"It isn't over yet."

"What isn't?"

"For Yongje, that night from seven years ago has never ended. I think he's planning to get his hands on me and Sowon at the same time, probably on the day of my execution. That's why I think you and Sowon haven't been able to stay anywhere. Who else would be out to ruin your lives like that? I don't know what exactly he's planning; it's just a theory at this point. I hope you can help me."

That was where their first visit ended. At the next, my father began telling his story. Mr. Ahn recorded it and began re-creating the incident, inserting my father's story into his old draft. Mr. Ahn went around, searching for people who could fill in the gaps. The story was mostly completed last winter, and Mr. Ahn sent Mun Hayong an unfinished manuscript without Yongje's part. With her assistance, the story developed. And as summer approached, Mr. Ahn succeeded in escaping writer's block. In the fall, my father read the bound manuscript, which was around the time he'd received a physical he believed meant he would soon be put to death. Mr. Ahn told him he hadn't been able to discover anything about my mother's fate.

"Oh Yongje will be your source."

"There's no way he'll tell me anything."

"No, but he'll talk to Sowon." My father laid out his plan. First, I would be sent the novel and the investigative materials. My father guessed that Mr. Ahn would be kidnapped first, and that if I read the novel I would make it my mission to face Oh Yongje personally. "Talk to the older detective who worked on the case. I think he'll help. He came to see me right after I was sentenced to death. He asked me what happened that night, if I really killed my wife. He said my execution will be set if I don't say anything. But I kept my mouth closed. I didn't have any desire to keep living."

Mr. Ahn shook his head. "Even if he helps, we can't put Sowon in danger like that. He's still so young and he's just barely managing. This is all too much."

"Seven years ago, Sowon was who I was trying to save. Now he's the one who can save himself. Do you understand? I'm going to send him a sign and he's going to finish it. It's his choice whether to accept it or shake it off. Give him that chance."

"Fine," Mr. Ahn told my father. "But there's no guarantee that Yongje is going to take me first. He might kidnap both of us at the same time. Everything could deteriorate really quickly."

"No, I think he'll let Sowon get the notice of my execution. He'll show up when it's time to pick up my body. I think he'll happily watch Sowon be tormented until then. Think about it. He showed me live footage of Sowon in the lake. He enjoyed watching me in agony. I doubt he's become more human in the last seven years."

"But there are other complications," Mr. Ahn protested. "I won't know in advance what that day will be."

"He will let you know somehow."

"But if you read this wrong . . ."

"It's possible," my father said. "But the end is the same whatever we do. He wins if we do nothing. He wins if we misjudged. But we can end this nightmare if we're right."

· · ·

IN EARLY NOVEMBER, Mr. Ahn went to the Sunchon police
station, though he had been unsure. He said Mun Hayong's
final letter made him act. The older detective who'd been on
the case was still there, and it didn't take long to convince
him. The detective reviewed Mr. Ahn's materials and agreed
to cooperate, telling him that this was the one unresolved incident in his career. We had to be kidnapped by Oh Yongje;
otherwise he had no basis to arrest him. The plan was to
catch Oh Yongje at the scene for kidnapping and investigate
my mother's death. The detective got Mr. Ahn two trackers
and Mr. Ahn slipped one into my jacket without my noticing.

On the afternoon of December 26, Mr. Ahn received a
phone call from someone requesting his ghostwriting services
for a memoir. It was a strange call; usually writing jobs came
through people he knew or publishing companies. Mr. Ahn
said that was when he realized: this was a sign that Oh Yongje
was putting his plan into motion. Mr. Ahn was told where to
meet his new client. He called the detective to let him know,
then placed the novel, materials, magazine, and Nike shoe in
boxes and asked the youth club president to deliver them to
me. The shoe wasn't mine, actually; he'd found it a while back
on the street, written my name in it, used rubbing alcohol to
make the marks faint, and kept it in the van. My father had
asked him to do this; he'd figured I wouldn't read the novel.
The shoe was my father's way of getting my attention.

After Mr. Ahn left the house, the detective and his partner were planning to be in Hwawon township, checking our
tracking devices. The team members would wait in Sunchon.
But the two trackers didn't go beyond Lighthouse Village for

two days. The detective had been confused, wondering if they'd gotten it all wrong. They'd expected we'd be taken to Seryong Lake or the arboretum.

When Mr. Ahn finished telling me everything, I sat back in my chair. I was enraged, but I didn't know who I was angry with or why.

Around nine in the morning, the detective called to tell us that he'd parked the van behind the hospital. He said reporters were on their way and that we should watch the news before we left. I turned the TV on. First, they reported that Choi Hyonsu had been executed. Then the Sunchon police chief began a press conference, announcing that Oh Yongje, who had long been missing, was alive and that he'd drugged and kidnapped Choi Hyonsu's son and his guardian, and had been about to kill them when he was arrested on the scene. He mentioned briefly the coffin found in Oh's van. Oh was arrested on charges of attempted murder, assault, kidnapping, imprisonment, and violation of medical laws. The Supporters were charged with the same. My mother wasn't mentioned at all. I turned off the TV. Choi Hyonsu was still a murderer and now he was dead. Nothing had changed. Oh Yongje was arrested, but I was still Choi Hyonsu's son.

Mr. Ahn pulled out his IVs and began to change his clothes.

"Are we really going to Uiwang?" I asked him sullenly.

Mr. Ahn put on a sweater.

"Didn't you hear what the doctors said?"

He glanced at me, his eyes stubborn. "They said I was fine."

That wasn't what they'd said. They'd said they hadn't discovered anything beyond a repression of the nervous system, arrhythmia, and a slight respiratory disturbance.

Mr. Ahn put his shoes on. Could he drive in this state? But without him, I'd have to go with a driver assigned by the detective or wait until Mr. Ahn was better. I didn't want to do the former and the latter was impossible. It would take over five hours to get there, and we had to get to the crematorium by five p.m.

In the back of the van, I found a large cardboard box and two black suits. I opened the box. Inside was a shroud and a portrait. When did Mr. Ahn prepare all of this? The portrait was the one described in the novel. My father was looking off to the side, smiling, holding his mask. I felt a lump in my throat. What was he smiling at?

"Go ahead and change," Mr. Ahn told me.

I looked up at him, dazed. The black suit looked unfamiliar, as did the mourning ribbon. I put down the portrait.

As we passed Namwon I finally opened my mouth. "So my father must have thought it would be all better once Oh Yongje was out of the picture."

"No. He just wanted you to do something for yourself."

"Why?"

"He was afraid of the hurt and anger inside you. That—" Mr. Ahn kept his eyes on the road for a while, silent. "That it could kill you or someone else. He was afraid it would turn you into a monster."

"And whose fault is that? He went through the exact same thing. He's the one who killed people. He became the monster."

"That's exactly why."

I shivered.

EPILOGUE

No final words," the prison guard told us. "He refused religious rites, too."

I opened the box containing my father's belongings. Among them I found six pictures of me.

"He didn't say anything?" Mr. Ahn asked.

"He said something, but it was so low that I couldn't hear it. I asked him to repeat himself, but he refused. The employee who put the hood over his head thought he said 'Thank you.' But we don't know for sure." The guard lowered his gaze.

I looked at the number written on the lid of the coffin. His inmate number.

"Would you like to see the body?" the guard asked.

I was afraid to face him, but before we could confer, Mr. Ahn asked, "Can we change him into his shroud?"

The volunteer undertaker came in. Mr. Ahn handed the shroud over. The coffin was opened. A hood was over his head, covering his face. I felt faint. Seeing the red inmate number on his prison uniform was a punch in the gut. He looked shrunken and thin, like Mr. Ahn had said. Still, the coffin looked too small for him. It reminded me of my father sitting in his Matiz, how he folded himself uncomfortably into the driver's seat. For such a big man, his world had been so narrow. He spent so much of it trapped: in the sorghum field, in an unhappy marriage, in his soju, in prison, and now in this narrow coffin.

I reached out and touched his inmate number. The undertaker changed him into his shroud and secured the coffin lid once more. I rubbed out the inmate number on the lid. I borrowed a marker from the guard and wrote something my father would much rather carry with him into the next world: *I believe in the church of baseball.*

To save money, we hadn't hired a hearse. We got into Mr. Ahn's van and drove off the prison grounds. But the press had caught wind of our movements and were blocking the road. This was the first execution in over a decade, and it had been the notorious Choi Hyonsu. The car with the coffin in it was right in front of their eyes, and his son, who had been kidnapped just the day before, was inside. There was no way they would move out of the way.

Mr. Ahn leaned on his forearms and looked out the window uneasily. We had to get going to make our appointment at the crematorium.

"I'll get out," I said. I had to give them something—otherwise, we'd never get through.

As I emerged from the van, the wind tore my hat away. Cameras began flashing against the gray sky. I didn't duck to avoid them. This darkness had begun seven years before, and it was time to step into the light. I held my father's portrait in my hands as I walked into the scrum. I had to wade into this ocean of light so that the world would finally let me and my father go. I advanced one step at a time as people shouted and shoved. Flashes burned my eyes. My ears rang with the noise and my face was numb. I swayed, my knees weak. The road looked endless. I stopped walking. I stopped breathing. I closed my eyes and tried to control myself. I was shaking. It'll be over soon, I told myself. I just have to put one foot in front of the other.

⁓

At five, my father's body entered the flames. The furnace door closed. I stood in front of the door. Why had he said thank you right before he died? What was he thankful for? To whom? Was he grateful that he was freed from his life? That he could send me one last assist? I didn't get it.

His remains came out after about an hour. I took the box; it was light and smelled of fire.

When we got back to Lighthouse Village, it was snowing outside. The youth club president's boat was waiting for us below the lighthouse. The ocean was dark and the waves were still. The youth club president drove the boat out. I changed into my diving suit on deck.

Mr. Ahn watched quietly. "Can I at least come with you to the cliff?"

I shook my head. He looked like a corpse himself, he was so exhausted. I didn't need to say goodbye to two fathers in a single day.

"It'll be low tide in about twenty minutes," Mr. Ahn said.

I nodded.

"You have to come up before then."

I nodded again.

The boat stopped at the western point of the rocky island. I turned my light to its brightest setting and put the box containing my father's remains in a mesh bag. I put my mouthpiece in and looked at my watch: 11:55 p.m.

I let myself fall backward into the water. It was cold, but the current was gentle. I floated down with the descending current, passed the ledge of the cliff, and continued farther down, past clusters of coral, redfin velvetfish glimmering among the seaweed, flatfish sleeping on a rock. I went deeper and deeper.

Midnight now. I was in the abyss. It was dark and everything was colorless. Gray fish circled above like storm clouds. I took out the box with my father's remains and cut the rubber band holding it closed. I opened the lid. The ashes ballooned up through the school of fish before scattering in the current. It was like an underwater snowstorm.

It had snowed forty-three years ago today, the day my father was born, he had told me. It had snowed, too, thirteen years ago, on his thirtieth birthday. That was the year he got his shoulder injury and his world was shattered. He had been in the hospital recovering. That afternoon, he put on a parka over his hospital gown, slipped out of the building, and took me to a nearby amusement park. The sky had been a sallow gray, snow scattered under leaden clouds. I gave him a smiling skull ornament I'd picked out for him to hang on his rearview mirror. I remember his face when he took it, and how, after, we marched together around the empty plaza, whistling the "Colonel Bogey March."

Now, as I watched his ashes float away in the dark water, I told him the same thing I had that day: "Happy birthday, Dad."

AUTHOR'S NOTE

Fate sometimes sends your life a sweet breeze and warm sunlight, while at other times a gust of misfortune. Sometimes we make the wrong decisions. There is a gray area between fact and truth, which isn't often talked about. Though uncomfortable and confusing, none of us can escape the gray.

This novel is about that gray area, about a man who made a single mistake that ruined his life. It's about the darkness within people, and the lightness made possible by sacrificing oneself for someone else. I am hopeful that we can say yes to life in spite of it all.

A novel can't be written alone. I would like to thank everyone who helped me with this book. The police investigator Park Juhwan, who shared his expertise and vivid experiences and even reviewed the manuscript; Kim Myonggon, the diving instructor of an emergency rescue team; Jong Ungi, a professional civil engineer. I am grateful to the operations staff of a certain dam. I send affection and thanks to my family; my friend Jiyong, who always cheered me on; the writer Ahn Sunghwan, who analyzed my disorderly drafts and ruthlessly and objectively diagnosed problems. I bow in gratitude to Cho Yongho, who mentored me, and Park Bomsin. I promise I will keep going, putting one foot in front of the other.

Seryong Lake and Lighthouse Village sprang from my imagination, and any likeness to existing locations is purely a coincidence.

For the two years I wrote this book, I was the mayor of two gloomy, unsettling towns, and I loved them with all my heart. For a while, I find myself unable to leave, pacing the neighborhoods in my head every night. I am thrilled that these towns are being revealed to the world.

Blessings to everyone.

Also by You-Jeong Jeong

THE GOOD SON

Yu-jin is a model student, a successful athlete and a good son.
But one day he wakes up covered in blood. There is no sign of
a break-in and there is a body downstairs. It is the body of
someone he knows all too well . . .

Yu-jin struggles to piece together fragments of what he can remember from the night before. He suffers from seizures and
blackouts. He knows he will be accused if he reports the body,
but what to do instead? Faced with an unthinkable choice,
Yu-jin makes an unthinkable decision.

'INGENIOUSLY TWISTED' *Entertainment Weekly*
'GRIPPING' *Cosmopolitan*
'INTENSE' *Telegraph*